**Also by Peter Høeg**

*Smilla's Sense of Snow*
*Borderliners*
*The History of Danish Dreams*
*The Woman and the Ape*
*Tales of the Night*

# The
# Quiet
# Girl

# The
# Quiet
# Girl

PETER HØEG

Translated from the Danish by Nadia Christensen

Farrar, Straus and Giroux  /  New York

Farrar, Straus and Giroux
19 Union Square West, New York 10003

Copyright © 2006 by Peter Høeg
Translation copyright © 2007 by Nadia Christensen
All rights reserved
Distributed in Canada by Douglas & McIntyre Ltd.
Printed in the United States of America
Originally published in 2006 by Rosinante, Denmark, as *Den stille pige*
Published in the United States by Farrar, Straus and Giroux
First American edition, 2007

Library of Congress Cataloging-in-Publication Data
Høeg, Peter, 1957–
    [Stille pige. English]
    The quiet girl / by Peter Høeg ; translated by Nadia Christensen.
— 1st American ed.
        p.    cm.
    ISBN-13: 978-0-374-26369-0 (hardcover : alk. paper)
    ISBN-10: 0-374-26369-8 (hardcover : alk paper)
    I. Christensen, Nadia.    II. Title.

PT8176.18.O335S7513 2007
839.8'1374—dc22

                                            2007008187


Designed by Jonathan D. Lippincott

www.fsgbooks.com

1   2   3   4   5   6   7   8   9   10

## Acknowledgments

Thank you to Jes Bertelsen, Erik Høeg, Karen Høeg, Nelly Jane, Jakob Malling Lambert, and Otto Moltke-Leth.

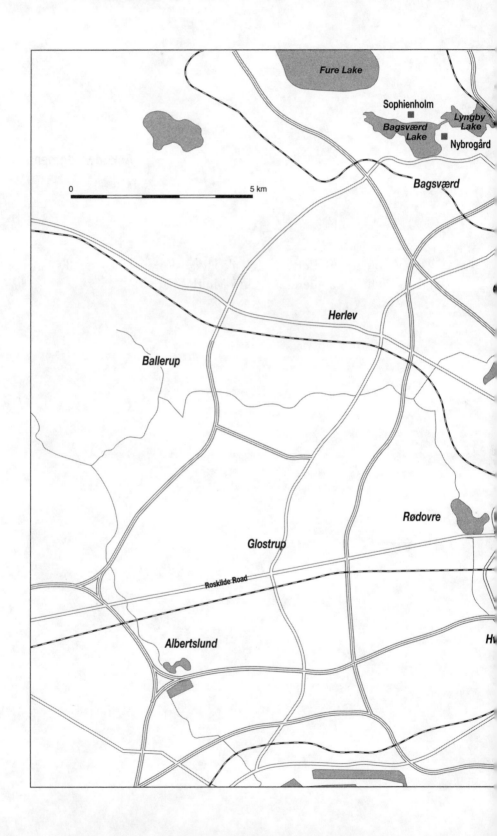

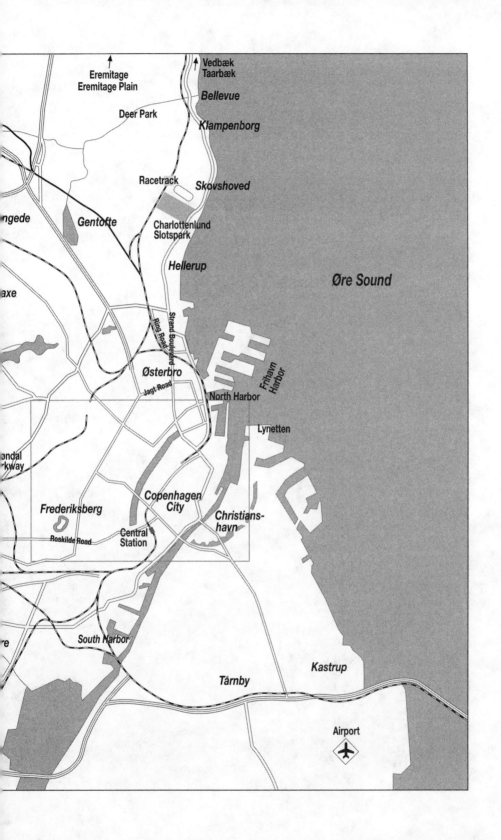

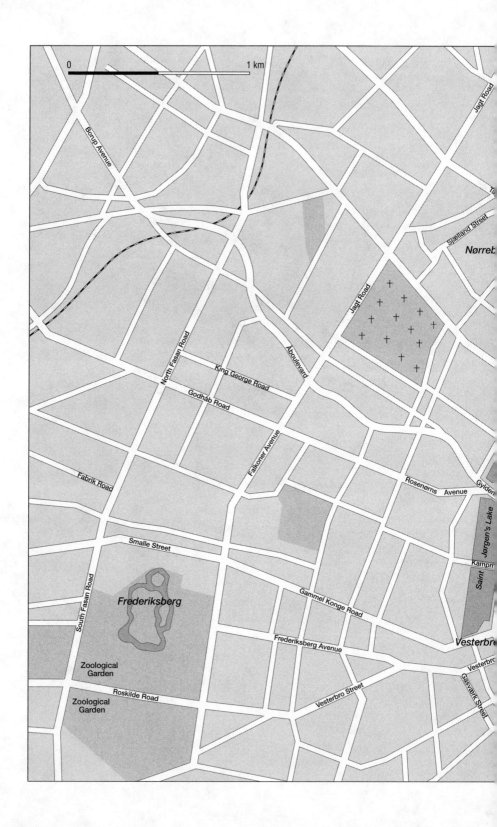

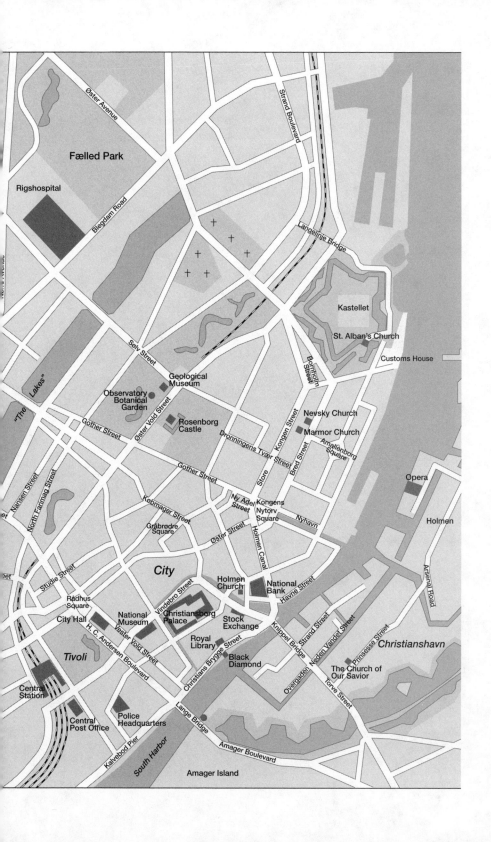

# Part
# One

# 1

SheAlmighty had tuned each person in a musical key, and Kasper could hear it. Best in the brief, unguarded moments when people were nearby but didn't yet know he was listening. So he waited by the window, as he was doing now.

It was cold. The way it could be only in Denmark, and only in April. When, in mad enthusiasm for the spring light, people turned off the central heating, brought their fur coats to the furrier, dispensed with their long underwear, and went outside. And only when it was too late, discovered that the temperature was at freezing, the relative humidity 90 percent, and the wind was from the north and went straight through clothing and skin, deep into the body, where it wrapped itself around the heart and filled it with Siberian sadness.

The rain was colder than snow, a heavy, fine rain that fell like a gray silk curtain. From behind that curtain a long black Volvo with tinted windows appeared. A man, a woman, and a child got out of the car, and at first it looked promising.

The man was tall, broad-shouldered, used to getting his own way—and capable of having a powerful impact on those around him if he didn't. The woman was blond as a glacier and looked like a million bucks; she also looked smart enough to have earned it herself. The little girl had dignity and wore expensive clothes. It was like a tableau of a holy, wealthy family.

They reached the center of the courtyard, and Kasper got his first sense of their musical key. It was D-minor, at its worst. As in Toccata and Fugue in D-Minor. Great fateful pillars of music.

Then he recognized the little girl. At that precise moment the silence occurred.

It was very brief, perhaps a second, perhaps not at all. But while it lasted, it obliterated reality. It took away the courtyard, the rehearsal ring, Daffy's office, the window. The bad weather, the April month. Denmark. The present time.

Then it was over. Vanished, as if it had never existed.

He clutched the door frame. There had to be a natural explanation. He'd suffered an attack of indisposition. A blackout. A temporary blood clot. No one survives with impunity two nights in a row, from eleven to eight in the morning, at the card table. Or it had been another tremor. The first big ones had been felt way out here.

He cautiously looked behind him. Daffy sat at the desk as if nothing had happened. Out in the courtyard the three figures struggled forward against the wind. It hadn't been a tremor. It had been something else.

The true mark of talent is the ability to recognize when to give things up. He'd had twenty-five years of experience in rightly choosing to part with things. He need only say the word, and Daffy would deny him a home.

He opened the door and extended his hand.

*"Avanti,"* he said. "I'm Kasper Krone. Welcome."

As the woman shook his hand, he met the little girl's eyes. With a slight motion, evident only to him and her, she shook her head.

He took them into the practice room; they stood there looking around. Their sunglasses gave them a blank air, but their tone was intense. They had expected more finesse. Something in the style of the main stage at the Royal Theater, where the Royal Danish Ballet rehearses. Something like the reception rooms at Amalienborg Palace. With merbau and soft colors and gilded panels.

"Her name is KlaraMaria," said the woman. "She's a nervous child. She gets very tense. You were recommended to us by people at Bispebjerg Hospital. In the children's psychiatric ward."

A lie causes a delicate jarring to the system, even in a trained liar. So too in this woman. The little girl's eyes focused on the floor.

"The fee is ten thousand kroner per session," he said.

That was to get things moving. When they protested, it would initiate a dialogue. He would get a chance to listen to their systems more deeply.

They didn't protest. The man took out his wallet. It opened like the bellows of an accordion. Kasper had seen wallets like that among the horse dealers when he was still performing at fairs. This one could have contained a small horse, a Falabella. From it emerged ten crisp, newly minted one-thousand-kroner bills.

"I must ask you to pay for two sessions in advance," he said. "My accountant insists on it."

Ten more bills saw the light of day.

He dug out his fountain pen and one of his old letterpress cards.

"I had a cancellation today," he said, "so as it happens, I can just manage to squeeze her in. I'll start by examining muscle tone and awareness of body rhythm. It will take less than twenty minutes."

"Not today," said the woman, "but soon."

He wrote his telephone number on the card.

"I must be in the room," she said.

He shook his head.

"I'm sorry. Not when one is working with children on a deep level."

Something happened in the room—the temperature plummeted, all oscillatory frequencies fell, everything congealed.

He closed his eyes. When he opened them again, fifteen seconds later, the bills were still lying there. He put them in his pocket, before it was too late.

The three visitors turned around. Walked out through the office. Daffy held the outer door for them. They crossed the courtyard without looking back. Seated themselves in the Volvo. The car drove off, disappearing into the rain.

He leaned his forehead against the cold glass of the window. He wanted to put his fountain pen back in his pocket, into the warmth of the money. The money was gone.

There was a sound from the desk. A riffling sound. Like when you shuffle brand-new cards for one of Piaget's games. On the desk in front of Daffy lay the small mahogany-colored stack of new bills.

"In your outer right-hand pocket," said the watchman, "there are two hundred kroner. For a shave. And a hot meal. There's also a message."

The message was a playing card, the two of spades. On the back, written with his own fountain pen, were the words "Rigshospital. Staircase 52.03. Ask for Vivian.—Daffy."

That night he slept in the stables.

There were about twenty animals left, horses and a camel, most of them old or worthless. All the others were still in winter season with circuses in France and southern Germany.

He had his violin with him. He spread out his sheet and duvet in the stall with Roselil, half Berber, half Arabian. She was left behind because she didn't obey anyone except her rider. And not even him.

He played the Partita in A-Minor. A single lightbulb in the ceiling cast a soft golden glow on the listening creatures. He had read in Martin Buber that the most spiritual people are those who are closest to animals. Also in Eckehart. In his sermon "The Kingdom of God Is at Hand." One should seek God among the animals. He thought about the little girl.

When he was about nineteen, and had started to make a name for himself, he had discovered that there was money in his ability to access people's acoustic essence, especially children's. He began to cash in on it at once. After a couple of years he'd had ten private students per day, like Bach in Leipzig.

There had been thousands of children. Spontaneous children, spoiled children, marvelous children, catastrophic children.

Finally, there had been the little girl.

He put the violin into its case and held it in his arms, like a mother nursing her child. It was a Cremonese, a Guarneri, the last thing that remained from the good years.

He said his bedtime prayer. The closeness of the animals had calmed most of his anxiety. He listened to the weariness; it converged from all sides simultaneously. Just as he was about to determine its key, it crystallized into sleep.

# 2

He awoke unreasonably early the next morning. The animals were restless. The lightbulb in the ceiling still burned. But now it was bleached by the dawn. Outside the stall stood a cardinal and his acolyte. In long black coats.

"I'm Moerk," said the older man. "From the Ministry of Justice. Can we give you a lift?"

It was as if they were driving him back to Moscow. In the early 1980s he had spent three winter seasons with the Moscow State Circus. He had lived in the Circus House on the corner of Tverskaya and Gnezdnikovski. The prerevolutionary elegance of that building was also evident in the mansion housing the Copenhagen Tax Authority on Kampmann Street. It was the third time in six months he had come here. But it was the first time they had sent a car to get him.

The building was dark and locked. But the cardinal had a key. It also worked for the blocked floors uppermost on the elevator control panel. Kierkegaard wrote somewhere that every person has a multi-story house, but no one goes up to the *bel étage*. He should have been along this morning—they rode all the way to the top.

The lobby downstairs had been decorated with marble and bronze sconces. That was just a prelude. The elevator opened to a staircase landing flooded with morning light from large dormer windows; it was big enough to hold a billiard tournament. Between the elevator and the staircase sat a young man in a glass booth. White shirt and tie, handsome as Little Jack Horner. But his tone was like a goose-step march. An electric lock hummed, the door in front of them opened.

A broad white corridor stretched ahead of them. It had a parquet floor, attractive lights, and a row of tall double doors leading to large smoke-free offices where people labored as if they were doing piece-work. It was a pleasure to see the taxpayers getting something for their money; the place hummed like a circus ground when tents were being set up. What made Kasper uneasy was the time of day. He had seen the clock at Nørrebro Station as they passed. It showed a quarter to six in the morning.

One of the last doors was closed. Moerk opened it and let Kasper enter first.

In a front office with acoustics like a church vestibule sat two broad-shouldered monks in suits, the younger one with a full beard and ponytail. They nodded to Moerk and stood up.

Beyond them was an open door. They all went in. The tempera-ture in the corridor had been comfortable; in here it was cold. The open window faced Saint Jørgens Lake; the wind that hit them was from Outer Mongolia. The woman behind the desk looked like a Cossack: muscular, beautiful, expressionless.

"Why is he here?" she asked.

Everyone sat down in a semicircle of chairs facing her desk.

The woman had three dossiers in front of her. On her lapel was a small pin. One worn by the happy few who have been knighted by Her Majesty the Queen. On the wall behind her was a shelf with a display of silver trophies engraved with figures of horses. Kasper put his glasses on. The trophies were for contemporary pentathlons. At least one of them was a Nordic championship.

She had been looking forward to a quick victory. All that lovely blond hair was pulled tightly onto the top of her head in a samurai's coiffure. Now confusion had crept into her sound system.

Moerk nodded toward the monks.

"He's applied to regain his Danish citizenship. The police depart-ment's Immigration Service is examining his case for the Naturaliza-tion Office."

The first time Kasper had been called in, a month after his arrival in Copenhagen, they had assigned him to an ordinary bailiff. The next time it had been the head of the department, Asta Borello. At their first meeting he and she had met alone in a little conference room several stories below. He had known that wasn't where she belonged. Now she was home. Beside her, an alert young man in a suit with blond curly hair sat at a word processor ready to take down a report. The office was brightly lit, and large enough to stage a stunt-cycling performance. Her bicycle leaned against the wall, a gray brushed light-alloy racing bike. Farther along the wall were low tables and couches for voluntary informal conversations. Also chairs placed at right angles and two studio tape recorders for depositions provided in the presence of witnesses.

"We got the U.S. figures," she said. "From the commissioner of internal revenue. With reference to the double taxation convention from May of '48. The figures go back to '71, the first year he was assessed for an independent income. They document honoraria of at least twenty million kroner. Of which less than seven hundred thousand is listed on his income tax returns."

"His current property?"

It was the older monk who asked.

"None. Since '91 we're entitled—under the tax compliance law—to freeze remaining assets abroad as well. When we contacted Spain we were turned down at first. They say that variety-show performers and flamenco dancers enjoy a form of illegal diplomatic immunity. But we went back with an international judicial ruling. It turns out that he liquidated what little real estate he still owned. The bank accounts that remain, a few million kroner in all, we now control."

"Might he have money somewhere else?"

"It's possible. In Switzerland, tax evasion isn't a crime. There, it's a religious act. But he'll never get money into this country. The National Bank will never permit him to make transactions. He'll never get another bank account. He'll never get so much as a gas card."

She folded her hands and leaned back.

"Paragraph Thirteen of the tax compliance law authorizes fines—as a rule, two hundred percent of the tax evasion—and imprisonment if the fraud is deliberate or grossly negligent. In this case it will be one full year in prison, and a combined fine and reimbursement of not less than forty million kroner. Since October we've been asking that he be taken into custody. Our request has been denied. We believe that decision can no longer be upheld."

The room became quiet. She had finished.

Moerk leaned forward. The atmosphere in the office changed. It-began to take on the feel of A-minor. At its best. Insistent and serious. In contrast to the woman, the official spoke directly to Kasper.

"We've been to London and, along with folks from Interpol, we spoke with the De Groewe law firm, which is examining your contracts. A year ago, in one twenty-four-hour period, you canceled all your signed contracts, using a medical certificate that WVVF did not approve. They have quietly barred you from all larger international stages while they prepare the lawsuit. The trial will be held in Spain. At the same time as the Spanish tax case. Our experts say both cases are very clear. The reimbursement claim will be at least two hundred and fifty million. And there will be an additional penalty for drunk driving. You have two previous judgments against you; the latter resulted in suspension of your driver's license. You will get a minimum of five years' imprisonment without parole. You will serve your sentence in Alhaurín el Grande. They say it hasn't changed since the Inquisition."

The woman tried not to show her shock. She didn't succeed.

"Tax evasion is plain theft," she said. "From the state! He's our case! He must be tried here!"

Emotion expanded her being. Kasper could hear her. She had some lovely aspects. Very Danish. Christian. Social Democrat. Hated economic turmoil. Excesses. Overconsumption. She had probably completed her master's degree in political science without going into debt. She already was saving for retirement. Bicycled to work. Knighted before the age of forty. It was very moving. He sympathized with her 100 percent; she had impeccable character. He wished he could live up to such standards himself.

Moerk ignored her. He was concentrating on Kasper.

"Jansson here has an order for your arrest in his pocket," he said. "They can take you to the airport right away. Just a quick trip home and a look around the hayloft. Get your toothbrush and your passport. Then off you go."

The tones of everyone else in the room faded. The young men and the functionaries had been purely ornamental. The woman had played the cadences. But the whole time Moerk had held the score.

"We may have another possibility," he said. "They say you're a person people keep coming back to. You once had a young student named KlaraMaria. We wondered if maybe she had come back again."

The room whirled around before Kasper's eyes. Like when you straighten up after a triple forward somersault. No chance to orient yourself in the forward bends.

"Children and adults," he said, "return to me in hordes. But the individual names . . ."

He leaned back in his chair, back into a feeling of no escape. The pressure in the room was enormous. Soon something would burst. He hoped it would not be him. He noticed the prayer begin by itself.

It was the woman who stumbled.

"Seventeen thousand kroner!" she burst out. "For a suit! When you owe all this?"

His prayer had been heard. It was a minimal blunder. But it would suffice.

His fingers closed around the arms of his jacket. Tailor-made jackets button at the wrist. Ready-to-wear suits have decorative buttons.

"Thirty-five thousand," he said mildly. "The seventeen thousand was for the material. It's a Casero. It cost seventeen thousand just to have it sewn."

Her earlier confusion reappeared in her system. Still under control.

For the first time, Kasper caught her eye. He nodded toward Moerk, toward the functionaries, toward the two young men.

"Can they leave the room for a minute?"

"They're here, among other reasons, to guarantee the legal rights of the accused."

Her voice was flat.

"It's about you and me, Asta."

She did not move.

"You shouldn't have said that about my clothes. It's only banks, businesses, and certain accounts that are required to report debt and interest. Now these people know."

Everyone in the room was quiet.

"It's hypocritical," said Kasper. "All these humiliating meetings.

Without our being able to touch each other. I can't stand it. I'm not as strong anymore."

"This is utterly absurd," she said.

"You must ask to be taken off the case, Asta."

She looked at Moerk.

"I had him followed," she said. "You'll get a report. I couldn't understand why you didn't arrest him. I couldn't understand why information was being withheld from us. Someone is protecting him."

Her voice was no longer controlled.

"That's how we knew about the clothes. But I've never met him privately. Never."

Kasper imagined her fragrance. The aroma of life on the steppes. Blended with wild Tajik herbs.

"I've come to a decision," he announced. "You resign your position. We work up an act. You lose thirty pounds. And appear in tulle."

He placed his hand on hers.

"We'll get married," he continued. "In the circus ring. Like Diana and Marek."

She sat paralyzed for a moment. Then she jerked her hand away. As if from an enormous spider.

She rose from her chair, walked around the desk, and headed toward him. With the physical sureness of an athlete, but with no clear motive. Perhaps she wanted to throw him out. Perhaps she wanted to silence him. Perhaps she only wanted to vent her anger.

She should have stayed seated. From the moment she stood up, she didn't have a chance.

Just as she reached his chair, it tipped over backward. To the others in the room it looked as though she knocked him over. Only he and she knew that she didn't manage even to touch him.

He rolled onto the floor.

"Asta!" he pleaded. "No violence!"

She was in motion; she tried to avoid him, without success. His body was flung across the floor. To those watching it appeared that she had kicked him. He rolled into the bicycle; it fell on top of him. She grabbed for the bike, and what they saw was her lift him off the floor and sling him against the door frame.

She tore open the door. Maybe she wanted to leave, maybe she wanted to call for help, but now it looked as though she threw him into the front office. She went after him. Grabbed for his arm. He determined the doors' position by dead reckoning, and crashed into first one and then another.

The doors opened. Two men came out. More people emerged from other offices. Little Jack Horner was on his way too.

Kasper got to his feet. Straightened his suit. He took his keys out of his pocket, loosened one from the ring, and dropped it on the floor in front of the woman.

"Here," he said, "is the key to your apartment."

She felt the eyes of her colleagues on her. Then she lunged toward him.

She didn't reach him. The senior monk had gripped one of her arms, Moerk had the other.

Kasper retreated backward toward the door to the landing.

"In spite of everything, Asta," he said, "you can't pawn my body."


Access to the staircase was through a dividing wall of reinforced glass with one door, next to the booth. Little Jack had left the door open. He followed Kasper out to the landing.

Kasper felt in his pocket for a piece of paper; he found a one-hundred-kroner bill. He held it against the glass and wrote: "I got an unlisted number. I had my locks changed. I'll return the ring. Leave me in peace. —Kasper."

"This is for Asta," he said. "I'm breaking up with her. What's the name of this setup here?"

"Department H."

There was no sign on the door. He handed the bill to the young man. He was in his late twenties. Kasper thought sadly about the pain that lay ahead for such a young person. And you couldn't prepare him. Couldn't spare him a thing. At most, you could cautiously try to let him suspect your own bitter experiences.

"Nothing lasts forever," he said. "Not even a department head's love."


Kampmann Street was grayish white with frost. But bright sunlight fell on him when he stepped onto the sidewalk. The world smiled at him. He had dripped clear water into the poisonous well of mistrust, and thereby transformed it into a healing spring. As Maxim Gorky so aptly said about the great animal trainer and clown Anatoly Anatolievich Durov.

He wanted to start running, but was about to collapse. He hadn't eaten for twenty-four hours. At the corner of Farimag Street was a newsstand that also sold lottery tickets; he escaped into it.

Through the fan of porn magazines on the shelves he could keep an eye on the street. It was deserted.

A clerk leaned toward him. He still had a hundred-kroner bill in his pocket; he should have bought a sandwich and a Coke, but he knew he wouldn't be able to eat, not right now. Instead he bought a lottery ticket, the cheapest kind, for the Danish Class Lottery.

The monks emerged onto the sidewalk. They were running, but their bodies were still stiff, and they were still confused by the way things had gone. They looked up and down the street. The older one was talking on a cell phone, perhaps to his mother. Then they got into a big Renault and drove away.

Kasper waited until a bus stopped at the railroad underpass. Then he crossed Farimag Street.


The bus was almost full, but he found a place in the back and sank down in the corner.

He knew he didn't have a real head start. He missed music, something definitive. So he began to hum. The woman sitting beside him edged away. You couldn't blame her. It was the rugged beginning of Bach's Toccata in D-Minor. Not the Doric, but the youthful work. He fingered the lottery ticket. The Danish Class Lottery was sophisticated. The prizes were big. Chance of winning, one to five. Percentage of return, sixty-five. It was one of the world's best lotteries. The ticket was a comfort. A tiny concentrated sphere of possibilities. A small challenge to the universe. With this ticket he dared She-Almighty. To reveal Her existence. To manifest Herself as winnings. In the midst of April's drab, statistical improbability.

To people with ordinary hearing and consciousness, Copenhagen and its suburbs stretch out horizontally from the center. To Kasper it had always seemed that the city lay inside a funnel.

Up at the edge, with light and air and sea breezes rustling in the treetops, lay Klampenborg, Søllerød, and, just barely, Holte and Virum. The downward spiral began already near Bagsværd and Gladsaxe, and far, far down lay Glostrup. A claustrophobic echo reverberated across its deserts of meager plots; Glostrup and Hvidovre preempted Amager, as if singing directly down into the drainpipe.

The great Polish nun Faustina Kowalska once said that if you pray fervently enough you can adapt yourself comfortably in hell. Earlier Kasper had thought that was because the saint had never been in Glostrup. Now he had lived here for six months. And he had grown to love it.

He loved the bar-and-grills. The jitterbug joints. The Hells Angels clubs. The coffin warehouses. The Cumberland sausages in the butcher shops. The discount stores. The special light over the gardens. The existential hunger in the faces he met on the street, a hunger for meaning in life, which he felt himself. And once in a while this recognition made him unnaturally happy. Even now, at the edge of the abyss. He got off the bus at Glostrup Main Street, unreasonably happy, but very hungry. It was impossible to keep walking. Even Buddha and Jesus had fasted for only thirty or forty days. And afterward said it was no fun. He stopped at the Chinese restaurant on the corner of Siesta Street and cast a discreet glance inside. The eldest daughter was working behind the counter. He went in.

"I've come to say goodbye," he said. "I've gotten an offer. From

Belgium. Circus Carré. Varieté Seebrügge. After that, American television."

He leaned across the counter.

"Next spring I'll come and get you. I'll buy an island. In the Ryukyu chain. I'll build you a temple pavilion. By a murmuring spring. Moss-covered rocks. No more standing by deep-fat fryers. As we gaze at the sun setting over the sea, I'll improvise."

He leaned in over her and sang softly:

> *The April moon glows*
> *on drops of dew*
> *her dress is damp*
> *she pays no mind*
> *she plays and plays*
> *her silver lute*
> *alone at home*
> *she fears the night*

Two truck drivers had stopped eating. The young woman gave him a serious look behind soft, curly coal-black eyelashes.

"And what," she asked, "must I do in return?"

He lowered his head so his lips almost touched her ear. A white ear. Like a limestone cliff. Curved like a cockleshell found on Gili Trawangan.

"A plate of sautéed vegetables," he whispered. "With rice and tamari. And my mail."


She set the food on the table, glided away like a temple dancer at the court in Jakarta. Returned with a letter opener, laid a bundle of envelopes beside him.

There were no personal letters. He opened nothing. But he sat for a moment with each letter in his hand before he let it drop. He listened to its freedom, its mobility, its travels.

There was a postcard inviting him to an exhibit of modern Italian furniture, where even the spumante couldn't disguise how uncomfortable the pieces would be; a chiropractor would have to escort you home. There were somber-looking envelopes from collection agencies with return addresses in the Northwest. And tickets to a Doko E premiere. Discount offers from American airline companies. A letter from an English reference work, *Great Personalities in 20th Century Comedy*. He dropped them all on the table.

A telephone rang. The young woman appeared with the telephone on a small gold-lacquered tray.

They exchanged glances. He used a P.O. box at a mail service on Gasværk Street. Any letters and packages that arrived were brought here to the restaurant twice a week. His address in the national register was c/o Circus Blaff on Grøndal Parkway. He picked up letters from government authorities there every two weeks. The mail service was required to maintain confidentiality. Sonja on Grøndal Parkway would burn at the stake for him. Nobody should have been able to find him. Even Customs and Taxes had been forced to give up. Now someone had found him anyway. He lifted the receiver.

"Would it be okay if we came in fifteen minutes?"

It was the blond woman from the day before.

"That would be fine," he said.

She hung up. He sat with the humming receiver in his hand.

He called the information desk at Bispebjerg Hospital and was transferred to the children's psychiatric ward. Along with the government's School Psychology Office, the ward handled essentially all referrals of children from the Copenhagen area.

The receptionist transferred him in turn to von Hessen.

She was a professor in child psychiatry—he had worked with her on some of the more difficult children he'd had as patients. For the children, the process had been healing. For her, it had been complicated.

"It's Kasper. I had a visit from a man, a woman, and a child. A ten-year-old girl named KlaraMaria. They say you referred them."

She was too surprised to ask anything.

"We haven't had a child by that name. Not while I've been here. And we would never refer anyone. Without a previous arrangement."

She began to sum up. Painful aspects of the past.

"In any case," she said, "we would try to avoid referring anyone to you. Even if we had a previous arrangement."

Somewhere behind her Schubert's Piano Trio in E-Flat Major was playing. In the foreground a computer hummed.

"Elizabeth," he said. "Are you sitting there writing a personal ad?"

Her breathing stopped abruptly.

"Ads are a far too limited channel," he said. "Love demands that you open yourself. It needs a broader form of contact than the Internet. What would be good for you is body therapy. And something with your voice. I could give you singing lessons."

There was no response. In the silence he heard that it was Isaac Stern playing the violin. The soft very soft. The hard very hard. The technique seemingly effortless. And sorrow that was almost more than one could bear.

Somebody stood beside him; it was the young woman. She put a piece of paper in front of him. It was blank.

"The song," she said, "the poem. Write it down."

# 4

Darf Blünow's Stables and Ateliers consisted of four buildings that enclosed a large courtyard: an administration building with three small offices, two dressing rooms, and a large practice room. A rehearsal ring built as an eight-sided tower. A low riding house, behind which were stables and exercise and longeing pens. A warehouse containing workshops, sewing rooms, and storage lofts.

The cement surface of the courtyard was covered with a thin layer of quiet, clear rainwater. Kasper stood inside the entrance. The sun came out, there was a pause between gusts of wind. The water's surface hardened to a mirror. Where the mirror ended, the black Volvo stopped.

He walked to the middle of the courtyard and stood there, in water up to his ankles. His shoes and socks absorbed it like a sponge. It was like wading out into the fjord opposite the tent grounds at Rørvig Harbor on the first of May.

The car door opened, the little girl pattered along the side of the building. She was wearing sunglasses. Behind her, the blond woman. He reached the building and opened the door for them.

He walked into the rehearsal ring; the little lamp on the piano was lit. He turned on the overhead light. Took his shoes and socks off.

There was a fourth person in the room, a man. Daffy must have let him in. He sat six rows back, bolt upright against the emergency exit. The fire department wouldn't have liked that. He had something by one ear; the light was poor—maybe it was a hearing aid.

Kasper opened a folding chair, took the woman by the arm, and led her to the edge of the ring.

"I have to stand very close," she said.

He smiled at her, at the child, at the man by the fire exit.

"You will sit here," he said quietly. "Or else all of you will have to leave."

She stood there for a moment. Then she sat down.

He went back to the piano, sat down, and wrung the water out of his socks. The little girl stood next to him. He lifted the fall board. The atmosphere was a little tense. The important thing was to spread sweetness and light. He chose the aria from Bach's *Goldberg Variations*. Written to soothe sleepless nights.

"I've been kidnapped," said the girl.

She stood very close to the piano. Her face was extremely pale. The theme modulated to a type of fugue, rhythmic as a guanaco's gait, charming as a cradle song.

"I'll take you away," he said.

"Then they'll do something to my mother."

"You don't have a mother."

His voice sounded to him as if it belonged to someone else.

"You just didn't know," she said.

"Do they have her too?"

"They can find her. They can find everyone."

"The police?"

She shook her head. The woman straightened up. The little CD player he used for morning practice stood on the piano. He chose a disc, turned the machine so the sound waves were in line with the man and woman. He led the girl into the shadow of the sound, and knelt in front of her. Behind him Sviatoslav Richter struck the first chords as if he wanted to pave the grand piano.

"How did you get them to bring you here?"

"I wouldn't do something for them otherwise."

"What?"

She didn't reply. He started from below. The tension in her legs, thighs, buttocks, hips, and abdomen was elevated. But not forcibly. No indication of sexual assault or anything like that. That would have caused stasis or a resigned lack of tension, even in her. But she was completely tight from just above the solar plexus, where the diaphragm attached to the stomach wall. The double sacrospinalis was as taut as two steel wires.

Her right hand, which the onlookers couldn't see, found his left hand. Against his palm he felt a tightly folded piece of paper.

"Find my mother. And then both of you come back for me."

The music faded.

"Lie down," he said. "It's going to hurt where my fingers are touching. Go into the pain, and listen to it. Then it will go away."

The sound came again. Richter played as if he wanted to pound the keys through the piano's iron frame. The man and woman had risen.

"Where are they keeping you?" he asked. "Where do you sleep?"

"Don't ask any more questions."

His fingers found a knotted muscle, double-sided, under the scapula. He listened to it; he heard pain of a magnitude a child should not know. A white, dangerous fury began to rise in him. The woman and the man walked into the ring. The girl straightened up and looked him in the eye.

"Do as I say," she said quietly. "Or else you'll never see me again."

He lifted his hands to her face and removed the sunglasses. The blow had struck the edge of her eyebrow; the blood had run down under her skin and collected above her jawbone. Her eye appeared to be unharmed.

She met his gaze. Without blinking. She took the sunglasses from his hands. Put them on.

He walked to the car with them, opened the door.

"Continuity is important in the beginning," he said. "It would be nice if she could come tomorrow."

"She goes to school."

"One works best within a context," he said. "I wonder what her situation is. Are her parents divorced, are there problems? A little information would help."

"We're just accompanying her," said the woman. "We need to get the family's permission first."

The girl's face was empty. Kasper stepped away from the car, and it rolled out into the sea.

He stuck his hand into his pocket to find something to write on. He found the playing card. He took his fountain pen and wrote down the license plate number. While he could still remember it. From the time one reaches forty, short-term memory slowly declines.

He felt the cold from below. It suddenly dawned on him that he was barefoot. The sawdust of the ring still stuck to the soles of his feet.

The trailer was parked behind the ring, by a row of electrical boxes and water connections. He turned on a light and sat down on the sofa. What the little girl had given him was a sheet of paper folded many times and pressed into a small, hard packet. He unfolded it very slowly. It was a post office receipt. She had drawn and written on the back of it.

The page looked like a child's version of a pirate map. There was a drawing of a house, flanked on each side with what looked like a toolshed; under the house she had written "hospital." Below the drawing were three words: "Lona Midwife." And "Kain." That was all. He turned the piece of paper over and read the receipt. The sender was the girl herself—she had written only her first name, Klara-Maria. He couldn't read the name of the addressee at first because his brain stopped functioning. He closed his eyes and sat for a while with his face in his hands. Then he read the name.

He stood up. From among the music scores in the bookcase he took a small bound copy of Bach's *Klavierbüchlein* and opened it. Inside was not the *Klavierbüchlein* but a passport; between its last two pages was a slip of paper with a series of telephone numbers written on it.

He carried the phone over to the coffee table and dialed the top number.

"Rabia Institute."

It was a young voice he hadn't heard before.

"This is the municipal health officer," he said. "May I speak to the deputy director?"

A minute went by. Then a body approached the telephone.

"Yes?"

It was an appetizing voice. A year ago he had met the woman to whom it belonged. A nibble could have cost him his upper and lower teeth. But not now. Her voice was hoarse and practically lifeless with sorrow.

He hung up. He had heard only the one word, but that was enough. It was the voice of someone who has lost a child.

He dialed the next number.

"The International School."

"This is Kasper Krone," he said, "leader of the Free Birds Troop. I have a message for one of my little girl scouts, KlaraMaria. Our patrol meeting has been changed."

The voice cleared its throat, tried to collect itself. Tried, despite the shock, to remember what someone had instructed it to say.

"She's in Jutland for a few days. Visiting some of her family. May I give her a message when she comes back? Is there a telephone number?"

"Just a scout greeting," he said. "From the Ballerup Division."

He leaned back on the sofa. And stayed like that. Until everything returned to normal. Except the tight, cold, little ball of anxiety in the pit of his stomach.

Ever since the mid-1700s, when James Stuart, the "Old Pretender," went to the guillotine in Paris and then picked up his severed head and left the Circus Medrano ring to apocalyptic applause, nobody had been able to take death onstage. It was the hardest thing to do. Kasper had tried for twenty years without success; he felt powerless, and now too.

He crossed Blegdam Road and took one of the side entrances facing Fælled Park. Rigshospital was like the gray backstage of a circus in the Underworld: the muffling effect of the white curtains, the patients' seminakedness, the uniformed employees. The hierarchies. The character roles. The quantity of polished steel. The sound of an invisible machine nearby. The taste of adrenaline in one's saliva. The sense of being at the edge.

He stepped out of the elevator. With the playing card in hand he made his way through the white labyrinth of bed units, found the right room, and opened the door.

Out in the hall there had been fluorescent lighting and smoking was prohibited. In the room he now entered, antique English Bestlites lamps swam in a cloud of tobacco smoke. On a low bed set in a wide cherrywood frame a man sat cross-legged, surrounded by silk pillows, smoking a cigarette. Unfiltered, but monogrammed in gold.

"I have to be in court in half an hour," he said. "Come in and say hello to Vivian the Terrible."

The woman was in her mid-sixties and wore a doctor's white coat. Her skin was pale, almost transparent, and quite thin; he could hear her blood through it, blood and life. She held out her hand; it was warm, dry, and firm. She was in A-flat major. Under other circumstances he could have listened to her for hours.

"It's only five months since you were here last," said the sick man. "I hope this isn't inconvenient for you."

"I've been performing down south."

"You haven't been advertised since Monte Carlo. You haven't been out of the country."

Kasper sat down in an easy chair. There were Karzamra carpets on the floor, shelves filled with books, a pianette, Richard Mortensen's circus paintings on the walls, a television large enough to be the box for the trick where the woman gets sawed in half.

"I look better than you expected, don't I?"

Kasper looked at his father. Maximillian Krone had lost at least thirty pounds. His glasses looked too big for him. The pillows weren't for the sake of comfort—they were to hold him upright.

"I've had a nice visitor. From the Ministry of Justice. Looked like an undertaker. Wanted your address. I told him to go to hell. He insisted they've got a tax case against you. And something worse in Spain. He said WVVF has blacklisted you. Is that true?"

The sick man gave him a questioning look.

"You were never very reliable. But you're not the suicidal type either."

He had some papers in his hand.

"Rigshospital has laboratories and annexes in the inner city," his father went on. "I'm a consultant on their insurance matters. That's why I can vegetate in this pantomime of *A Thousand and One Nights*. While Vivian's patients bleed to death in the hallways. I filched a list of the experts the state and county have summoned."

There were five sheets of paper, perhaps two hundred names, Danish and foreign, companies and individuals. One was underlined.

Kasper read it, handed back the paper. He stood up, and let his hands glide over the room's props. The Brazilian rosewood bookcases, the lamps' chrome plating. The white-lacquered frames around the large canvases.

"It must be her," said Maximillian.

New curtains had been hung, like stage curtains. Kasper gathered the heavy brocade between his fingers.

"What is Department H?" he asked.

A delicate tone of anxiety began to sing somewhere in the room, as if a tuning fork had been struck.

"It doesn't exist—it's a rumor. Where did you hear about it? It was supposedly established in the nineties. Grew out of collaboration among the Serious Economic Crime office, the police's mobile patrol unit, the Financial Supervision Authority, the Customs and Tax Administration. The local tax authorities and the Danish Competition Authority. Along with the board of supervisors at the Copenhagen Stock Exchange. After major companies were drained. The goal was to counteract new ways of making illegal profits. People say they discovered something. Something big. Which they didn't make public. Something that made them set up a special office. I don't believe a damn word of it. And in any case, they wouldn't be mixed up in a small-time con man's boring tax case. Where did you hear about it?"

Serious illness begins outside the physical. Kasper had noticed this before, sometimes months before the illness broke through. The same was true of Maximillian. There was a change; an unfamiliar element had been added to his tonal picture.

"What about child abuse? How hard is one allowed to hit?"

"Law number three eighty-seven of June fourteenth, 1995, amended in 1997. 'The child shall be treated with respect for its person, and must not be subjected to physical punishment or other offensive treatment.' In practice this means you can certainly lead them with a firm grip. But no karate chop. Are you expecting a child?"

"There's a student."

"A new little Footit?"

The English clown Tudor Hall, alias Footit, was the first to make serious money by taking a child, his three-year-old son, into the ring with him.

Kasper stood up.

"How much is it?" asked Maximillian. "How much do you owe? Actually, I know. The undertaker told me. It's forty million kroner. I'll pay it. I'll sell all the crap. I can raise forty million. I'll get my license back. I'll go to court for you. With my IV stand and all. I'll make them back down."

Kasper shook his head.

Maximillian's hand fell on the papers.

"They'll throw you in jail! They'll deport you! You won't be able to meet her!"

He pressed himself up on the bed. Like a gymnast preparing to do a handstand on the parallel bars.

"A bad heart," he said hoarsely. "Not a good thing for a clown. Pisses on the helping hand. Burns the opportunity. After she's been out of range of any damage from you for years."

He turned toward the woman.

"When he dies—and his turn will come too—he'll have wheels put under his coffin. So he can pole himself out of the chapel and into the crematorium. And won't have to ask anyone for help."

His anger was monumental, as it always had been. But the physical underpinning was gone. The sick man began to cough, deeply, dangerously.

The doctor let him finish coughing and then carefully lifted his upper body. Kasper put the playing card on the edge of the bed.

"If," he said, "you still know someone who can get into the main motor-vehicle registration files. Then you could find the address. That goes with this license plate number."

Maximillian had closed his eyes. Kasper started toward the door.

"We saw the broadcast from Monte Carlo," said the sick man. "Both the award presentation and your performance."

Kasper stopped. Maximillian reached backward. Took the woman's hand. The skin around his eyes had become smooth, like a *graciosa* in the Spanish theater.

"We wished the show would never end. It was like when I was a child. It's the only thing that must never end. Love. And great performances."

Father and son looked straight at each other. There were no masks. The sick man held out for a few seconds, then it became too much.

He put his hands up to his hair. It was red, bristly as a badger's. He lifted it off. It was a wig. Underneath he was as bald as a watermelon.

"Disappointed, eh? Had it made after the chemo. From my own hair. Hats off! To a great artist!"

Kasper walked back to the bed. Took hold of the large bald head and drew it close to him. He listened into the tragedy that thickly surrounds most people. The sound of all that could have been, but never will be.

Maximillian had stiffened at Kasper's touch. After a moment he pulled himself free.

"Enough," he said. "I feel like Lazarus. The dogs lick me. When will I see you again? In six months?"

The doctor held the door for Kasper.

"The little girl," Maximillian said from the bed. "The student. Wasn't that the real reason you came? Wasn't it?"

The door shut behind Kasper; the doctor stood beside him.

"I'll drive you home," she said.

The most successful white-face clowns Kasper had seen had based their effect on having their partner play up to them from below. Self-reliant authority is very rare. The woman in front of him had it. It radiated from her. Cleared corridors and opened doors.

She wanted to do something for him, but couldn't express it. She sat behind the wheel in the underground garage without moving, and waited for the words. They didn't come.

The vehicle was as long as a railroad car. Kasper loved how rich people sniffed their way to each other. It was like Romeo and Juliet. Even in the heat of passion and love at first sight, in the upper right-hand corner there was always a space set aside for balancing the account.

He handed her the girl's map. She decoded it immediately, without asking any questions.

"There are thirteen county hospitals and sanatoriums," she said. "Køge, Gentofte, Herlev, Glostrup, Hvidovre, Rigshospital, Frederiksberg, Amager, Roskilde, Hillerød, plus the smaller ones in Hørsholm, Helsingør, and Frederikssund. None of them are by the water. None of the private hospitals are either."

"Clinics?"

"North of Copenhagen and south of Avedøre Holme, all together perhaps a hundred health centers and special clinics. How old was the person who drew this?"

"Ten years old."

She pointed at what he had interpreted as outbuildings.

"They could be wings of the building. Children first start to understand perspective when they're about eight. That would make the building too big to be a private office. It doesn't look like anyplace I know."

She started the car.

"How many midwives in Copenhagen?"

"Perhaps fifteen hundred."

"How many are named Lona?"

"They're registered with the Midwives Association. I can find out for you."

"Within an hour?"

She nodded.

They drove to the other side of the lakes, down Gother Street. He listened to her; she didn't know where she was going. She pulled over to the side, blinded by something or other. She sat fumbling with the steering wheel. He got out of the car in order to give her time and peace. They were parked by a barricade.

The barrier was made of watertight plywood, like a fence around a building site; it blocked off part of the road and a row of houses facing Gammel Mønt Street. Some fifty yards ahead it was interrupted by a glass booth, a gate, and two attendants in overalls.

He walked over to the booth; a woman in a civil-defense uniform sat behind the speaker.

"May I deliver a note to someone I know?" he asked. "Close family. A matter of life and death."

She shook her head.

"We have seven hundred journalists swarming around here. From all over the world."

"A telephone call?"

She shook her head. Out of the corner of his eye he caught sight of the top name on a board with a list of salvage companies, relief organizations, and entrepreneurs.

"I'm the son of the senior Mr. Hannemann," he said. "He's just become an honorary member of the Søllerød Golf Club. The lifelong dream of an old man."

"He won't be able to appreciate it," she said. "He died in the eighties."

Kasper caught sight of his own face in the window. It was as white as a full makeup job. The woman's eyes grew worried.

"Shall I call a taxi for you?"

Her sympathy went to his blood like a shot of glucose. He wanted to sit on her lap and tell her everything. He nodded toward the car.

"My chauffeur and personal physician are waiting."

"Did you have another name besides Hannemann?"

"Stina Claussen. Engineer."

"Dark-haired?"

He nodded.

"Something to do with water?"

"She's made of water."

She looked at a printout lying in front of her.

"She has a pickup agreement. With the taxi companies. That's a special arrangement for the VIPs. It means she lives at a hotel. The Three Falcons or the Royal. If word gets out that you got this from me, I'll be fired."

He drew a deep breath.

"Angels," he said, "can't be dismissed."

He got into the car beside the doctor. She was sitting in the same position as when he left her.

"He's going to die now," she said.

He had known that was what she wanted to say. For him personally it wasn't a problem. He had reconciled himself to death long ago. Padre Pio once said that, seen from a slightly larger perspective, we all lie at death's door. The only difference is that some lie a little closer than others.

So it wasn't that something happened to him; it was the surroundings that changed. One moment the city was a picture postcard with no reflections, the next moment the car sailed through a world of destruction where all sound had died.

"He looked well."

"Prednisone. A chemical veneer."

"Does he know it himself?"

They had passed the zoological garden and Solbjerg cemetery. He didn't know how they had reached Roskilde Road.

"As a rule there's a part of oneself that knows. And a larger part that doesn't want to know."

She turned toward Glostrup, took the ring road, turned off, and drove through the industrial section, parked behind the market square.

She started to cry. Quietly, but unrestrained. She pointed to the glove compartment—he handed her a packet of tissues.

He had been mistaken about the money. Her sorrow came from somewhere deep down, farther down than the safe deposit box with securities in it.

She blew her nose.

"Tell me something about him," she said. "From when you were little."

He listened out over his childhood; he heard the sound of potatoes.

"I was ten years old—we lived in Skodsborg. They were always nomads, even after he began to earn money. They never furnished more than one room each, plus my room, like in the trailers. All the other rooms were closed off to save heat. They moved once a year. Skodsborg was the record—we lived there almost four. They had three places to escape to there, the Sound, the Coastal Railway, and Strand Road. I started to juggle there. I practiced with potatoes. I put quilts and blankets on the floor, but it still vibrated when I didn't grab correctly. One day he must have heard that, because suddenly he stood in the doorway."

Kasper closed his eyes and saw the scene before him.

"It was the early seventies, there was no real poverty anymore, but he had experienced it. As a boy he had been hungry—he sold carnations and sang in the streets. He never got over it, just like the artists who were in concentration camps during the war; it never goes away. So he left the circus; he saw only one way out: a higher education and a secure income. And now he stood in the doorway. My schoolbooks lay on the table—they hadn't been opened. He looked at me. It's more than thirty years ago. He could have sent me to the Herlufsholm boarding school, he could have sent me to learn to be a paint dealer, he could have wiped the floor with me. But he just stood there in the doorway, absolutely still. And then I could sense what was going on in him. We could both sense it. He understood that sometimes the longing is greater than you are. And if you choke it, you'll be destroyed. Finally he backed away without saying anything, and very quietly shut the door. We never spoke of it. But he never again came into my room without knocking."

Her eyes were fixed on his lips. When one is sixty-five and falls in love it must be the same as when one was fifteen. If he had shown slides and related anecdotes about Maximillian she would have sat at his feet for three months.

"Because of moments like those, I love him," he said.

The situation was full-toned. It's important to exit at a high point. He got out of the car.

She got out on her side, walked around the hood.

"And aside from those moments," she said, "what was it like?"

He was mistaken, apparently, about being in love. When one is sixty-five, one wants a more comprehensive picture.

"They tried to chop each other's head off," he said. "Aside from those moments, it was like the Viking battle at Bravalla."

He had started to walk; she came up beside him.

"What about forgiveness?"

"That was thirty years ago. I've forgiven everything."

She took his arm.

"You've forgiven a certain percent. If we can increase that percent, it's never too late to find a happy childhood."

He tried to pull loose, without success; she had a grip like a paramedic.

"It's too sensitive," he said. "He and I, we're both deeply traumatized."

"You're a couple of hooligans. You've fought for forty years. Now you have three weeks, at the most, to make your peace."

She walked back toward the car. He followed her.

"Three weeks?"

She got in.

"He's strong as a workhorse," he said.

"I'm the head of the Rigshospital hospice service. I've watched fifteen hundred people die. There are three weeks left at the most."

She wanted to close the door; he blocked it.

"Death isn't the end. I'm very religious. After the last breath there's a general intermission. Then consciousness starts out in a new physical body and the music plays again."

She looked him straight in the eye.

"What good is it to me," she asked, "when I'm lying alone in bed, to know that somewhere on this earth a newborn baby is nursing at its mother's breast, and in that baby lives my lover's consciousness?"

He leaned against the car. There was still hoarfrost on the grass in the empty lots.

"I love him," he said.

"I do too," she said.

He bent down to her.

"Could the fact that we share this deep feeling create a starting point for a loan of five thousand kroner?"

She found her purse, opened it, handed him two thousand-kroner bills. Closed the door, rolled down the window.

"What's all this about the child?" she asked. "And the drawing?"

Her eyes were expansive. He could have put himself in them with all his sorrow, and there would still have been space remaining. He shook his head.

"Don't be mistaken about me," she said. "I charge interest. Bank discount rate plus two percent."

The window closed, the car started and accelerated. As if up the long side of the Jutland racetrack. He felt an involuntary admiration for his father. For the fact that, despite his deviant psychology, Maximillian had still been able to capture a she-elephant.

He walked into the office and placed the woman's two thousand kroner in front of Daffy.

"Installment payment on the rent," he said.

The watchman handed him a letter, without postage, stamped by a messenger service. Gave him a letter opener from the desk.

The envelope had an extrasensory feel that can't be scientifically explained, but that results when its contents are both a letter and a check. The letter was two typed lines.

"We hereby inform you that KlaraMaria will no longer come to instruction. Enclosed find twenty thousand kroner for your trouble."

No signature. The check was a money order.

He sat down on a chair. The good thing about having reached the bottom is that you can't fall any farther.

The door opened. A young man with censers held it. Moerk walked in.

"You're going to be deported," he said. "You have ten hours to get everything in order. You'll be put on a plane for Madrid tomorrow morning."

Maybe there is no bottom. Maybe it's an endless fall. Kasper stood up. Opened the door. Walked out into the courtyard.

He stripped off his jacket. His shirt. Two groups of workmen were lounging on the benches by the warehouses. Some costume makers on break were drinking coffee at one of the tables. He took off his shoes and socks. His pants. He was now in just his harlequin-pattern boxer shorts. Made of silk. He had a thing about silk, as Wagner did.

"Everything must go," he said to the seamstresses. "It's a matter of giving away everything. Our Savior did it. Liszt did it. Wittgenstein. The fourteenth-century Tibetan Buddhist Longchen Rabjam did it seven times. When there's nothing more anyone can take away from you, then you're free."

He waited. Maybe he had frightened Moerk. To be legally valid, deportation must also be communicated in writing.

Paper rustled; Moerk stood behind him.

"Does the name Kain mean anything to you?"

"It's right at my fingertips. From the Bible story."

"Josef Kain."

Kasper didn't respond.

"Here's the deportation order," said the official. "In your jacket you'll find a taxi voucher. With a telephone number on it. In case you should remember something. About your little student."

Kasper shut his eyes. When he opened them, Moerk was gone. Someone put a blanket around his shoulders. It was Daffy.


They sat across the desk from each other. Kasper had wrapped himself in the blanket; it was as long as a ball gown. He was numb. Perhaps it was the cold.

The letter lay in front of Daffy. He must have read it.

"She's a student who means something to me," said Kasper. "They owe me money, they aren't coming back. I have no address, no trace of them."

The watchman raised one hand. It was empty. He turned it around. Nothing behind it. He moved it along the desk. From the top of the desk a card appeared.

"The tall man. The emperor. He had this in his wallet."

Kasper picked up the card. A name was printed on it. ASKE BRODERSEN. Beneath it, written in pencil, was a telephone number beginning with 70. He turned over the card. On the back the same pencil had written the name of a person or a place, BOHRFELDT.

"The names aren't listed," said Daffy. "The number isn't either."

When Kasper was a child, tent workers and craftsmen were called "circus specialists." They were Danish. At the beginning of the season they emerged from the ground; in October they disappeared without a trace. Since then the name had been changed to "technical workers." Now they were groups of Poles and Moroccans who traveled through Europe led by a team boss, like highly specialized ships' crews. When a circus docked, they went on to the next job. Their tone had remained the same, a tone of discipline, professional self-confidence, and raw effectiveness. He had always loved the sound—he had heard it ever since he first met Daffy, and also heard it now.

But there had been another sound too; he had missed it. Until now.

The watchman set the telephone in front of him. Kasper looked out the window.

"I wonder what time the sun will set," he said.

Daffy turned toward the bookshelf. It held many manuals. Too many for a watchman who had gone to school for seven years at most. There was also an almanac. He looked up sunset times.

"In fifteen minutes," he said.

"Then I'd like to wait fifteen minutes. I express myself best at sunset."

The watchman raised both hands. Brought them over the desk. Out of nothing appeared the fountain pen, visiting cards, loose change. The lottery ticket. The keys. Minus the one Kasper had given to Asta Borello.

"Montblanc Meisterstück," said Daffy. "For important signatures. But the other pockets don't match up. No credit card. No wallet. Loose bills. Money is just passing through. No driver's license. No permanent address. Someone without roots. My professional opinion. Don't take it personally."

It wasn't Kasper's own will that made him stand up. He would actually have preferred to stay seated. It was the orange impersonal rage that's awakened by criticism when it's justified.

The desk was less than three feet away. In short distances he was as fast as a Chinese Ping-Pong player.

He didn't reach it. Daffy's right hand dissolved. Rematerialized instantly. With a leather-covered conical stick two-thirds the length of a billiard cue. Made like a riding crop. With a shiny ball at the end about the size of a glass eye.

It was an animal trainer's baton. Kasper remembered them from the early sixties, before carnivore menageries were prohibited. A man with a good forehand who knew where to strike could smash a lion's skull.

He stopped in his tracks. He heard the refined tones he had ignored in Daffy. They were like those in the young Beethoven. The world was about to discover him now. The muted treasures had been drowned in subsequent events.

The watchman's hands dropped out of sight. Appeared again. With a laboratory stand, a dish of uncut diamonds, a box of toothpicks, two glasses, a bottle of slivovitz. He fastened a diamond to the stand, filled a glass with liquor, warmed it in his hand, and lit a match. Held it to the liquid mirror. A voracious, restless blue flame crept along the edge of the glass. He pushed it in under the diamond. The flame caught the mineral, which began to melt and drip down into the glass. It was rock candy.

Kasper listened toward the sunset outside. He pulled the telephone over to himself, collected his thoughts, and dialed the number on the card.

"Yes?"

It was a woman in her early forties.

"I'm a very close friend of Aske," he said. "I had a dream I want to tell him about."

She left the phone but did not hang up; she was away for fifteen seconds. He could have hung up—he had all the information he needed. A feeling of helplessness and an absurd hope of hearing KlaraMaria's voice from somewhere in the background made him stay on the line.

The woman came back.

"He's away on a trip."

"To the men's room at most," he said. "I think you should go and get him there. This is a profound dream. He would hate to miss it."

He must have been standing beside her. Now he took the receiver.

"You got your money. How did you get this telephone number?"

"The little girl. I want to talk to her."

He heard his voice from outside himself. It belonged to a person who was about to lose his composure.

"She's been hit," he added. "This is assault and battery. I've spoken with a lawyer."

The man hung up.

Drops of boiling-hot sugar hissed down into the slivovitz. Daffy slid a glass over to him.

"A vagabond existence is fine until the age of forty," said the watchman. "After that, one needs a permanent address to stop the decline. Especially if it's as rapid as yours."

Kasper drank. Closed his eyes. It gave him a physical lift, similar to what large birds of prey must feel when they are flying. The concentrated fruit, the alcohol, the sugar, and the tropical heat rushed through his body out to the farthest capillaries. Chased away hunger, cold, and weariness. Bathed his suffering in a golden light.

"And this profound philosophy," he said, "has led you to a meteoric career as a janitor in Glostrup."

Daffy smiled. It was the first time Kasper had seen him smile in the six months he had known the man.

"With help from the judge. I got four years' suspended sentence. Provided I changed my occupation."

Kasper gathered together his things. Picked up the glass, which was still hot. Laid the check on the table.

"An installment payment on what I owe," he said.

Daffy came around the desk. Opened the door for him.

"Why at sunset? Why do you express yourself best at sunset?"

Kasper looked at the watchman's hands. Daffy could have been famous, as Bach was only after his death. Wealthy, as Richter never was. And now he stood holding the door.

He pointed toward the sunset sky above the city.

"Listen," he said.

There was no loud or distinct sound. It was an intricate curtain of muffled ringing tones. The city's church bells chiming the sun to rest.

"The key they are tuned to becomes the tonic in a major or minor triad. An overtone, which is an octave plus a minor or major third, varies along with the tonic. The city is a sound map. Grundtvig Church. Tuned in D. And above that, the F-sharp is heard just as strongly. The church has only the one huge bell. Its chimes could never be confused with those of the Church of Our Savior. Each is unique in its own way. So if you talk on the phone at sunset, and listen beyond the voice and compensate for the flat sound picture, you get an impression of where the person at the other end is located on the sound map."

# 9

He sat down on the bed. He drank slowly. The dark amber liquid had everything. It calmed you and filled you up, brought clarity and ecstasy. It anesthetized bad nerves and stimulated healthy ones. He raised the glass and let it refract the last light coming through the window. April light was unlike any other. It had a charming, optimistic unreliability, like an overbid hand in poker. It gave a promise of spring that it wasn't sure it could keep.

He opened a large shallow rectangular drawer, the kind architects keep their elevations in; it was Stina's. He had asked Rud Rasmussen to make it for her.

Before the drawer she had never left anything at his place. In the morning she would methodically gather up everything, often while he was still asleep. When he woke up everything was gone, no physical trace of her; only her sound remained.

He had looked for her when she was away. He hoped she would have left a toothbrush or some lotion in the bathroom; there was nothing. One evening he put it into words as they sat eating.

"I could clear out a couple of shelves in the closet."

She put down her knife and fork and wiped her lips. She did it delicately, but at the same time like an animal, the way a cat washes itself, the way a jaguar is delicate.

"You've heard about voodoo," she said. "Some years ago we purified groundwater in Haiti. We were warned by our department head and by COWI, an international consulting firm, that we must never leave personal belongings behind. If a sorcerer wants to put a spell on you and gets hold of anything of yours, he'll have power over you."

The food had turned to sawdust in his mouth.

"We can't see each other anymore," he said. "If that's how you view me. I can't stand humiliation. We've known each other for a month and a half. I've behaved with total respect. Toward you. Toward all women. Like a little boy who peeks over the hedge at the neighbor girl. But never jumps over it. Always waits for her to want to play."

"But who, deep inside," she said, "is hatching a plan. About how to take over the whole neighborhood."

A week later he'd had the drawer made. He hadn't said anything. She arrived, the cabinet was attached to a wall in the trailer, and the drawer was pulled out slightly. Her hands glided over the wood, pulled out the drawer, pushed it in, without a word. He had taken its measurements from the drawers in her apartment. It exactly fit a four-centimeter-scale map.

The next time she brought a briefcase with her. Without saying anything she left a small stack of maps, copy paper, an etui containing a bow compass. The things had been there ever since.

One of the maps was of Copenhagen Harbor, 1:25,000. Now he took the compass, and recalled the sound picture from the telephone conversation.

Foremost were the Marble Church bells, electrically amplified, but muted so as not to awaken Amalienborg Palace. In open surroundings the sound pressure level decreases six decibels each time the distance to the sound maker doubles. With the compass he measured two and a half miles according to the scale at the bottom of the map. Using the church as the center, he drew a circle with this distance as the radius.

Grundtvig Church lay far back in the sound picture, but it was very clear. The huge vibrating bell seemed to be playing, quite alone, "Christmas Bells Are Ringing." It was also in D; the composer had imitated the sound of the church bell. So it was likely that the telephone had been located high up. Above the sixty-five feet that would have made it higher than the roofs of Nørrebro and Østerbro. He estimated the distance at three miles. He heard the Church of Our Savior chimes. Farther out in the sound picture were the City Hall chimes; he must have caught their quarter-hour tolling. They were made of iron ore instead of bronze, and had a hard clang. The frequency wasn't as pure as that of the church bells. Their distance from the telephone was three miles. Using Grundtvig Church as the center, he drew a new circle with this radius. The two circles shared a common area that included all of outer Østerbro.

He listened again. He identified the English Church and St. Jacob's Church; their interference created a corona of suggested major keys from A to D. He drew two additional circles.

They intersected the two original circles fifty-five yards offshore. North of the entrance to Copenhagen Harbor. Beyond the tip of the peninsula, at a depth of thirty-nine feet. He hadn't heard correctly.


He drank from the glass. In the midst of failure all the sounds he heard seemed very near. The sounds of April were unlike any others. No leaves on the trees. No vegetation to dampen reflection and diffusion. He heard the last rush-hour traffic from Glostrup. The distant drone from Ring Road 4. The birds in the bogs. Voices of the seamstresses. Cheered by the sunset. By closing time. Yet, not completely present. A part of their systems was already on the way home. Most of them had children. Women's voices developed a certain gravity when they had children. An ostinato.

The first day when the sun was warm enough to sit outside for fifteen minutes he had crossed the courtyard during the lunch break. He had heard the women's voices from far away. Not the words, but the tone; they were talking about children. They had called to him, and he had seated himself on a bench with them. Their eyes were affectionate and teasing, the kind of risk-free flirting that comes from knowing you have a dependable husband at home. Normally he loved it like a warm bath. One of them had asked: "Why don't you have children?"

He had noticed her before.

"I haven't been able to find a woman."

They smiled, he smiled. They didn't understand that it was true.

"That's one reason," he said. "The other is that in a little while we're gone, in a little while the children are old. Just imagine it—they're eighty years old, their spouses are dead, there are no witnesses to the first thirty years of their lives, and then they're gone. That's the other reason."

They edged away from him. The woman who had asked the question before spoke again.

"I thought you were a clown."

He rose to his feet.

"I'm a musician," he said. "I have a deal with SheAlmighty. To play all the notes. Including the black ones."

After that the latent eroticism had cooled. Some of it had heated up again. But things had never been completely the same.

He placed a book on top of the glass. To reduce evaporation. The book was Jung's memoirs. Jung had written that people seek their spirituality in alcohol. Jung must have known what he was talking about. He must have known how it felt to sit across from two cases of Krug Magnum and be unable to stop after the first case. Alcohol is a violin; it's impossible to leave it alone. He lifted the book and emptied the glass.

He changed places. So he would be sitting across from the sofa. Across from where KlaraMaria had sat. The first time he saw her.

## 10

It had been exactly one year ago.

He had returned from a performance a little later than usual; it was April, midnight. The trailer stood on a plot of land near the coastal community of Vedbæk. He had owned the property for twenty years without applying for a building permit. Its twelve thousand square yards of quack grass stretched down to the beach, encircled by fir trees.

The trailer stood in the middle of the grass; he drove over to it, parked, opened the door, and listened.

Nature always plays one or more musical themes, or that might just be imagination. That night it was the Ricercare from *Ein Musikalisches Opfer*, orchestrated by Anton Webern with text by Tagore: "Not hammer blows, but the dance of the waves sings small stones into perfection."

It had been years since Stina had disappeared. She hadn't taken the meaning of life with her—that had begun to wander away of its own accord much earlier. But she had slowed down the process.

From the trailer came a sound that shouldn't have been there. He ducked out of the car. One can't have twenty years of gentle ascent in show business without becoming a victim of projections.

He reached the door on all fours. He felt under the trailer for the key; it was gone.

Someone who had progressed further in his development would have left. Or would have pressed a couple of buttons beside the door. Artist's insurance had given him a direct line to the security services of both Falck and Securitas. But we are no farther than where we are. From under the steps he fished out a thirty-inch pipe from the good old days when they were still made of lead.

He entered the doorway silently. He could hear one person, a resting pulse between eighty and ninety, a circus dwarf.

"Come in."

It was a child, a girl. He didn't know how she had been able to hear him. He walked in.

She was perhaps eight or nine years old. She hadn't turned on the lights, but the shutters were open; she sat in moonlight, on the sofa, with her legs crossed. Like a little Buddha.

He stood there and listened. In the history of crime there have been examples of young children working with grown men who had very poor ethics. He didn't hear anything. He sat down across from her.

"How did you find the key?"

"I guessed."

It lay on the table in front of her. He had found such a good crack to hide it in that sometimes he couldn't find it himself. There was no chance that she could have guessed where it was hidden.

"How long have you been here?"

"Not very long."

"How did you get here?"

"By bus and train."

He nodded.

"Of course," he said. "Around midnight a big city lies wide open. For a little eight-year-old girl."

"Nine," she said. "And they're free. The bus and train. When you're under twelve."

Something was wrong with her system. Her intensity didn't match her age.

Not that other children didn't have energy. He had lived in the midst of the other artists' children for thirty-five years. Children woke up at six-thirty in the morning and shifted directly into fourth gear. Fourteen hours later they rushed straight into sleep at more than a hundred miles an hour without decelerating. If one could attach electrodes and draw energy directly from children, one could make a fortune.

But the systems of those children had been unfocused; it had been a flea circus. The girl in front of him was utterly composed.

"I've seen you in the circus. I could see that it would be good for you to talk with me."

He didn't believe his own ears. She spoke like a queen. Without taking his eyes off her, he found the drawer of opening-night gifts with his right hand. He opened it, and put a two-pound box of Neuhaus chocolates on the table.

"Have a child-molester candy," he said. "Why would it be good for me?"

"You have a sick heart."

She was deadly serious.

She opened the candies. Closed her eyes while the chocolate melted in her mouth.

"Maybe you're a doctor?" he said. "What's wrong with my heart?"

"You have to find her, the woman. Who left you. And that's just the beginning."

There were no letters. No pictures she could have seen. Not five people who would remember anything. And none of them would have told it to a child.

"Where are your parents?"

"I don't have any."

Her voice was as unconcerned as a loudspeaker announcement.

"Where do you live?"

"I promised not to tell."

"Who did you promise?"

She shook her head.

"Don't push me," she said. "I'm only nine years old."

Just a fraction of his attention was on her words. He tried to determine her musical key. It wasn't constant. Something happened to it whenever she wasn't speaking. He didn't know what it was. But it was something he had never heard before.

"Where did you get my address?"

She shook her head. He noticed an anxiety in himself that he didn't understand. He let his hearing become unfocused, spread it out, scanned the surroundings.

He heard Strand Road. The waves and the gravel at the edge of the water. The wind in the fir trees. In the withered grass. Nothing else. It was just the two of them.

"Play for me," she said.

He sat down at the piano. She followed him. Took the chocolates along. She curled up in the easy chair and pulled a blanket over her.

He played the Ricercare, the entire piece, perhaps nine minutes. She had stopped chewing. She sucked in the tones just as fast as they left the piano.

When he had finished she waited for a long time, longer than a concert audience. Longer than people usually do.

"Did you compose that?"

"Bach."

"Is he in the circus too?"

"He's dead."

She considered that. Took another piece of chocolate.

"Why don't you have any children?"

She reached out one hand and turned on a lightbulb. It was placed behind a piece of glass with a matte finish. On the glass plate was a child's drawing. Fastened with metal clamps. For years he had received hundreds of drawings each month. He had installed a place to hang them, and each week had changed the drawing. Sometimes more often.

"I haven't been able to find a woman who wanted to be a mother."

She looked at him. It was the most aggressive gaze he had met in any child. Perhaps in any human being.

"You're lying. And to a small child at that."

He felt his anxiety increase.

"I could move in," she said.

"This is all the space I have. And I don't have much money at the moment."

"I don't eat very much."

He had sat across from all kinds of children. Juvenile offenders, fifteen-year-old desperadoes who had double-edged daggers strapped to their legs under camouflage trousers and suspended sentences for violent crimes against innocent people. That hadn't been a problem. He'd had them on a short leash the whole time. This was something different. He started to perspire.

One moment her face was pure and austere as an angel's. Then it broke into a demonic smile.

"I'm testing you," she said. "I'm not going to move in. You wouldn't be able to take care of a child. It's not true either that I don't eat. I eat like a horse. The matron calls me 'The Tapeworm.'"

She had risen from the chair.

"You can drive me home now."

She didn't talk on the way, except to give directions about where to go. She was as concise as a rally navigator; from Strand Road they turned inland via Skodsborg Road.

The road ran along the border between the city and the woods, between the highway and deserted stretches, between row houses and country estates. They drove across Frederiksdal.

"Turn right," she said.

They drove down along the lake. After half a mile she signaled him to stop.

It was a stretch without any houses.

They sat silently beside each other. The girl stared up into the night sky.

"I'd like to be an astronaut," she said. "And a pilot. What did you want to be? When you were little?"

"A clown."

She looked at him.

"That's what you became. That's important. That a person becomes what they most want to be."

Somewhere deep in the night sky a dot of light moved. Perhaps it was a shooting star, perhaps a spacecraft, perhaps an airplane.

"I'll drive you all the way home," he said.

She got out of the car, he opened his door. When he got to the other side, she was gone.

He felt with his hearing. Behind him were rows of small houses leading toward Bagsværd, behind them the night traffic on the main highways. To his right, the wind in Lyngby Radio's installations. From the lake, the sound of the last ice that had broken up and was tinkling at the shore, like ice cubes in a glass. Ahead of him, dogs had awakened one another somewhere around the regatta pavilion. He heard the rushes rustling. The night creatures. The wind in the trees in Slotspark. In just one place, a voice in a garden. An otter fishing near the canal connection to Lyngby Lake.

But no sound of the girl. She was gone.

A powerful motor started up from somewhere just inside the forest nursery. He started to run. Although tragically out of condition, he had it in him to do one hundred meters in less than thirteen seconds. He made it up the steep slope just as the car drove by. A woman sat at the wheel. Perhaps someone with very refined hearing would have been able to hear the girl curled up in the backseat. He could not. Nevertheless, he noted the license plate number. He pulled out his fountain pen and a card.

He walked back and forth along the lake for nearly fifteen minutes. In order to try to hear her. In order to catch his breath. He succeeded in neither.

He got into the car. Dialed his father's number. Maximillian answered immediately. His father whispered.

"I'm at the casino; you're not allowed to have cell phones turned on. Why the hell are you calling me—did you wet your bed?"

"Despite your decrepitude," said Kasper, "can you still get into the central registry for the Department of Motor Vehicles?"

He gave Maximillian the number. The line went dead.

He had driven home slowly.

## 11

A sound shattered his memories and restored the trailer; it was the telephone. At first there was only a hoarse breathing on the line, as if the caller needed thirty seconds to recoup the oxygen it cost to make such an effort.

"I'll be completely well on Friday," said Maximillian. "I've found the best Filipino healer—he gets marvelous results. I'm having him flown here. Within a week, I'll be checked out of the hospital."

Kasper didn't say anything.

"What are you blubbering about?" asked Maximillian. "Next summer we'll be doing cartwheels on the beach."

There was quiet on the line.

"The license plate number," said the sick man. "That you gave me. It's a restricted number. In the central registry. Described as 'stolen' and 'investigation in progress.' With a link to the police commissioner. And the Intelligence Service."

The hoarse breathing became labored for a few seconds.

"Josef Kain?" asked Kasper.

As a boy he had learned great things about improvisation from his father. Maximillian Krone had been able to get up from a devastating quarrel with Kasper's mother, or a twelve-course dinner with his hunting pals that had lasted six hours, and go straight into court or straight into the Industrial Council.

But now he was silent.

Father and son listened to each other in silence.

"The occult," said Maximillian. "That was supposedly part of the reason they established Department H. Damn. It shows you how lily-livered the police are becoming."

"And is it found in the circus?"

"It isn't found anywhere."

"There was a woman. Both you and Mother mentioned her. Even at that time she was old. Something about birds. And a remarkable ability to remember things."

His father didn't seem to hear him.

"Vivian is standing here beside me," said Maximillian. "She says you and I should talk together. 'Why the hell should I talk with that idiot,' I say. 'He collapses. He's as soft as shit.' But she insists."

"She says you're sick."

"She's the head of the hospice program. She has a professional interest in convincing people that they are at death's door."

The hoarse breathing again became labored.

"She wants to talk to you."

The receiver changed hands.

"There was no Lona in the Midwives Association register," said the woman. "But I had a thought. There was a midwife whose name may have been Lona. It was fifteen years ago. Quite young. Talented. A lot of original ideas. Very critical of the system. Led efforts to establish experimental birth environments. The environment rooms here at Rigshospital. The underwater-birth rooms in Gentofte. At some point she completed medical studies. Became a very young chief physician. Obstetrics. That's why I didn't think of her as a midwife. Very aware of economic issues. Left her position at the hospital. Worked first for the pharmaceutical industry. Still does, as far as I know. In addition, opened a very exclusive—and well-patronized— maternity clinic in Charlottenlund. Could it be her?"

"What was her last name?"

"It's so long ago. I think it was Bohrfeldt."

Kasper looked at his knuckles. They were white like a medical-school skeleton. He loosened his grip.

"I don't know," he said. "It's not too likely. But thanks very much."

He hung up.

There was nothing in the ordinary telephone directory. But he found the address in the Yellow Pages; it was the only listing under "Maternity Clinics."

It was at the beginning of Strand Road. The ad showed a vignette of the building. He unfolded KlaraMaria's drawing and placed it beside the telephone book. She had included many details. The stairway curving up toward what must have been the main entrance of a mansion. The number of windows. The characteristic way each window was divided into six panes.

The address had five telephone numbers listed: main office, on call, pediatrician, labs, infirmary.

For a moment he considered calling the police. Then he rang for a taxi.

From the small cabinet above the toilet he took out a large bottle of pills; from the bottle he took two pills, as big as communion wafers, twelve hundred milligrams of caffeine in each, with warm greetings on the prescription from La Mour, the Royal Theater's physician. He filled a glass with water. In fifteen minutes the pills would commence spreading an outer layer of big-band wakefulness over the inner counterpoint of alcohol and fatigue.

Just to be sure, he took out two more pills. He gave a toast in the mirror. To all the doctors who, like Lona Bohrfeldt, help us into the world. Those at the Rigshospital hospice, who go with us out of it. And those like La Mour, who help us to endure the waiting time.

A vehicle turned from the Ring Road. It couldn't be a taxi because he thought he heard twelve cylinders. But it slowed down, searching. He swallowed the tablets with water. Put the glass upside down on the shelf.

Twice he had shared a dressing room with Jacques Tati, the second time in Stockholm after the master had lost everything on *Playtime* and had gone back to variety shows. After removing his makeup he had placed his glass upside down; Kasper had asked why.

"The dust, *la poussière*."

"We'll be back tomorrow."

The mime had smiled. The smile had not reached his eyes.

"We can hope so," he said. "But can we plan on it?"

# 12

It was the first time he had seen a Jaguar used as a taxi. The rear door burst open by itself, the backseat took him into its embrace like a woman. The car smelled like an expensive harness, but the light was strange. The driver was a young man wearing a clerical collar. Kasper tried to determine what sort of man he was by his sound. Probably from a small farm on Mors Island, studying theology without any financial help from home. Theology department during the day, taxi at night, and a use for every krone he could scrape together.

"Strand Road," said Kasper. "And as far as I'm concerned you don't have to start the meter."

He needed only fifteen seconds with a new orchestra conductor to know if he had any verve, and the same was true with taxi drivers. This one was off the scale, a Furtwängler of cab driving. The vehicle flowed forward like a river toward the sea, Fabrik Road melting into the darkness behind them.

"Christ will exist for eternity," said the driver. "According to the Gospel of John. Everything else will change. Now there are sensors in the seats. Connected to the taxi meter. No more unmetered trips."

Kasper closed his eyes. He loved taxis. Even when, like now, they were driven by a rural simpleton. It was like having a coach and coachman, only better. Because when the trip was over, the coachman disappeared, the repair bills disappeared, the scrap heap disappeared. Leaving just a car—and no responsibilities.

The driver whistled a scrap of melody, very purely, which was unusual, even among musicians. The melody was also unusual—it was BWV Anhang 127, one of Bach's two or three marches, in E-flat major, almost never played, especially in this version, a circus orchestration by John Cage. It had been Kasper's signature tune during his two seasons in the U.S. with Barnum & Bailey.

"We saw all five of your evening performances," said the driver. "At Madison Square Garden. We left the stage at eleven-thirty p.m. I wiped off my makeup with a towel. Put an overcoat over my costume. I had a wonderful car waiting. A Mustang. When I greased it with Vaseline and kept to the right, I could drive from Fourteenth to Forty-second Street without seeing red. The police let the traffic flow. If you stay away from the highway and Riverside Drive, you can drive for years without seeing even the shadow of a speeding ticket."

The clerical collar wasn't a collar. It was a fine-tooled web of scar tissue, as if a new head had been transplanted onto the body.

"Fieber," said Kasper. "Franz Fieber."

It had been an automobile stunt. A triple somersault from the ramp. In a rebuilt Volkswagen. Performed as a comedy routine for the first and last time in world history. Kasper had carefully avoided reading about the accident; he had been less than ten miles away when it happened. Both occupants were supposed to have died.

He moved his head a fraction of an inch. The glow in the vehicle came from a votive candle; it was burning between the gearshift and a small icon of the Virgin Mary with Baby Jesus.

The man noticed Kasper's movement.

"I pray constantly. It's a trait that stuck with me. I first noticed it right after the accident. I started to pray. After I came to on the respirator I prayed all the time. And have ever since."

Kasper leaned forward. To listen to the system in the front seat. He let his hand glide appreciatively over the upholstery.

"Twelve cylinders," said the man. "There are only seven Jaguars used as taxis. In the whole world. As far as anyone knows. I have all seven."

"So you recovered."

"I started with a Lincoln Town Car limousine. It cost forty thousand dollars. And a fake license. After I was discharged from the hospital. By next year I'll have ninety-five percent of the limousine business in Copenhagen."

"You must have seen very . . ."

Young people do not know how to parry compliments. The spine in front of Kasper straightened.

"It's very clear to me now what Paul means by saying it's through suffering we become united with Christ."

"Like Eckehart," said Kasper. "Are you familiar with Eckehart? 'Suffering is the swiftest horse to heaven.' It was this awareness, of course, that made you realize I was the one who ordered a taxi."

They turned off the Ring Road into Vangede, then from Vangede into Gentofte. The sounds changed; Gentofte had an old clang of porous optimism. An expectation that when the polar caps melt and the "bridge neighborhoods" of Østerbro, Nørrebro, and Vesterbro sink to the bottom, then the area from Gova to the Blidah Park housing complex will float on top like an inner tube.

The car turned and stopped. It was parked discreetly in the dark on one of the roads leading to the racetrack. The clinic lay about fifty yards away.

Kasper pulled out the taxi voucher from Moerk, his glasses, and the fountain pen; he filled in the blanks with the maximum amount, signed it, tore the voucher in two, held out one half toward the young man.

"I'll be gone twenty minutes at the most. Will you still be here when I come out?"

"This is a maternity clinic."

"I'm going to assist in a birth."

The young man took the yellow paper.

"It must be a great experience," he said. "For the baby. And the mother."

Kasper looked into the impudent yellow eyes.

"I ordered the taxi from my home," he said. "For tax reasons, the telephone isn't listed in my name. So my name never appeared on the screen. The question is: How did you find me? And why?"

He crossed Strand Road and passed through the sound of his most basic traumas. The salty coolness from the Sound, the parklike silence of the surroundings, childhood memories from twelve different addresses between Charlottenlund Fort and Rungsted Harbor. The silent weight of the buildings' affluence, granite, marble, brass. His own unresolved relationship to wealth.

The glass door was as heavy as the door to a vault, the floor mahogany. Not genetically engineered wood, but the dark kind that has

stood on its roots for two hundred years and looked down at the car-
nivals in Santiago de Cuba. The room was lit by Poul Henningsen
vintage lamps. The woman behind the desk had steel-gray eyes and
steel-gray hair; in order to make sure he got by her, he should have
put down two hundred thousand kroner and made an appointment
two years before he became pregnant.

She was the epitome of the Bad Mother archetype he had not yet
integrated. It is extremely depressing to have turned forty-two and
still be performing among fragments of your parents that have yet to
be carried out of the ring.

"There's less than a minute between the labor pains," he said.
"How do we get hold of Lona Bohrfeldt?"

"She went off duty. Did you call here?"

Part of the woman's system had shifted to listening toward the
corridor to her left. Lona Bohrfeldt might have gone off duty. But she
was still in the building.

"My wife is hysterical," he said. "She doesn't want to come in
here. She's sitting out in the car."

The woman stood up. With an authority that, in forty years, had
never met a case of hysteria it couldn't neutralize. She walked out the
front door. He closed it behind her, and locked it. She turned around
and stared at him through the glass.

The desk was empty, but in the first drawer he opened were the
telephone lists. He found Lona Bohrfeldt's number and dialed it. She
answered the phone immediately.

"Reception desk," he said. "There's a young man standing here
with an insured package. He looks trustworthy. I'll let him in."

He hung up. Beneath the number was her home address; the
postal district was Raadvad. He copied it onto his lottery ticket. The
woman outside watched his movements. He waved to her reassuringly. The important thing is to keep our hearts open. To the outward
expression of our Unconscious, which we must separate ourselves
from temporarily.


The corridor had oak doors with plaques giving names and titles,
marble floors, and acoustics that made it sound as if the visitor were
tap dancing and had come at an inconvenient time. It all made one

question whether there's been nothing but progress since the Savior was born in a stable. At the end of the corridor was a set of double doors; he walked in and locked them behind him.

Ninety-nine out of a hundred women are afraid of strange men who come in and lock the door behind them. The woman behind the desk was number one hundred. There was not so much as a whisper of concern in her system. He could have unzipped his trousers and exposed himself, and she would not have taken her feet off the desk.

"I work with children," he said. "I have a little ten-year-old student who has talked about you."

She had everything. She couldn't be forty yet. She had the age, the self-confidence, the education, the title, the money, the business, and even though she was wearing loose black wool clothing and was mostly hidden behind the desk, he sensed that with her build she could stroll down a catwalk modeling swimsuits whenever she pleased. And would do it, if she could charge for it.

The only sign of the price we must all pay was two long furrows that had etched themselves along each side of her mouth ten years ago.

"This is a busy workplace," she said. "People usually call first. Or write."

"Her name is KlaraMaria. From the children's home. From Rabia Institute. She's been kidnapped. We don't know by whom. She got a message out. The message was your name. And a drawing of this place."

She took her feet off the desk.

"The name may ring a bell," she said. "Will you repeat it?"

It didn't ring a bell. It rang a fire alarm. He did not reply.

"I think there was a preliminary study for a survey. At the institute. For the Research Council. It was years ago. Perhaps a girl with that name was part of the empirical data. She must have remembered that for some reason or other. There was very little personal contact."

"What survey?"

"It's a long time ago."

"Is it available for one to read?"

Normally she wouldn't have answered, but the shock had made her more open.

"It was never finished."

"Even so."

"It's a stack of pages in rough draft."

He seated himself on the desk. If he had been wearing a dress he would have hiked it up. So she could have seen some of his thigh.

"I'm rolling in money," he said. "Unmarried. Unrestrained. How about inviting me home? For a cup of tea. And sixty pages from the drawer?"

The two furrows turned black. She pushed the swivel chair away from the desk. So he could see her entire figure.

"You're speaking to a woman who is eight months pregnant!"

She had gained weight only around the fetus itself. Her stomach was shaped like a roc's egg.

"That doesn't matter," he said.

Her jaw began to drop. He knelt between her legs and put his ear to her stomach.

"A boy," he said. "A slightly more rapid pulse beat, around a hundred and thirty, D-flat major. With a premonition of D-major. Where Gemini slides over into Cancer. Your due date must be about Midsummer's Eve."

She pushed the chair backward, tried to get away from him. He followed her.

"Why did she give your name?"

Steps were approaching, one woman and two men. Just when a bubble of intimacy is about to be created around a man and a woman, the outer world has a way of interfering, head nurses, angry men, the collective unconscious. It's tragic.

"There's very little time," he said. "The authorities have no clues. You're probably the last chance."

He placed his hands on the arms of her chair, his face next to hers; he spoke softly.

"What if they kill her. And you know you could have prevented it. Every time you look at your own child, you'll think about that."

She managed to stand up. There was a chink in her armor; she was on the verge of opening up.

"Who is Kain?" he asked.

Someone rattled the office door. Without taking his eyes off her, he tried a glass door; it wasn't locked. It opened onto a balcony. The kind Romeo and Juliet had enjoyed. As long as that lasted.

Someone tried to push in the door, without success. Footsteps moved away to get a key.

In eight hours he would be sitting on an airplane bound for Madrid. He bent down toward her. Her face became transparent. He suddenly realized that she was too frightened to speak. He let her go.

He felt in his pockets, found the lottery ticket, tore off a corner, wrote down the telephone number at the trailer. She did not move. He opened her hand and placed the scrap of paper in her palm.

A key slid into the lock. He opened the terrace door and swung himself over the balustrade.

Romeo had better odds; he hadn't needed to contend with sea fog and acid rain. The copper was coated with verdigris; there was nearly half an inch of green algae on the marble rail. He slid as if in green soap.

He hit the lawn flat; the air was completely knocked out of him. When you're six years old and it happens the first time, you think you are going to die. When you're forty-two you know you don't get off that easily. He focused on the starry sky to keep from losing consciousness. Just over the horizon was Taurus, his own persistent constellation. If he'd had a telescope, and if it had been another time of year, in the sympathetic Pisces he could have seen Uranus, the planet of sudden impulsive behavior.

"The survey," he whispered. "It wasn't just a medical survey. You weren't alone. Someone else was involved."

She looked down at him. Because of the fall his voice was still breathless. Nonetheless she had heard him.

Beside her, three unknown faces came into view; the youngest sprang up on the balustrade. He lost his footing and hit the ground like a BASE jumper whose parachute has failed to open. Three feet to the right of Kasper, where the lawn ended and the natural stone chips began. It's these small differences in people's karma that determine if we get up or remain lying on the ground.

"A female friend," Kasper added. "Blond as the chalk cliffs of Møn. Cold as an icy winter. Sharp as a German razor."

She looked like Ophelia standing there above him. Well into Act IV. Where the process has become irreversible. He had hit home.

He got to his feet. Like Bambi on the ice. He wanted to start running. But found the strength only for a fast walk.

## 13

He rolled over the garden wall and into one of the narrow passages between Strand Road and Kyst Road. He got up, reached the road. The taxi was gone. He crossed the road, increased his speed. Right now the important thing was to gain the darkness around the race-track. Headlights blinked far back in a driveway; he ducked into the shadows. The Jaguar was backed up all the way to the house. The car door opened, he toppled into the backseat.

"I have the radio set at seventy-one megahertz," said Franz Fieber. "The police change the signal codes once a month. The taxi drivers break them in less than twenty-four hours. They've called the Gentofte police station; two squad cars are on their way."

A patrol car passed the driveway and stopped in front of the clinic. Three officers ran into the building, one woman and two men. Another vehicle stopped behind the first one.

"Let us pray together," said Kasper.

The yellow eyes stared at him in the rearview mirror. Anxiously. Young people begin to fall apart when confronted with a situation where there seems to be no means of escape.

"The woman. Whom you locked out. She saw me back up into this driveway."

"Just a minute," said Kasper.

He leaned back. Prayed. Silently. In sync with his heartbeat. "Lord have pity on me."

He confronted his exhaustion. His fear for the child. His hunger. The alcohol. The caffeine. The pain from the fall. The tax return. The humiliation. At being wanted by the police and wandering on foot through streets and alleys at the age of forty-two. And he confronted the unnatural consolation of prayer.

A knuckle rapped on the window. The young man stiffened. Kasper pressed the button and the window rolled down.

It was a woman in her sixties with her hair in a French braid. It was too dark to see what she was wearing, but even if it had been sackcloth and ashes she would have looked like an aristocrat.

"I don't think I ordered a taxi."

"The day may come," said Kasper, "when you will wish you had."

She smiled. It was a beautiful mouth. It looked as if it had practiced smiling and kissing for the last sixty years and had reached perfection.

"Will you promise to stay here until then?" she asked.

A flashlight beam flickered over the gateposts. There was no escape.

"I'm trying to save a child," he said. "There's no time to go into details. Due to a mistake, the police are looking for me."

She stared straight at him. Like an eye doctor during an exam. Then suddenly she straightened up. Turned. Walked toward the officers.

She moved like a prima ballerina walking *à la couronne*. She reached the gateposts. Stood so she blocked the sidewalk and their view. Said something. Gave a gracious order. Turned around.

The policemen crossed Strand Road without looking back. Franz Fieber slumped behind the wheel.

Kasper leaned out the window.

"When I've completed my mission," he said, "and served my Spanish prison term, I'll come back. And invite you to dinner."

"What will I say to my husband?"

"Can't we keep it under our hats?"

She shook her head.

"Frankness is crucial. Our silver wedding anniversary was ten years ago. We're going for the gold."

Two policemen stood on the sidewalk. The exit was still blocked.

"A generous heart like yours," said Kasper, "knows the neighbors. Including Lona Bohrfeldt across the road."

"Yes, for twenty years," she said. "Since before she became famous. And moved out here."

"She's been there when each of my four boys was born," he said. "My wife and I have wondered: What drives her? What is it about births? Why would anyone want to share in them two thousand times?"

She bit her lip.

"It could be money," she said. "And the premature babies. She's interested in them."

The officers got into a patrol car, and the vehicles drove away. Franz Fieber started the Jaguar. The way was clear.

"May I have your autograph?" she asked.

He felt in his pockets; he needed to keep the voucher, and it was also wise to hold on to the lottery ticket. He tore out his pocket. His fountain pen wrote just fine on material.

"I'm writing on my silk underwear," he said.

"I'll keep it next to my skin."

The Jaguar leaped forward.

"Stop at the gate," said Kasper. "I have to blow her a kiss."

The car stopped. He leaned out and blew a kiss. And read the nameplate on the gatepost. It had been taken down. And replaced with a FOR SALE sign. He looked up the road. Fifty yards ahead toward the racetrack stood a dark Ford.

"Please park just around the corner," he said.


The Jaguar rounded the corner and stopped. Kasper got out, walked back, peered cautiously over the wall. The Ford had started up and moved forward. The ballerina came out of the driveway, running like a twenty-year-old, and seated herself beside the driver.

Kasper got into the Jaguar.

"There's somebody after us," he said, "who surpasses your skills."

The Jaguar shot forward as if a huge hand had grabbed it from underneath. Behind them, headlights swept over the houses and out to the promenade. The Jaguar's motor began a crescendo, Franz Fieber whipped the wheel to the right, the world tilted, the car raced up the slope toward Slotspark and broke through the hedge. Kasper found a couple of handles and clung to them; there were trees and bushes everywhere. He looked at the young man ahead of him—he was focused but relaxed. Hands and legs danced over the pedals and keys; this was what it must have been like to sit behind Helmut

Walcha at the big grand piano in St. Laurent's Church in Alkmaar during his recording of *Die Kunst der Fuge*. Hundreds of pneumatic hammers pummeled the car from outside. The Jaguar began braking and ended with a crash that sounded as if they'd driven straight into a shredder. Everything grew dark.

In the darkness beyond them were points of light, which condensed into a small circular area. The car had stopped in the middle of a rhododendron bush; the bush was as big as a garage.

The dark Ford drove past the lighted area, searching.

"We could have killed ourselves," said Kasper.

"I pray constantly. Jesus hears me."

Every automobile has an acoustic signature. Kasper heard the Ford coming back; it must have turned around. It passed them slowly.

"An expert like you," said Kasper. "Tell me, if a customer was to be picked up inside the barricaded area, could you find out where and when?"

"Have you got a name?"

He gave Stina's name. Franz Fieber spoke briefly on his mobile phone.

"The unions run taxi clubs. Cafeteria food, slot machines, wild rumors. And information. We'll have her in a couple of minutes."

Kasper listened out across the Strand Road traffic. It was in a different galaxy than Glostrup after all. The sound around him was tasteful and muted. The soft click of the hydraulic pump in a Rolls-Royce. The complex and yet gently controlled intensity in eight-cylinder common-rail engines. Cars that were manufactured not to be heard, but to appear, suddenly, out of the silence. And if the silence was ever broken, it was by something personal, a Ferrari's bestial rumble or the nostalgic roar of a veteran Volkswagen four-cylinder air-cooled boxer engine.

And there was room for the sound between the houses; reverberation is proportional to the volume of the space. Kasper closed his eyes. He could have owned automobiles like Chaplin. Like Bhagwan Shree Rajneesh. He could have employed people to drive them and repair them. Instead he sat here.

It was time to lay a little golden egg.

"Happiness," he said, "doesn't consist so much of what one has scraped together and gotten off the ground, but of what one has been able to let go of."

He heard a nearly silent diesel motor, a Mercedes, the quietest of all cars. He heard the wind softly flapping a convertible top. A Mercedes coupe. The kind of car he would have bought if he had been Lona Bohrfeldt. It drove slowly and unevenly. As he would have driven if he had met himself. And then the police.

The car entered the lighted area and passed in front of Café Jorden Rundt. A woman sat behind the wheel. Kasper put on his glasses. There was a little white cross on the license plate.

Kasper pointed; the young man understood immediately. The Jaguar crept forward out of the rhododendron, then accelerated. Kasper could not understand which sense Franz Fieber used in driving; everything was dark. The car struck the hedge, slid across the bicycle path, and stopped for a moment on the road between the Ved Stalden restaurant and Denmark's aquarium. Two hundred people were sitting on the glass-enclosed terrace; they had stopped eating. The Jaguar started again, turned onto Strand Road. There were five cars behind the coupe.

Franz Fieber spoke into his mobile phone.

"She's to be picked up in forty-five minutes," he said. "And I took the trip."


The Jaguar kept its distance heading toward Strand Boulevard. The car in front of them turned on its left blinker; there was roadwork ahead, traffic directed into just one lane. Now there were ten cars between them and the little Mercedes; when they reached Middelfart Street, it had disappeared.

Kasper remembered the area. He had walked around here to rest his ears during the first circus performances in the gasworks building, back when there scarcely were dressing rooms. He pointed; the Jaguar made a U-turn across the road, glided along the gasworks grounds, and stopped.

Kasper was out of the car before it came to a complete stop. He jumped over the hedge along the railroad gradient, and clambered up the steep clayish slope to the train tracks above. He ran north, leaping from one railroad tie to the next, until he had the open playing field on the left. Then he squatted down.

He heard her before he saw her. She hadn't turned into Frihavn Harbor; she was headed out Skudehavn Road.

The car disappeared behind the office buildings around the container harbor. But he knew where she was going. She was going out toward Tippen, at the end of the peninsula that juts into Skudehavn.

Tippen wasn't there anymore. The nature preserve had disappeared since he last left Denmark. But something else had appeared instead.

The new construction blocked the view to the sea. But in a space between two buildings he could see the landfill. It lay in front of a complex of four-story office buildings and extended fifty to a hundred yards out into the sea.

It covered the area where the circles on Stina's four-centimeter-scale map had intersected. He had heard correctly after all.

He walked back slowly. Copenhagen stretched out ahead of him. Long yellowish chains of light from the radial roads. Over the inner city, a calcium-white and diode-blue glow, with a black hole, a vacuum, where the barricaded area lay. Behind it, illuminated by halogen spotlights, the white walls of the incineration plant, monumental as temples. Farther back, Amager Island, like an orange circuit board of light. Framed by long lines of airplane headlights approaching Kastrup Airport, like shining bridges swaying just above the sea.

He slid down the slope to the wire fence by the playing field; this brought him out on Middelfart Street behind the Jaguar. He walked hunched over. Outside the driver's side he straightened up. Put his elbows in the open window.

"I still have some of my childhood hearing," he said. "Before, when you talked on the phone, when you got information about where she should be picked up. There wasn't anybody at the other end. So we've got two breaches of confidence. This latest one, and the question of how you got my order for a taxi. It grieves my heart."

He yanked open the door, grabbed the front of the other man's shirt, and lifted him out of his seat. His body followed for about eight inches, then would go no farther. Kasper looked down; both of the man's legs were amputated just below the knee and strapped tightly to extended pedals. In the door were two plastic prostheses and two retracted telescopic crutches.

He let go of the torso. Franz Fieber slid back into his seat. The yellow eyes gleamed.

"You were an artist too," said the young man. "I know everything about you. A few more technical mishaps and it could have been you who had this disabled driver's license. You're looking at yourself."

Kasper turned around and started to walk away, toward Strand Boulevard. The Jaguar pulled up beside him.

"She's supposed to be picked up in thirty minutes. And only taxis can get in. So you can walk your grieving heart back to Glostrup. Or you can accept a lift. From a white liar."

Kasper got in.

They stopped for a red light at Århus Street.

"What have they built at Tippen?" Kasper asked.

"Some sort of bank. That's where the doctor was headed. I've driven her. Over there. Twice."

"You might be mistaken."

The spine in front of Kasper straightened up like the *Brave Soldier* statue in Fredericia.

Kasper looked at the vehicle's clock.

"Can we manage to see the ocean in only thirty minutes?"

A tidal wave of cars was approaching them from Oslo Square. Ahead of the wave, just before it broke, the Jaguar ran the red light.

# 14

They passed the entrance to Frihavn Harbor. The pension fund buildings, the Paustian furniture showroom and offices. When Kasper was a child a couple of smaller circuses had spent the winter season at the north and south harbors. At that time the area had the sound of poorly greased windlasses, coal cranes, wooden-soled boots, two-stroke diesel engines, steam whistles. Now he heard fast elevators. Muffled ventilation systems. The cosmic whisper of a thousand tons of I.T.

They turned east. On the other side of Kalkbrænderi Harbor the Svanemølle power plant rose like an electric cathedral. The Jaguar pulled off to the side.

"Welcome home," said Franz Fieber. "To where the money lives."

Back then there had been a few rusty cutters on a grassy stretch leading down to the beach at Tippen. Now it had been built up.

The road where they were parked was newly paved and straight as an arrow. The asphalt had a deep luster, like a dull black pearl. Toward the north, out toward the Sound, mixed-use buildings had been constructed. Expensive, timeless, in glass and granite, like seven-story gravestones. To the left were stores and restaurants that had opened recently; a few were not yet rented out. The Jaguar was parked outside a display window, sixteen by twenty-six feet, an unbroken piece of plate glass; behind it, on a dark background, one lonely tie was illuminated by a spotlight. Next door was a chocolate shop. In four windowpanes, against a dark-blue setting, huge filled Easter eggs, three feet long and two feet in diameter, rested on hemispherical brass bases nesting in monkey-tree boxes.

Kasper listened to the music in front of him. From the restaurants. The people. In a few hours the area would close down. But right now it was at its best.

"Jesus," said Franz Fieber, "drove the money changers out of the temple."

"He had a bad day," said Kasper. "He'd probably spent all his cash."

He pointed. The Jaguar rolled forward slowly. Kasper looked at the signs. The buildings housed advertising agencies, accounting firms, large law offices.

The car stopped.

"There," said Franz Fieber.

It was the group of buildings Kasper had seen from the elevated train tracks. A complex of black and dark-gray buildings, some of them built on the landfill. The whole area was surrounded by a wall. It was low enough not to seem aggressive. But high enough to stop a pole vaulter. And to block most of the view. By the water's edge stood a tower; it was supported by pillars and as tall as the power plant chimneys, striving upward as if it were about to take off. It could have been a piece of scenery for the grail fortress in *Parsifal*.

"Konon," said Franz Fieber. "It's some sort of bank. They work day and night. They use taxis a lot."

"I like the name," said Kasper. "It has something to do with wholeness. For those of us who are fluent in Latin."

A patrol car passed them slowly, decreased its speed, but drove on, reassured by the taxi sign. A delivery van drove past them, searching. The name JONEX was painted on it. Kasper sized up the buildings. Two thirds of the façades were glass.

"We need to see where that truck goes," he said.

The Jaguar rolled forward about three hundred feet. The van turned the corner, moving slowly. The street was bordered by magnolia trees that went all the way down to the water. Fifty yards down the road, a section of the wall swung open and the van drove in. Kasper caught a glimpse of a wrought-iron gate, surveillance cameras, and men in green uniforms. And far back in the darkness, something that could have been a Mercedes coupe.

"When I was a child," he said, "the artists' children did whatever work came along. Before they were old enough to perform. I had a talent for climbing. So I cleaned windows. At that time too, the equipment came from Jonex, Inc., in Vesterbro. It's only your generation and later that have gotten everything handed to them on a platter."

The Jaguar turned the corner. The wall hadn't swung back again. Through the gate came first one, and then a second, delivery van; they were black and well maintained, like hearses. LEISEMEER CATERING was written in gold letters on the sides.

Kasper rolled down the window and listened as they drove by the building. He heard rubber against glass. A window washer's working cage stalled for the night. He estimated the façade had roughly sixty-five hundred square feet of glass.

"I've been working from the time I was twelve," said Franz Fieber. "Until now. Constantly."


They turned down toward the building that housed the *Berlingske* newspaper offices. Franz Fieber tossed a fire blanket into the back-seat. Kasper lay down on the floor of the car and pulled the blanket over him. The Jaguar stopped, he heard muted speaking outside, the car started again, drove slowly, stopped, drove, stopped. The motor got turned off. Kasper sat up. They were parked on a small unlighted parking lot surrounded by a plywood barrier. The ground shook; a sound he could not identify preceded the vibrations. He looked at the clock on the dashboard. There were ten minutes left before he was due to pick her up.

Franz Fieber reached back with a bottle. Kasper sniffed it and drank; it was Armagnac. G. I. Gurdjieff's drink. Not as many overtones as Cognac. But with the soft rustic bass of its single distillation in continuous stills. Franz Fieber poured something from a thermos into a paper cup; Kasper drank it. It was scalding-hot espresso, more brutal than the brandy.

"What do you hear when you listen to the city?"

Very few people knew enough to ask him that question; the young man should not have been one of them.

"Life and happy days."

"And behind that?"

The impudent light was turned off. The question came from deep down. When people ask something from a deep place, one must reply.

"Angst," said Kasper. "The same angst that's in every human being. But multiplied by one and a half million."

"And behind the angst?"

"Who says there's anything behind it? Maybe the angst is the end."

Kasper got out of the car.

"We sent a note backstage," said Franz Fieber. "After the performance. All five evenings. We would have liked to shake your hand."

The car door opened. Franz Fieber detached himself from the
pedals, put on his prostheses, expanded his crutches, and got to his
feet. All in one, flowing movement.

"They weren't delivered," said Kasper.

"I saw you for the first time in '99. In the Circus Building. That
was one of the reasons I shifted to variety shows. Not just for the
money. There were two thousand people. You heard every one of us."

Kasper walked backward.

"Nobody can hear two thousand people," he said.

Franz Fieber followed him.

"After maybe twenty minutes, there came a moment. Perhaps
two minutes. It was love. You loved each one of us."

"You must be crazy," said Kasper. "Nobody can love so many
people."

His back was toward the plywood. The young man was right in
front of him.

"I know that. That's why I drove race cars. Do you know what my
method was? It was the curves. I started to brake there, where the
other tracks ended. I could hear twenty thousand people gasp. And
then scream. They knew I had done it for them. Not just for the
money and myself. That was what I lived for. It was love. I'm a seeker.
Looking for love."

He smiled. It was a smile that, in Kasper's opinion, should have
revoked his driver's license.

The young man had a key in his hand. He opened a door in the
barrier. Pointed to the left.

"Five minutes. Be careful of her."

Without losing his balance, and without losing his crutches, he
took off his jacket with the taxi badge and handed it to Kasper. The
yellow warning light was back in his eyes.

"Think how many famous artists have died in traffic accidents," he said. "You leave a sidewalk. It's only thirty feet over to the other side. But you never reach it."

He turned to leave.

"I thought you were looking for love," said Kasper.

"God's love," replied the young man without turning around. "One doesn't need an individual person."

Kasper stared after his retreating back. It's unpleasant for a great artist not to have the final line.

"Remember your prayers," he said. "Because suddenly one day you'll find that something has stuck with you again."

He put on the uniform jacket and walked through the door.

# 15

He had seen hundreds of pictures; still, the scene took him un-
awares. He stopped short. With an aching heart. Because of the
beauty and tragedy of the sight.

The sea had overflowed Copenhagen. The canals were gone, the
sidewalks were gone, the road. At his feet an unbroken surface of
water stretched from Holmen Canal to the Renaissance façades of
Strand Street.

In that water, the Stock Exchange, Christiansborg Palace, and
Holmen Church floated like the trunks of huge oak trees.

He stood by the Public Guardianship office building. In front of
him lay what must be the geological fault line; it was now a steep
slope, perhaps ten feet deep, down to the water. Smooth. But with
scraps of split cables and gas lines.

The acoustics went straight to his heart. Smooth water surfaces
are very reflective. The space in front of him was as filled with sound
as the Musikvereinsaal in Vienna multiplied by one hundred. Without any traffic. Like Venice.

The area was illuminated by work lights. He now could identify
the vibrations beneath him. They must come from hundreds of hydraulic drainage pumps.

Their deep bass was interrupted by louder booms, as sharp as ex-
plosions. From a floating platform outside the National Bank building several groups of men in orange security suits were pounding
down sheet piling with a pile driver.

A heavy fiberglass boat with a low railing set one of the orange
figures ashore. It moved quickly up the slope, like a flame across
gasoline. Kasper began to run.

The boat driver looked at him uneasily when he went by; the man had the complexion of a freshly cooked beet, into which two turquoises had been set as eyes. Kasper pointed to his uniform jacket; the man nodded.

The figure was just a minute ahead of him when he reached the work shed that had been cobbled together against a structure that must be part of what was left of the Royal Theater. The stairs made no sound under him. The door was not locked; he went in.

Inside, the atmosphere was dripping wet. The air was hot, damp, and impenetrable, like a steam bath. A splashing sound swallowed his footsteps. Swallowed the little click when he locked the door behind him. The Divine is partial to saunas. There was a steam bath in Gurdjieff's chateau, Le Prieuré. Three saunas in the Vallemo cloister in Sweden. A Russian bathhouse connected with Nevsky Church on Bred Street. Sweat huts for the shamans.

He saw light through the steam. At the end of the hall a coverall was stripped off.

The figure in front of him walked backward. It was a woman.

Without turning around she took a towel and walked into the shower room. He followed her slowly.

The room had six shower heads. Hot water flowed from all of them. The steam was so thick that his neck was perspiring. At first he couldn't see her. Then she walked backward out of the shower. She lathered herself up, using a long curved brush with a wooden handle. Methodically. Gradually she dissolved in a thin layer of bubbles. She went back into the steam, dissolved completely, and disappeared.

He didn't move. The water was turned off. A vent drew out the steam. The room was empty.

He felt a touch like a caress. From behind him, a towel was wrapped around his ankles. Then his legs were pulled out from under him.

He managed to get his hands up to his face. Nevertheless, it was a hard fall. Only with difficulty was he able to sit up.

"Did you get lost?"

She had the heavy curved brush in her hand.

Then she recognized him. She took a step backward, as if she'd been struck. Water ran down her face from her wet hair; for a brief moment she looked as if she were drowning. Then she regained control.

"I need to talk with you," he said.

"That's out of the question."

There was a knock on the door.

"Journalists," he said. "It's me they're after."

She grew paler than she was before.

"What's your telephone number?" he said. "Your address?"

"It's over. It's completely over."

"I'm a new person. Reborn. Everything is changed."

She bared her teeth. Like an animal. The situation was about to get out of hand.

"I'll throw myself into the arms of the press," he said. "I'll tell them everything. My wild longing. How I defied the armed guard. The bloodhounds. The electric fences. In order to give you a brief, vital message. How you threw me out. Called in the executioners. We'll be on the front page."

Her eyes were filled with wonder.

"You would do that," she said. "You would actually do that."

"Half an hour. Just half an hour."

She found a carpentry pencil in her coveralls. He handed her the lottery ticket. Her hand shook slightly as she wrote.

There was loud knocking at the door. She wrapped a towel around herself. Walked ahead of him through the shower room, opened a door he hadn't seen. They came out into a narrow hallway where yet another door opened to what once had been Tordenskjold Street. Behind them, a door was unlocked.

She had carefully avoided even brushing against him. Now she placed the carpenter pencil's point against his cheek like a switchblade knife.

"A half hour," she whispered. "And after that, I'll never see you again."

# 16

There is a dangerous black hole of two freezing hours between the last bus at night and the first one in the morning. He didn't fall into it; he had caught the last bus. He had walked around the grounds in a large arc and now stood by the thick row of poplar trees. Every living thing leaves an echo. He hadn't heard anything. There were two hours until the deportation order went into effect. He should have eaten and slept; he didn't do either. He got out his training outfit and changed clothes.

In the ring he turned on Richter and the music lamp on the piano.

He began with the balancing exercises. He had done them every morning for thirty years, hardly missing a day. First the tenacious, liturgically based vertical movements of classic barre training. Then long, gliding legato series around the edge of the ring. Finally, he would put on his performance shoes. Made for him. Size seventeen. Large without being presumptuous.

Balance and prayer are self-confrontational. Behind the muscular and spiritual exertion there must be a point of effortless calm. At that point you meet yourself.

The prayer began spontaneously, in sync with his heartbeat at first. Soon it would break away from that. He felt grateful. He was alive. He had a body. He had Richter's recording of *Wohltemperiertes*. He had two more hours. And best of all, he had a telephone number. A door partly open. Leading to her.

And somewhere he still had an audience. "The public is half of my personality," Grock once said. He spread out his arms toward the spectators' seats. He loved them all. Even now when they were not there.

But they were there. The space wasn't empty.

Most circus rings have dry acoustics because of the poisonous combination of sand on the floor and a tent overhead. A musical clown's great, depressing mission in life is to try to liven up a circus ring. But not this ring. The walls were veneer panels with space behind them; they absorbed the deep tones, which gave many horizontal reflections. In this space he could always orient himself like a bat, and now too.

He turned off Richter, walked backward over to the post with all the electric switches, and turned on the lights.

There were two. The man with the hearing aid, who sat as if he had never left his seat by the fire exit. The other man, tall and blond, came rushing down the center aisle with outstretched hand.

"This is an honor. I saw you for the first time when I was a boy. I've followed you ever since."

Kasper stepped to one side and leaned against the piano. To get it between them and him.

"We're here on pleasant business," said the blond man. "We represent the board of a nonprofit organization. It awards grants to artists. The board has awarded you a grant of twenty-five thousand kroner."

Kasper's hands found the piano cover. Over thirty pounds of Brazilian rosewood with a brass edge that was as sharp as the blade of an old-fashioned bread cutter.

A bundle of one-thousand-kroner bills appeared on the piano.

"What organization?"

"The board wants to remain anonymous. Will you please sign a receipt?"

A piece of paper was placed in the light, on top of the bills. It did not have a letterhead. Kasper put on his glasses. He lifted the paper so he could read it and at the same time keep an eye on both men.

It was a "Declaration of Trust and Confidence." Stating that when he taught KlaraMaria in April she was fine and healthy, with no sign of physical molestation.

"Do you have an address?" he asked. "So I can send you tickets to the premiere?"

The blond man shook his head.

Kasper's hands found the piano keys. Coaxed a choral arrangement of *Jesu bleibet meine Freude* out of the piano. One had to admire Bach for his sense of reality. For the way he had composed and performed without forgetting that he also had to make a living from his music. There had been a balance. All his talents stretched to the utmost. And at his very core, a point of absolute repose. A point which knows that no matter what is happening now, we'll have enough to eat tomorrow too.

But anyway. The chorale flowed through his fingers. One couldn't commit perjury to that music. One could only express declarations of love.

"I practice numerology," he said. "Quantum numerology. I never sign anything on odd-numbered dates."

The blond man smiled.

"Maybe fifteen thousand are missing."

"Maybe."

An additional stack of bills was laid on the piano.

"That didn't help," said Kasper.

The smile in front of him grew thinner. The man with the hearing aid had risen.

Without moving anything but his fingers, Kasper unhinged the cover. Rested it against the music rack.

"You can keep the money anyway," said the blond man.

The two men began walking toward the exit. Kasper balanced the cover on the piano keys. Followed the men.

They had entered through the door facing the railroad—the chain lock had been cut with a bolt cutter and lay in the grass. Outside stood a BMW. Long, low, royal blue. Like the color the sky had now become.

Kasper held the car door for them. They got in. The man with the hearing aid hadn't taken his eyes off Kasper's face.

"He's staring at me," said Kasper.

"You have a well-known face—something Ernst appreciates. And a smooth face. That no one has ever harmed."

The car door slammed. The window was rolled down.

"What we're buying," said the blond man, "is an end to the telephone calls. To the Institute and elsewhere."

Harlequin can absorb an endless series of humiliations. He who is without pride is invulnerable. Harlequin was an ideal. But still far off.

"I'm thinking of buying a share in Johnny Reimar's Smurf show," said Kasper. "Using the grant money. I'll need stuffing. For the Smurf dolls. You guys could go right onstage. Give me a call. When you need a job."

The window rolled up, the car drove away. Kasper bowed low in respect.

It was the least one could do. It's what Bach would have done. For forty thousand kroner.

# 17

His legs were trembling as he walked back to the ring. He had his hand on the door when he heard the car, a Ford Granada station wagon.

He went inside, turned off the CD player, gathered up the money, turned out the lights, and locked the door.

There was no chance of reaching the trailer; he ran into the stable, grabbed his bedding, climbed up the ladder to the loft, tumbled into it. He pulled up the ladder and shut the trapdoor.

The loft stretched the length of the building. Aside from a narrow passage along the space under the eaves, it was covered from one sloping wall to the other with piles of folded canvas that, together with steel and wooden reinforcements, would make two medium-size tents. Just above the floor on the gable wall was a row of stable windows, from which he could see the trailer.

There were six men plus Daffy, all in civilian clothes. Moerk, the two monks from Immigration, and three technicians with thick black attaché cases. One of them carried four light stands.

They knocked, but they knew he wasn't there. Kasper saw Daffy protest. The watchman was wearing a camel-hair coat Kasper hadn't seen before, a coat suitable for the head of an advertising agency. They opened the door with a pick gun; Daffy must have refused to give them the key. He squeezed in behind the technicians, but after a moment was led out.

Kasper made a bed on a pile of canvas. Tucked himself into his duvet.

The monks came out and sat down on the bench by the trailer. The technicians hooked up electricity for the lights from another box. Kasper set the alarm on his watch. Took out his cell phone. And the ticket Stina had written on. Dialed her number.

She answered immediately. She hadn't been able to get to sleep. Yet her voice gave no indication of fatigue.

He looked over at the trailer. They had turned on the lamps inside. Light filtered through the shutters, white and gleaming.

"Could we meet at your place?" he said. "I've got workmen here."

"It has to be a public place. There have to be other people."

He gave her a name, Copenhagen Dolce Vita, and the address.

"Is it an ordinary place?"

"Like a coffee shop."

"Eight o'clock," she said.

Then she hung up.

Kasper dialed the number on the taxi voucher. A hundred feet away Moerk came out of the trailer with a telephone to his ear.

"Tell me about Kain," said Kasper.

At first there was no reply.

"What will I get in return?" asked the official.

"Something about the girl."

In the silence Kasper heard the other man calculating how the cards had been dealt.

"Since 2006, Europol has assessed crime in Europe. A common pattern now is that international crime is no longer hierarchical. It's organized into cells; one cell doesn't know the others. But the threads have to come together somewhere. Kain is a place like that. And now, what about the girl?"

"She came to see me the day before yesterday. Accompanied by two adults. Said she'd been kidnapped. They arrived and drove away in a stolen Volvo. I haven't seen her since."

Out the window Kasper saw Moerk signal one of the monks. Kasper knew they would try to trace the call now. He broke the connection.


He leaned against the canvas behind him. It would have been safer to hide in a crowd of people. But he didn't have strength for that. He had to sleep. He closed his eyes. Prayed his evening prayer. The words were "Herz und Mund und Tat und Leben," the music was Bach's cantata BWV 147, Kasper's favorite among the Leipzig cantatas. On this escape chute he slid down toward sleep.

As he fell asleep, KlaraMaria sat there. Just as she had the second time he saw her.

# Part
# Two

# 1

It had been night, the dark night of the soul. C. F. Rich Road was empty and deserted. Behind drawn curtains untroubled parents and red-cheeked children were asleep, his public, unaware that out here in the cold, Kasper Krone walked his *via dolorosa*, freezing, with no money for a taxi after having lost in poker for the first time in ten years.

Poker was Kasper's game, and had always been. Poker had depth and complexity like Bach's music; a sure bet and a rhythmically played hand lasted about as long as one of his small choral arrangements. Bach would have been a great poker player, if he hadn't been so busy. More than fifteen hundred works, many of them under constant revision up until his death.

Kasper had played in all the major capitals, but for him poker belonged in the Frederiksberg section of Copenhagen on C. F. Rich Road. Where the doorman wasn't a foreign legionnaire and serial killer, but a former boxer with fists like sugar beets. Where there was mutual familiarity, as in a community-garden club. And concentration, like musicians auditioning for the Radio Symphony Orchestra, each man and woman bent over his or her sheet music.

But tonight he had lost, even the Saab at the end; when he handed over the car keys he'd felt like he was turned to stone. He hadn't had enough humility to borrow money for a taxi. As the bus drove through the woods, he went through the night's games in his mind; he found no mistakes—he could not understand it.

When he crossed Strand Road he saw there was light in the trailer. He approached in a half circle; the light flickered like a fire. As he was getting out the lead pipe he identified the sound. It was E-flat major, happy, playful, uninhibited, like the first movement of Trio Sonata in E-Flat Major. He put the pipe back in place and walked in.

KlaraMaria stood with her back to him. She must have been lighting the stove, and then come to a standstill before the undulating world of the live coals. The light of the small flames flickered over her face; she did not turn around.

"You found me," she said. "Tell me how you did it."

"I drew a circle," he said.


He had awakened in the trailer the morning after their first meeting, after she had disappeared by Bagsværd Lake.

He had slept only a couple of hours. He took out one of the four-centimeter-scale maps. Stina's compass. Using as the center the spot where he let the little girl off, he had drawn a circle with a radius of three miles. Maybe she had been driven away in a car. But she had been ready to walk—he could tell that.

No ordinary child walks three miles at two a.m. from somewhere on the outskirts of Bagsværd when the temperature is around freezing. She had not been an ordinary child.

The circle enclosed Bagsværd, Lyngby, some of Vangede, a corner of Gentofte, the southern part of Virum, Fure Lake, and Hareskovby, some of Gladsaxe. It was seven in the morning; he took out his violin and played the beginning of Beethoven's Opus 131. It begins in darkness as a fugue, but then climbs upward and into Paradise. When the sky grew light and office hours had begun, he picked up the telephone.

He had planned to call the Ministry for Social Affairs, but with the receiver in his hand, before dialing the number, he could suddenly hear how he would sound to an outsider. A middle-aged single man is looking for little girls, without being able to explain why, even to himself. He held a weak hand and had tough opponents. He put down the receiver and took two copies of his last CD, the solo partitas and sonatas, recorded in St. Mary's Church outside Lübeck. Then he got into his car and drove to Grøndal Parkway. To Circus Blaff. To Sonja.


Sonja had started at the bottom. Kasper had met her when they were very young, in the Sans Souci variety theater in Kolding and then the Damhus Inn owned by the Stefansen dynasty. From the very beginning, he could hear that she was driven by something. Her system had a sound like a motor that can't stop and just keeps running until it burns out, the sound by which life's desperadoes recognize each other. Her desperation was directed toward wealth. She had left the ring, studied economics, and then returned to the circus. The building on Grøndal Parkway had three floors, four hundred employees, administration offices for four circuses, several music halls and theaters, a booking agency, an advertising company that had followed in the footsteps of Erik Stockmarr, the famed circus poster artist of the fifties, when nobody else could. And an accounting office. She owned all of it.

She was a little older than he. A little taller, a little heavier. She had three children. A splendid husband, deep and vigorous and in C-major, like Mozart's last symphony. And besides the husband, lovers too.

Twenty years ago Sonja and Kasper had been lovers; they had not lost contact since then, and never would as long as they lived. SheAlmighty awards lifetime partners to some people. Brahms got Clara Schumann, Mozart got the clarinetist Anton Stadler as a lifelong partner in pin billiards. Maybe it has something to do with the thing called love.

Sonja's office resembled the Defense Command in Vedbæk, where Kasper had performed several times; the military love clowns— Grock met Hitler personally twice. Everything was in its proper place here, and orders were not to be questioned. A large pair of binoculars lay on the window ledge; the Bellahøj circus grounds were just opposite the office, and Sonja liked to keep up with things. On her desk were four telephones and the remainder of an Italian lunch, including a whole bottle of Brunello. He laid the four-centimeter-scale map and the CD in front of her, and explained the situation.

She turned the CD over in her hands.

"You never went for little girls," she said. "You went for grown-up women. So what can she do? Is it talent? Does it have something to do with money?"


It wasn't he who had left Sonja, and it wasn't she who had left him. They had known it simultaneously.

She'd had an apartment in Frederiksberg, on King George Road.

The last night he had been awakened about two o'clock in the morning by the city's atmosphere; it had felt like a blister on his brain and heart. He'd had to sit up and hum the arpeggio from BWV 4, "Christ Lay in the Bonds of Death." The Danish philosopher Martinus once said that to endure living in Frederiksberg he needed to pray constantly.

Sonja had already been awake. They were both in their early twenties. He hadn't had a word for it, but he had known, they both had known, that they were in the path of a storm it would be hard to ride out.

"We can't cope with it," she had said. "Soon I'll want to have children, and a dog, a female dog, and a fire in the fireplace, and will need to turn off the hearing aid and say the sound won't get better now."

He had gotten up and put on his clothes. She had followed him to the door; she moved in a free and easy manner, when she was naked, when she was clothed, through life as a whole.

"Since you believe in something," she had said, "can't you pray for help for us?"

"One can't pray for something," he had said. "At least not for different musical notes. One can only ask to play as well as possible the notes one is given."

It had been a dignified exit line and departure. He had gone out into the night with eyes dim with tears; it had felt like singing Wotan's farewell scene with Brynhild from Wagner's *Ring*. Then dawn came, and he had discovered that when there first is love, it does not go away when the sun comes up and the curtain goes down. It remains. Now twenty years had passed, and somehow both his happiness that she existed, and his sorrow that it couldn't be more, were not diminished.


He had laid his hands on the city map in front of him.

"I've always been searching for something," he said.

"Does she have it?"

He shook his head.

"She's nine years old. But she knows something. About where one can find it."

Sonja did not ask any more questions. She drew a telephone over to her and gave him headphones to listen in. Then she took a stack of green books out of a drawer.

"Mostrup's municipal directories," she explained. "We need to look at all of Copenhagen County."

She looked up and wrote down while she talked. There were two children's homes within the circle on the map.

"We can't call them directly—it's sensitive personal information. We'll get a flat refusal. We have to go via the county's Health and Social Welfare Administration. What's our story?"

He listened outward; necessary lies come from the same place as the ideas in the ring, from outer space.

"We found a small purse after the show. A brocade purse. With feathers on it. The kind little girls love. It was a benefit performance. For institutions. The name inside the purse is KlaraMaria. We'd like to send it to her. May we have the address?"

She made the call. The woman at the other end was cooperative. Kasper could hear her sympathy, for both children and adults. As so often before, he felt a longing to live in a world administered to a greater extent by women. It was a warm day; the woman on the phone had a window open.

"I'm sorry," she said. "We have forty-seven children on our list. No KlaraMaria. Could she be with a foster family?"

On Sonja's piece of paper Kasper wrote: "Matron."

"I believe there was a matron."

"She might be living with other children in some sort of family arrangement. I'll give you the telephone numbers for the foster home associations."

Through the telephone Kasper recognized the sound from the open window. It was the sound of Glostrup. He stood up and looked over Sonja's shoulder at what she had written. The Health and Social Welfare Administration address was Amstgården County Courthouse in Glostrup.

"Ten numbers!" said Sonja. "Fourteen thousand children are placed outside their parental homes. I'll get you the numbers for boarding schools too. It's hard to find them in one place; institutions are listed under each community."

———

For a quarter of an hour Sonja looked up numbers, telephoned, wrote. Kasper sat absolutely quiet. She hung up the receiver. Pushed the telephone away.

"Eight hundred children. Divided among two children's homes, eighteen foster families, three boarding schools, and one children's hospital. No KlaraMaria."

"Could there be some type of institution we don't know about? An institution that's registered some other way?"

She telephoned the county courthouse again. Spoke with the woman. Hung up.

"All the private institutions get a county subsidy, or at least fall under county supervision. So they are listed with the county. The one exception is institutions that—especially after September eleventh— are designated as possible terrorist targets. Their telephone numbers and addresses are released only by the police. But she doesn't think any of them are in our area."

Kasper stood up. They had reached the end of the road. Then he sat down again.

"Try the police."


Sonja telephoned police headquarters. She was transferred three times. Then she got a woman who was the same age as her. The woman's voice had a secret. Don't we all? She was sorry, but the police did not have any institutions listed in that area. She too had a window open; she hung up.


Sonja accompanied him to the door; the office was so large that the distance was a hike. She gave him his mail. One letter had a window envelope. He opened it with a feeling of distaste; the unknown often arrives by mail and frequently in a window envelope. It was from Maximillian, a sheet of letter paper with a woman's name and an address printed on it. At first he did not understand anything. He looked at the envelope. It was postmarked with that day's date, by the central post office on Bernstorff Street. Then he understood. Maximillian had been to the main office of the Department of Motor Vehicles. He got out his glasses. The printout was from the database of a large insurance company; they too had access to the records now, along with Customs and Taxes. As access to large databases grows more liberal, Danish national feeling becomes more intimate. Soon we will all know everything about one another.

Maximillian must have gone to the main post office to try to reach him immediately. He read the name.

"Andrea Fink," he said. "Does that name mean anything to us?"

Sonja's face grew blank.

"It's the name of the woman," she said, "from police headquarters. The woman we just talked to."


He had gone back to the desk, sat down, and put on the headphones.

"Our story now," he said, "is that we're married. The world doesn't feel safe with single people."

Sonja dialed the number.

"It's me again. I have my husband on the line. There's no Klara-Maria anywhere."

"And what do you want me to do about it?"

The secret was a tragedy in C-minor; it had something to do with children. She was childless; A-major perfectionism had not been softened. With increasing age a person integrates the next higher musical key in the circle of fifths, the acoustical equivalent of what we call maturation. Something in her had impeded that process.

"My wife and I met her," said Kasper. "After the performance. She made a deep impression on both of us. Also on our three children."

Sonja had closed her eyes. There are few women among the great poker players. No woman would care to bluff, as he was doing now, a royal straight flush in hearts. Against an opponent who was acting in good faith. On a hand that was as thin as bouillon.

"All five of us in the family," he said, "had the—perhaps completely crazy—feeling that we could give her a new home."

At first there was no response at the other end of the line. He tuned in to the traffic noise from her open window. She had a body of water outside, closer than police headquarters did. He heard traffic crossing a bridge, crossing two bridges. A siren howled past; the shift in sound-wave frequency known as the Doppler effect gave him a sense of the nearest bridge's length. It could be Knippel Bridge. The woman cleared her throat.

"Our agreements," she said, "regarding institutions are related to how we evaluate the threat. If, for example, there were diplomats' children, it would mean tighter security."

"I'm a clown," Kasper said. "Do I sound like a terrorist?"

"I don't know what terrorists sound like. They say Nero loved circuses. Heliogabalus did too."

"May we stop by?" he asked. "Then you could experience our credibility firsthand."

"Call me tomorrow."

She hung up.

He helped himself to a piece of paper, took out his fountain pen. He drew Knippel Bridge. Lange Bridge. The National Museum, the Royal Library, and the Black Diamond, the library's modern extension on the waterfront. He put a check mark next to the government building on Christians Brygge Street. Pushed the paper over to Sonja.

"What do the police have here?"

Her sound grew uneasy.

"Their Intelligence Service," she said. "Most of it is located above the Gladsaxe police station. But some of the administrative offices are over on Slotsholm Island. They approve the circus security plans. For gala performances. When the royal family and government officials attend."


He took the binoculars from the window ledge. Borrowed cardboard and tape and wrapped up the other CD. Sonja didn't ask any questions.

"You'll have to go there alone," she said. "I've left the circus ring."

He wanted to leave—she blocked his way.

"I have more than you," she said. "Children. A home. Accounts all in order. More love. You have very little talent when it comes to being satisfied in everyday life. But your longing. Sometimes I envy you that."

She put her arms around him.

Touching doesn't help; we never reach each other anyway.

But still—

He parked behind the Stock Exchange after driving from Sonja's office. When he got out of the car the city wrapped itself around him like a wall of sounds. No harmony, no concentric waves, no tone center. One and a half million people, all with individual, uncoordinated refrains.

He turned down Christians Brygge Street. The building had a glass entranceway with an intercom. He remembered his childhood, when one could walk right in to see people and government authorities. Since then, life had become less free; now we all keep one another under surveillance. Or perhaps he remembered incorrectly. From the time we are forty we all gild our memories.

Beyond the entrance a civilian official was sitting in a glass booth. Kasper wished he had a partner; the task ahead was not a solo job. He walked along Frederiksholm Canal, across the Parliament grounds, past his own automobile, and back. Next to the Royal Danish Arsenal Museum and the *Isted Lion* sculpture was a daycare center; a boy about five or six years old was standing just behind the gate.

"Where are you going?" asked the boy.

"I'm going over to warm a cold angel."

Colored lights lit in the boy's eyes.

"Can I come along?"

The child's sound was interesting. The world is rarely able to block the openness of children before they are seven or eight years old. Kasper looked up and down the street; it was empty and deserted.

"The grown-ups will miss you."

"They just went for nap time. I'm the only one outside."

The boy's system interfered with Kasper's. But anyway. One needs to choose one's partners carefully.

"What if I'm a child molester?"

"They're different," said the boy. "They've tried to get me to go with them."

Kasper leaned forward and lifted him over the fence.

He pressed the button by the door; from somewhere inside behind many layers of glass he was asked to identify himself. He acted as if the intercom was broken, lifted the boy in his arms, and pointed at him. The presence of children casts a legitimate light on adults; the door buzzed and they were inside.

Kasper set the boy on the counter.

"Andrea Fink's son," he said. "He has a high fever. Over in the daycare center we think it may be gastroenteritis. We telephoned Andrea and agreed that we should come immediately."

The attendant behind the counter pushed his chair backward, away from the source of infection. The situation was uncertain; it could go either way. On the wall behind him was a list of offices. Andrea Fink's was on the third floor.

"I want my mommy," said the boy. "I'm hot. I don't feel well. I'm going to throw up."

The attendant reached for the telephone. Kasper shook his head.

"She's in an important meeting. They don't want to be disturbed. She told us to go right up, and she'll come out."

He knocked, and walked in without waiting for an answer. The woman behind the desk was surprised, but composed. The room was not in keeping with his prejudice against the Intelligence Service; it was large and friendly. There was a potted palm about as tall as a man. The white paint on the walls had a hint of pink pigment. On the desk was a figure of Buddha.

He set the boy on the desk beside the statue and the telephone; as he put the child down, his fingers detached the phone cord. In a little while, when the attendant from the glass booth telephoned, his call would not go through.

"I'm Kasper Krone," he said. "I'm the one who called you earlier, about KlaraMaria."

The woman laid two open books on top of each other and moved them. Her face grew cold. The temperature in the room fell to something that called for caps and mittens.

"I inquired about you," she said. "You're not married. You don't have any children either."

Part of her mind was still on the open books. It was important that he get a look at them. He took the boy's arm. Ran a finger lightly over the Buddha.

"One of Buddha's teachings that I like very much," he said, "is that all living beings have been each other's mothers. In an earlier life. And will be again. I've thought about that. It must mean we have all been each other's lovers. And will be again. Including you and me."

She began to blush, faintly, like the walls.

"I don't know how you got in," she said. "But now you must leave."


Outside the office door he put the boy down and knelt beside him.

"Can you get her out here?" he said. "And keep her out here for a little while?"

The boy opened the door. Kasper crouched behind it.

"I have to pee," he heard the boy say. "My daddy left without me. I'm going to pee my pants."

The woman did not move.

"Can I pee in the palm tree?"

Kasper heard him unzip his trousers. The woman stood up.

"I'll take you to the bathroom."

They disappeared down the hall. Kasper slipped into the office.

The two books she had moved were Krak's map of Copenhagen and something that looked like an address book.

Behind the desk he saw a small scanner and copy machine; it was turned on. He put the opened pages on the machine, folded both copies, and stuck them in his pocket. A toilet flushed. He walked out into the hall and went to meet the woman and the child. She was pale. He took the boy by the hand and headed toward the stairway.

"I'll call for someone to show you out," she said.

The door to her office closed.

Kasper winked at the boy. Laid his finger to his lips. He took off his shoes, stole across the herringbone parquet floor in stocking feet, and put his ear to her door.

She was about to dial a number. Every push button has a tone; sufficiently refined hearing would have been able to catch both the number she dialed and the voice that now answered on the other end. His could not.

But he heard her whisper.

"He's been here," she said. "He just left."

Something was said on the other end.

"Very Puccini," she said. "Seems like a bit of a Lothario to me. I got rid of him. He's out of the picture now."

Kasper stole back to the boy. Put on his shoes.

The attendant from the glass booth now stood behind them. Kasper picked up the boy in his arms. The glass door opened automatically.

They were out in the open air; the city sounded better than before. In the deepest sense, do we ever hear anything but the pitch of our own voice?

"Why didn't you want to go to nap time?" asked Kasper.

"I can't lie still," said the boy.

"Why not?"

"They don't know why. They're investigating it. Maybe I've got DAMP syndrome. Or water on the brain."

Some children weren't children; they were very old. Kasper had begun to hear this twenty years ago. Some children were ancient souls with a thin infantile veneer. This boy was at least twelve hundred years old; his sound rang like one of Bach's great pieces.

Kasper lifted him back over the fence.

"You did well," he said. "For someone five years old. With water on the brain."

"Six," said the boy. "Six years old. And it's good to praise children. But money is good too."

His eyes were dark, with experience perhaps. There hadn't been a day in the last twenty years—with the possible exception of the three months with Stina—when Kasper hadn't wanted to give up at some point. Withdraw his savings. Take off for the Fiji Islands. Develop an opium habit. Listen to cello sonatas on the stereo, and fade out on the beach.

It was eyes like those in front of him now that made him keep going. They had always been there. In the audience, in himself. Stina's eyes had sometimes been like that.

He felt in his pockets; there was no money, just his fountain pen. He handed it over the gate.


Back in the car, he spread out the two photocopies on the dashboard. The map covered Bagsværd Lake, Lyngby Lake, and the southern end of Fure Lake. The other page had more than forty addresses. Only one of them was in the map's postal district, and it was just a fragment: "Track 3, 2800 Lyngby," along with a telephone number. No institution name, street name, or house number. He called Information from his cell phone; the number was unlisted. He looked at his own Krak map. "Track 3" had a set of geographic coordinates, but no street name. At first he couldn't see anything on the map, but then he faintly saw three needle-thin lines. He opened the car door and held the book in direct sunlight. Every day that passes after one turns forty, the old folks' home and the lighted magnifying glass draw closer. Tracks 1 to 3 were three parallel paths in the wooded area between Bagsværd Lake and Fure Lake.


He had taken the last pieces of firewood out of KlaraMaria's hands and closed the potbellied stove. She had seated herself on the sofa. He had told her about Sonja and his visit to Slotsholm Island. About the policewoman from the Intelligence Service. She had listened without moving, absorbed in what he was saying.

"And the nuns?" she asked.

"I drove straight out there," he said. "I went according to the map."

# 3

He had parked by the Nybrogård psychiatric residence, taken Sonja's binoculars and the wrapped CD, and walked along Bagsværd Lake. The signs numbering the boat race lanes were newly painted. He had been here before, in the good years, twice. He had opened an exhibition of circus paintings at Sophienholm, together with the queen. And he had fired the opening pistol shot for an international regatta.

Track 3 was a gravel road north of Sophienholm, a fire lane cut into a hillside to reduce the incline for fire engines. The roadsides were steep; an oncoming car would have seen him. So he went into the woods and found an animal track above the road.

He knew from the map that there were three peninsulas. Buildings had been constructed on all three, but they were hidden behind the vegetation. As he neared the third peninsula he found a spot above a sharp drop on the hillside, laid his jacket on the ground, and crawled forward to the edge.

His mouth was dry from anxiety. The sound picture was unreal, but he couldn't have explained why. He let his hearing expand; he heard nothing that could cause his anxiety. Toward the east lay the prime minister's official residence, out in the open like a large summer house. Behind him were Fure Lake and the North Zealand forest preserves with their wild stock of corn-fed, ring-marked ducks waddling around on mowed grounds. In front of him lay Bagsværd Lake and small suburban houses. Beyond them, the low, bearable city. Everything was peaceful. Around him, within a radius of three miles, at this moment twenty thousand people lived and breathed who thought Bagsværd and Denmark were cozy little corners of the world and it was not they who would die, but other people.

He pulled himself to the edge of the drop-off.

The original building was a large house, perhaps a hundred years old. More recently, low white rectangular structures had been added to it. He heard the faint hum of a small transformer station and felt from somewhere underground the vibrations of a large natural-gas furnace. A small machine building had a chimney tall enough for a diesel-driven emergency generator, which suggested this was a hospital.

His anxiety had intensified. It would last a little while longer. The idyll was about to be compressed; soon it would leap an octave, and disintegrate.

To the right he could see a group of children playing. It would happen around them.

His hair was standing on end. He couldn't identify the individual children; he could only hear their collective sound. It was completely harmonious.

The children had established a family of sorts, or maybe a tribal solidarity. They had placed small bowls, made of clay perhaps, on a plank resting on two trestles. In another spot, where the ground was sandy, they had dug a hole. All eleven children were active. There was no adult in sight. The play was spontaneous, without any rules; it was improvised before his eyes.

He looked down at the impossible. No other person would have understood that, except maybe Stina. And it wasn't certain that even she would have understood.

Play is an interference phenomenon. Two children playing together create a balanced binary opposition. Three children is a more fluid, but also more dynamic, harmony. Four children polarize again in two doubled units, more stable than the triangle. Five is again fluid; six is normally the largest number of children that can play an improvised game that isn't organized by a dominant leader among them. Only once had Kasper seen seven children play together in a fair and balanced way. That had been artists' children who had traveled with the circus a whole summer; it had been at the end of the season, they had known they would be leaving each other, and it had lasted less than an hour. Games for more than seven children required rules set and supervised by adults, like ball games, for example.

There were no adults in the scene before him, and no dominant sound. There were eleven children. And they played in perfect harmony.

He had put down the binoculars. Without them he could not see faces, but he wanted to sense the children as directly as possible. Most of them were between nine and twelve years old. Two were African, three or four were Asian, two or three might have come from the Middle East. He heard a few English words, also something that could have been Arabic; the children did not speak the same language.

Their sound was as soft as a baby's, completely uninhibited, like the sounds from a playpen in a nursery. And at the same time it was much too intense, blew around him like a strong wind; it would have reached the spectators in the back row of a soccer stadium. He was sure it was the same phenomenon as the quiet girl. And he had no idea what it was.

Nature usually has a dry sound because of a lack of perpendicular surfaces. In nature there is no lateral fraction, no sound energy from the horizontal plane. The scene before him was an exception. Perhaps due to the trees, perhaps due to the buildings, he heard everything very clearly. And what he heard made his hair stand on end.

Usually the sound we hear is a direct signal from the source of the sound plus innumerable reflections from the surroundings. But not the sound from the children below him.

There was a wooden porch facing the lawn where the children were playing; a woman in a blue nurse's uniform came out onto the porch. The children saw her coming and stopped playing.

On the alert. Simultaneously. Without losing their mutual interference. He had never seen children stop playing that way. He noticed how their tone changed. The woman raised one hand and opened her mouth to call to them.

Then the silence began.

The woman on the porch kept standing there with her hand raised and her mouth slightly open, completely motionless.

Kasper had never seen immobility like that before. She did not stand like a wax doll. Nor like a French mime. She stood as if in a film where the projector suddenly broke and a single image remained on the screen.

Below the steps leading to the lawn a rambler rose climbed upward; it would take still another season to reach the porch. But its leaves should have been moving in the breeze. They were motionless.

Behind the children, the spring-green foliage of the beech trees was motionless too.

Then the children moved. At first he thought this would change the situation; it didn't. It intensified the sense of unreality. They turned around simultaneously and, like strictly choreographed dancers, resumed their play as if it had never been interrupted. But their movement did not release the woman; she kept standing there. The leaves did not move. On the roof above the porch one could see the exhaust pipe for the gas furnace, a stainless-steel chimney with a thin stream of vapor above it. The vapor was at a standstill; it had lost its direction and was suspended, motionless, above the building.

A large clock hung on the wall of the porch. It was very visible, like a clock at a railroad station, with black numbers on a white background and a red second hand; it did not move.

Kasper shifted his focus toward the lake. He saw a fine interference system of small ripples out on the water's surface. So the phenomenon before him was localized; farther out the water was moving.

He tried to move his arm to look at his watch. Movement was possible but painfully slow; the relationship between his mind and body had changed. Above and ahead of him was an area in which the foliage had become rigid. The area was shaped like a ball.

He tried to tune in to the sound. His hearing switched off. He tried again. It switched off. There was nothing to hear. Everything was silent.

The children made ordinary sounds, physical sounds, like all children, like all people. But behind these sounds another level had opened. A level that extended into the silence. The children's systems interacted in this silence, Kasper could hear.

Their interference was a type of friendliness. But not the friendliness of advertisements for Jehovah's Witnesses, where the lion grazes with the lamb in a place that looks like Frederiksberg Garden. They were interacting in a medium of powerful intensity.

Ordinary physical sound does not have much energy; it causes only a minimal increase in the general atmospheric pressure. Even a hundred-person symphony orchestra that goes wild in one of Wagner's greatly inflated passages does not produce enough sound energy in an hour to warm a cup of coffee.

It was different with these children. They had spread the strange silence in a spherical area of perhaps fifty yards in diameter. Within this space, Kasper knew, the acoustic organization of reality in time and space did not exist.

The children's games ended. With no warning, they all suddenly straightened up and walked out of their roles in an unspoken synchronous realization that now it was over. The woman on the porch opened her mouth and shouted, kindly. The rosebush leaves stirred, the beech foliage trembled, above the roof white vapor floated up toward the sky.

Kasper's body was tingling, like when anesthesia wears off, and he was terrified that he'd gone crazy. He discovered he'd pissed in his pants from fright.

The children moved toward the porch; everything was as usual. He had heard incorrectly; he had been imagining things. One child was still standing there, a girl. She was looking at something, at the clock on the wall.

As she and Kasper watched, the red second hand began to move, intermittently at first, then faster. And after that, the minute hand.

The girl caught up with the others. Kasper put the palms of his hands against his closed eyes. He lay there until his breathing calmed down.

Under more private circumstances he would have taken off his trousers but, considering the situation, it would not be a suitable way to present himself, so he tied his jacket in front of him like a maid's apron.

Then he walked down to the gate.

It was locked. There was an intercom and a buzzer; he leaned against the button.

After a minute, she came. It was the woman from the porch. At close range he could hear she was not an ordinary nurse. She had a young sound, perhaps in her mid-twenties. But tense.

He handed the CD through the gate.

"I think it says KlaraMaria," he said.

She was not older than she seemed after all. She took the CD. She should not have done that; one should not take anything from a stranger, especially not from the great clowns. That, plus her hesitation, told him what he wanted to know. KlaraMaria was, or had been, somewhere behind the gate.

"We have a post box," she said. "We pick up the mail ourselves."

"I'm parcel post," he said. "We bring packages right to the house and put them in the customer's lap."

He turned and began to walk away. After the first turn he ran straight up the hill and back to where he had been lying; he threw himself on his stomach and crawled forward to the edge.

She was headed toward the building, walking as if she were drugged. The door opened and another woman came out, also wearing a uniform. A tall African. They exchanged words; he could not hear what was said because his heart was hammering so loudly. The African took the CD.

He had wrapped it solidly; the tape was the kind the post office used, and could have supported a man's weight. The African took hold of the paper and peeled the flat package the way one peels a banana. She looked at the cover. Turned her face in the direction where he had disappeared. She stood like a totem pole. He could not detect any uneasiness in her system.

# 4

It had taken three weeks before they came.

That spring he was with Benneweis in the Circus Building. He was taking off his makeup in the green dressing room when she arrived.

The green dressing room had been Rivel's. It had been Grock's. And Buster Larsen's, when he performed as an Auguste clown. Tardi had used that dressing room. Callas. Birgit Nilsson. Irene Papas. If Castaneda had understood opera, he would have called the room a musical power spot. Even the Copenhagen municipality had needed to watch its step when it renovated the building after taking it over in the eighties.

The room also had preserved Stina's vibration.

She had often gone along to the performances; she must have seen more than twenty during the three months. Afterward she would come down into the dressing room. She would stand behind him in the dark, not saying a word, while he took off his makeup. And sometimes, without any special reason or warning, she had gone over to his chair, put her hands over his eyes, and drawn him close.

The first few times he had thought, Now she'll get makeup and nose putty on her pashmina and it won't come out in the wash, but later he stopped thinking. It was part of what he had begun to learn from her, to stop thinking and let himself go; he had been on the verge of understanding how to do that. And then she had left.

She stood there again now. For a tone memory like his, there was no difference between past and present. That's what was painful— he could never turn off the sound of loss. It was tragic, but it was also wonderfully sentimental; the day he died it would be just as bad as now, or worse.

Above her tone he heard a pentatonic scale. Exotic, like drums from a tropical jungle, and also deep breathing, like a blacksmith's bellows in the Friland Museum in Århus. It wasn't Stina; he was not alone.

He swiveled his chair around; it was the African. She stood where Stina had always stood, in the darkness just inside the door.

She was graceful like a photographer's model. Big like a rower. Dressed in expensive businesslike attire, like the head of a corporate board.

Someone burst open the door without knocking; it was Madsen, who was in a panic. The woman withdrew farther into the darkness.

Madsen was six feet, six inches tall and broad as an upright piano; he had been in charge of security in the Circus Building for twenty years without any outsiders ever getting in. If Macbeth had gotten hold of Madsen, it's not certain that Banquo's ghost would have slipped through.

Now he was as pale as a Pierrot; the fourth and fifth fingers of his right hand stuck straight out, as if he were about to propose a champagne toast.

"They're broken," he said. "By a black woman. Wanted to talk with you. I told her she could leave a message. I tried to get her to leave. She's in the building somewhere."

"I'll lock the door," said Kasper.

The door closed. He locked it. He and the woman looked at each other.

"We have tape recordings," she said. "Of your telephone calls to us, as well as the two calls to the Intelligence Service. We've got witnesses to your visit on Slotsholm Island. We have good lawyers. At the very least, the police will arrest you. We'll leak the recordings to the press. They will make an impression. On the nine-tenths of your public who are children and their parents."

"She came looking for me," he said.

The woman did not hear him. That was the problem with the totem pole; communication went just one way.

"You will write a message," she said. "Now, right this minute. To KlaraMaria. You will tell her that you've gotten a job; you have to leave the country; you will be away for a long time, maybe a year. But you will try to keep in touch. After this you will stay away. Forever. And everyone will be happy."

He took the envelope from a large congratulations card from the dressing table, and on the back wrote with a lipstick what she had demanded. He handed the envelope to the woman.

"In the movies," he said, "women put perfumed notes like this into their bosom. Could I help you do that?"

It was an attempt to open her system so he could listen to her. It did not succeed. She merely gave him a thoughtful look. The kind of look with which men with chain saws determine what trees are going to be cut down.

He held the dressing-room door for her, and accompanied her to the exit.

She walked like a sea horse swimming in an eighty-five-degree ocean, in time to a mambo beat that only she could hear.

"What is it about the children?" he asked. "What is it they're able to do?"

She did not reply. He opened the fire-exit door leading to Studie Street.

"Why tell me this here?" he asked. "Why not at my home?"

She made a sweeping gesture that included the restaurants, the palace, the traffic on H. C. Andersen Boulevard. The people streaming into the city's nightlife.

"Right here," she said, "you can tell how it would feel to be on the front page of the morning papers with a pedophile charge against you."

She stepped out onto the sidewalk.

"And Madsen's fingers?" he asked.

"They're not broken," she said.

She looked down at her hands. They were larger than Kasper's; they were piano hands. Each of them could have stretched across an octave plus a diminished fifth.

"Little necessary tricks," she said. "In order to live as a black woman. In a white man's world."


The next three weeks he had existed in a state of semiparalysis; he was completely present only in the ring. At the end of the third week he came to his senses just as he was entering a store to buy a television. At that point he understood how serious the situation was. Jung has written somewhere that the quickest path to psychosis is seeing visions from afar. He turned around and left the store.

In periods of depression it is important to hold on to one's healthy leisure-time interests. The same evening he went to C. F. Rich Road. And lost in poker. A couple of hours later he stood in front of the quiet girl.

# 5

"I had a visit," he had said. "From the African."

"Nurse Gloria?"

"That's not a good name for her," he said. "It means 'honor.'"

"What's honor?"

"It's when one does something very good. She didn't do something good. She forced me to lie. To write to you that I was going to leave the country."

"I didn't believe her," she said. "I saw right through her."

She looked straight at him. It was a look that went through everything, his skull, his brain, the trailer. Her sound changed, and reality began to slip away; his hair stood on end. And then it was over; everything was the same as always.

"I'm hungry," she said.


He prepared food for her.

He had learned that from Stina. He had been sitting on the chair where KlaraMaria now sat and Stina had been standing by the stove; they had known each other for fourteen days, and then she told him:

"You have to learn."

He hadn't understood what she meant.

"You've never really moved away from home," she said. "You've been living in a trailer; you've found women to cook for you. Again and again you've raised your mother from the grave to stand by a hot stove. This time, it's not going to be that way."

He had leaped to his feet and taken a step toward her. She put both hands on the handle of the large sauté pan she had brought over on one of her first visits. Eleven pounds of cast iron plus a pound of vegetables in nearly four-hundred-degree oil. He stepped back, turned around, got as far away from her as he could; it was less than twenty feet. In a minute he would have packed a suitcase and been on his way to the airport, but suddenly everything grew dark before his eyes. He began to pray. That the ground would open and swallow her; that SheAlmighty would write her out of the libretto. But nothing happened. When he tried to make prayer function that way he was never successful.

The darkness lifted. He stood with his nose against the bookcase; before his eyes were Kierkegaard's collected works, a fugue on the theme that none of us wants to listen to the sound within us because it's so hellish.

He had turned around and looked at her. Kierkegaard would never have dared to go closer than these twenty feet. But since his time, progress has been made. Even if only a little.

He had gone back to the table and stood beside her. She had placed a handful of Jerusalem artichokes in front of him. And a stiff brush.

For KlaraMaria he sliced vegetables—carrots, celery, and leeks—and then added a touch of bouillon and some herbs. He and Stina had prepared food in silence. Stina had understood that he didn't have extra reserves of energy; he had enough to contend with already. The discomfort of feeling like a pupil at a time when one thought one was finished with school. The fear that his public would see him like this, wearing an apron. Kasper Krone, the only artist who couldn't find a woman who prepared his food and served it to him.

Now and then she said something anyway. Succinct. Basic sentences he had remembered ever since.

"The richness," she said, "in taste and smell comes only if the herbs are fresh."

The next day he had placed a plastic tray on top of the Fazioli and filled herb pots with coriander, green and purple sweet basil, Greek thyme, curly and flat-leaf parsley, dill, chives, lemongrass, marjoram. It had looked as if the piano had a big green wig, and still did now, an eternity after she left. He had continued to keep the refrigerator filled. It was like a mantra, buying the things she had bought. For other people it would have been compulsive behavior. For him it had been a form of prayer, a way toward her image.

He filled his hands with herbs and buried his face in them for a moment.

The little girl on the chair watched him constantly.

"The lady," she said, "the woman, did she do that too?"

He nodded. Stina had always wanted to experience the scent of everything. She had wanted to touch everything with her lips. Herbs, textiles, his skin, his hair, flowers. She had even held the sheet music up to her face.

He added a dash of butter to the pasta, set the table, poured water into a carafe. He took an airtight glass jar out of the refrigerator; on top were three eggs, and under them, uncooked rice. Three large white truffles were buried in the rice. Stina had loved truffles.

"The problem is their aroma," she had said. "It's so very fleeting, like the most volatile hydrocarbons. If you store them in a jar like this, in a few days their scent will saturate the rice and penetrate the eggshells. And you preserve their fresh flavor."

While she had talked she had filled the jar; he had followed the movement of her hands, delicate, absolutely precise. And at the same time they had an artisan's strength and sureness. As when a carpenter handles wood, or a toolmaker touches metal. Richter at the keyboard.

He tore up a small piece of the truffle over the pasta.

"What do you want with me?" asked the girl. "Why did you look for me?"

He sat down at the table. She sat down across from him. They began their meal. She concentrated entirely on eating; he could hear her body's growth processes, tissue building up, the future reprogramming of her hormonal system—still a few years away, but nevertheless begun. Her plate was empty. She licked the fork, licked the knife, used the last piece of bread to wipe her plate; it was white and shiny, ready to put away with the clean dishes.

"People make noise," he said. "Their bodies make noise. But so do their thoughts, their feelings. We all make noise. I hear very well, sort of like an animal, and it's been that way ever since I was a child. It isn't always fun; you can't shut it out. It's easiest when people are asleep. So I'm often awake at night. That's when the world is most quiet. But the noise never goes away completely; I've often listened to people who were asleep."

"To the lady?"

"Also to her. When people sleep there's a sound that may come from their dreams; it sounds as if you've taken away the whole orchestra and only the thin notes of a flute remain. Can you imagine what that's like?"

She nodded.

"Even death makes noise," he said. "I've been with at least ten people when they died. Even when they had taken their last breath, it wasn't quiet; their sound continued. You don't die when you die."

He listened into her as he spoke. There was no change when he mentioned death.

He scanned the nearby surroundings. The blustery weather outside, the slight friction of the rubber tires against the trailer's ground sheet. The wind in the tarpaulin around the Lotus Elise. He still had not paid the vehicle registration fee; you could tell that by the sound, the metallic clang of the temporary license plates. He heard the wall panels shifting. The crackling of the hornbeam log as it carbonized in the potbellied stove.

Behind it all was a homey sound. The aria from the *Goldberg Variations*.

He had always regarded families differently from the way most other people did; what he heard was their balanced intensity. It had never been music to fall asleep to, like the *Goldberg Variations*. The real opportunity in family life was not the security, not the monotony, not the predictability. The real opportunity lay in the fact that sometimes there were no pretenses, no masks, no reservations; suddenly everybody took out his earplugs, it was quiet, and one could hear the others as they really were. That was why Bach had hurried to get a wife and enough children to furnish a chamber choir.

Perhaps it was a joke on the part of SheAlmighty that Kasper was the one who could hear this. Kasper, who had never succeeded in having a family.

"The noise doesn't stop for a second as long as people live," he said. "But your system is different. Once in a while there's a pause. Once in a while you're absolutely quiet. I'd really like to know why. And how. I've been searching for that silence. All my life."

Her face became expressionless. Perhaps he was mistaken about her. She had empty eyes. Pigtails. Knock knees. She was just like every other nine-year-old girl.

"What about earplugs?" she asked.

He forced himself to answer.

"There would still be noise. The noise from my body, the noise from what people are thinking. What I myself am thinking. The silence I'm looking for is another kind. It's the silence behind all noise. The silence that existed before SheAlmighty put in the first CD."

Her expression was more blank than blank.

"Is it over?" she asked.

"Is what over?"

"The dinner."

He dished up more food.

"It's too bad," she said, "that you can't meet the Blue Lady."


He drove her home in the Elise. He recognized Skodsborg Road only by the street signs; the landscape was unfamiliar. The woods along the edge of the road were quiet, white and frozen. Spring had hidden a Siberian night up its sleeve.

"I fit nicely in a sports car," she said.

The car was warm inside. The climate control sounded like the fire in the potbellied stove; the motor played the *Goldberg Variations*. He didn't want to let her get out; he wanted to keep driving for hours and hours, with her beside him. For the first time in his life he understood something of what it must feel like to have a child.

"You really like to drive," she said.

"No telephones. Silence. Nobody can get hold of me. I can drive wherever I want to. No borders. To the end of the world. Shall we do that?"

"That's just your imagination," she said. "You're dreaming. You can't drive away from your contracts, from the money. You're stuck in the money. And from the people you like a lot. There aren't many. The lady. Your father. Maybe one or two more. Not many. For somebody as old as you. But anyway."

For a moment he was afraid of having an accident. He hadn't told her about Maximillian. He hadn't invited such crudeness. From a child. He prayed. For strength not to give her a good whack.

His prayer was heard; his anger disappeared. But the music was gone.

"I'm testing you," she said. "To see what you can stand."


He parked where the fire road turned off. Already the ground frost was so thick he could feel the cold through the soles of his shoes. The girl must have a different metabolism from him; in her thin sweater she seemed to be carrying summer around with her.

The property was dark; even the outdoor lighting was turned off. The only light in the building was in two gable windows.

"The gate is locked now," she said. "Give me a boost."

"Who is the Blue Lady?" he asked.

She shook her head.

"You probably won't see me again either. This was to say goodbye."

He could hardly breathe. She stepped onto his interlocked hands and took off. She weighed nothing; she flew into the air like a butterfly and landed weightlessly on the other side of the wire fence.

He knelt down. Their faces were close to each other. But on separate sides of the fence.

"Did you see me fly?" she asked.

He nodded.

"In a way, I'd like to take you along. Flying. Out in space. Can you help me become an astronaut?"

"Easy as a snap of my fingers."

They stared at each other. Then her face expanded. Her smile started around her mouth, spread to her face, then to her whole head, then to the rest of her body.

"You couldn't even help yourself get over this fence," she said.

She was serious again.

"It's strange," she said. "That you're so close. She's sitting there behind the windows. Where there's light. She's the only one awake at this hour. It's her room. So close by. And still you'll never meet her."

She reached her fingers through the wire mesh and touched his face.

"Sleep well," she said. "And sweet dreams."

Then she was gone.


He stood there by the fence. The night had been quiet. In freezing temperatures everything becomes stiff and silent. Stina had explained the reason to him; all the surfaces that reflect sound become both hard and elastic, like ice and glass. Hence the frost-night koan: Everything can be heard and there is not a sound.

He prayed for a sign. It did not come. Perhaps the same was true with SheAlmighty as with cell phones. The range is not always the best.

He took hold of the wire fence. And leaped. Like a gibbon.

# 6

He did not meet any opposition. The door he tried was not locked; the hall inside was lighted. He passed an industrial kitchen. A quiet elevator asleep in a glass shaft. The hallway on the top floor had track lights, but they were turned off; light came from candles burning in niches a few feet apart.

The corridor ended in a dark door. He opened it without knocking.

He entered the attic room. At a desk by the dark windows sat the head nurse. She had come directly from the operating room, and was still wearing blue scrubs and a white bonnet covering her hair.

"I'm reading the reports right now," she said. "You'll get at least three years in prison. No matter how you look at it. You haven't fallen between two chairs. You've fallen into an abyss."

She was in B-minor.

Bach had chosen B-minor for his great mass. Beethoven too. For the last part of *Missa Solemnis.* Somewhere he had written that each time he encountered Goethe he had heard him in D-major, the parallel key. B-minor was deep. Dramatic, introverted, spiritual. Bluish to the point of being black. The woman in front of him was bluish-black. Not just her clothing, but her being. The same color as deep water. He had never seen her before.

"Spain will never be Europe," she said. "Europe stops at the Pyrenees. Spain is the Middle East. The tax laws are based on the fifth book of Genesis. Anything over five million pesetas is gross tax evasion, and will get you two years. To that we add your withdrawal of all the funds in your offshore companies in Gibraltar. Our attorneys say that probably you have already been reported to the police and summoned to the investigative tribunal in Torremolinos."

"Where am I?" he asked.

"At the Rabia Institute. A convent. We are the Praying Sisters Order. Our head convent is in Audebo. The mother convent is in Egypt. Alexandria."

In Kasper's mind, nuns belonged in southern Europe. From Munich's Maria Church, across from Varieté Plön, and farther south. Where religion was a circus. High ceilings, the public dressed to the nines, smoke, stage lighting, a ringmaster in white and gold, sold out every evening. The Danish church was an attic filled with stage scenery.

She spoke directly into his mind.

"There are about forty or fifty orders of nuns in Denmark. The Cistercians at Sostrup Castle. Clarissa Convent in Randers and Odense. The Benedictine Order's Leoba sisters in Frederiksberg and Ordrup. Carmelites in Hillerød. Les Beatitudes in Brønderslev and Århus. Little Sisters of Jesus at Øm Cloister. And on Vesterbro Street in Copenhagen. Focoler Sisters on the islands of Møn and Langeland. Charismatics on Bornholm Island and in Århus. Missionaries of Love in the Nørrebro neighborhood. The Sisters of the Precious Blood Community in Birkerød. It's said that even Our Lord does not know the number of congregations. Three convents near the Russian Orthodox churches in Råstad, Gislinge, and Blommenslyst. The Russian Orthodox Church has been in Denmark since 1866. That was when Dagmar, a daughter of Christian the Ninth, married Alexander the Third of Russia, who became emperor in 1881. The Nevsky Church on Bred Street dates from that time."

"And are all of them," he said, "experts in Spanish criminal law?"

"We have six convents on the Costa del Sol. Children's hospitals. Counseling for illegal immigrants from Morocco. We have our own attorneys in the Torremolinos administration. We cooperate with the Catholic Church. With the patriarchate in Paris."

She must have been in her late sixties, but she had kept some aspects of her earlier years. Behind her thinness and deep wrinkles was a younger woman's vitality. In her movements, a child's impulsiveness.

"The children," he said. "What is it about the children? About the girl, KlaraMaria?"

"What did you observe," she asked, "when you sat across from her?"

"She's quiet. The other children too. Now and then they're quiet. In a way that no ordinary children are. No normal people."

She stood up and began pacing back and forth. He could not get into her sound; it was inaccessible; he lacked the acoustic password.

"I've baptized nearly a thousand children," she said. "What do you say to the idea that some children are born with a gift for coming close to God faster than others?"

He did not respond.

"KlaraMaria may be such a child," she said. "Perhaps some of the other children as well."

He could tell why she was moving. It was an excess of energy. Not an ordinary excess, not ordinary muscular restlessness, but something else. A slight quivering surrounded her, like around a transformer station. As if she were an organ pipe, as if she contained a standing wave.

"We wanted to tell you about this," she said. "It's not very often that people from outside have perceived something themselves. However, there's no future in it for us. Don't be offended. But you're a bad bet. They're about to bring a tax fraud case against you here at home. In Spain, a subpoena is waiting for you. The situation is hopeless. You'll be gone in a flash."

"I'll appeal," he said. "To the district court in Granada. It will be several years before the case comes up."

"They will charge you with attempted bribery of the public prosecutor in Torremolinos. Bribery cases have first priority. After the big scandals in the nineties. Our lawyers say you'll be sentenced this summer."

He didn't say anything. There was nothing to add.

"It's a desperate situation," she said. "Nevertheless, there may still be hope. We've talked about it. The sisters feel they know you. There's nothing they would rather do than help a great artist. What if powers within the Church interceded for you? If we brought the verdict from Granada to the Supreme Court in Madrid. It doesn't mete out punishment. But it makes the final decision in determining guilt. What if the patriarch from the patriarchate in Paris went to the pardon office in Madrid on your behalf? The king has the power to give pardons. What if we could document that you had donated most of the defrauded funds to our convent? And if all of us here prayed intercessory prayers for you?"

He was flooded with gratitude. What streamed toward him from this total stranger was some of the Christian love for your neighbor that flowed from the cantatas.

He knelt down and laid his forehead against her hand. Old-fashioned, perhaps. But for one whose love is spontaneous there are no limits.

"I think we'll do it," she said. "There's just one little thing we'll request. In return."

He stiffened. Slowly he raised himself backward onto the chair.

"What's wrong?" she asked.

"My basic traumas are exposed,"

"The sisters and I," she said, "are self-reliant. But we need a man."

"Love is never unconditional," he said. "There's always some small thing."

"We're worried about the children," she said.


"A year ago," she said, "one of the novices in our lay order disappeared, Sister Lila; she worked closely with me, caring for the children. She was dragged into an automobile, blindfolded, and driven away. She was gone for two days and nights. She had been tied up and mistreated. Beaten. Questioned about the children. After two days she was driven to Amager Commons and left there. She still hasn't recovered completely. A number of talents lie in what you call the silence. We're afraid somebody wants to exploit those talents."

"The police," he said.

"They're involved. The Institute has been identified as a possible terrorist target. Which means there are contingency plans. And a patrol car drives past our entrance twice a week. That's all the protection one can get. It's quite understandable. There's nothing concrete to go on."

"Where do the children come from?"

"Families connected to the lay order in various parts of the world where the Russian Orthodox Church has a long tradition: Jerusalem, Ethiopia, Australia. Some places in the East. France. The families take no vows and don't wear habits. They can choose how close their connection to the convent will be."

"What do the children do here?"

She looked out the window. As if she were waiting for She-Almighty to prompt her.

"We could call it a training camp," she said. "An expanded international Sunday school. We bring them here once a year. We're finished for this year. It's next year that frightens us."

He tried to get past her voice. Right now it was hoarse, coarse-sounding, like fine shingle on a conveyer belt in a quarry. And it was definitive. A voice for final announcements, blessings, or excommunication. He could not open it.

"We're a modern convent. We're well prepared for many challenges. Very many, in fact. But not for this one."

"You'll have protection," he said. "I can arrange a contact."

She came around the desk, drew a chair over to him, and sat down. She was very close; he wanted to edge away. But the signal from his brain to his muscles was poorly transmitted.

"These aren't ordinary children," she said. "The people we're dealing with aren't ordinary criminals either. We don't know what's out there. But it's far-reaching."

He succeeded in pushing his chair backward.

"I'm an artist," he said. "I have my public to think about. I'm drowning in debt. I have contracts for the next two and a half years. Outside Denmark."

He didn't know if she heard him.

"In the Russian Orthodox Church we work with role models," she said. "That's what the saints are. Following the Savior's example, they allow others to feed them in order to wander among sinners and thieves. In the East they're called bodhisattvas. What we need here is a little saint. A reflection of a saint. Someone who will allow these people to contact him. Whoever they may be. Someone who will solve the situation. Mediate between us and the public authorities. That's what we need."

He moved his chair still farther back.

"You need a police informant," he said. "I'm a man with an international career. And at that point I'll be touring on the Côte d'Azur."

"Not if you break your unfulfilled contracts. That would put a stigma on you. Publicly. You'd seem like a fallen angel. They might try to use you. Whoever they are. You're known for being good at working with children."

The atmosphere was homelike. Like the *Goldberg Variations*. She spoke as if they had known each other for a very long time. She spoke like a big sister. Deadly frank.

"They're the two biggest variety-show companies in Spain," he said. "And on the Côte d'Azur. They would file a claim for damages."

"For a very large sum," she said.

"I'd be blacklisted," he said.

"In most of the world."

They laughed at each other.

"So I come here to the Institute," he said. "It's one year later. I've killed my career."

"A mercy killing. It's about to die anyway. The spiritual part of you is searching for something deeper."

"My future is about to fold. Lawsuits being prepared here and in Spain. So I come to the Institute. And then what?"

"You wait. We come and find you. Or KlaraMaria does. She's very taken with you. I was there in the Circus Building when she saw you the first time. We almost didn't get her home with us. You will be nearby. When we need you. And you will seem like a bankrupt soul. They will contact you. Maybe we can find a way to point you out."

"You'll give me a Judas kiss."

"We'll just glance in your direction. Maybe they will come. Maybe they won't. The crucial thing is that you're nearby. When we ask for help."

"What kind of help?"

She shook her head.

"I'm the *hegumena*. That's the same as the abbess. And from time to time I function as the *staretza*, the spiritual director. But this business here. This isn't my area. However, the sisters believe in you."

"And afterward?"

"There are two possibilities. We follow the plan. Intercession. Write to the pardon office. Contribute to your fine from our charity fund. Move heaven and earth. From the White Russian Metropolitan to the Danish Ministry of Justice. You apologize. An out-of-court settlement is made. You complete your tour belatedly. You're back onstage."

"And the other possibility?"

"Is that it's not enough. Nobody, not the variety shows nor the hacienda nor the tax administration, will agree to a settlement. So you end up with five years in Alhaurín el Grande after all."

She wasn't smiling anymore.

"And when I'm sitting there," he said, "in the long Andalusian winter nights, what will I tell myself was the reason for all of this?"

"The silence," she said. "Was the reason for all of it."


She accompanied him downstairs; he was grateful, because he couldn't have found the way by himself. He had lost his sense of direction, externally and internally.

They walked through the industrial kitchen and a canteen. The candles had replaced themselves and received reinforcement from the moon.

"The terrace," she said. "The dining hall."

She opened a door that led out to the cloister garden. The sound there made you want to settle down on a stone bench and stay, even now, in forty-six-degree weather.

The garden was surrounded by four wings; the fourth wing was a church, diminutive and well kept, like a large community-garden house. The church was built in the form of a cross and had a large onion dome that glistened in the moonlight.

He listened into the scene; a caring tone pervaded everything.

"It's part of our training," she said. "One tries to sanctify all the everyday things. The garden. The maintenance. One prays while sitting on the toilet."

He felt a longing begin to grow. Probably in his own heart, but it was so far-reaching that it spread to the surroundings. Like a dissonant tension.

"For most of my life," he said, "I've searched for silence. Within oneself, and between people. I know it's to be found. I've never been totally within it myself, but I know it exists. You have it. You are standing in it; I can hear that your voice comes out of the silence.

Also the little girl, KlaraMaria. She's close to the same silence. I want to be in there. Otherwise I'll go crazy."

She listened to him. He felt his knees knocking against each other slightly.

"It's undoubtedly true," she said, "that you will go crazy if you don't find the silence."

She closed the garden door; they walked toward the front exit. He held back. He was almost paralyzed with anger. She was a Christian. But not one compassionate word had she given him. Not one blessing. Not even a little kiss on the cheek.

Nevertheless, he had to listen to her body. She walked the way Ekaterina Gordeeva had danced on ice. With a twelve-year-old's joy in moving. The young figure skater had performed a number with the state circus during his three seasons in Moscow. Still, the woman in front of him had a different kind of flow. As if she weren't camped directly in her body, but around it. He had listened to bodies all his life; he had never heard anything like it.

"The African woman," he said. "She threatened me. To make me stay away."

"It's my understanding that in both the circus and the theater it's common to have an audition. In order to find those who take the profession seriously."

He stopped short. His body grew icy. In spite of that, he managed to make his voice purr like a Siamese.

"To be the abbess," he said, "must demand a very high level of trustworthiness."

She turned toward him. He had sat in cafés in southern Europe and listened to nuns walking past. Most of them had a great deal of Monteverdi from the top of their heads and down to their heart. But below that, they were laced up tightly. The woman ahead of him was a different phenomenon.

"Ideally," she said. "In reality, we're all human."

"So I'm going to ask you to put it in writing," he said. "Everything. The bishop and the patriarch. And the intercession and the five million."

They were back in the attic room. She wrote fluidly, with total concentration, went into the next room, a photocopy machine hummed; she came back, gave him the document. He read it and signed it. He'd had many contracts in his life, but none like this.

"Do you trust me?" she asked.

He nodded.


She opened the front door. Held out her hand. He shook it. They stood there in the doorway.

The sounds around them began to change. First they became clearer. He heard his own body, and hers. He noticed the scarcely audible whisper of an electronic device on standby. He heard the building, the constant, minimal settling of stone and cement. The vibration of sleeping people.

He heard the sounds harmonize. Transpose into the same key. He was witness to some form of orchestration.

He could no longer hear the woman's keynote. He looked at her. She had become colorless. He knew they were standing upright and were both on the same journey, in through all the sound boxes and wind instrument bells, toward where he had always wanted to go, toward silence.

Longing and terror hit him simultaneously, like a single beat on a kettledrum. He nearly let out a scream. At that instant, the phenomenon ended.

He leaned against the wall. It took a while before he was able to speak.

"A year is a long time," he said. "You might forget the agreement."

"We may also remember it," she said.

"You may also be mistaken. Maybe no one is after the children. In that case, I will have ruined my life."

"What has characterized great men and women," she said, "is that when it came down to it, they were willing to put everything on one number on the roulette wheel. Our Savior's number. And with no guarantee that it would win."

The room spun around before Kasper's eyes, like a carousel, a cloister carousel.

"It will be a long year," he said. "And not the easiest one in my life. Do you have any advice?"

She looked at him.

"Have you ever tried to pray?"

"I've asked for things. Most of my life."

"That's why you haven't gotten farther."

Anger took away his breath again.

Her sound was now like the aria from the *Goldberg Variations*. Familial. He could tell that she liked him. As few, perhaps very few, people could. It was what he had noticed with KlaraMaria. With Stina. A person who could tolerate the noise from his system. And more than tolerate it.

Love makes people equal. For a moment he and she were completely on the same level.

"To whom shall I pray?" he asked. "Who says there's someone out there? Who says the universe isn't just one big hurdy-gurdy?"

"Maybe it's not necessary to pray to anyone. The early desert mothers said that God is without form, color, or content. Perhaps prayer isn't a matter of praying to anyone. Perhaps it's an active way of giving up. Maybe that's precisely what you need: to give up, without going under."

She opened the door.

"The words could be anything whatsoever," she said, "as long as they speak to the heart. For example, they could be from Bach's cantatas."

He noticed a movement; the African stood behind him.


She accompanied him to the gate and opened it for him. He turned and looked at the building.

"The guest wing," said the African.

The building had three stories; he counted seven windows on each floor, each with its small balcony.

"Very hospitable," he said.

"*Philoxenia*. In love for the stranger one finds love for Christ."

He began walking toward Frederiksdal Road. She stood watching him through the open gate.

He experienced her tone, her reaction to him. What she saw made her sound like a person standing at the roulette table, after *Rien ne va plus*, calculating the odds, and knowing that since it's roulette, the odds are less than 50 percent in any case.

Or perhaps it was his imagination; on cold moonlit nights especially, the world easily becomes a screen on which each of us plays our own home video. He got into his car; he had always regarded his automobile as a separate, but utterly safe, part of his living room, with two easy chairs and a sofa.

Even when he had reached Klampenborg and the Elise was warm and there were other night owls on the road, he continued to hear, from the seats and motor and body of the car and from the traffic and the suburbs around him, the utterly simple and yet incredibly complex theme of the *Goldberg Variations*. As it begins to sound when you have gotten well into the variations and begin to notice that now you cannot leave, now Bach has hold of you, now you must go on, regardless of where it leads you.

# Part
# Three

# 1

Copenhagen Dolce Vita was located on the ground floor of a building that faced what had been Kongens Nytorv, the city's most elegant square.

Kasper had never doubted that spiritual longing and food belonged together, and that in principle there were two approaches: One could either starve or eat oneself toward Paradise.

Great religious traditions had perfected both extremes. The early desert fathers and mothers had sometimes looked as if their skeletons were outside their clothing; the Taoists had said, "Empty the mind and fill the belly," and a series of smart Tibetan Dzogchen and Mahamudra stars had looked like managers of the Gluttons Club. Buddha had proposed a path between the two extremes, and that was what Kasper was looking for, this evening and many times before, as he sat at Bobech Leisemeer's restaurant, where the food was like the circus in the old days—thoroughly spiritualized, shocking, and on the border between equilibristic and unconscionable.

Nevertheless, a point between the heart and the solar plexus would not relax, and never would relax in this life. A point which knows that in an environment like this, surrounded by gold and white and damask and annual incomes never below a million kroner, if one has been born a Gypsy, one must have come to the wrong place.

But still he had kept coming back. Because the food was the way it was, because one who seeks the highest must not leave any path untried. And because Kasper had always been able to hear himself in the chef: a proletarian boy born to play the buffoon at fairs who had to spend the rest of his life trying to understand why fate had dressed him in a white uniform and chef's hat, made him the darling of the upper class, and set him up as some sort of high priest before an altar to food.

Kasper looked out over the water.

He had awakened two hours earlier; it was pitch-dark around him.

He climbed down from the loft and went over to the trailer. No one was inside. He tried to let himself in, but there was steel wire on the door handle; he struck a match, and saw the wire had a lead seal marked COPENHAGEN POLICE.

He broke the seal. Inside the trailer he struck another match. They had cleaned up after themselves. The way a corpse looks nice on the outside after embalming, but there's no longer anything inside. His violin was gone, the strongbox had been opened, his papers were gone. *Klavierbüchlein* was no longer on the shelf.

But his clothes were still there. He gathered up his suit, shoes, towel, and toiletries. Next he tore a little piece of cardboard from the cover of Carl Nielsen's memoir about his childhood on Funen Island. He turned out the light, walked outside, pressed the piece of cardboard firmly in the door at knee height. Connected the two halves of the seal as well as he could.

In the lavatory building he took a shower and shaved, first with an electric shaver and then with a safety razor. The face that looked out at him from the mirror was affected by aging and by five to seven thousand complete makeup jobs over thirty years.

Once Stina had stood behind him. Put her hands around his face. Looked at him in the mirror.

"A little of the Savior," she said. "A little of Holberg's *The Pawned Farmer's Helper*. A little of Grev Danilo in *The Merry Widow*."

He would have liked to have said goodbye to Daffy, but the risk was too great. If the police were waiting for him, they would wait by the door. He went into the stable.

The lightbulb was burning in the ceiling; he took a couple of apples from the crate and stood outside Roselil's stall. The horse took a small leap toward him, like a little girl who wants to play. He placed his hands on the animal's neck. In fourteen days it would be killed.

Somewhere outside the light something moved that wasn't a horse.

He released the stall's double bolt. He would kick the door open, buzz like a Vespa crabro hornet, and they would get Roselil in the head like a thirteen-hundred-pound projectile.

Daffy emerged from the darkness. He must have stood very quietly.

He came over to the stall. Shoved the bolt into place. Laid the violin, the documents, and *Klavierbüchlein* in front of Kasper.

"I put on a big coat. And went into the trailer with them. This is what I had time to rescue."

One of the watchman's hands left the lath board. Disappeared out of sight. Reappeared with an apple.

"Your sentence back then," said Kasper. "What was it for?"

"For three million, at Nydahl's. During business hours."

Kasper had tried to give Stina a ring from Markus Nydahl, but she had refused; it had been difficult or impossible to get her to accept gifts. But the visit to the store had been spectacular. It was located on Ny Øster Street. There were two guards at the door. Jewelry and watches lay in bulletproof glass cases that were ready to sink into fireproof vaults under the floor if anyone so much as rustled a bag of candy.

"And the profession?" asked Kasper. "That you had to leave? What was that?"

"I was an apprentice to Boras."

Boras had been the Johann Sebastian Bach of gentlemen thieves. He'd had one student, an apostle, a dharma heir. Something stirred in Kasper's memory. The heir had begun to help himself to the inheritance. And then he had suddenly disappeared.

He opened the case; the violin was intact.

"Why run this risk?" he asked.

The watchman had paused in the doorway. He stood looking around the stable.

"They will be put out to pasture," he said. "I bought them this morning. For what the slaughterhouse and the riding school would have paid, minus the veterinarian's bill. Boras and I had some conversations before he died. I felt he gave me an unwritten will. I started buying the animals' freedom then. It didn't fit with an apprentice's salary. He said, 'You'll pull yourself together, Daffy. Life is no prayer meeting.'"

"That's nice," said Kasper. "You've acted compassionately. But I was hurt in my childhood, so I have a hard time accepting anything; there's always just one little thing. What can it be in this case?"

He spoke to an empty doorway, and a horse. Daffy was gone.

He looked out across the water. It was an unbroken surface, from the National Bank to where the Krinsen garden had been.

The statue of Christian V on horseback had been taken away. On the sidewalk leading to the barricade, a chamber orchestra was playing appetizing morsels from the *Brandenburg Concertos* to begin Copenhagen's municipal spring and summer entertainment. People streamed past the musicians into the city's night, as if they had a mission and direction in life.

He closed his eyes and listened inside the music. Inside the space around him. Under the surface there was enough fear to open a psych ward.

He opened his eyes and looked out across the water. It did not appear like the end of the world, Pompeii, Santorini, the Deluge. It could have been a natural lake. Or major water damage.

The city's anxiety had existed before the earthquakes too. He had heard it from the time he was a child, since the accident, since his hearing became more acute; it was an old acquaintance. From deaths, from serious accidents in the ring, from himself. It wasn't so much fear of the catastrophes themselves as for what they led to. The tragic events were doors that opened to understanding that we all are living on borrowed time and the things that are important to hold on to—life, happiness, death, love, inspiration—are completely out of control.

He felt a sudden anger at SheAlmighty. People around him could have been happy. He could have been happy himself. At Leisemeer's restaurant they could all have felt like absolute kings. Or better yet, like gods, for after eating and drinking and receiving royal service, the tableware disappeared, the footmen disappeared, the whole feudal illusion disappeared, and one was out in the carefree Copenhagen night.

Instead, one found natural catastrophes. Children mistreated. Kidnappings. Loneliness. Separation of people who love each other.

His anger increased. The problem with anger against God is that it's impossible to go higher in the system to complain.

He turned his chair and tried to escape both the place and the view. That only made the situation worse. Across the zinc counter dividing the kitchen from the restaurant he caught sight of Leisemeer.

When Kasper left Denmark the previous time, believing it was for forever, he had left behind, partly by accident, a huge unpaid bill here at Leisemeer's. He had been sure the debt must have been rescheduled. Because Leisemeer had risen beyond the restaurant work itself, into a white shirt and tie and the managing director's chair. Instead, here he was, bent over the convection oven, strong and coarse as a herdsman. Like circus owner Eli Benneweis, who had never learned to stay in his office either, but had continued to hang around the stables.

Kasper heard a sound he remembered, but couldn't identify. At the farthest end of the restaurant sat a woman and a man; the woman's back was to him; he zoomed in. It was the aristocrat from Strand Road. But now Our Lord or fate or the cosmetic industry had given her long black hair and a stylish suit. The man across from her was ten years younger than she and had shoulders nearly five feet across; his sound was awkward, as if he wasn't used to dining in a place where it cost five hundred kroner or more to eat one's fill.

Two-hundred-pound footsteps approached Kasper. A couple of champagne glasses were placed in front of him, and something was poured into one; he listened to the polyphony of the bubbles; it was Krug champagne.

He looked up at the completely bald head and waxed mustache, the same as Gurdjieff. It was Leisemeer.

"I've come to pay for everything," said Kasper.

The chef let the large drop-shaped bottle glide down into the wine bucket. Then he turned around.

Kasper reached him in a single movement. The chef would have walked away, but his left foot got stuck in a crook; the crook was

Kasper's left foot. Leisemeer began to fall. In order to stop falling he tried to move his right foot. That too was stuck, in a crook created by Kasper's right foot.

It would have been a bad fall, but Kasper slid out of his chair, caught the massive figure, and drew it toward him.

"You're not at work today. You have a day off. I asked when I reserved a table."

They had known each other for twenty-five years; there had always been mutual respect, warmth and courtesy. Now suddenly there was no courtesy anymore. That is one of the clown's tasks. To release the dark sides of the moment too.

"I wanted to be here myself. With a meat cleaver. To see if you would pay up completely."

"I didn't give my own name."

Leisemeer pulled himself free. They faced each other at close range.

"The police," said the chef quietly. "They're waiting outside. They're going to nab you when you leave. They want to find out who you're meeting."

Kasper suddenly remembered that Gurdjieff wrote somewhere that he had been to an Easter meal. Incarnated as Judas.

"So you fingered me."

Two red patches appeared on the smoothly shaven cheeks in front of Kasper, like warning lights. Leisemeer grabbed his lapels; he had hands as big and thick as pizzas.

"Your regular customers are looking at us," said Kasper. "And they don't like what they see."

Leisemeer let him go.

"They knew you were coming. There's also somebody from the Ministry of Justice. I didn't have your telephone number. What would you have done?"

Kasper smiled reassuringly to the nearest tables. People fell back into the vaudeville act. Leisemeer left. Kasper looked out the windows. Out through the coatroom and the glass door. They could be anywhere in the crowd. In a car.

Something happened in the restaurant, on the deeper levels too; for a moment, the anxiety gave way. He looked up, and saw Stina.

She was in the middle of the restaurant. On her way toward him. She moved awkwardly, as she always did in a group of people, like a schoolgirl at the last dance of the season.

Nevertheless, people had stopped eating for a moment. Even those who were choosing from Leisemeer's dessert trolley. Behind her, two young waiters broke into a quick trot. Coming over to pull out her chair. He could have sworn that a spotlight followed her. Until he realized it was his own attention, and that of the other guests, that illuminated her.

He stretched out his arms for an embrace. It was never completed. She looked at him. With a look that could have stopped a runaway circus elephant. He was left hanging in the air. Like a wounded bird. She was the one person for whom he could never time his entrance.

She sat down. Her being was E-major. The higher aspect of E-major. He had always heard a shining green color around her.

She removed a large diver's watch from her left wrist and laid it on the table.

"Half an hour," she said.

She had changed. He couldn't say how. His preparations disappeared. All the time he hadn't seen her disappeared. Ten years meant nothing. A whole life hadn't meant anything.

He nodded toward the dark-golden water.

"What's happening there? What's your involvement?"

At first he didn't think she would answer.

"When you walk on the beach," she said, "without shoes, what happens to the sand in front of your foot when you step down on it?"

"It's years since I've been in the mood to walk on the beach."

Her eyes narrowed.

"But if you did?"

He thought about it.

"The sand will become sort of dry."

She nodded.

"The water is sucked away. Because increased pressure creates increased porousness around the pressure area. It's called Vatanjan's theory. The theory posits something to the effect that accumulation of stress in the Earth's crust will cause changes in groundwater conditions. We're trying to refine that hypothesis. We work with figures related to water depths when wells are dug. Anywhere in Zealand. In order to predict whether new earthquakes will occur. And to understand the earlier ones."

He barely paid attention to the words. Just their color. During her explanation she glided toward her subdominant key, A-major; the mental aspect of her sound followed. Her color shifted toward a bluish tint.

"There won't be another earthquake," he said. "That's what the papers say. Holes in the limestone collapsed. They don't think there are any more holes."

"True," she said. "There are certainly no more holes."

Her sound had changed. Only very briefly, a quarter of a second. But that was a quarter of a second too long. It had shifted to F-minor. The suicidal key.

"What's wrong?" he said. "Something is wrong."

She looked over her shoulder. As if she were looking for a creditor. But that was impossible. She had always lived on next to nothing.

"What about the earthquakes?" she asked.

"They write that it's unclear. If it was earthquakes. Or just the collapse of cave systems. They write that there have always been earthquakes in Denmark. Something to do with crustal tension from the Ice Age. They just haven't attracted public attention."

"Where did you get that information?"

"From your group."

Her sound shifted again.

"This is a 'civil catastrophe.' All information is cleared by a special office of the Danish Police."

Something had been put on the table in front of them, appetizers, perhaps; she swept them aside.

"Put your hands on the table."

He complied.

"Earthquakes are measured according to the Richter scale. Magnitudes of three or less can't be felt. They are only recorded by a seismograph. And even those can be read only by a trained seismographer. At a magnitude of four there are noticeable vibrations. But in a city you'd confuse them with heavy traffic."

She shook the tabletop against his hands. The vibrations increased.

"At five on the Richter scale, cracks develop in masonry. With a magnitude of six, things begin to go badly. It starts as an explosion. At a particular spot. The epicenter. From there, irregular rings of secondary waves spread out. They are what cause damage."

The table thumped against his body.

"With magnitudes of seven and up, there's chaos. Everything except bits of buildings topples. There's a sound like thunder. But you can't locate its source."

The table twisted back and forth under his hands. His champagne glass tipped and broke. She leaned back.

"I was at the San Andreas fault. Some years ago. At UCLA. We sprayed high-pressure steam at the tectonic plate borders. To release the tension in the Earth's crust. It failed. We worked at Antonada. Twelve miles outside San Francisco. There was an earthquake. One moment there was life—everyday life, children. The next moment, death and destruction. Fire from burst gas pipes. That was a small earthquake. But it measured seven on the Richter scale."

He hadn't seen her like this before, not even when she left him. Her sound had become more dense.

"One determines the quake's epicenter by an ordinary trigonometric measurement. GEUS, the Geological Survey of Denmark and Greenland, participates in the European seismographic warning system. They have the European numbers on the screen as soon as the blast wave strikes Zurich or Gothenburg. There weren't any waves. GEUS has a measuring station on the Vestvolden ramparts. They have RefTek seismic recorders there. Complete equipment. Radar there can register a spider's movement on the Knippel Bridge railing. It didn't register a thing."

He understood what she said. And at the same time, he didn't understand.

"Half a square mile of Earth crust and ocean floor sink," she said. "More than a hundred million tons of stone, chalk, and sand are set in motion. And it's all caused by an underground vibration."

"The flooding? There was water."

"There was a blast wave. That reached to Helsingør, and no farther. But no terrain movement. No trace of a mass transfer."

"The holes?"

"There were no holes."

She was now completely in F-minor. Just like Schubert's last string quartet. First E-major in its heavenly purity. And then suddenly F-minor. At that point something in Schubert must have known that he was soon to die.

"GEUS and Denmark's Space Center detonated over three thousand pounds of dynamite. Last summer. Two months before the first quake. In order to map the deeper strata beneath Copenhagen. They detonated in several places at the bottom of the Sound. And recorded the blast wave's movements with geophones. Do you remember them?"

He nodded. He had calibrated four hundred geophones for her, using his hearing. They were sensitive microphones designed to be sunk into the ground. He felt a stab of joy that she at least acknowledged this little piece of the past.

"The same procedure as was used in recording the Silkeborg anomaly in 2004. Sound waves have different rates of diffusion in various layers of sediment. There were no holes in the limestone. It wasn't a collapse."

"What was it then?"

She didn't reply. She just looked at him. She wanted to tell him something. He didn't understand what it was. But for a brief moment she let her guard down.

He spread out the post office receipt between his hands. She read it slowly. Read her name. A child's handwriting. But still personal and very clear.

"KlaraMaria," he said. "A student of mine, a girl nine years old, turned up a year ago; now she's been kidnapped. I had brief contact with her. She gave me this."

Her face had been glowing. From her many outdoor activities. From excitement. Now all the color had drained out of it. She started to get up.

He grabbed her wrist.

"It's a child," he said. "She's in mortal danger. What sent her to you?"

She tried to pull her hand back. He tightened his grip.

There was movement near the door; it was one of the two monks and another man in civilian clothes. The woman with the dark hair and the man across from her had risen from their table. Their timing indicated they were working for the police.

There was no way out. It was Easter. He thought about the Savior. Things weren't much fun for Him on Friday evening either. But He had continued to make an effort nonetheless.

Kasper raised his voice.

"I've suffered," he said. "All these years, I've suffered beyond words."

She lifted the champagne bottle out of the cooler and held it like a juggler's mallet. It was his grip on her wrist, the sensation of physical pressure; she had never been able to stand that. He let her go.

"I've changed," he said. "I'm a new person. Reborn. I'm sorry for everything."

She began to turn around. The officers were headed toward him. It was hopeless to try to get past them.

"I can't pay," he said. "I'm completely broke."

The room had good acoustics. A bit dry, but the ceiling was grooved, which made for excellent dispersion of sounds with high frequencies. Sound needs to be frustrated; smooth ceilings are a nightmare. People at the nearest tables had stopped eating. Two waiters had started moving.

She swayed back and forth. Like a tiger in a menagerie crate.

He raised the broken champagne glass. It was transformed into a wreath of razor blades on a crystal stem.

"I can't live without you," he said. "I'll kill myself!"

There were about one hundred people in the restaurant. They absorbed some of the sound. Nevertheless, he now had nearly everyone's attention. Three of the waiters plus Leisemeer had almost reached the table. The officers had come to a halt.

"Well, do it then!" she whispered. "Do it, goddamn it!"

The champagne in her glass on the table released a cloud of bubbles. He didn't understand that. Krug was made with more than 50 percent old wine. It didn't have the restlessness of modern champagnes. The glass began to dance. The small plates levitated; their liberated contents floated in the air: snails in parsley sauce on small pressed medallions of what looked like spring leeks, pieces of Danish lobster with Serrano ham.

Then the shaking began.

Porcelain and glass were swept off the table. People screamed. One of the large front windows cracked, broke into pieces, and fell to the ground in a cascade of pulverized glass.

He had been flung over the table. Those in the restaurant who had been standing up were now lying down. Except Stina.

"It's a sign," he said. "That our fates are bound together. People have always taken earthquakes as a sign."

She straightened up effortlessly. If he tried to follow her he would end up on the floor. The room was swimming before his eyes.

"It's karma," he said. "We were lovers in an earlier life."

He was grabbed from behind. Leisemeer and the waiters had reached him. The officers were still down on all fours. The way to the exit was open.

"Take me to the kitchen!" he shouted. "I'll wash dishes. I'll stay till I've paid for everything."

Leisemeer put his coat around Kasper's shoulders.

"We have dishwashing machines," he said.

They led Kasper toward the exit. He caught a glimpse of Stina's down jacket in the coatroom. The waiters formed a circle around him. Leisemeer's lips were by his ear.

"Half a minute," he whispered. "I'll block their way for half a minute. Now get going."

Kasper was pushed past Stina's jacket. The dark-haired woman and her companion struggled toward him, past overturned chairs and panicked customers. He put his hand into Stina's pocket, without looking directly at the jacket. Still ten seconds. And he wanted to be prepared.

"You are witnesses," he shouted. "To my confession. This woman. Whose life I devastated in the past. I had a hidden purpose when I forced her to come to this meeting."

Leisemeer clapped his hand over Kasper's mouth. It smelled of garlic and sage.

"I'll make bouillon out of you," whispered the chef.

The door opened. Kasper's heels left the earth.

They had pushed him with all their might. A person who hadn't learned falling routines would have broken something. Kasper met the sidewalk with a forward rolling fall. The crowd made room around him.

Three groups of two men moved toward him. There was no open area between them.

He stripped off his jacket and shirt; people drew away from him, and the plainclothes policemen were pressed backward. With naked torso and outstretched arms he began moving sideways along the restaurant's broken window. Hundreds of faces stared at him from inside.

"A penitential pilgrimage," he cried. "Two hundred times around the restaurant! I invoke double pneumonia!"

He stood in front of the orchestra. A uniformed policeman came toward him, hesitantly. Kasper took a handful of bills from his jacket and threw them in front of the musicians; they were thousand-kroner bills. They fluttered to the ground like mahogany-colored doves. The policeman stopped at the sight of the money.

A taxi halted at the curb facing Hovedvagt Street. The restaurant door opened. Stina came out and got into the taxi. He reached the vehicle as the door slammed. It was headed in the wrong direction, toward the policemen. But he couldn't control himself.

He pounded on her door. The window was rolled down.

"Let's get married," he said. "This is a proposal. I've changed my attitude. I want a family. I want that very much."

The blow struck him under the cheekbone. It came as a surprise; he hadn't seen her lift her hand. But at any rate she had raised the champagne bottle.

"Wake up!" she said.

He held out the postal receipt toward her.

"What was in the letter?" he asked.

The taxi pulled away from the curb, accelerated, and was gone.

He straightened up. People around him were still paralyzed. By the earthquake. By the events. He walked toward the orchestra.

A woman was standing at the curb. Pushed forward by the crowd behind her. She was wheeling a bicycle. It was the head of Department H, Asta Borello.

She stared at his naked torso. As if at a poltergeist.

To meet her was magnificent synchronicity. Of the sort that Jung says happens only for those who have taken a seven-mile step toward the unknown in their process of individuation.

He listened to her. Perhaps she was on her way to meet a girl-friend. To go to the theater. She was wearing a skirt. Panty hose. Tall high-heeled leather boots. Nonetheless, she had taken her bicycle. No reason to throw money away and interfere with her savings. On a Good Friday evening.

"Asta," he said. "Do you have a mobile bailiff business?"

She tried to get away from him, without success.

He walked over to the orchestra. Leaned down. Picked up the bills. Took half of them. That still left enough for a thousand for each of the musicians.

"When you practice charity," he said, "it's important not to over-dose."

At that moment the collective paralysis lifted. People started running toward him.

If the race had been more than sixteen hundred yards on a well-lit artificial-turf track, they would have caught him. But it was a sprinting distance through a black labyrinth.

He turned into the first open gate, where two cooks were empty-ing two Leisemeer hearses; an external staircase led up two stories to the roof of a low rear building, and after that came more than a thou-sand feet of tall hedge that separated the wooden fences and garbage containers of the yards behind the apartment buildings along Ny Øster Street and Ny Adel Street. He crossed Ny Øster Street and Købmager Street; only when he reached the open squares, where people would have spotted someone running, did he start to walk.

# 2

On the surface the city looked like itself, aside from the television crews' vans double-parked in front of the hotels. But the sound picture was different. At first he thought it was because of the barricades. On the way to the restaurant he had seen that the city center was now closed to traffic from the embankments on in; only taxis and buses were allowed through the inner city, perhaps out of fear of new tremors.

He had always loved the few cities without traffic, first and foremost Venice. One could hear them; the city space took on the sound of people's footsteps and voices. It was the same now. He crossed Gråbrødre Square and five hundred pigeons flew up; their flapping wings made the whole square vibrate. And in Rådhus Square there wasn't a single automobile. He had never heard Vesterbro like this, quiet and solemn.

Then he felt the silence draw itself together, and the sounds got more dense; he heard a flute theme; it was *Actus Tragicus*, Bach's only funeral mass. Perhaps it was just imagination, perhaps Bach had captured some of the background music that accompanies every apocalypse. And he had been only twenty-two at the time.

The traffic on Vesterbro Street closed around him. He turned down a side street toward the old shooting range; he had to find a place to rest. The distances in between were the worst; after four hundred yards anaerobic sprint reserves are used up, and there is still far to go. His heart was beating too fast for the prayer to keep up.

A woman went in a door leading to a stairway; he reached the door before it closed.

He stood just inside the entrance until her steps reached an upstairs apartment and a door slammed. Then he started up the stairs;

there was no elevator. He continued past the fifth floor and sat down on the uppermost step, in front of the attic door. He turned on the hall light and took out the folded piece of letter paper that he had fished out of Stina's pocket.

It was a fax, signed with unreadable Gothic script and marked BERLIN and EUROPÄISCHES MEDITERRANISCHES SEISMOGRAPHISCHES ZENTRUM. He wished he knew more German; he was able to understand Bach's cantata texts, and even then just barely. But the address was legible; it was Stina's name and two locations. One was Hotel Scandinavia, with a room number. The other was "Pylon 5, Copenhagen Harbor."

He folded the paper and put it back in his pocket. He listened to the building below him. To the sound of family life.

He had made one last attempt at establishing a real home. It was midway in their relationship, about a month and a half before Stina disappeared. A late autumn night. She fixed dinner for him. He sat and listened. It was like listening to the pauses in Mozart's Adagio in B-Minor. Peaceful, meditative. Completely satisfying,

"I had a profound insight," he said. "A moment ago. It came like a ringing sound. From deep within me. I saw that you could give up your job."

She stopped what she was doing.

"This isn't the usual situation," he said. "It's not a case of an ordinary man making the usual attempt to control a woman. What it's about is that the truly great men—Grock, Beethoven, Schubert—have needed women who totally developed their talent for providing loving care. Bach as well. Two women. And Jesus: the Virgin Mary and Mary Magdalene. When a man has an artistic or spiritual mission, he needs total female devotion."

It was a gamble. But one is always willing to take a risk when trying to bring home big prizes.

She stared at him intently.

"You mean it," she said. "Ninety percent of you means it."

She put down the knife. Turned off the stove.

"I have an insight," she said. "That tonight you'll eat crap."

He stood up. Grabbed her wrist; squeezed it. Her sound and her look changed. He let go of her. She turned around and left.

He had known somehow that it was the beginning of the end.

---

His pulse was becoming manageable again. He heard voices in the yard behind the building: children.

There is no sound more complex and unfathomable, no sound more individualized, than the human voice. Normally the vocal cords are relaxed within their entire register. But if the volume is increased, the tension and *internus* activity is also increased, and with that comes a change in pitch; this is how one does Tyrolean yodeling, how gentlemen with fruit stalls offer bananas for sale, how clowns reach the rows farthest back, how children shout, how KlaraMaria had laughed.

It had been his last performance; he was leaving the next morning, going back to Spain, back to fulfilling the first part of his contract with the Blue Lady. Near the end of his act he heard her laughter—free, uninhibited, rippling, and with the characteristic raw huskiness of a change in pitch.

Back in the dressing room, he took off his makeup; there was no time to change clothes. When the finale was over he walked along the edge of the ring in his bathrobe; the audience was leaving, but she still sat there, alone. He sat down beside her.

"I get happy," she said, "when I see you perform."

He wished she would keep talking. How do you explain the sweetness of the miracle of a voice? It was like when a great coloratura soprano hits a note that's clear as a bell; he could have sat listening for hours, a whole lifetime, just to the color of her tone.

She gazed into the deserted ring.

"Why did you start to play music?" she asked.

He listened backward across his childhood; he heard "The Pilgrim's Chorus" from *Tannhäuser*.

"I was at the Royal Theater," he said. "I was six years old. Sometimes the theater uses artists' children, and I had a role as a child acrobat; we'd had afternoon rehearsals, but I didn't want to go home. I persuaded my mother to wait; I wanted to hear an opera. They performed *Tannhäuser*. The hero is a mama's boy, but even so I'll take you to hear it. We were a small group of children, from the circus and the ballet. We had climbed up to the iron supports of the scenery towers, way out at the edge of the proscenium. There we saw the director of the chorus. He waved the singers forward. There were a hundred. A hundred singers! 'The Pilgrim's Chorus.' The music got louder. It was as if it grew out of the ground. And at the end there came a crescendo. Full force. I almost fell onto the stage. I was blissful. Absolutely blissful. And it wasn't just the chorus; it was the sound of the audience too. I could hear the hair rise on the backs of their necks. And at that moment I felt the decision inside me. Not even a decision. A knowledge. That I wanted to be able to evoke a phenomenon like that. As great a sound. As many tears. Do you understand?"

She nodded.

"I told this to my mother in the bus on our way home. She asked if I wanted to sing. I said I wanted to play the violin. The next week she brought me a violin. We didn't have any money. Still, she brought me a violin."

He noticed that she was listening toward the empty ring. He listened with her.

"All the great clowns have been there," he said. "That's what we hear. I've learned from all of them, those I saw as a child. Grock, August Miehe, Enrico and Erneste Caroli, Buster Larsen, Charlie Rivel. Now they are gone."

She waited. He nodded toward the tent poles above them.

"My mother fell," he said. "Her sound is always in there too. And the sound of the great ones she learned from. She walked on a high wire. She danced on a high wire. She learned from the Swedish wire artist Reino. The Australian Con Colleano. Linon, the rope-walking clown from Paris. The truly great ones."

He tried to smile. The girl did not smile in return.

"And that's why," she said. "Why you have so few friends."

He didn't believe his own ears.

"I have a hundred million friends. My public."

"You think people will always be abandoned. Because your mother left you. But that's wrong. Actually, people are never abandoned."

It is very difficult for an adult to accept wisdom from a child. He had lost his bearings.

She took his hand.

"Is it true?" she asked. "That you'll take me to hear a hundred people singing?"

The wisdom was gone. Only the child remained.

He nodded.

"Everything except the overture," he said. "I'll cover your ears while they play that. There's too much sex in the overture; it ought to be forbidden for children under sixteen."

A kind of peace settled over him. Love has something to do with peace. He felt at home. Here in the empty tent, in one of the most transient buildings imaginable. He felt a solidarity with the child beside him. A feeling that must be the essence of home and family.

She looked up at him obliquely, from lowered eyes.

"If I have problems sometime," she said, "if things are bad, will you come and help me?"

She had spoken quickly, casually. But he caught the tone behind the words. It was the most serious thing he had ever heard a child say.

When people make promises it's always with only a percentage of themselves; he had heard it many times, weddings, confirmations, sworn blood brotherhoods. There is never more than 10 percent of the total persona behind the golden promises, because that is as much of ourselves as we control; it was true of himself as well.

But not this moment. This moment there was suddenly more. He could hear his body vibrate, like a wind instrument when the embouchure all at once succeeds and a great deal of the energy becomes tone.

"Always," he said.


The door above him opened. A boy and a girl stood there, perhaps about six years old; they had come through the attic space used for drying laundry. It was their voices he had heard earlier, but he had not heard them arrive. Now they did not move.

"Who are you?" asked the girl.

"I'll whisper it to you both," said Kasper, "but only if you don't tell anyone else. I'm Santa Claus."

The children shook their heads.

"You don't look like Santa Claus."

"When spring comes," said Kasper, "then Santa gets his hair cut and his beard shaved off; he has his hair dyed, loses almost ninety pounds, stables the reindeer, and lives in people's drying attics."

"What about the presents?"

He felt in his pockets. All he found was money, nothing smaller than a thousand-kroner bill. He gave them that.

"I mustn't take it," said the boy. "That's what my mother says."

Kasper stood up.

"From Santa Claus," he said, "you can take anything. Tell your mother that. Say that Santa is going to come and nibble her earlobe."

"What about my father?"

Kasper began heading down toward the earth's surface.

"Santa Claus will come and nibble him as well."

"I've got a dog too," said the little girl hopefully.

"I'm sorry," said Kasper. "Even Santa Claus has to set limits."

"You don't talk very nice," said the girl.

Kasper turned toward her.

"For children to know where the abyss is, and be careful," he said, "you need to take them all the way out and show them the edge."

He continued down the stairs. The children followed him, hesitantly.

"Santa Claus?"

"Yes."

"Thank you for the money. And Merry Christmas."

The pitch of their voices changed. They disappeared up toward heaven. In a cascade of laughter. Kasper stepped onto the sidewalk. He began walking.

# 3

Kierkegaard wrote somewhere that if one just goes walking, everything goes well. He should have been along this evening. Behind every pair of approaching headlights he heard one of the police's Ford Mondeos. In every passing drunk he saw a plainclothes officer. He looked for a taxi.

A green light came toward him in the darkness; green is the color of hope and the heart; it was a taxi. The taxi stopped. It was a Jaguar. The back door opened; Kasper did not move. The traffic was heavy, flowing fast. There was no way an automobile could have followed a pedestrian.

"They've issued an arrest warrant," said Franz Fieber. "On the police home page. And broadcast a radio description to taxis and Greater Copenhagen Authority buses. If you continue on foot you'll be nabbed in ten minutes. I suggest you get in. One of my drivers has a motorboat in Sweden. He can have it ready in an hour. Ten thousand kroner, which includes his picking up the boat in Malmø. Late tomorrow afternoon you'll be lying low in Umeå."

A feeling of no escape is in D-minor. It was Mozart who discovered that. And developed it. In *Don Giovanni*. Around the statue. Before Mozart, there had always been a way out. One could always pray to God for help. Doubt about the Divine begins with Mozart.

Kasper got into the Jaguar.

"We're going out to Tippen," he said. "Through the inner city. Where we'll change cars."

Franz Fieber shook his head.

"I've got orders. To take you away."

Kasper folded his hands. He prayed. For forgiveness for what he would be forced to do. If the car didn't start in ten seconds.

Kierkegaard writes somewhere that there is something disturbing about praying for forgiveness. It's as though one doesn't really believe that God has already granted forgiveness. But what shall we do?

The Jaguar started up and moved into the flow of traffic.

"I can sense my passengers," said Franz Fieber. "Through the seats. You would have slugged me. If I hadn't cooperated."

The Jaguar drove down Studie Street. In the side streets adjacent to the barricaded area, homeland-security cars were parked with dark windows and their headlights turned off.

"There are two," said Franz Fieber.

"Two what?"

"Two children. They've disappeared."

If one listens into the truly big shocks one can hear what effort it takes to hold the world together. When for a moment we let ourselves feel deep, sudden joy or sudden sorrow, reality begins to disintegrate.

"How long ago?"

"Simultaneously—they disappeared simultaneously."

"Why hasn't this been in the media?"

"That was a police decision. Probably to protect the investigation."

Kasper listened backward, toward the place in his heart and mind that prayer came from. Slowly, reality returned.

"Tell me about the city," said Franz Fieber. "What it really sounds like."

Kasper heard himself speaking, perhaps to reassure the young man ahead of him, perhaps to reassure himself.

"It sounds like the way people treat their children."

Perhaps that was true. Perhaps it was part of the truth.

The area was as full of motorcycle cops as during a state visit. The police's small Dutch armored cars, built to drive straight into a war zone, were parked at every other corner. To help prevent plundering in apartments and stores.

In the northern suburbs there is a tendency toward discipline without empathy. Coddling instead of love. Closer in, there is inferiority and bewilderment. The volume increases according to the population density. From Park Cinema on into the city center, Copenhagen sounds like an acetylene torch.

The yellow eyes regarded him in the rearview mirror.

Kasper kept his face expressionless. Generalizations have an inhuman touch. But without them it is difficult, or perhaps impossible, for great clowns to create energy. The Savior also painted with broad brushstrokes and plenty of tar on the palette.

"I earn two hundred fifty thousand a month," said Franz Fieber. "On the city. Is that a sin?"

"Before or after taxes?"

"After."

"It would be a sin not to earn it."

The mobile phone rang; Franz Fieber lifted the receiver, listened, hung up.

"They're searching for this vehicle," he said.

Kasper pointed; the Jaguar turned across Ny Adel Street and drove through an open gate. The two hearses still stood there. The back door of one was open.

"I'm borrowing a friend's van," said Kasper. "Still, I'm not sure the key is in the ignition. If not, could you help me?"

The Jaguar stopped. Franz Fieber took out a small toolbox from a space between the seats.

"I outshine every auto mechanic," he said. "Every auto electrician."

A young man in a cook's uniform came out from what had to be the kitchen's delivery entrance. He took a tray from the open van. It held puff-pastry canapés. Hunger hit Kasper like a blow.

"We've got perhaps a couple of minutes," he said.

"I can take out the motor and do major repairs in that time."

They got out of the Jaguar; Kasper was just a little ahead of Franz Fieber. It was like watching the sorcerer's apprentice, as crutches and prostheses fell into place of their own accord. Kasper was about to get behind the wheel; the young man put his hand on the door handle.

"I'll drive."

They looked at each other. Then Kasper heard the sound. It's not just that people themselves can be identified by their tone. The feelings they awaken in others also create a watermark of sound. Kasper had always been able to hear Bach's love for Maria Barbara in works from 1710 and on. And in the "Chaconne," Bach's wild and yet transfigured sorrow over her death. Now in the system in front of him he heard the quiet girl. He let go of the door. Franz Fieber swung himself into the driver's seat. Kasper walked around the vehicle and got in the other side. The key was in the ignition. The van glided out through the gate.

A cell phone lay on the dashboard. Kasper leaned out the window and read the restaurant's telephone number on the side of the van. He dialed the number and was transferred to Leisemeer.

"This is Kasper. I had to borrow one of your delivery vans from the yard."

The chef breathed heavily into the receiver.

"It is," he said slowly, "a long way down the list from you to the customer who pissed next-most on me."

"It's also a long way down the list to the customer who comes next closest to loving your crisp fried vegetables as much as I do. And that's one reason you will wait an hour before reporting the van stolen."

"And the other reason?"

"When I get over these temporary difficulties, I'll attract customers. In droves. You can recognize a trendsetter when you see one."

"You won't get over them," said Leisemeer. "This isn't temporary. I can recognize a big loser when I see one."

The telephone hummed. The line was dead.

# 4

Night is not a time of day, night is not an intensity of light; night is a sound. The clock on the dashboard showed 9:30. Although a scrap of daylight still hung in the sky, it was no longer evening; night had fallen.

Kasper heard children fall asleep, dogs go to sleep, machines get turned off. He heard the strain on the electricity grid decrease, the water usage diminish. He heard television sets get turned on, and adults prepare to end a long working day.

He rolled down the window. The city sounded like a single organism. It had been up early, and now it was weary. Now it sank down into the furniture, heavy as a moving man. And under the weight he heard the uneasiness that is always there, because yet another day is over, and what was accomplished, where are we headed?

Or else it was his imagination. Do we ever hear anything other than our own monstrous ego and the immense filter of our personality?

They stopped at Frihavn Harbor. Beyond the Oslo boat quay and UNICEF warehouses they could see the landfill. And behind the container ship harbor, the gray contours of Konon.

Around them and behind them rose the harbor's new construction. Stacks of apartments for seventy thousand kroner a month, designed like space stations on Mars.

The van was high enough that they could look into the first-floor apartments. Wherever there was light, people sat on sofas watching television. Kasper let his hearing sweep over the buildings like radar; there were hundreds of apartments. But the human sounds, of bodies, of personal contact, were very weak, barely audible behind the TV programs.

He heard the fabulous wealth. From the apartments, the auction houses, the offices. Right here was the greatest concentration of temporal liquidity anywhere in the country. It was a sound that made the affluent suburbs of Søllerød and Nærum sound like the Klondyke nightclub.

"Before I was born," he said, "my father left the circus to get out of poverty. He studied law and had a career; he opened his own law office. We had money, we were flush. It was the mid-sixties. My mother forced him to drive her and me on tour; we had a Vanguard Estate with a trailer and those yellow-and-black commercial plates. I can remember when we got a refrigerator—at that time the highway went only the first thirty miles toward Holbæk. Now that's all standard for welfare clients. And what do we do with our wealth? We watch television. One thing I've never understood: How do you go from the TV to the bed; how can you get something going with your beloved after staring into the electron cannon?"

Kasper heard the other man's system contract with this sudden intimacy. Heard it expand in an attempt to relax.

"I've never had a TV set," said Franz Fieber. "I've never lived with a woman either. Not really."

Kasper could hear him blush, the sound of blood pricking the skin's surface. He leaned forward, to respect the other man's modesty. The intimacy between them was a realm in F-major; it expanded into the night.

"You work for the sisters," said Kasper.

"I drive for them. As much as I can. What are we waiting for?"

"I can hear the little girl. Sometimes I can hear people in ways beyond the physical sounds. I'm waiting for the right timing."

Kasper closed his eyes.

"Let us pray," he said. "Just for a couple of minutes."

Franz Fieber set the icon of Mary in front of the gearshift; he must have taken it from the Jaguar. He lit a votive candle by it. They closed their eyes.

The words that came were, *"Grant me a pure heart."* That had been the favorite prayer of Saint Catherine of Siena; she lived to be only thirty-three, like the Savior. Kasper had already outlived them both by nine years. How much can one expect?

The prayer brought a memory. Kasper remembered how as a child he had fallen asleep in the Vanguard between his mother and father. On the days they moved the tent site they never left until after midnight. He had awakened just as his father carried him into the cool night air to go to the trailer. He looked up into Maximillian's face and saw a weariness that had been accumulating for ten years. A weariness caused first by working full-time and taking his final university exams, then by completing his law studies with top grades, then by being unable to persuade his wife to leave the circus, and then by always being stretched between two worlds, the artisan's and the bourgeoisie.

"I can walk myself," Kasper said.

Maximillian laid him carefully on the bed; it was summer. The trailer had the brittle sound of glass that's cooled and crackles; it was the sound of veneer on the wood panels giving way. His father tucked the duvet around him, and sat down on the bed.

"When I was a child," he said, "we had horse-drawn carriages and the work was very hard. I remember being seven or eight, as you are now, and being awakened at midnight to be carried inside. You know the fairy tales about people who promise the fairies something or other if only they can have a child. I promised myself something then. I promised that if I had a child who fell asleep in the carriage, I would always carry the child inside."

Maximillian had gotten up from the bed then. Kasper could feel him as if he stood beside him; it wasn't thirty-five years ago, but now. This was what Bach had meant with *Actus Tragicus*; it was in both the music and the text: "SheAlmighty's time is the best time"; there is no past, only the present.

He listened. It was as if the universe hesitated. There was nothing to do; one can't press SheAlmighty for a solution.

"Stina," said the young man. "How do you know her?"

He could have replied dismissively; he could have replied negatively; he could have not replied at all. Now, to his surprise, he heard himself answering with the truth. With one of the possible versions of the truth.

"She rose out of the sea," he said.

# 5

He had been sitting outside the trailer; it was three o'clock in the afternoon. A warm September day. He had tried to repair a couple of Cro-Magnon-like hangovers with Haydn's symphonies. They had a more powerful detoxifying effect than Mozart's, perhaps because of the surgical horns, perhaps because of the shock effects, perhaps because of Haydn's ability to create interferences that made the instruments sound like something unknown, Divinely sent, from another, better, less alcoholic world.

There had been a seal out in the water.

The seal had risen out of the sea; it was a diver. He waded toward the shore backward, removed his flippers in shallow water, turned around, and walked onto the beach. He took off his Aqua-Lung and air tanks, unzipped his wet suit. It was a woman. She looked around; she had lost her bearings.

Kasper got up and walked toward her. Somewhere Eckehart had written that even if we are transported to seventh heaven, if a traveler is lost we must be there immediately.

"The current," she said. "It's strong along the coast. The dive boat is outside Rungsted Harbor."

"You've drifted more than a mile north," he said. "Your fiancé in the boat must be in tears now. But with my car, we'll be there in a minute."

She looked at him. As if she wanted to determine his molecular weight.

"I'll take the bus," she said.

He gathered up the gas tanks and the harness backpack; she gave up trying to get the equipment from him. They walked up toward the road.

"It's Sunday," he said. "The buses run only every two hours. One just left."

She didn't say anything; he was sure she would give up. There's no woman alive who would ride six stops along Strand Road in dive socks and a neoprene suit, carrying two five-gallon cylinders and a mask and a snorkel.

The bus came after five minutes.

"I don't have money for the bus ticket," she said.

He gave her a five-hundred-kroner bill. And a bus card.

"This threatens my household budget," he said. "I need to get the money back. Perhaps you could write your address on the envelope."

The bus door slammed; he began to run back to his car.

The bus had been out of sight less than three minutes when he caught up to it. But then he fell behind a semi truck. No one got out at Rungsted Harbor. He began to worry. At the last stop in Klampenborg he got on the bus and walked through it. She was gone. He found where she must have sat; the seat was still wet, the floor too. He put a drop on his finger and tasted salt water; it must have touched her skin. The bus driver stared at him.

He telephoned the Rungsted Harbor office, but it was closed on Sunday. He telephoned the harbormaster at home; he told Kasper that they did not keep a record of diving outside the harbor basin.

He didn't sleep that night. Monday morning he checked with the Danish Sport Diving Association. They had no record of diving outside the harbor in the last two weeks.

He evoked her image, her sound. The core of her being was E-major. Behind that, the deeper tone of her instincts; people's instincts normally were less nuanced, not yet formed into musical keys, but hers were. He heard A-major, a professional key. She wasn't a sport diver. She had been at work. On a Sunday.

He telephoned the Danish Maritime Authority. He got a trained mermaid on the line. Accommodating, but chilly and smooth.

"We keep records of all commercial diving," she said. "But we don't give out that information. To anyone except the proper authorities."

"I'm going to have a mole built," he said. "For my swan. Outside my villa on the coast. I want that firm to do it. I saw them working.

They were marvelous. So could you give me the name of the company?"

"It wasn't a company," she said. "It was divers from an institution. And how did you see them working? In Denmark one can't see more than three yards underwater in any direction because of the mire."

"I was inspired that day," he said.

She hung up.


He had gone out to the road and picked up his mail. There was a letter with no return address; the envelope contained a five-hundred-kroner bill. Nothing else. He had driven in to see Sonja.


Sonja had brewed tea for him, slowly and carefully, then she stood beside his chair and stirred until all the honey was dissolved. He sank into her loving care. He knew it had a price. A lesson would soon be forthcoming.

"You've seen her only once," she said. "Five minutes at the most. Have we lost our senses?"

"It's her sound," he said.

She stroked his hair; somewhere within him he felt an inkling of tranquillity.

"You reacted to my sound too, after all," she said. "Back then. And you were damn lucky in that. But we can't deny there have been other times when you've made a mistake."

He sipped his tea; it was first-flush, made in a Japanese cast-iron pot. It stood on a hot plate on the table in front of her. Even with milk and honey, it was something entirely different from what he could get out of tea bags at home.

She turned over the envelope that had contained the kroner bills.

"It's stamped," she said.

He didn't understand what she meant. She handed him a headset for monitoring phone conversations.

"The franking machines," she said, "leave an identification number."

She telephoned the postal service. Got transferred to the franking-machines team in Fredericia.

"I'm calling from the law firm of Krone and Krone," she said. "We received our postage machine from you. We think we got someone else's machine. May I give you the number?"

She gave the number.

"Yes, that's a mistake," said the woman's voice at the other end. "That machine should have been one of four. For the Map and Land Registry office. Where did you say you were calling from?"

"I spoke incorrectly," said Sonja. "I'm calling from the Registry."

She hung up.


She had accompanied him down the stairs. Out on the sidewalk she took his arm. She still had a dancer's posture. She led him into a flower shop across from the fire station, where she chose sprays of peonies that hadn't yet burst into full bloom. Large, round, perfect flowers.

She carried the flowers to his car, laid them carefully on the seat beside him. Her fingers caressed the back of his neck.

"You've been alone for a long time," she said.

He didn't answer. There was nothing to say.

"I don't know the Map and Land Registry office," she said. "But I'm sure the peonies will be a good beginning. Maybe you should wait awhile before telling her where you got them."


The Map and Land Registry was on Rentemester Road. On the ground floor, a middle-aged woman was selling maps behind the counter; if she had been a dog there would have been a sign saying, PROCEED AT YOUR OWN RISK.

He placed the flowers in front of the woman. The bouquet was as big as a tuba.

"It's her birthday," he whispered. "I want so much to surprise her."

She melted, and he got past her. That's how one can measure spiritual progress. The guardians of the threshold become more and more cooperative.

The building had four additional stories, and on each floor there were between ten and twenty offices plus laboratories; he peered into all of them. On the top floor was a cafeteria with a roof terrace, where large seagulls waited for a chance to clear the tables. The terrace had a view out to sea, over to Sweden.

She sat alone at a table. He laid the flowers in front of her and sat down. For a while neither of them said anything.

"The first meeting," he said, "is risky. What do we hear—is it anything but what we hope to hear? On the other hand, we have no history together. We haven't put up our guard. Anyway, here are some flowers. Maybe you can put them in water at home. Without hurting the man in the diving boat."

She looked out over the roofs. Over the elevated railway, Harald Street, out over the sea.

"It was a colleague," she said. "A woman."

He stood up. If there was one thing Bach could do, it was leave at a high point.

"You can stay a little longer," she said. "I've just started my lunch break."

# 6

Someone had said something, the memories thinned out, and then they were gone. Franz Fieber's eyes hung on Kasper's lips; Kasper wasn't certain what he had said and what he had only remembered.

"They're dead," said Franz Fieber. "We'll never find them."

"Who is the other child?"

"Bastian. He and KlaraMaria disappeared at the same time. From the school yard. In the middle of the day. They went in a car."

"Where are the police in all of this?"

"They've got many officers on the case. All of us were questioned. At the Lyngby police station. And downtown."

"Where downtown?"

"On Blegdam Road. At the jail."

Kasper's temples were throbbing. He had to telephone his father. It's unfortunate. To be forty-two. And the only way out is still to call your father.

Maximillian answered the phone immediately. His voice was almost gone.

"If two children have been kidnapped," said Kasper, "and the police are questioning people at the Blegdam Road jail, what's going on?"

"Is the person being questioned a potential suspect?"

Kasper looked over at Franz Fieber.

"No," he said.

"Then they've activated VISAR. The international profiling register for serious criminals. It's administered by the Danish police force. In collaboration with external criminologists, behaviorial psychologists, and court psychiatrists. They have a large advisory panel. Vivian sits on it. She's sitting beside me. She's studying my dying process. I'll call you back in a minute."

He hung up.


A clip attached to the dashboard held receipts and address slips. Kasper leafed through them, to no effect. Another clip held a thinner bundle; it was consignment notes. Leisemeer had his own imports of wine and delicacies; some notes were for the following week. Kasper found what he was looking for at the bottom of the pile. It was an order from Konon for an Italian lunch on the following Wednesday. The order was attached to a brochure printed on handmade paper. The kind one would give to guests on the Concorde or at the Ritz with a warm welcome and a description of the flight plan and an assurance in four languages that this is simply to comply with the law because we will never die, at least not in this place and at this ticket price.

The brochure showed a cross section of Konon's buildings, plus a ground plan. He put on his glasses. Everything was labeled: stairs, emergency exit, library and archives, meeting rooms, administrative offices, two cafeterias, four restrooms on each floor, technical buildings, company boathouse and jetty. Someone had also added directions, in red India ink, about how the Italian lunch should be served.

The telephone rang.

"You know about the children," said Vivian. "That hasn't been made public. Perhaps to protect them. Perhaps to conceal the investigation. The one child, the girl, it must have been she who drew the map?"

She was silent for a moment.

"I was asked to sit on the advisory panel," she said. "But I declined. Usually we get all the information the police have, but in this case it was on a need-to-know basis. Far too little information. I said no. But one of my girlfriends is in on it. A child cardiologist. One of the children had surgery. I've telephoned my friend. The police are trying to link the two children with four or six others. Who have disappeared other places in the world. Boys and girls. Seven to fourteen years old. Two from a Buddhist convent school in Nepal. One in Thailand. A Senegalese girl from a Catholic girls' school in France. No reported connection among the children. Now comes the bad news. One child has been found. She was strangled. No sign of sexual molestation. But tortured. The second joint of the fingers on her left hand had been cut off. While she was alive."

They were both quiet for a moment. Maximillian took the phone.

"You wouldn't believe it. But I still have a friend or two. I asked them to take a look at Kain. I've got a report on him. He's about the same age as you. We don't know anything about his childhood. He first comes to light in the navy. Merchant marine, seamen's school, coxswain candidate, navigation school, and shipmaster. After that, he gets a shipping trade certificate and passes the military shipmaster exam. Then joins IMO, the International Maritime Organization. And studies economics. Youngest flag skipper ever in the Royal Danish Navigation and Hydrography Administration. Leaves the government. Suspected of smuggling. He's been able to draw on his knowledge of international radar and report systems. Wanted since '95 for illegal shipping operations outside international security regulations. Probably involved in illegal financial activities too. Hasn't been seen, identified, or photographed since '95. He's thought to be living in England. And to be carrying on illegal trade through a front organization in Denmark."

"What might the name of that organization be?"

"Konon."

Kasper closed his eyes.

"The occult," he said. "If it has ever existed. In the circus. Who would know that?"

"The genuine article doesn't exist."

Kasper didn't say anything.

"Have you tried the Amusement Museum archives in Frederiksberg? Barley's collection? Boomhoff's circus agency?"

"The woman," said Kasper. "Who you and Mother talked about. Something to do with birds."

Maximillian was silent. Somewhere in the silence there was anxiety.

"Feodora," he said. "Jensen. The world's greatest bird act. The world's greatest circus collection. The world's greatest memory. But in the first place, she won't talk with you. And in the second place, it's a blind alley."

Kasper didn't say anything.

"The Artists Association apartments," said Maximillian, "in Christianshavn."

"Christianshavn has been evacuated."

"On a voluntary basis. She's no longer able to leave her home. She's there. If she's alive."

Vivian was back on the line.

"Lona Bohrfeldt," said Kasper. "Where was she employed? What organization did she work with?"

"It's a long time ago. As far as I recall it was a collaboration. Between the university's Panum Institute for Social Medicine and the Mind Institute."

Kasper heard a motorboat going through the Stokke Channel. He heard reflections from the thousand TV sets around him. If all the screens around us are hard and unfeeling and powerfully reflect sound, the strength of the sound is essentially independent of distance. So the unmerciful world presses in on us at full volume.

"I've sat on the VISAR panel," said Vivian. "Perhaps twenty times. I know the crime folks. From both the Intelligence Service and Department A. They are level-headed people. But not this time. They're afraid. Big, tall police folks. So whatever you do, be careful."

She hung up. He sat there looking at the receiver. Then he took out his lottery ticket. He turned it over. On the back was Lona Bohrfeldt's home address.


They passed Charlottenlund Fort; beyond the public swimming pool they turned inland and drove past Deer Park toward the cliffs behind Raadvad.

The distances between houses became greater, and then the houses ended. To the right, the valley stretched toward the Sound; to the left were the sharply rising hills. Kasper had rolled down the window. He gave a sign; they stopped and got out.

All they could see was a tall wire fence. Behind it, nearly two hundred feet of lawn leading right up to the steep hill, no house.

There were large bushes on the lawn. One of them covered a double carport, where the little Mercedes was parked. Next to a black Jeep that was as big as a tractor. The motor's cooling system was still running; perhaps that was what he had heard.

They leaned their heads back. The window was right in the hill, fifty feet above them. It was shaped like an ellipse, with about twenty feet between the focal points. The house must have been dug into the hill. The windowpane had a faint bluish glow. Like a huge eye.

They found a tall narrow gate in the fence. On the gatepost were a sunken doorbell and a scarcely visible intercom box. Kasper pressed the doorbell.

In the beginning of *Either/Or* Kierkegaard writes that his favorite sense is hearing. He could permit himself to write that because intercoms had not yet been invented in the 1800s. He should have been here this evening. The loudspeaker gurgled like a stuffed turkey.

"It's me," said Kasper. "The situation has gotten worse. Since the last time. Now there are two children. They still haven't been found. There's also been a murder."

"I don't want to talk with you," she said.

Franz Fieber had opened his toolbox. He found a panel on the gatepost and opened it.

"Closed circuit," he said softly. "If I cut it the alarm will go off. Keep talking. I need to find the control box."

"From the time I was a boy," Kasper said into the intercom, "ever since I was born, I knew I had come to the wrong place. Right family, but wrong planet. So I started to search. For a way out. A way home. A door. I've spent my life looking for it. I haven't found it. But the little girl. Maybe she's standing in the doorway."

The intercom was silent. But he knew she was listening. Franz Fieber had pulled himself up the fence by his arms; he rolled over the top and fell onto the other side. He landed on his arms and the stumps of his legs, as softly as a cat. He crawled over the ground like an inchworm. Brushed aside a camelia bush. Behind the bush was a metal box. He signaled to Kasper.

"I'm measuring the impedance," he whispered. "If you put a conductor with the wrong impedance, the alarm will go off. Let the golden gift of gab flow."

"I haven't had children," said Kasper. "Have never been present at a birth. But I think that door must be open at a birth. Just like when a person dies. For a moment, the door is open. And you can hear what's behind it. That's why you've made birthing your profession."

"Go home," said the intercom.

Franz Fieber rose inside the gate. His hands came through the bars. Punched the code pad. The gate opened.

"Something in you is like me," Kasper said into the microphone. "You're searching. You've been searching near a door."

"I want to be rich," said the intercom.

"Of course," he said. "We all do. Bach too."

Franz Fieber hobbled across the lawn on his crutches. At the foot of the hill you could see the elevator entrance, a rectangle of stainless steel.

"Very rich," said the intercom.

"That's true of all humans," said Kasper. "Look at Verdi. The Scrooge McDuck of classical music."

"It's too late," said the voice.

"It's never too late. And I know what I'm talking about. Everything has been too late for me. Several times."

Franz Fieber gave him a thumbs-up from the elevator.

"We subscribe to a security guard service," said the woman. "I'm going to call them now."

The connection went dead.


The elevator was cylindrical; it shot up like New Year's fireworks.

"I could be approved by the Danish Insurance Association," said Franz Fieber. "They license security electricians. I do all the electrical work on the Jaguar myself. To stay in shape."

The elevator door opened. They stood in the midst of men's overcoats and women's furs. It was the first time Kasper had been in an elevator that opened directly into the entry, in the middle of the floor, like a sentry box.

He opened a double door and they found themselves in the living room.

The room was elliptical, like the window, with a double curvature similar to a ship's hull. The floorboards were twenty inches wide. Whatever furniture Kasper had time to identify was Eames.

Lona Bohrfeldt sat on the sofa. In the middle of the room stood the owner of the Jeep; he looked like his vehicle, shiny black hair, traction on all four wheels, and not expecting anything to get in his way. Both he and the woman were in shock.

The man threw off his surprise and headed toward them.

"We're very sensitive," he said. "We're expecting a child."

"Are you sure you're the father?" said Kasper.

The shock returned. But just for a moment. The man grabbed Kasper's shirt.

Many people have an incorrect image of clowns. They think that because a clown has a child's sweetness he also has a child's physique.

Kasper hit him with the underside of his elbow, from below and upward. The man was unprepared for the blow; it pressed through his abdominal muscles and reached the lower tip of his lungs. He fell to his knees.

Kasper set an Eames stool behind the man. In the kitchen he found a basin, and filled a glass with water from the tap. Wrung out a tea towel. Franz Fieber was leaning against the wall.

Kasper placed the basin in front of the man. He handed the glass and tea towel to Franz Fieber. Sat down across from the woman. She had taken to wearing dark eyeliner since the last time he had seen her.

On closer inspection, it wasn't eyeliner. It was twenty-four, or more likely forty-eight, hours without sleep.

"What is it about the premature babies?" he asked.

"It's that some survive," she said.

Kasper moved his chair. So she could not see the man on the stool. It was part of the circus ring routine. From the standpoint of sound, married couples act like buffalo; with their rear ends toward each other they present a united front against a wicked world. If they are going to do their best for an audience, one must separate the love partners.

"It has always fascinated doctors and midwives," she said. "In the past, when one treated newborns more summarily, it regularly happened that premature babies who were declared dead and taken from the mother came to life and screamed. They wanted to live. And to be loved."

"So you went looking. For someone who might know where those babies come from. Why some come into the world with such a strong will to live."

She nodded.

"And so you contacted the Institute. You contacted the Blue Lady."

"They suggested that I follow twelve children. At that time they were between six months and four years old. Of various nationalities. But they came together at the Institute once a year. I was to analyze their births. All the obstetrical details. Also facts that are otherwise never reported. The relationship between the father and mother. People present at the birth. Even the weather. And then I was to monitor their general health."

The sorrow around her grew denser. A mother close to giving birth should not have sounded like that; it bordered on resignation.

"You sold the information to Kain," said Kasper. "He financed you. He must have financed the clinic."

She leaned forward as far as she could, given her stomach, and hid her face. The man on the floor leaned over the stool and threw up in the basin.

Kasper rose and walked over to the window. The view was unique. Not like Denmark. Mountainlike. You looked down the whole stretch of coastline, from Vedbæk to Amager.

There was a telescope by the window, an astronomical telescope, very powerful; he put his eye to the ocular and the field of vision vibrated nervously. In focus was a polished blue emerald in a black setting. It was a lighted swimming pool; it must be Taarbæk Sanatorium, a combination of private hospital and spa that had been built while he was out of the country. He had heard of it, but never seen it.

He turned the telescope. Found Konon's tower. There was light in the two top floors.

He took out the map that had been attached to the consignment note. The light was in the administrative offices.

"You were supposed to examine the children," he said. "During the past few days. That's what they were going to use you for. They were going to use a doctor."

"Two," she said. "Professor Frank and me."

"From the Mind Institute?"

She nodded.

Kasper looked over at Franz Fieber.

"Øster Vold Street," he said. "Next to the botanical garden. In the buildings that were once the Copenhagen Observatory."

Kasper turned the telescope. Found Rosenborg Castle. The Copenhagen Observatory was the city's highest point, right next to the castle. He found the observatory tower. Focused sharply. Around and outside the tower, glass offices had been built, like greenhouses.

"Where did you examine them?"

"I'll lose everything," she said.

Her face was white, almost fluorescent.

"We all lose everything anyway," said Kasper. "We have just one option. We can try to lose in a somewhat housebroken manner."

He was glad that both Franz Fieber and the kneeling father of the child were present. It gave him a sense of having a slightly bigger audience. For these brilliant rejoinders.

"Look at me," he said. "I don't have an øre. I've lost everything. No wife. No children. My career ended. A deportation order. Wanted by the police in twelve countries. But I'm in the process of cleaning up my life. Can you see that? That somewhere deep within me there's a growing honesty?"

"I think you look like a bum," she said.

He drew erect.

"They brought the children here," she said. "Their condition was good. They're still alive. They're going to be used for something or other. It has to do with the earthquakes. I don't know what."

He adjusted the telescope. On the roof of the Konon building were two davits. On wheels. Behind them, a machine shed.

"What kind of a business is Konon?"

"Officially, a financial institution. But they deal only with options."

"Where is Kain?"

She shook her head.

"What about the murder?" she asked.

"The police believe there is a connection between a series of kidnappings. One of the children has been found. Tortured and strangled."

He was on his way out. She followed him.

"I want to make things good. I want to be able to look my child in the eye."

"Wait until after the baby is born. We who are making a penitential pilgrimage take one step at a time."

Kasper helped the kneeling man to stand up and get over to the sofa. On the coffee table lay a small stack of typed pages.

"What," he asked, "was common to all the births?"

"They were harmonious. Calmer than the average. And then there was something about the weather."

She stood close to him.

"There were rainbows," she said. "In every instance, those who assisted at the birth had seen rainbows. Outside the window. I spoke with them independently of one another. There were rainbows at night too. There are nocturnal rainbow phenomena. Haloes around the moon. White rainbows in the night sky, moonlight reflected in cloud formations."

He opened the door to the elevator.

"We must hope there was gold at the end," he said. "Of the rainbows."

She blocked the door.

"Those two children," she said, "the boy and the girl—they aren't ordinary children."

He didn't know what he should say.

"They were calm," she said. "Not happy. But much too calm. I can't explain it. But it wasn't natural. They should have been depressed."

He removed her hand from the elevator door, gently.

"Kain," she said. "He owns the sanatorium. That's where he is. He telephoned from there. Five minutes ago."

"How do you know where the telephone call came from?"

"The sound of the large Jacuzzis. I could hear them."

He caught a sound from her system. Deep, old. As if from a persistent longing.

"You were born prematurely," he said.

"In the seventh month. Declared dead. Laid in the rinse room. Where they say I pounded on the lid that had been placed over the tray. When I began as a midwife there was a retiring obstetrician who remembered my case. He called me Rinse Room Lona."

He couldn't stop his hand. It tore itself loose, floated up, stroked her cheek. Knowing full well that one should be very cautious about caressing pregnant women in front of their husbands.

"Franz and I," he said, "we're wild about those who want to survive."

"I'm not the fearful type," she said. "But I'm afraid of him. Of Kain."


Kasper motioned; Franz Fieber pulled the van over at a rest stop. Kasper pointed to the flat metal flask.

"How about a little more lighter fluid," he said, "for us two bachelors, after our meeting with the young couple in happy circumstances?"

Franz Fieber poured; the aroma of fresh grapes filled the vehicle.

"What does it sound like inside a person who has killed a child?"

Kasper would have crawled a long way around to avoid the question. But the young man's yellow eyes shone intensely in the dark.

"Twice in my life," he said, "I've sat across from a person who had killed a child; both were artists. One had run down a child by accident, the other had beaten his child to death. Around each of them there was silence."

He sensed helplessness. Confronted by great horror and great miracles—the Mass in B-Minor, world wars—we are powerless; there is nothing an individual person can do.

But he could hear that the young man's helplessness was greater than his own. And in this lost world does not the person with one eye have a duty to try to help the blind man?

"There are two types of silence," said Kasper, "or at least that's how it has sounded to me. There is the high silence, the silence behind prayer. The silence when one is close to the Divine. The silence that is the dense, unborn presence of all sounds. And then there is the other silence. Hopelessly far from God. And from other people. The silence of absence. The silence of loneliness."

He felt the young man's openness. There was contact. Interference. They were very close to each other.

"I know them," said Franz Fieber. "The two kinds of silence. I know them both."

"Those two people I sat across from, they were acoustically dead," said Kasper. "Something had gone out of them."

He grasped the other man's upper arm. If you are going to send a signal through clearly, it's best to have physical contact.

"But behind their silence, behind the isolation," he added, "they sounded like all other people. Like you and me. So if you and I, if we got in that situation, if the world had withdrawn from us. Or if we had withdrawn from the world. Then it could have been us. It could be us. That's what I thought when I sat across from them. That it could have been me."

For a moment they were open and candid. For a moment Kasper knew they were both looking into the source of the darkest demonic power, which the great enema syringe gives us all a dose of occasionally. The young man bore it for a moment, but then it became too much.

"Can't we call the police?"

"In a minute," said Kasper. "When we've followed our guiding star."

He drank from the silver-plated flask cap. It may well be that liquor doesn't work as deeply as heartfelt prayer. But it works just as quickly.

Headlights swept over the bushes; the Jeep passed them at about ninety miles an hour. Franz Fieber stared at him. Only now did Kasper hear that the other man was about to reach his limit.

"She lied," said Kasper. "When she said they brought the children to her. Now she wants to go in and make things good again. When women in her weight class get excited they believe they are indestructible."

# 7

The driveway to the sanatorium was flanked by two square granite pillars and luxuriant shrubbery. Kasper gave a signal; the van stopped about two hundred feet from the pillars.

The buildings were constructed above six granite terraces that led down toward the fine old homes in the suburb of Taarbæk. The granite was so dark that at night it looked black. The terraces were lit from below, and on them were stone urns from which tumbled a tropical profusion of flowers and climbing vines that resembled Babylon's hanging gardens—a miracle in April in Denmark, where the final frost nights are still smiling expectantly in the wings.

"That's for the clients," said Kasper, "the profusion of flowers. To tell them that modern technology has removed all lack of generosity in nature, and there is no reason to get old when every three months you can get a nice shot of Botox for the bags under your eyes."

"This is not a biblical place," said Franz Fieber.

Kasper took two double-breasted chef jackets from a coat hook behind the driver's seat and handed one to the young man.

"Let's not be too holy," he said. "Can we be sure that the Mother of God would have refused a face-lift and a tooth straightening? If she had been offered the chance."

The young man put on the chef's jacket. His hands had started to tremble.

Kasper put his hand on the man's shoulder. Turned him so he could look straight at him.

"Think about the children. See them before you. Their parents aren't there. They are away from home. They are surrounded by something they don't understand. They're helpless. Can you hear that? When I saw her last, she had been hit. Even those children are helpless, by and large. And they are dependent on you and me. Can you feel that?"

The young man slumped a little.

"And in addition to them. Thousands of other children. Equally helpless. Or more so. And within us. In you and me. There are two little boys. Can you hear them? Can you empathize with them? It's a fuel. The only thing that can keep one going. Through a whole symphony."

Franz Fieber stared at him. The moment had nobility. Like Kempff playing the slow movement of Opus 109. In a situation like this, the important thing isn't to be filled with emotion. But to act and go in another direction. Like Beethoven. To try to enhance the sentimentality.

Kasper gave a signal. The van drove forward. Kasper rolled down the window.


Out of the shrubbery emerged a man in a dark uniform, the same color as the granite. Kasper pointed to the back of the vehicle.

"There's a steaming-hot steak in the back. Saddle of veal à la Count Metternich. It must still be a hundred and forty degrees when it's served to Kain. Delay me three minutes and you'll be out in the cold."

The tropical shrubbery swallowed the man.


They walked through a reception area with curved walls like the Salle Pleyel, then through a waiting room with acoustics like Mantzius Hall. Past the infirmary section, where you would have to listen very carefully to discover that you were in a hospital. There wasn't a single room where you could not have recorded your next piece of chamber music without further ado.

But it wasn't chamber music that the walls reflected. It was confusion and perplexity, in people who hope, but can't seriously believe, that at a cosmetic clinic you can come just a hairsbreadth closer to the meaning of everything.

They entered a room with a sloping floor, like an amphitheater;

on the steps some fifty women lay or sat in front of a large fireplace. They were all wearing white bathrobes.

A woman came through a door in a cloud of steam. She had red hair and green eyes and a white smock and a bundle of fresh birch boughs in her hand; she had to be the sauna master. She had a tone of grace and authority that made Kasper wish he had time and opportunity to pull down his trousers and ask for twelve blows with the birch boughs on his bare bottom.

"What are you doing?" the woman asked.

"We're enjoying the acoustics," said Kasper. "My heart bleeds for the poor. But my ears love Brazilian rosewood. And five inches of acoustic headroom."

"You're in the women's section."

"We're here professionally. We left our sexuality outside the door."

He heard her sound soften up.

"It's not well disciplined," she said. "Your sexuality. A little of it has slipped in with you."

Kasper held out the tray he had taken from the van.

"Have a canapé. Forget the rabbit diet. Trust the natural regulation of your appetite."

The woman took one of the small puff pastries. Kasper offered some to those sitting around him too.

"I wonder where Kain is," he said.

"He's going to have his hair cut. By Heidi."

Kasper followed her glance. Through a large window he could see a glass summerhouse built on a granite platform that seemed to sway in the air. Through the glass he saw green plants and hairstylist chairs. A man was sitting in one of the chairs.

Kasper leaned toward the red-haired woman.

"Some people would think that a relationship like yours and mine, which may be the beginning of a lifelong friendship, should not be spoiled by money. I don't agree. A few kroner can give an internal accompaniment to the natural harmony of two hearts."

He handed the woman four thousand-kroner bills.

"If you delay Heidi just ten minutes. Kain and I went to dancing school together. Happy memories. Which we'd like to have a chance to refresh for ten minutes alone. He always danced the woman's part."

The woman folded the bills.

"Will you stop in on your way back?"

Kasper looked at Franz Fieber. The young man's face was bathed in a thin layer of perspiration. Maybe it was the warmth from the sauna.

Part of the secret of love is concentration and setting voluntary limits.

"In the next incarnation," he said.

He looked out across the women. The room's acoustics were a small version of the Carl Nielsen Hall. The sound of fifty women was like the caress of a warm breeze. He could speak to the whole group without raising his voice.

"The heart of every person emits a sound," he said. "It has a wonderful ring, but unfortunately we dampen it. Right now all of you sound marvelous. There isn't a single one of you for whom Franz and I wouldn't break our clerical vows. If you just listened ten minutes each day. To your heart. And let go of the tension that keeps the wave front from spreading. My God, you would sound like Bach."

The women stared at him. He put down the canapés. Took off the chef's hat. Bowed. Walked backward out the door.


Franz Fieber was right behind him. His voice shook.

"We're on a mission. We're going to rescue children. We're trespassing. And you're acting like an idiot."

They crossed a recital hall with a Steinway. The summerhouse was just ahead of them.

"Wait outside," said Kasper. "In case the women have followed us."


He walked into the room. Its walls were all glass. Outside the wall at one end lay the swimming pool, shining like a blue jewel. Behind the pool was a decline of about a hundred feet that sloped down toward the lights of Taarbæk. Behind the lights, the sea. Kasper pulled the long white drapes on the windows.

The man in the chair was not turned toward the view; he was turned toward his own reflection in a large mirror. He wore a white dressing gown, and his skin still glowed from the dry-air bath.

Kasper took a comb and a hairdresser's scissors from the shelf under the mirror.

The man's eyes in the mirror fell on Kasper. Noted the white jacket. The interest in his eyes turned off.

That's where we humans make a mistake. We don't see the utterly amazing when it comes to us disguised as the ordinary.

"Heidi has been delayed a few minutes," said Kasper.

He positioned himself behind the man.

He was about Kasper's age. He had the body of an athlete. Or a circus artist.

Out of view of the man in the mirror, Kasper lifted the hair on the back of his head with the tooth edge of the comb. And cut off the tuft close to the scalp.

He opened his hearing for the other man's sound.

He heard his relationship to the physical world. Those were the deep tones, the frequencies that set most mass in motion.

He heard money, more than he had ever heard before. He heard real estate. Cars. He heard the future. Golden economic virtualities.

He heard the man's sexuality. It was more than interesting. Masculine, with a strong feminine overtone. He would have been able to get any woman. And most men.

Kasper heard the man's emotional register; it was broad, nuanced, and explosive. Very light and very dark, evenly divided, as in the case of Mozart.

He heard his heart. It was a large sound. Generous. Warm.

He heard the higher frequencies. Inventiveness. Intuition. Spirituality. They were rich sounds; the man vibrated with inner life.

Tuft after tuft Kasper gathered the hair at the back of the man's head. And smoothly, very satisfactorily, in view of the fact it was the first time he had cut another person's hair, he gave the finely curved back of the head a crew cut.

Josef Kain's eyes in the mirror were vacant. He didn't see himself. He was looking inward.

Then Kasper heard the hole. It was a form of internal acoustic shadow. An area in the man's system where the sound was dead. Somewhere between the heart and the solar plexus.

He put down the scissors. On a shelf behind the chair was a plastic holder with a variety of colored pastes. He opened one of them. It was henna. Ten years before it became common, Helene Krone had used henna to paint Moorish swirls on the tops of her strong feet once every six months.

Kasper found a small brush. Slowly and carefully, still out of view of the mirror, he began applying a thin layer of the red coloring to the crew-cut head.

"I cut Wilhelm Kempff's hair," he said. "In the early seventies. When I was still a young comet at beauty school. He told me about Hitler. He had met him in '44. At the Berghof, Hitler's home in the Alps. Eva Braun had gotten Kempff together with Furtwängler. And the great pianist Walter Gieseking. To plan a concert that would please the Führer. It never came to anything. But they put together the repertoire. Hitler's favorite pieces of music. Something from Lehár's operettas. A couple of Strauss's lieder. 'The Badenweiler March.' 'Donkey Serenade.' Excerpts from *Die Meistersinger*. Kempff was able to listen to Hitler's system. He told me the man's personality was all right as far as that goes. Small, but all right. But there was a hole somewhere. And destructive collective noise streamed through that hole. Do you understand? There are no evil personalities. A personality always has a basically sympathetic sound. It's those places where there are holes in our humanity, where we don't resonate, that are dangerous. Where we feel we're serving a higher cause. There we must ask ourselves if the cause really is higher. There we become possessed. In other cultures they call it demons. We don't have a good word for it. But I can hear it. It's the noise of war. Collective fury."

The man's eyes in the mirror rested on Kasper.

"Who the hell are you?" he said.

The voice was as black as a night sky. Soft as five hundred square yards of costume velvet.

Kasper picked up a hand mirror from the shelf. Let the man see the back of his head.

Josef Kain went rigid. Hitler would also have lost his composure. If he had seen himself with a crew cut and a henna tint. Kain's jaw began to drop. His sound opened. Kasper spoke into the openness.

"There's a hole in your sound. There are damaged places in all of us. But in you it's huge. Not to compare with Hitler. We should not compare ourselves with the great ones. But big enough. It has something to do with your childhood. It always has something to do with one's childhood. Maybe you grew up poor. Maybe there was no father in the picture. That could explain your lust for money. Longing for power. The hole has something to do with these two things. It turns off the heart. Can you feel the children? Can you remember when you were a child yourself? Did you cut off the little girl's fingers?"

The man's face in the mirror was expressionless. Now his sound was closed, encrypted.

Franz Fieber entered the room. Pulled the curtains aside. A man was on his way toward the summerhouse. The thickset man with the hearing aid.

Kasper leaned down. His face was a fraction of an inch away from Kain's.

"I'm forty-two. Do you know what I've concluded from my life until now? Hell: It's not a place. Hell is transportable. All of us carry it around with us. It opens up and stays with us from the moment we lose contact with our own natural sympathy."

Kasper remembered the scissors in his hand. He looked at the man's throat. Where the sterno-cleido muscle passes behind the jawbone. It would take one thrust. The point of the scissors would go through the base of the skull and into the brain. There would be one less black sound hole in the world.

He closed his eyes. He heard the anger. It was not his. It had entered through a hole in his system. All of us are acoustically perforated, like Swiss cheese. Who has the right to be another's executioner?

He straightened up.

The man in the chair brought a hand to the back of his neck. Looked at his hand. It was red from the henna.

"It doesn't much matter," said Kain, "who you are. You were dead and buried long ago."

Kasper felt the pain around his heart. Because—once again—he had failed to reach a fellow human being. With the simplest and most important of all truths.

Franz Fieber opened a glass door; behind the door a merciful winding staircase descended toward the spot where they had parked the van.

"Ten minutes in the hair dryer," said Kasper, "and nothing will rub off on your bonnet."

# 8

They drove past Svanemølle Harbor out onto the wharf area itself. They passed warehouses, rows of full-rigged wooden ships. Franz Fieber's eyes kept glancing at the mirrors, scanning the road behind them for pursuers. They reached the promenade and pulled over.

"Call the police."

His voice shook.

"Tell them that you know where the children are. That they should storm the building. You'd be able to get them to do it. You could talk your way into Paradise."

"And if the children aren't there?"

The young man slumped. A tone of despondency had begun to pervade his sound profile. Kasper didn't like it. They still had a way to go before reaching the end of the road.

A patrol car passed them slowly. Three dark-haired young men on a corner withdrew into the darkness. After the car passed they popped up again. They had high energy, like small-time gangsters in embryo. Kasper felt a sudden joy at the cosmos's tendency to create unified entities. As soon as we have built a neighborhood for the best circles and cleansed it of foreign elements, darkness tumbles out of all the corners.

He listened out over the scene before him. He could hear the last shops with evening hours balancing their cash accounts. He could hear the windmill park outside Lynetten at the northern tip of Amager Island. The seagulls. The deep whisper of turbines at the power station. The late customers at the restaurants. He listened for the true sound structure. Timing is not a specific time; timing is a sound. He would not have been able to explain it, except perhaps to the Blue

Lady. Musicality often knows when, but often doesn't know why. It was not yet the moment.

His hearing was clear because it was evening and because of his hunger. Somewhere Saint Catherine wrote that fasting is an excellent instrument through which to see God. The problem with that aphorism is that what's important is to see God without an instrument.

He reached back in the van and found a loaf of bread, cheese, pesto. A bottle of springwater. A paring knife. He tore off some pieces of bread and spread them with pesto and cheese on the ledge under the windshield. He handed a piece to Franz Fieber; the young man shook his head.

"We've done what we could; they're looking for both of us. The people we're after aren't ordinary people; they're devils."

He opened the Armagnac, took a swig, handed the bottle to Kasper, poured coffee. His hands shook.

"How does liquor mix with continual prayer?" asked Kasper.

"What do you mean, man? The Trappists brew beer. The Benedictines make liqueur. Our Savior changed water into wine. And on a night like tonight, what the hell do you want me to do?"

A new sound was added to the previous collage, the sound of wind in something that might have been telephone wires.

"I don't know if you're familiar with *Parsifal*," said Kasper. "If not, I'd recommend that you listen to it. Wagner was in a tight spot. Fleeing from his creditors. That happens to the greatest ones. He was given sanctuary. With a view out to the water. The way we have now. There he wrote *Parsifal*. There's a wonderful scene. It's Good Friday. Like today. Third act. The castle of the Knights of the Grail rises around them. One understands that it's not a physical place. It's in the mind. So Parsifal will succeed."

Franz Fieber stared at Kasper. At the granite wall in front of them.

"That wall is rock solid," he said. "It's got nothing to do with the mind."

Kasper opened the door of the van; Franz Fieber grabbed his arm.

"You're not going in, are you, man? You must be absolutely crazy!"

"I must have made a promise to KlaraMaria," said Kasper. "Also to the little boy, even if I haven't met him. I must have promised to carry them from the car. And inside into safety."

The yellow eyes stared at him. The last bit of trust, which had never really been there, was now gone.

"I've driven more than ten trips out here. It's secured like a military test station. Armed guards. Video cameras. Infrared sensors. You won't get even three feet inside."

Kasper stepped onto the pavement.

The other man's hands grasped his jacket like claws.

"They were wrong, the sisters. You're mentally ill!"

They crossed the road. Kasper could hear that there was very little time. Favorable sound constellations are fleeting.

## 9

Kasper tried the door of the chocolate shop; it was locked. The angel at the cash register shook her head with a smile.

"Turn around please," said Kasper.

Franz Fieber turned around. On the back of his white shirt Kasper wrote with his fountain pen: "My sweetheart sails tonight. Only chocolate can express my sorrow. Show mercy."

"What are you doing?" asked Franz Fieber.

The girl came closer. She read what was written on the shirt, laughed, and opened the door.

"I didn't know ships sailed from here," she said.

"It's from Konon," said Kasper. "We're sending the top administrators on a business trip tonight. From our own jetty. My sweetheart needs a large chocolate egg. And twelve mocha balls."

The girl packed up the egg.

"It's going to be a surprise for them," said Kasper. "What's the best way to go in, would you say?"

She nodded toward a road lined with magnolia trees.

"That's the rear entrance. There's just one man there. And no cameras. The main entrance is locked. And at the delivery entrances there are cameras and lots of guards."

The mocha balls went into a box; each one got wrapped in a piece of pink tissue paper.

"Shall I put it on the account?"

A patrol car drove by. Kasper took Franz Fieber's arm. If he hadn't, the other man would have crumpled to the floor.

"As usual," said Kasper. "And if you blow me a kiss, can we put that on the account too?"

The girl blushed. She was eighteen at the most.

They went out the door. The girl blew Kasper a kiss.

"That's free of charge," she said.

The door closed behind them. Franz Fieber stared at him, and for a moment his fear gave way to amazement.

"What are you—almost fifty years old?" he said. "A failure. Forgotten by everybody."

"Many of the great ones have been good to young girls," said Kasper. "Elvis. Kierkegaard. Regine Olsen was thirteen. Priscilla fourteen."

They approached a group of dark-haired boys.

"We'll be slashed to pieces," said Franz Fieber.

Kasper immersed himself in their sound; he liked it. There are many reasons for dropping out of society. One is that it has little space for wildness. At least two of the boys sounded as if they had a large square in their horoscope. In ten years they would be dead, deported, or in leadership positions.

The boy on watch was the youngest, fourteen at the most, with eyes that had seen more than was good for him. Kasper stopped a few yards from him. Put the box of mocha balls on the ground and nodded toward the road lined with magnolia trees.

"We need to go in," he said. "Before the next patrol car goes by. In order to do that, you boys need to get the guard out of his booth. The question is whether you can do that."

The boy shook his head.

"That's not the question," he said. "The question is what's in it for us?"

Kasper laid a five-hundred-kroner bill from the Institute's resources on the box of mocha balls.

"When I was a kid," he said, "we would have done it for a cream puff."

"That was before World War One," said the boy. "The cost of living has gone up since then."

Kasper laid another bill on the box.

"I'll get a head start," he said. "The guard mustn't see me go in."

Franz Fieber leaned against a lamppost for support.

"Wait half an hour," Kasper told him. "If I'm not back, call the police. And notify my heirs."

"There aren't any heirs. And no inheritance."

Kasper crossed the promenade. The sound of crutches followed him. The young man had tears in his eyes.

"I don't dare to be alone out here."


The rear entrance lay about fifty yards down the tree-lined road. Kasper held the egg up in front of the booth.

"We're very close friends of Aske Brodersen," he said. "We wrote him a secret Easter letter and he guessed who sent it. So now we're coming with his Easter egg."

The guard was in his late fifties; he had a well-pressed green uniform, gray eyes, and nearly an inch of laminated bulletproof glass between him and the visitor.

"I want to give it to him myself," said Kasper.

"I'll telephone him."

"That would ruin the surprise."

The gray eyes grew blank. Kasper raised a hand.

A mocha ball hit the glass booth. The balls were large and homemade, with a thick outer layer, like ostrich eggs.

With a little less self-importance he might have handled it. But self-importance is one of the most difficult things to lay aside. Everyone would like to be an admiral on the royal yacht. And all we have been given command over is a glass booth on the jetty.

For a moment the guard sat motionless. Then another mocha ball struck, this time the door. At that he got out of his chair. And out of the booth.

Kasper looked backward. The dark-haired spokesman had taken a position in the middle of the road; he used his whole body in throwing.

A mocha ball hit the guard in his chest, near his heart; the impact threw him backward for an instant. Then he started to run.

Kasper and Franz Fieber walked in through the open door; a second door to the left led to a room with video monitors above a sink and a coffee machine. Beyond that was still another door, through which they entered the Konon grounds.

# 10

The sound of the wind blowing over sandblasted granite was affectionate. Even in the dark the buildings were beautiful. All the surfaces had a silky finish; a third of the horizontal area was covered by low stone basins containing a thin film of water. They were surrounded by plants Kasper wished his mother could have seen.

The building that had been constructed on the landfill was rectangular at the bottom. Five stories up the tower began; it was so tall the upper floors merged with the darkness.

The building seemed to float on the sea, like an island, or a very large ship. Kasper could well imagine that a former naval officer would choose to build such a structure. If he suddenly got his hands on four hundred million kroner.

The lower floors were dark; light shone only in a few windows higher up. Kasper tried the door. It was locked. They went around the building; on the side facing the water a scaffold had been raised, but only up to the second floor. There were no other doors, and all the windows were locked.

Kasper listened to the sound of the wind in wires. He climbed onto the scaffold. On the last plank was a large box covered with a tarp, which he removed. Under it was the window washer's modular work cage: a little open cabin, like a chairlift, which glided against the façade on two sets of rubber wheels. There must be a rail-mounted winch and a continuous loop rigging on the roof. Inside the cabin were a bucket, a pole sponge, and two mops. Also a small instrument panel with four buttons.

Franz Fieber climbed onto the scaffold like a weeping ape, entering the cabin after Kasper. Kasper pushed the start button. The lift glided upward.

In the glow of the instrument panel Kasper studied the building's floor plan. There was light in the meeting rooms, a faint light in what was indicated as the "library," and light at the beginning of the tower in what must be the administrative offices.

The cabin swayed slightly in the wind. Franz Fieber's face shone whitely in the darkness. Kasper stopped the lift beneath the first row of lighted windows. A voice that belonged to a woman he knew said, "We didn't get offered anything in Brønshøj."

The window was open a crack; Kasper thought he heard ten or twelve people in the room, but he didn't dare peek.

"Contour line thirty-seven goes through the Brønshøj neighborhood," the voice continued. "Even the sewers are dry. There won't be any government land for sale either, because the government insures itself."

It was the blond woman who had brought KlaraMaria to him. Someone asked her something.

"Seven thousand plots," she said. "Divided by twenty-two companies. In two weeks they will close the harbor. Close the Avedøre embankment. And start pumping out. Very slowly. To prevent settling damage. They've had to fill fifteen hundred homes with water. So they won't collapse. Or float away."

She had a lovely voice, like Irene Papas. But she was feeling very tense about something.

"How can we be sure?"

Kasper couldn't catch her answer. But it was evasive.

"We all saw the fault area," said the man. "During the assessment. How does one explain that?"

"By unique conditions that made the limestone more transmissive."

"We saw the papers from Pylon Five. And the Land Registry office. There are soft sediments under Copenhagen. A zone of fifty to a hundred and fifty feet would have been realistic."

"Our own geologists have looked at it. The grain size of Copenhagen lime is different from sand lime. That could explain a skid like that. Against the white chalk beneath."

"And the earthquakes?"

"People need to reevaluate Copenhagen. Experts are considering whether fault zones may be active. There were tremors in the Sound in the nineties. Maybe they were stronger than previously thought. There is a fault line in Sweden under the Barsebäck nuclear power plant. Stronger movements than assumed until now in the lime zones that intersect the baseline on Amager. The differing beach ridge heights on Saltholm Island suggest there have been larger quakes than previously assumed. The problem is that geological memory is short. There are no written records of an earthquake that occurred only a thousand years ago."

No one said anything. She had not reached them. With whatever it was she wanted to say.

"We can do many things," she said. "But we can't order an earthquake."

"And if we could nevertheless?" said the man. "If the earthquake were manufactured somehow. And it was discovered. We'd get life imprisonment."

Kasper touched a button on the panel; they glided upward. He counted the rows of dark windows. Beneath them, the ground first grew dark, and then disappeared. There was light in front of them.


Only one desk lamp was on in the room. Lona Bohrfeldt sat in a chair and her husband sat next to a radiator; they looked straight ahead out the window, like two people in a movie theater. They both had bandages around their jaws. The man had undergone a remarkable transformation. His face had become longer, longer than any human's; he laughed toward the window.

Aske Brodersen stood with his back to the window; in his hand he held a little crowbar. A sheet of plastic covering had been unrolled on the floor under the three people. Kasper put on his glasses. The seated man's face hadn't gotten longer. His mouth was split open to his ears; the blows had damaged both chewing muscles, and his jaw had dropped onto his throat.

Kasper felt the body next to him grow limp. Franz Fieber slumped to the bottom of the cabin.

Aske Brodersen struck the seated man with the crowbar. He was standing about three feet from the window. Kasper knew that even in his prime he would not have been able to climb in over the windowsill before the other man got to him.

He pressed the button, and the elevator glided sideways.

"I want to go down," said Franz Fieber.

"Pray. Keep praying."

"I can't. I can't concentrate."

"There's a story about Saint Lutgarde, a Cistercian nun. I hope it's okay that she was Catholic. She couldn't keep her mind on things. But SheAlmighty revealed herself to the nun. And said: 'Relax—it's all right if there are holes, because I will fill them up.'"

The office was empty; Kasper secured the lift and crawled in the window. He pulled Franz Fieber in after him.

The doors in the office must lead out to a corridor. And there must be access to the library from the corridor; he reached for the door handle.

The door was kicked open. It hit Kasper in the chest and flung him against the wall.

The stocky man with the hearing aid came through the door. He had a flat weapon in his hand; it looked like a child's gun, but with a long barrel.

When Kasper was a child, guards had been recruited among the poorest classes of society. Since then, concern for the common good had risen to the surface; it had become a high-status profession to guard people's money. The man coming toward him moved fluidly, like a dancer at a royal ball. Close at hand his sound had a tone of massive presence and great inner authority.

He stopped with his legs apart, raised his weapon, and relaxed his muscles against the recoil. Kasper saw why the barrel was long. A perforated metal cylinder had been screwed onto it, and you could see the hole was stuffed with glass wool; it was a silencer. Kasper remembered them from the circus. They were used when killing had to be done quickly—for example, if a horse struck the edge of the ring and one of its legs got an open fracture.

The prayer began of its own accord, wordless, but the meaning was: "May SheAlmighty grant me an open heart, and give me strength to meet the great light."

Behind the open door, Franz Fieber was hidden from the man.

Now he walked out, thrust one crutch between the man's legs, and twisted.

The sound of the shot was dampened. But Kasper heard a surprising sound behind him, like a hammer against stone. At first he didn't notice any pain, but the middle of his body felt paralyzed. His legs gave way under him, and he slid to the floor. The assailant's face was less than an inch from his own.

Kasper grabbed the other man's head, and bit him in the nose. He bit in order to survive, but at the same time he felt sympathy; part of his mind prayed, "May SheAlmighty let this man fall into the hands of a skilled plastic surgeon, because that's the minimum requirement if he's ever to be a male model again."

The man opened his mouth to scream. Kasper stuck the Easter egg into it.

Kasper got up. His abdominal muscles felt like one continuous disc-shaped pain. He took the egg's brass holder and struck the fallen man on the back of his head, as hard as he could. The man's head flopped back on the floor, and he lay still.

Kasper took the pistol from him. It was the first time in his life he had held a firearm; he wouldn't have had any idea how to use it. He handed it to Franz Fieber.

Doubled over with pain, he walked out the door and down the corridor; it wasn't possible to straighten up. There were three doors to the library. He tried one carefully. It was locked. So the others would be locked too.

He crawled back to the office. He would have to get into the library from the lift outside.

He had thought that pneumatic tubes had gone out of style; this system must be the second generation. There were no buttons to push, just a black screen; he brushed it with the tips of his fingers, and red numbers came to life. A list of dispatch addresses hung on the wall; he found the library's. He took out his fountain pen. Got the egg from the man on the floor. On the wrapping paper he wrote: "A price has been placed on my head. I'm coming to get you instead." He put the egg into the tube.

"Count to twenty," he said. "Then send it."

"You've been shot in the stomach," said Franz Fieber.

Kasper pulled up his shirt. There was a small swollen hole beside his navel.

"Also on your back," said Franz Fieber. "The bullet went through you."

Kasper climbed back on the lift, and glided sideways to the library.

In just the short time he had been away, the man had bled a great deal. Kasper couldn't tell for sure if he was alive. Aske Brodersen had now turned toward the woman.

Kasper listened inwardly to the prayer for a moment; it hadn't stopped at any time. He turned it toward his inner picture of Saint Genesius, patron saint of actors and entertainers; he had suffered martyrdom in A.D. 303, but before that had freed numerous souls from torment.

The pneumatic tube hummed. Aske Brodersen stopped short. He went over to the terminal. We are, all of us, information addicts. All of us have to listen immediately to our telephone messages. Look at our e-mail. Empty the mailbox. In the middle of a meal. In the middle of making love. In the middle of an interrogation.

Kasper opened the window. He got up onto the windowsill, slid onto the floor. Aske Brodersen stood with the egg in his hand.

# 11

Aske Brodersen had taken off his jacket. Underneath he was wearing suspenders.

"I want to see the girl," said Kasper.

The other man stood with the egg in his hand.

"She's in the room next door."

Kasper placed his fingers on one side of the husband's neck; the man was alive. Lona Bohrfeldt was gagged with sports tape, which had also been used to tie her to the chair. The roll of tape and a scissors lay on the table. Kasper cut her free.

Aske Brodersen led the way toward a door. Kasper couldn't hear any discord. Maybe the world was really so simple when one had deep contact with one's musicality. Maybe he would see KlaraMaria now.

The tall man opened the door and let Kasper walk in.

At first the room seemed completely dark, but then Kasper noticed a gentle light coming from the sea. One entire wall was glass. He looked around; KlaraMaria would be sitting somewhere on the floor with her dolls.

He heard the egg hit the floor. Then he was grabbed from behind.

The other man had a good grip; he was holding Kasper's upper arms. He lifted him off the floor and smashed him against the windowpane.

The window must have been laminated, like bulletproof glass; it had no elasticity; it was like hitting a cement wall.

Aske Brodersen didn't say anything, but Kasper could hear him nonetheless. Or actually, not him, because he wasn't there anymore. When feelings become strong enough, the ordinary personality disappears: The sound of the heart disappears; the compassionate aspect of the frequency field disappears. What is left is an extreme form of the impersonal. Kasper could hear that the figure behind him wanted to kill him.

He was flung against the glass again, this time much harder. He saw something being drawn across the lighted windowpane. At first he thought it was Venetian blinds or a blackout curtain, but then he felt the warmth on his eyelids; it was blood.

The next time the window struck him there was no pain and no sound; he knew he was very close to the end. The prayer in his heart began by itself. What he heard himself pray was: "May SheAlmighty give me strength to strike back."

The windowpane came toward him again. But this time he flexed his hands and feet; his palms and soles took the blow. It sounded like an explosion; he heard one wrist break, but his head was not struck.

He let his body go limp like a rag doll, let his head fall forward. The man behind him took a deep breath for the final effort. In drawing the breath, he lowered Kasper. The instant his feet touched the floor, Kasper gave the man behind him a backward head butt.

The backward head butt is the Dom Pérignon of stage fighting and onstage violence. Kasper had practiced for two years on a swinging sandbag before he learned to perform a knockout with one blow. And then he practiced for months to learn to stop the movement just before his partner's head. But now he didn't stop; now he followed through.

The man didn't go down immediately. He was still standing upright when Kasper slipped out of his grasp and swept his feet from under him. But his eyes were blank.

He hit the floor without bracing himself. On the way down, Kasper ripped off the man's suspenders and wrapped them around his throat. He put a knee against the back under him and tightened the suspenders. He could use only his right hand.

The door opened, and the ceiling light was turned on; the blond woman stood in the room.

Actual violence against real people is terrible. But stylized scenic violence is necessary. For those of us who haven't come farther than we have.

"Please come in," said Kasper.

She walked in, like a robot.

The light had transformed the panorama pane into a mirror; in it one saw the face of the man on the floor.

"When a person is strangled," said Kasper, "it's not primarily be-cause he can't get his breath. The first thing that happens is that the supply of oxygen to the brain stops. Because of the pressure on the large veins in the throat. If you look in the mirror, you can already see sort of avocado-colored, burst blood vessels in the whites of his eyes. Do you see that?"

The woman's legs collapsed under her; she slid down along the wall until she was sitting on the floor.

"Where is KlaraMaria?" Kasper said.

She tried to say something, but had to give up.

A broad stream of perspiration was running down into Kasper's eyes. He rubbed his face against the back under him; the shirt be-came colored as if he had used a paint roller. It was blood.

He heard something unexpected. He heard love. It came from the woman. He looked down at the man beneath him. It was the man she loved.

"Tell me where she is," he said. "And we won't have to pull the suspenders tighter."

"They're both down in the basement," she said.

"So the boy is alive too?"

She nodded.

"What are you going to do with them?"

Something clinked like pieces of glass when Kasper spoke; at least two of his teeth were broken or knocked loose.

The blond woman didn't say anything. He tightened the sus-penders.

"I don't know," she said, "I swear. I look after her, after them— please don't do anything, please don't."

He stood up.

"Take my arm," he said.

She obeyed mechanically. She opened the door. They went down the hall. The door to the office was open. He pointed; she led him over to the desk, to a telephone.

He dialed the Institute's number.

"I want to talk with the Blue Lady," he said.

Half a minute went by until she came to the phone. He fell in and out of consciousness.

"Yes?"

It was a year since he had last heard her voice.

"Both children may be alive," he said. "They may be in the basement at Konon, a place built on the landfill beyond Tippen in North Harbor. I'd like to go and get them myself. But I've encountered a slight problem which prevents that."

Her sound did not change. Perhaps she could receive news of the end of the world without modulating.

"We'll contact the police," she said.

He supported himself against the desk. The telephone connection was poor; the small receiver and speaker holes were filled with blood.

"I have a couple of errands to do," he said. "And then I'll come and collect the payment."

"We'll be glad to see you."

He hung up.

The elevator worked; they rode down three floors, stopped, the door opened. Franz Fieber stood outside. He got in. The elevator continued down. Franz Fieber stretched up and looked at the top of Kasper's head.

"Your head is split open," he said. "You've got a fractured skull."

Kasper gave Franz Fieber his other arm; they half carried him across the yard. He could hear blood dripping on the flagstones, a brittle, slightly ringing sound, very different from drops of water, because of the fluid's greater viscosity.

The moment they walked into the shadow of the outer wall, floodlights illuminated the yard. Through his feet he could feel many running steps. They opened the door and walked into the glass booth. The green admiral was still shaken. Kasper could hear that. But it was nothing compared to what he now became. He stared at Kasper, at the woman, recognized her, could not move. Kasper felt he needed to say a few words. When we have inconvenienced our fellow human beings, we can't leave them completely confused.

There are many people who believe they have bought a ticket to Gilbert and Sullivan in this life. And only when it's almost too late do they discover that existence is a piece of doomsday music by Schnittke instead.

"Aske didn't think the egg was big enough," Kasper said. "And you know his temper."

Out on the sidewalk Kasper let go of the woman's arm; she just stood there. He and Franz Fieber reached the van. The woman behind him hadn't moved. Kasper managed to get up into the front seat.

"We're going to take a ring road," he said.

"You're bleeding to death," said Franz Fieber.

"All bleeding from the veins can be stopped. With gentle but firm pressure maintained for ten minutes."

"You've got only two hands."

At the end of Sundkrog Street they turned north. The lights all blurred together before Kasper's eyes. Franz Fieber made a U-turn; Kasper was thrown against the door.

"A police blockade," said the young man.

They drove along Strand Boulevard. Continued along Jagt Road. Kasper found a stack of linen. He folded cloth napkins like a compress. Tried to tie them on his head with tea towels. As fast as he applied them they got soaked with blood. He was beginning to run a fever. The young man beside him started to cry.

That was the trouble with apprenticeships. When the master lights the afterburner the student may get flattened. Just look at the Bach sons. None of them ever rose to their father's level. And think of Jung. He could never completely wipe away the footprints after Freud had walked all over him.

"Both children are alive," said Kasper.

"You need to go to a hospital."

"Later. We have a couple of quick errands."

"Just look at you."

"We're so close. I say, like Saint Thérèse of Lisieux, 'Je choisis tout,' I want to have everything."

Kasper rolled down the window. The fever was a reaction to physical injury; he remembered it from his accidents in the ring, from when he was still performing as an acrobat. The cool wind helped. His weariness was a more serious matter; it was related to the loss of blood.

They drove along Jagt Road, on the border between central and greater Copenhagen. Turned onto Tagen Road, drove past the lakes. The city had never sounded like this before. It had acquired a bit of focus. The sound reminded him of Christmas Eve, of the times a decisive final soccer match was on TV. But darker. Far more tense. People listened toward the barricaded area. Toward the possibility of new earthquakes. They listened in solidarity. It was, however reluctant one is to say it, the solidarity of people who see in one another's eyes that perhaps they will die together. Pater Pio once told believers that the best place to pray is in an airplane during a crash. "If you truly unite in prayer then," he said, "you cannot help but realize the Divine."

"I've met many crazy people," said Franz Fieber. "But so help me, I've never . . ."

Kasper pointed; the vehicle turned from Øster Vold Street, past the Geological Museum, up a 15 percent incline and through the low, open wrought-iron gate of the Mind Institute.

There was light inside the glass door. A blond Prince Valiant was sitting at the desk.

"Please drive all the way into the office," said Kasper.

Franz Fieber shook his head.

"In my condition," said Kasper, "it's nice to not have to go out into the cold."

Franz Fieber pressed down on the accelerator. The van struck the glass door, broke through it like a paper screen, stopped with the front of the van inside the office.

Kasper struggled down from the high seat. Seated himself in a chair by the desk. The man on the other side of the desk was immobilized.

When Kasper was a child many professors had had an unfortunate clang that made people look around for something to plug their ears with—rugs, for example. At that time, having an academic career required neurotic, biased mental overexertion. Kasper had met professors who were in the audience with Maximillian at premier performances. They had been fragmented.

Time had changed the sound; the man on the other side of the desk had a broad spectrum. But still.

"Many artists," said Kasper, "are afraid of academics. But not me. My favorite figure in commedia dell'arte is *Il Dottore*. Do you know him? 'Learning can cure everything.'"

The blond man cast a sidelong glance toward the shattered front door. Kasper could hear him calculating his chances for a successful escape.

"I don't recommend it," said Kasper. "I don't have anything to lose."

The sound across from him gave up.

"What were you supposed to do?"

The other man didn't answer.

"You were supposed to give scientific luster to the demonstration. What did they demonstrate?"

The blond man looked out at the van. Franz Fieber was still sitting behind the wheel. The doors and windows were locked.

"There's no witness to this," he said.

"God hears everything," said Kasper. "But He doesn't testify in municipal court."

The professor moistened his lips.

"They didn't demonstrate anything. The little girl just said, 'There won't be any more earthquakes.' There were twenty buyers. Foreigners. Everything was translated into English. That was all. It took five minutes."

Kasper could hear he was telling the truth.

"What do you get out of it?"

"Scholarly information."

"Can we get a little closer to the truth?"

The professor looked down at the desk.

"You are extremely talented," said Kasper. "I can hear that. You also came with King Kong to try to bribe me. You aren't the violent type. But I am. Just look at me. I've come directly from the battlefield."

The professor looked at him.

"The university is a flat structure," he said. "If you want to move up in earnest, it has to be outside the university."

There is a pleasant firmness of tone when one is in harmony with oneself. Even when it's a weak ethic one is resonating with.

"What can the children do?"

"We've scanned them. They have interesting brain waves. That's all."

"What can the Blue Lady do? Mother Maria."

The man's tone changed to something Kasper remembered from the marketplace, a tone that preceded steer trading.

Kasper rose, with difficulty. On the desk in front of the professor lay a blue folder. He drummed on it.

"There is free exchange of information among institutions of higher learning," said the professor.

The folder was from the police department; Kasper recognized the cover from Asta Borello's office.

"That's nice," said Kasper.

"We could do business. You worked with Danish Technical University. In the eighties. At the Institute for Mathematical Acoustics. As a consultant, it says. In connection with planning and renovating large concert halls. They evaluated you. Here it says you could perceive variations in three- to thirty-five-thousand-hertz frequency fields. One-hundredth-of-a-decibel changes in the sound pressure level. That's quite unusual, if it's true. It says that they can't understand it. That they constructed one-hundredth models. Put you in them. And you were able to tell them immediately what was needed. Whether they should pour sine profiles into the concrete. Or some damn thing. Is that true?"

The post-traumatic shock from the van's entrance into the office was about to wear off the man's system. That attested to his robustness. Kasper felt a touch of respect for the entourage Kain had assembled.

"They were dreaming," he said. "And it was in my early youth."

"They write that you say physical sound is only a door. Behind it is another sound. A world of sounds. Is that true? Could you tell me a little about it? Maybe I might know something about the children in return. And about the *staretza* too."

Now Kasper heard the other man's misfortune. The theoretician's longing to rescind his separation from reality.

"You got the folder from Moerk," said Kasper. "You've bet on two horses. Or on three. You've worked for Kain. And had your time at the Institute. And kept Department H informed."

The other man's tone began to get thinner.

"You wanted to try to avoid anything happening to the children," said Kasper. "But you also wanted to be near the money. And to Kain's reason for getting the children. While at the same time, you wanted to look out for yourself. You tried to bet on all the horses. The entire track at once."

Along the back wall of the room were showcases containing optical instruments, possibly from the time the building had functioned as an observatory. And the world had been simpler. Perhaps.

"We humans," said Kasper. "We bet on too many horses. That way one never fully comes up into the light. But on the other hand, never fully down into the dark either. We stay right here. Where it's just clear enough to be able to fumble our way forward."

He hoisted himself into the van.

"It's the reptile brain," said the professor, "that contains acoustic memory. They say reptiles can also recognize the sound of prey. That is a primitive function in the deepest sense."

"You went along to see if I was for sale. To see if you would strike anything firm. When the instruments were thrust in deeply."

"Everyone can be bought. That's the ultimate reality."

Behind the anger Kasper heard the despair.

"I think you were the one," said Kasper. "Who killed the little girl. I checked with Immigration. You were in Nepal at that time."

The man leaped up like a jack-in-the-box, flailing his arms and legs.

"It was Ernst. Josef's bodyguard. I had no idea that was going to happen. I was miles away when it occurred."

Then the professor sank back down into the chair.

Kasper listened. The other man had possibly told the truth.

"I tried to explain something to them," he said. "At the university. We orient ourselves in measurable aural space because of the subtle time difference between when the right and left ear perceive the sound. But in the larger context, a little information has disappeared. The actual sound is perceived by both ears at the same time. By the mind, so to speak. And it doesn't get lost. It exists outside time and space. And it's free. You don't have to buy it. All you have to do is prick up your ears."

The man on the other side of the desk suddenly appeared much older. As if he had aged in five minutes. His hair looked white.

"I'm afraid," he said, "that Kain will fly the children out of the country."

## 12

They were out on the Ring Road.

On the seat beside Kasper, Franz Fieber sniffled. It is important, even while making large arm movements, to remember to show consideration for what is close at hand. Bach also did that. In the midst of constructing his cosmic tonal cathedral he had shown concern for each individual brick. A preoccupation with always making everything sound good. Gentleness with Maria Barbara, with Anna Magdalena, with the children, one could hear that. Kasper laid a reassuring hand on the young man's shoulder.

"In a few minutes," he said, "both children will be sitting between us."

He stroked the trembling muscles; his hand left a sticky trail of blood. They passed Roskilde Road, Glostrup, the first fields. Kasper pointed; the van turned left down a dirt road just before the go-cart track. The road became steep, and then stopped. They parked on an artificial embankment across from the water purification plant. Below the plant lay the courtyard and stables, utterly quiet, with only a single floodlight on.

"You can't go down there. They're waiting for you."

Kasper crawled out of the van.

"I'm flowing with Tao."

"How can you know that?"

The yellow eyes had given up on him.

"I can hear it. It's the sound of a gentle fair wind."

# 13

Between the field and the road there was a thick hedge of poplars; between the poplars and the yard a vehicle was parked. Kasper got down on all fours.

The car was half a tone too high. Half a tone is not much, but to a person with absolute hearing it is annoying. Throughout the seventies Kasper had wondered about Richter's recording of *The Well-Tempered Clavier*; it had been half a tone too high. At first Kasper had thought it must be the record, or the master tape; there must have been a faulty transposition. Later, Richter's recording of Prokofiev's sonatas had trickled through the Iron Curtain; they also had been half a tone too high. So Kasper had realized there was a reason behind it.

When a car has contents, people or baggage, the number of natural vibrations rises, or it feels like that. Kasper crawled sideways, and got the car between him and the floodlight; in it sat two men.

The explanation came first in the nineties, after the only long interview with Richter was published. Toward the end of the interview the great pianist said that age, in addition to the other damage it had wrought, had lowered his keynote perception almost half a tone.

Then Kasper had understood. Richter had tuned the grand piano up to compensate.

That had deeply moved him. Not that age corrodes a person's hearing; age corrodes everything—think only of Beethoven. But that a man can possess such great willfulness that he raises all classical music half a tone in order to accommodate his own system.

He remained on all fours until he was around the corner. He let himself in by the little door on the south side of the courtyard. Stood up, wanted to run; it was impossible. Hunched over, moving with difficulty, he went around behind the corral and the riding house. In the stable only Roselil heard him. He stroked the horse soothingly, leaving blood on the horse's coat; then he felt around in the hay. The violin and his papers were gone.

He made it through the courtyard in the shadow of the wall, tried the door to the office; it was not locked.

The room looked the same, but its tone was too resonant. He felt along the shelf under the desk; the three-legged stand was gone, as well as the Bunsen burner and the nightstick.

The shelves looked just as always. In the faint light he spelled his way along the ring binders to *K*; he took the volume from the shelf and opened it. It was empty.

He put the binder back in its place, tried the door to the private office. It was unlocked, and he went in. The room was too quiet.

He opened the door of the refrigerator; it was turned off. The door of the freezer; it was defrosted.

He went back to the outer office. Sat down in the desk chair. Lifted the telephone receiver. It was still connected.

He dialed Sonja's number; she answered immediately. He lifted the turban of tea towels and napkins on his head. He could hear she was lying down. The voice becomes deeper when the anti-gravity muscles don't press against the lungs and decrease the spatial tone. A man was lying beside her; Kasper could sense his breathing.

"The trailer space," he said, "at Daffy's. How did you find it for me?"

"I got a special offer. As far as I recall. An insert. In the Scandinavian issue of *Circus Zeitung*."

"Your office gets thirty special offers a day. You don't even look at them. Why this one?"

She was quiet at first.

"It was addressed to me," she said. "It was half price. I should have wondered about those two things."

He paused, tried to collect himself.

"Have I done anything wrong?" she asked. "Have I hurt you somehow?"

"A guardian angel," he said, "can only do good."

"Is there anybody with you? You shouldn't be alone."

"I have company," he said. "SheAlmighty's piano tuners. I'm about to be taken down a half tone."

He hung up.


He approached the trailer cautiously, and stood listening; there was nothing to hear. He felt around for the little piece of cardboard, which was still just the way he had left it. Then he walked in.

He didn't dare turn on the light. He sat down for a moment in the easy chair. The lighting on the grounds streamed in through the windows.

He could have had a castle, like Grock's in Oneglia. He could have owned a housing complex outside Paris, like Rivel. He could have had a nine-thousand-square-foot penthouse overlooking Kongens Nytorv Square, like the place Oleg Popov had in Moscow overlooking MKhAT, Chekhov's old theater. Instead, for twenty years he'd had only this trailer. Two hundred square feet plus a small entry, minus the space taken up by the prop cabinet, the costume closet, the piano, and the bookshelves.

He looked at the sheet music. The little potbellied stove. The washbasin. The electric kettle. The firewood. The hot plates. The small stainless-steel refrigerator, condenser-cooled without a compressor; he had never been able to stand the sound of compressors. He looked at the toilet. The Fazioli. He looked over at the sofa.

The winter after they met each other, Stina had sometimes been waiting for him when he returned from the performance. Often, but not always. And never planned. It had been difficult or impossible to make an appointment with her. She could lay out a work schedule and an on-duty plan six months in advance. But when it came to planning to meet in the evening, she couldn't make up her mind about it the same afternoon. He'd never been able to understand that.

He'd arrived at midnight. It had snowed. He saw her tracks leading to the trailer.

He was supposed to leave the country, but never had. That winter changed his relationship to the seasons. Before, he had wished that Denmark would be closed and evacuated five months of the year, from November to March. For ten years he had not accepted any winter contracts farther north than Cannes. Her footprints in the snow changed everything. The outer seasons became irrelevant.

Smoke was coming from the chimney. Her down jacket and boots filled the entire entry; she didn't want to get cold. Since the beginning of November she had been dressed for Nanga Parbat.

The windows were white with steam; she had cooked food. She had a lifetime contract with the physical world. All she had to work with were two hot plates and an iron ring on the potbellied stove. Nevertheless, she had made something straight out of Leisemeer's vegetarian cookbook.

She sat on the sofa, across from where he now sat. Wearing ski socks. With her legs drawn up under her. With her papers, or her computer. Or with empty hands.

He stood just inside the door.

Femininity does not have a specific sound. Nor a specific musical key. Nor a specific color. Femininity is a process. The moment a dominant seventh chord rings out in the subdominant major key, one hears femininity.

Until then he had lived in dissonance. Now his trailer was no longer a trailer. No longer a woodshed on wheels. It was a home.

Her presence brought out colors he had never seen before. It rounded sharp corners; it created surfaces that hadn't been there. It altered the contents of his books. Of his sheet music. Bach would have sounded different without women. Obviously, he would not have sounded at all. And the only thing she had done was be there.

Now the space around him was hard. Square. Dead. He knew he was seeing it for the last time. He noticed how his thoughts roamed around in his body, like a caged beast unable to find a way out.

He opened the door to the driver's cabin and slid behind the wheel. They were searching for the van now. But not for the trailer. It was seized but not sought by the police. While the police stormed Konon he could visit Maximillian one last time. And then turn himself in. Get medical treatment. Start the repatriation process with the police. His mind could go no further.

He turned the ignition key. Nothing happened.

"They had a mechanic with them," said Daffy.

He was wearing the camel-hair coat; it appeared to be woven

from rock wool that had smothered all sounds, which was why Kasper hadn't heard him.

Something was placed in his lap; it was the violin case. On top of it was the envelope with his papers, birth certificate, Spanish passport, insurance policies. The Swiss bank account, his temporary health-insurance card.

He opened the case and ran his hand along the instrument's curves—his right hand; he couldn't move the left one.

Guarneri and Stradivari had something in common. They had always incorporated a small variation. Like a type of research. In the midst of the bankruptcies. In the midst of the turmoil of the Spanish War of Succession. Never an exact replica. Never monotony. The small, continual experiment. To see if one could create just a minimal improvement.

"My last season during the court hearings," said Daffy, "was at the Retz in Hamburg. There was a young clown. He had a forty-five-minute appearance. At that time Carl was the only clown in Europe whose solo act could hold people's attention for more than twenty minutes. This clown hadn't even opened his violin case after twenty minutes. Some nights we had to get the firemen into the ring. To prevent the audience from devouring him. There could be eighteen hundred people at the Retz. After I was convicted and left, they kept him on for three months. I said to myself: In ten years he will have his own circus. In twenty years he will have an empire. That was twenty years ago. And you owe me six months' rent."

Now Kasper remembered. A dark-haired man in a tuxedo. Boras's heir. Just as Daffy must remember a much younger clown.

He placed the ignition key on the dashboard in front of the watchman.

"This trailer here. Have it towed away tonight. You'll get seven hundred thousand for it. At Classic Vintages in Helsingør."

Daffy did not touch the key.

"I looked in the private office. The refrigerator is turned off and defrosted."

"I'm about to leave on vacation."

Kasper opened the door. They got out. The night was quiet.

Daffy held a set of car keys in his hand; they were keys to the company pickup.

"I'll drive you to the hospital."

One could hear the southern highway. Traffic noise is strange. It isn't stopped by sound barriers, just lifted. And comes down somewhere else. Like fallout from a chemical disaster.

"I was maneuvered here," said Kasper. "To this place. You sent a message. To Sonja at Circus Blaff. Who arranges things for me. A year ago. So we're involved in something far-reaching."

The other man did not say anything. Kasper scanned the surroundings. Everything was half a tone too dead. There should have been the call of a heron from down in the wetlands. Around eighty decibels, a deep glottal sound like a kettledrum. And a night owl hooting in the gardens near Glostrup. Instead, everything was quiet.

"There's a Renault parked in front of those poplars, with two men inside," he said.

The circus is a piece of the Middle Ages that has survived on the fringes of the modern world. Artists are outdated, like foxes that have adapted themselves to the city and garbage cans. But not simply as lonely wanderers, also as a brotherhood, a brotherhood of half-wild animals. Outside the system of grants and awards. Outside ARTE cultural subsidies. Outside Customs and Tax Administration control. With very few rules, one of which is: You always support one another in life's hide-and-seek with the public authorities.

Daffy rocked back and forth on the balls of his feet.

Kasper put out his hand.

Daffy handed him the car keys. Walked with him to the gate. Opened it.


They were waiting for Kasper; he didn't hear them. Even if he had, it would not have helped.

They got out of a car that was parked fifty yards farther ahead; it was the two monks. A door opened behind him also, outside the yard. He had the wire fence behind him and Snow White's hawthorn hedge on the other side of the road. And he was having a hard time holding himself upright. He walked over to the monks and got into the car.

# 14

The open area in front of the police station was blocked off all the way down to the Arla administration building. A gate had been set up facing Bernstorff Street; one of the monks put an ID card in the front window, and the gate went up.

They passed military vehicles, civil-defense trailer trucks, ambulances. The monks parked on the sidewalk near the driving-test examiners' red barracks. They took Kasper under his arms and half led, half carried him. Across the street, through a door that faced the harbor, into an elevator.

The elevator opened to a narrow corridor; the first thing he heard was music. It was faint, came from a distance away, yet was very clear. It was a Bach cantata, BWV 106, sung by the Copenhagen Police Women's Chorus. He remembered the recording; on that CD the soloist was the patroness of the chorus, Police Chief Hanne Bech Hansen. Kasper recognized her lovely soprano voice, which had almost no vibrato.

An open door led into a rectangular room with a high ceiling, like a school gymnasium. Along the back wall were desks where four officers were sorting papers. At the other end of the room, in front of shelves filled with binders, two female officers sat at what appeared to be a switchboard.

The room had six large windows facing the harbor. Next to one of them sat a heavy, motionless old man who looked as if he had been dressed by the Men's Fashion Council and then lowered into the chair by a crane. Moerk stood by another window; beside him was a little boom box, which was the source of the music.

Moerk turned and looked at Kasper. At the bloody bandages.

He took some newspapers from a table and placed them on the chair beside him. Kasper sat down on the newspapers.

"Weidebühl," said Moerk, nodding toward the older man. "He represents the Church Ministry. And is our contact with the Institute."

The CD case lay on the boom box; pictured on the front was the golden lyre that all police bands carry. Blood dripped onto the plastic case. Moerk moved it and turned off the music.

"We need Kejsa up here," he said. "And Cokes. Coffee."

"A brandy," said Kasper.

The monks disappeared. Moerk looked out again across the barricaded area.

"We've got Konon surrounded," he said. "Two hundred men from the anti-terror unit. Four motorboats. Navy combat swimmers. Two military helicopters in case they should try to fly out the children. Thirty men to check doorbells at the administrators' home addresses and get statements from witnesses. They went in ten minutes ago."

Kasper tried to listen to Moerk, but couldn't; his hearing was unstable; it seemed to be falling out.

"Total Defense Concept," said Moerk. "That's the official name. It's a nice concept, very Danish. It covers unlimited collaboration. When a catastrophe occurs, like this here, everyone works together. The police, emergency services, civil defense, firefighters. The military. In Denmark we're afraid to declare any situation an exception. The politicians think they can legislate themselves out of everything, including a coup d'état. So what we have is a civil emergency. The police head up the investigation at the core. The National Guard sets up blockades. Civil defense cleans up. The military provides muscle power. And on top of all that, we have the Church Ministry with us. That's a nice idea. They don't have radio equipment, of course, so they can't communicate with one another. And they haven't linked their IT, so they can't exchange information in writing either. And they're bound by seven thousand laws and statutes that must be obeyed. But still, after a week at most, the connections are somewhat established. That was the time it took. One week. After the first earthquake."

Something was placed on the broad windowsill next to Kasper; Moerk handed him a glass. Kasper drank. It was a Spanish brandy, slightly sweet. Tears came to his eyes; the liquor burned the open sores in his mouth, like when flying paraffin wax incorrectly ignites for a fire-eater.

"The police are the same way," said Moerk. "Built on collaboration and open lines. A unified force. The Serious Economic Crime office, narcotics, fraud, theft, technical departments, all under the same umbrella. Regulations and plans for everything, no problems. So when they're looking for the girl and boy and call the Lyngby station, a level-headed officer tells them not to worry because ninety-nine percent of the children who disappear have just wanted to take a little walk. When they telephone again a couple of hours later, the officer investigates whether the mother and father have been divorced, or if there are young siblings; most children who leave home have wanted only to express their dissatisfaction with something. When this time there is pressure on the other end, the policeman asks that someone from the Institute come to the station with the parents and a picture. There are no parents, he is told. Then the officer asks to speak with a representative from the school. And only then does someone become aware that the Intelligence Service and the police chief have assessed this institution to be a possible terrorist target. Among eighty others in Bagsværd and Lyngby. From then on, things start to happen, so to speak. A couple of police officers search the Institute thoroughly. Nine out of ten children who remain missing after a while have hidden themselves up in an attic or something. When that doesn't pay off either, the Intelligence Service is contacted. We get out the plans for precisely this situation. Advise the patrol cars. Establish a search management team. Get hold of the police chief in Lyngby. The deputy crime commissioner in charge of the case. The police commissioner, who wants to stay in the background as long as possible. An inspector from the Intelligence Service. Line up all the basic investigative measures, which must proceed according to law and order. So that when Weidebühl here starts to be frightened and advises the Ministry of Justice police department, which gets hold of me, a week has gone by, and it's too late."

A woman stood behind Kasper. It was the aristocrat from Strand Road; she was wearing a white lab coat now, and had a small trolley with what appeared to be first-aid equipment.

She began to remove the tea towels and napkins from around his head. He vaguely noticed that she took his pulse. Measured his blood pressure. His world had begun to fade away. Some of his hearing was intact. But his field of vision was disturbed; he could focus only on a limited area.

"I started with the police force," said Moerk. "I've been through it all. Foot patrolman. Dog handler. Denmark's youngest criminal-investigation assistant. I love it. It's one of the best, most honest police forces in the world. There's just one thing wrong: It's so damn slow."

Moerk had forgotten to put up his acoustical guard; his system opened. What Kasper heard was weariness. Not temporary fatigue. Weariness that was twenty or thirty years old. He had heard it in some of the great circus directors, those who wanted something other, something more, than earning money. It was the weariness of a person who doesn't just have a job, but a mission, and who has let that mission absorb him totally. And is now slowly burning up from within.

The woman pulled up Kasper's shirt; he heard her catch her breath. She placed a hand on his midriff. Normally he would have been pleased by the touch, and especially from her. But not now.

"The Ministry of Justice normally never gets involved," said Moerk. "We've got a measly five men in the police division. It's only when there's a very big case, and when politics are involved, that we get called in. And even then we know that we're putting our heads on the chopping block."

"Department H?" asked Kasper.

He heard his own voice; it sounded like a tree frog croaking.

Moerk stood up. Walked over to the window.

"The police have always used astrologers," he said. "Mediums, clairvoyants. Quietly, you understand. But toward the end of the nineties we noticed that something was changing. I could feel it brewing like a bad storm. We knew there would be new types of illegal profits. Related to mind control."

"Like trading options," said Kasper.

The official nodded.

"Time," he said. "To be able to foresee the future. That's become paramount. Intuition. It's gotten to be one of the highest-paid resources. I'm constantly trying to get the Danish police to understand this."

The woman made Kasper open his mouth. He felt the coolness of a dentist's mirror against his tongue. She straightened up.

"He needs to go to intensive care," she said. "Immediately. He has a bullet wound in his stomach. His skull is fractured. Left wrist is broken. Maybe two ribs. Maybe his nose. Three teeth have been knocked loose. He needs to be sewn up; he's lost a lot of blood. He needs to get a transfusion. And be examined for internal bleeding."

He recognized her voice from another context; he had heard it sing. It was a refined alto, from the CD. She sang in the cantata.

"I need him for twenty minutes more," said Moerk.

"If an organ has been damaged, if the liver is torn, he'll be dead in twenty minutes."

"He won't die. He's made of something different than other people are. Maybe some sort of plastic."

"I'll report this," she said.

"Give him a shot," said Moerk. "I'll take responsibility."

She left. Moerk watched her go.

"They hate me," he said. "I took the investigation from Lyngby and moved it here, to police headquarters. We set up a command station. I've sat on them here for a week. Technically, we're just observers. But they're afraid, they're afraid of the publicity. And the politicians. Still, they're waiting for a chance to get rid of us."

"What about the rest of the children?" asked Kasper. "Those who disappeared in other countries."

The official's surprise could not have been registered on an oscillograph; not a muscle moved. But Kasper heard it.

Normally Moerk would not have replied; it's those who keep their mouth shut who rise to the top. But when one is close to the grand prize, it's virtually impossible to remain hermetic.

"Five were reported missing. All the reports have been withdrawn."

"Except for the dead girl."

A shadow of pain crossed the official's face; it darkened his unified tone for a moment.

"I originally wanted to be a judge," he said. "I've always longed for justice. Sometimes the longing feels like thirst. Can you imagine that? Why am I telling you this?"

"I immediately inspire confidence," said Kasper. "After five minutes people usually tell me their life story. Women. Children. Taxi drivers. Bailiffs."

The woman was back. Far away, like something that didn't concern him, Kasper felt the hypodermic needle.

"Prednisone," she said.

He began to smile. Maximillian was also full of prednisone. It's frightening and fascinating the way the fates of children and parents merge, all the way to the autopsy.

He felt the chemical relief in his body. Something was wound around his head; it was gauze binding. The woman was doing it. Moerk squatted in front of him.

"We got the request for your extradition," he said. "From Spain. Modifying punishment is not part of the official Danish penal code. Nor is money under the table. The few times the police have bought a rock star for a couple thousand kroner the issue went straight to the police commissioner's desk. So the police can't do a damn thing for you. But in the ministry we can. We can appeal the Spanish request. Get it overruled. Expedite a vote on your Danish citizenship in Parliament. Weidebühl here can speak with the Interior Ministry. We'll work out a settlement with the tax authorities. In half a year you can be back here. On the major stages. Do you understand what I'm saying?"

Kasper nodded. The other man's tone was completely open. They had reached what they had been going toward the whole time.

"In a little while. When they've got the children. And we pray that they've got them. This whole operation. We set it up relying on you. And now, when we have the children, we'll still need you. To talk with them. I have some female assistants, from Department A's morality office. And from Glostrup, where they specialize in incest hearings. But these children are different. So before anyone else talks to them, I want you and me to speak with the children. I want to understand what they were supposed to be used for. Are we agreed?"

Kasper nodded.

Moerk straightened up.

"Are you going to die on us?" he asked.

Kasper listened. Not to his body but outward and upward; death comes from outside.

He shook his head.

"The music," he said.

Moerk gave him a thoughtful look.

"It's true," said the official. "What you said about inspiring confidence. Though who could understand it. If you skid in the curve now, Saint Peter will start telling you his personal concerns."

"They're in Copenhagen," said Kasper. "The five surviving children. Somebody brought them to Copenhagen. And it wasn't the Institute. Wasn't the abbess. Who brought them here?"

Moerk pushed the button on the boom box.

It was the last part of the cantata. Still sorrowful, but more like the New Testament than the first part. Slowly the police chief's soprano voice opened an escape. Death is a door where there is something on the other side.

Kasper heard the harmony among the music, the building, and the men before him. The hall had the same reverberation and acoustic clarity as a church. He heard how religious the police actually were. He heard the sense of justice. The idea of cosmic justice. Moerk could have held any leadership position in Danish business life. Instead he was here. Gray with fatigue. Sustained by an internal carbon arc lamp. Kasper could hear it whispering. What it whispered was a credo: Evil is not necessary; it's a tumor; it can be removed.

Moerk was the human community's head surgeon. The police station was its cloister hospital.

It was a beautiful philosophy; Kasper sensed it within himself. The belief that if we just have the discipline, energy, and courage to clean out the muck, we will reach the goal. For a moment he wished he could have believed it.

A cell phone rang; it was Moerk's. He spoke briefly. Broke off the conversation. Stood looking out the window.

He pulled a chair over next to Kasper and sat down.

"They've taken the place apart," he said. "The children aren't there. No sign that they have been there. No sign that you have been there. My people say there are guards; the wall has infrared security;

there's no place you could have entered. They've located all personnel, and several passersby. The only person who saw you is a young
girl from a chocolate shop. Who says you bought an Easter egg for
your sweetheart."

Kasper looked at the brandy glass. It was empty.

"I was mistaken about you," said Moerk. "You screwed me. Was
it to buy time?"

"There was a way out of the place," said Kasper. "Which you
didn't manage to close."

For a moment Moerk lost his composure. His left hand tightened
around the back of Kasper's neck. The pain exceeded what Kasper
thought possible. Pain is never depleted; it always has room for more.
He lost consciousness.


The world was restored; perhaps he had been unconscious only a few
seconds. Moerk supported the bandaged head with both hands, carefully now. His face was right next to Kasper's.

"I would have liked to question you," he said. "But you understand. I've sent two hundred men from the anti-terror unit on a wild-
goose chase. After having taken the case away from the local police.
Now they will all be after me. The minister. The police. The families.
So now you won't be questioned. You will explain."

The monks stood behind Kasper; they lifted him up.

"Were you in there?" whispered Moerk. "Were the children there?"

The monks closed in on him. This time they carried him.


The car rolled past the fire engines and the trailer trucks carrying Pi-
oneer Corps rubber boats. If he could get them to stop somewhere
with low buildings, there might be a chance.

"My father is dying," he said. "I'd like to see him one last time.
Could we please stop at Rigshospital? It will take only a couple of
minutes."

They did not reply; they drove across the Zealand Bridge, onto
the highway leading to the airport. His consciousness flickered.

"In my obituary," he said to the two silent backs, "they will write that he contributed two hundred million in taxes for the benefit of the common good, and that he gave Denmark more free international publicity than Niels Bohr and a million pallets of bacon ever did. Nonetheless, the men who accompanied him—when he was taken away to torture and execution—were as boorish as hip-hop gangsters. And as unshaven as Indian swamis."

# Part
Four

# 1

They gave him a cell in the Third Bardo, between one nightmare and the next. On the second floor in the immigration-police facilities at Kastrup Airport.

The cell was one of six that, along with two toilets, adjoined a reception room in which there were benches, a counter, two cubicles for body searches, and three armed officers, two men and a woman. Everything was white concrete, even the counter. You could hear a child crying in one of the cells. Somewhere a person in severe pain groaned rhythmically. Elsewhere a woman softly sang *La illaaha illa llah*, There is no other god than God.

The place had no windows. From far away came the penetrating mechanical roar of accelerating jet engines.

An officer set a metal tray on the counter; the monks emptied Kasper's pockets and placed the contents there. The officer took the violin case, counted the objects, and handed Kasper the paper money, the lottery ticket, and a receipt. The man's face was like a mask. In commedia dell'arte he would have played Kassander, a stern, powerful father figure. Even in the Third Bardo state we do not escape our deep-seated Oedipal conflicts.

The cell contained a wooden table and a chair; the monks sat him in the chair and disappeared. He heard their footsteps retreating through the building. He stared at the white wall. He had reached the point where great operas end.

Every stage artist knows the letdown that comes around midnight. The transition from theater lights to the darkness outside. From being idolized to not knowing a soul. And walking alone through a city where you can hardly find your way back to the hotel. Where the only people who speak to you are the prostitutes.

He had learned to live with this loneliness. It had been temporary. It rarely lasted more than twenty-four hours. And while it lasted he was already reloading the barrel for the next shot. Polishing a detail for his next performance. Adding an extra movement. In his mind he already had the company of his future audience.

It was different now. Now there was no future audience. Now there was a Bardo night. An airplane trip. Four *guardia civil*. Five years in the Central Prison in Madrid. Or in Alhaurín el Grande. With possible time off for good behavior.

He listened into the situation. Every moment contains an opportunity. The present opportunity was to hear how the mind is tuned near the point where it cracks.

Someone looked at him through the window in the cell door. The door opened, and Kassander walked in. He laid the violin case on the table.

"I'd like to make a phone call," said Kasper.

The officer did not move.

"In Madrid," said Kasper, "reporters are waiting for me. I'll show them the bloody bandages. And say I was mistreated by the Danish police. I'll remember to describe you specifically."

He heard faint anxiety awaken in the other man's system—anxiety, and a kind of involuntary admiration. Not for the threat itself, but for the madness behind it.

"I'll make it even worse now," said Kasper. "I'll start banging my head against the wall."

"We'll strap you down," said the officer.

"I'll swallow my tongue."

The officer placed a cordless phone on the table. He left the cell slowly, deep in thought. Kasper dialed. The one number he had never forgotten.

"Yes?"

It was a coarse voice, like crushed rock on a conveyor belt. But still. It was the Blue Lady.

"The police didn't find them," he said. "I'm on my way out of the country. There's nothing more I can do."

"Where are you?"

"At Kastrup."

"We know that. Fieber followed you. Where in the airport?"

"It doesn't matter."

"It's crucial."

"With the immigration police."

"We'll be there in twenty minutes."

"I'll be gone in fifteen," he said. "This place is in the departure area. Nobody can come in here from outside."

She had hung up.

He opened the case, took out the violin, kissed its smooth wood, tuned the strings. The fractured wrist made it almost impossible to use his left hand—he could move his fingers, but there was little strength to summon in the hand itself. He supported the violin against the wall. The "Chaconne" came of its own accord. Where is memory stored? Not in the mind, at any rate, because his did not function. Perhaps in central warehouses.

The music streamed through him, in through his right arm and out through the left one, the way God streams through whirling dervishes. He was drowning in sound. He remembered what Bach had written when he came home after Maria Barbara and two of his children had died: "Dear God, let me never lose my joy."

It was silent all around him. Those being deported listened. The officers listened. The woman's prayer had become wordless, the child's crying had stopped. There was even a divine interval between the arriving and departing planes.

His left wrist wasn't broken. The bow was an extension of his mind. He was in contact with his audience. He was very close to Bach.

A brief moment, then it was over. A child screamed. Somebody threw a chair against the wall. One door burst open, another got kicked. Four Hercules airplanes loaded with Tiger tanks went aloft. Still, for that short time, he was completely happy.

Happiness has a timeless character. The moments when our hearts are entirely open we step out of temporal sequence. Stina was with him in the cell, along with the "Chaconne," just as she had been the last night before she disappeared.

# 2

It had been the same time of night as now. They sat letting the silence take effect while darkness fell. Something important was going on inside her; he didn't know what it was, but he knew he should not interfere. Finally, she rose and went over to stand behind him. He expected that she would put her hands on his head and draw it toward her. His hearing reached out for her; the female abdomen had always sounded to him like a bronze Tibetan singing bowl filled with fruit.

But what happened was something different. She turned on the light, unbuttoned her shirt sleeve, and showed him her arm.

The blue marks had turned yellow.

"It's been a week," she said.

He didn't answer. What could one say?

"It's building up," she said. "You're getting closer and closer to hitting me. Do you have an explanation?"

Her voice was flat. Almost hopeless. He had never heard her like that before.

"I thought love had a fixed shape," he said. "I thought it was feelings that focus on a particular body. A particular heart. A face. A sound. With you, it's different. It's something that opens up. A door. Candidness. Something that helps me grow. And it varies all the time. Your sound always keeps changing. It's like dope. I'm hooked on it. I'm afraid of losing it."

"I can't stand violence," she said. "If it's playful, that's all right. But this wasn't playful. The other times weren't either."

They were silent. He felt he was in free fall.

"Something happened to me in the past," she said. "Someday I'll tell you about it. I just can't stand violence."

He rose from the chair. She was almost exactly the same height as he. He pulled together the parts of himself he could access. At that moment he felt it was all of them.

"It will never happen again," he said.


Later that night he had danced.

An expansive happiness had been spreading over Rungsted and the surrounding countryside. Nature played the Quartet in C-Major, the culmination of Mozart's series of string quartets dedicated to Haydn. It was also the music Kasper had put on the record player; he could tell that he needed to dance. His earlier sorrow was gone. He was reborn.

Stina sat straight up in bed. He pushed the furniture against the wall and began to take off his pajamas. Slowly, lingeringly, without looking at her. Soon he was completely naked.

He began to warm up, to do pliés and breathing exercises. He could hear her breathing become more rapid. He heard her begin to take off her nightclothes; he did not look in her direction. She stepped onto the floor in front of him; he saw right through her. He heard a tone louder than all the others. The sound of her love, and her wildness. Something in her wanted to throw herself at him and tear pieces of raw meat off his bones with her teeth. He was glad no one from the artists' insurance company was present; his policy would have been canceled.

He turned slowly in a circle, as if she did not exist. She let her hands glide over her body, caressed herself.

He squatted down and put on his performance shoes. She walked over to him; her fingers opened her labia in front of his face, gathered a little of the flowing honey and wrote something on her inner thigh. He knew it was the word NOW!

He moved away from her, around the bed, and put on his clown nose. It was a good costume: clown nose, clown shoes, and a hard-on. But one should probably think twice before introducing it in the Benneweis Circus. The quartet flowed into the allegro movement, soaring, triumphant, complex; Mozart alone knew what was up and what was down.

Stina glided across the bed like a leopard but he looked straight through her. He kept hearing her love both as a smooth surface of water and as desire that could have howled with rage.

He put the clown nose on his erection. Looked into her eyes. He sat down on the bed, close to her. When one tries to rouse feminine instincts it's important not to overdo it.

She slid down onto him. He heard the sea. They were about to be swallowed up. Women are better at being swallowed up than men. Their two bodies began to disappear—only his heart remained. His manhood was also his heart; it was his heart pulsing inside her. He heard the fear they each had of losing the other. He heard himself pray: "May SheAlmighty let me stay in this without becoming afraid."

She stopped.

"People never reach each other."

He didn't believe his ears. He still heard her hunger for him, her love, but now a new, utterly unexpected chord had been added.

"No matter how close people get," she said, "they never reach each other. Including us now. Even now, there's a place where each of us is alone."

He had no idea what she was talking about. Femininity is an ocean; even if one has both a life jacket and a preserver, the risk of drowning is overwhelming. He wanted to escape from her. But it wasn't easy; his rigid heart was still inside her, and she was holding tight.

"Do you know the requirements of a chemical analysis?" she said. "It must be comprehensive, free of contradictions, and the simplest possible. That's nice—I love it. Unfortunately, it can't be done. Not even in mathematics."

He pulled free from her and pushed himself back against the wall. She came after him.

"When you're able to sense another person's smell," she said, "you feel like you're close. Active substances—esters and fatty acids—dissolve in the skin's fat, get loosened by the evaporation of sweat, and condense again in the open mucous membranes of the nose and mouth. We can sense that moment. And at that moment, when we are fluid and fragrance, we are very close to merging. And we get the feeling it must be possible. It must be possible to rupture the final membrane that separates people. But it doesn't happen. Never. Do you understand?"

This was important for her; it was crucial. Her voice was tense and low, and almost breathless.

"I understand completely," he said. "It's simply a question of finding a partner who is comprehensive and without contradictions. And in the meantime, you'll settle for me."

He crawled over to her and gripped her upper arms. Her sound shifted; it became life-threatening.

"On some level you're a very violent man," she said. "You will control that violence. Or else you will never see me again."

He got up and went out to the entryway. It was the only way to escape from her in two hundred square feet. Unless you crawled into the refrigerator. Nature had given up on Mozart. The wind in the needles of the fir trees sounded like diamonds in a glass.

He was imprisoned in her sound, locked in her fragrance, like the pit in a peach.

She stood in the doorway.

"Loneliness," she said. "Why shouldn't it be allowed here too?"

He did not understand what she meant. He did not understand the mood shift. The sea had changed its appearance again. But at the same time, he could hear all the moods from before. Love, sorrow, desire, disappointment.

He put on his bathrobe. And flip-flops. And went outside.


He walked a couple of miles along Strand Road, but then it got too cold. So he went into the Rungsted Hotel. The teenage boy at the reception desk possessed the fearlessness and class of the Little Bugler. He showed no sign of disapproval, of either the bathrobe or the flip-flops.

"I've left behind me in the darkness," said Kasper, "a woman who missed her train. I left without my credit card. Can I get a room with an ocean view?"

"Your face," said the boy, "is surely as good as cash."

He didn't sleep that night; he sat looking out across the water. When morning came, as a sound, not yet as light, he went down to the reception desk. The boy was standing where Kasper had left him.

"The church fathers had a saying," Kasper said. "'*Credenti et oranti.*' I don't know how much Latin you know; it means, 'Let your prayer guide you.' Last night I watched and prayed, and I have come to the conclusion that in reality the train never leaves. In reality, one way or another, we will spend our whole lives on the railway platform with those we love. What do you say to that?"

"I'm fifteen years old," said the boy. "I absorb the wisdom of life with gratitude. But that doesn't mean I wouldn't appreciate a fiver as a tip. When you transfer the money."

"It will be more than a fiver," said Kasper, "if you'll also call a taxi. And pay for it."

The boy called a taxi.

"They want to know where you're going."

Kasper expected to hear himself say: "Out along Strand Road."

But that wasn't what came out of his mouth.

"Into town," he said. "To the darkest part of Nørrebro."


Stina's apartment was on Sjælland Street, on the ninth and top floor. He asked the taxi to wait. There were a few drunks on the street; they looked quizzically at his bathrobe and flip-flops.

The building had no elevator, and he climbed the last flights slowly; her sound hovered over everything. He had plumbed the depths of only a hopelessly small part of her.

He stood for a while outside her door listening to the sleeping building, then his fingers found the key above the door. Inside, he stood for a while again, without turning on a light.

It was one square room plus a small kitchen and bathroom, with sloping white walls, a bay-window seat, and very few pieces of furniture. The furnishing was not only Spartan—it was like a cell. Nevertheless, the room was alive.

Part of the secret was that the few things in the room were placed with precision, like stones in a sand garden. He had worn out more set designers and prop masters than he could remember; only a handful of them had what Stina had. And they, like her, used very few pieces of furniture, few lamps, few props.

He could hear the echo of her bare feet on the floorboards; he could sense some of her fragrance. But on other levels the apartment provided almost no information. A scoured oak desk. A brown Poul Henningsen lamp from the thirties. One chair. A large double bed. A flat file designed for architects and graphic artists, which he'd used to take the measurements for the drawer in the trailer. On the desk, a few writing materials. And two computers. On a low table, two printers. A large bulletin board with maps and charts hung on one wall. Pieces of driftwood lay in various places, wood that had turned black, then silvery gray. Beach rocks. Conch shells. Flowers, orchids—not those found in flower shops, but muted, rare botanical species that he had seen here for the first time. A low shelf held professional books. Hanging on another wall was a rug made of fine black wool with an intricately woven geometric design. No pictures on the walls. No photographs.

She had told him essentially nothing about her past. And he had not asked. They had danced around each other, after an unspoken agreement to avoid those places where the past was archived. And where the future is planned.

It had been a beautiful dance, moving, respectful. The flip side of respect is unnecessary distance. He slid down from the windowseat and opened one of the flat drawers; it was filled with letters.


One time, they had taken a shower together, here in the apartment; he had gotten out first. She had turned off the water. The drops from the walls and the shower curtain had played Chopin's Prelude in A-Major, drops of passion, oxygen-filled heart blood falling on black marble. She had lathered her palms, thinned the lather with water, and blown a soap bubble from her hands, as large as a coconut.

She put lather on one forearm and held it tight against her body under her left breast, outside her heart. She began to blow. He had never seen anything like it; the bubble was large, twelve inches in diameter, and floated like the sea lions' ball in the circus.

It did not pop. She captured it with the other arm, and now it formed a tube straight across her body. She stretched the tube; its sides curved inward, as if it wanted to expand and deflate simultaneously.

"Dirichlet's theorem," she said, "of minimal surfaces. A very nice proof. When we increase a surface, at the same time it gives way it will try to stretch over the least possible area."

She had come toward him. With the long, concave, shining bubble.

"Everything alive," she said. "And everything dead. Tries simultaneously to expand and hold back. Including love. It's a mystery. How does one go into free fall? And at the same time keep one's hand on the emergency brake?"

She was right next to him. It was as if there were an invisible layer of clear oil on her skin. Water could not stay on it; the film of water contracted and divided into drops, like on a dolphin.

"Is there a solution?" he said.

"Even if there were, you wouldn't want it."

The bubble touched him.

"And you've never wanted it. Even when you were very close to it."

The bubble burst.

It had been just a small mistake. But it had been enough. For a moment her sound had been different. Full of knowledge. He had sensed that she knew something about him. That she must have been inside a space in his system that he hadn't given her permission to enter. And that she must have taken something out of it. It was that memory this night had activated.


A person with good upbringing doesn't read other people's letters; he hadn't even read Bach's letters that were reprinted in the Groce edition. And he read Kierkegaard's only for academic reasons. But if one is to gain insights into feminine nature one must take advantage of every opportunity.

He lifted out the letters in piles and riffled through them. Someone who has shuffled and dealt cards with a lucky hand throughout a long life can quickly orient himself in a stack of papers.

The first pile was technical letters, Seismic Studies, Lund University, Lund, Sweden; British Geological Survey, Edinburgh. Stacks of letters from the European Mediterranean Seismological Center, EMSC, in Bruyères-le-Châtel. UCLA Institute of Geophysics and Planetary Physics. On cheap copy paper. He came to the private letters; there weren't many. Or she kept them somewhere else. Or she didn't keep them. There was a thin bundle of handwritten letters on heavy off-white stationery. They were signed "Mother" or "Your Mother." There was no return address, but "Holte" was written next to the date. He found one envelope with a return address and stuck it in his pocket.

He continued looking. The sound in the room shifted. He knew he was getting close. He listened into several piles organized with large paper clips. There were letters from previous lovers; he shut his hearing hurriedly. Deep down, isn't it totally unacceptable for any woman to have had any lover but you?

Two pages touched his fingers and his hearing like a thorn. They were stapled together; the tiny pieces of metal had stuck him. He separated the pages. They were photocopies. He recognized the handwriting. It was his own. Carefully written more than twenty years ago. By a person that in some sense must have been him.

He had known he would find them. That was what he had heard in her voice that day in the shower. It was the sound of these letters.

A third letter was attached. Also handwritten. It was a photocopy of the reply he had received back then. The handwriting of the answer was uneven, slightly wavy. Like the handwriting in Mozart's musical scores had been. When you played Mozart you absolutely had to have a copy of the original; his scores were full of information. The same was true of the handwriting in front of him now.

He should have stopped at that point. But he continued. His fingers found a thicker shape. On a thin piece of paper were what looked like fingerprints, in purple ink. Five fingers, but broader than fingers' normal thickness. The print was protected with a clear adhesive coating and marked NATIONAL POLICE, CFI. Directly under it lay another printed sheet with numbers and combinations of letters marked CRIME LABORATORY. The address was Slotsherrens Road.

He drew a last card. It was a receipt for "various effects" marked MINISTRY OF JUSTICE, KIF, HORSENS.

He looked at his watch. It was Sunday morning. Not yet seven o'clock. He dialed Sonja's cell phone number.

It took a long time before she answered. Wherever she was, she wasn't at home; the acoustics were different, fewer surfaces to dampen the sound. She was in bed; he could hear the friction of textiles. There was a man beside her. She had alcohol in her voice, warm alcohol; it must be glogg, so close to Christmas.

He thought about what it must be like to be Sonja's husband, sitting there at home with the children. While she worked through the night and far into Sunday.

He thought about the tiny burst capillaries in her cheeks. The first small sign that one can get too much even of all the good things. Too many men, too much money, too much success. Too much Brunello wine.

He had never before used her cell phone number this way. She didn't ask any questions; she felt the seriousness immediately.

"I have five fingerprints," he said. "Unusually broad. Marked NATIONAL POLICE, CFI. I have some numbers and letters of the alphabet from the crime lab. And a receipt from the Ministry of Justice marked KIF and HORSENS. What am I getting into?"

"I need a little time. Can I call you back?"

He gave her Stina's number.

Sonja planned tours for large circuses and big rock concerts. Each circus visited an average of eighty cities during a summer season, using logistics that were deeply rooted in tradition and based on trust and personal acquaintance. There wasn't a police chief in the country that she did not know well.

He sat on the windowseat. Stina and he had sat opposite each other here, naked. The curved window looked across outer Østerbro and out over the Sound. It was the only place in Nørrebro from which one could see the water. He knew that must have been the reason she chose the apartment. From down in the street he heard the taxi's horn.

The telephone rang.

"CFI," said Sonja, "is the Central Bureau for Identification. Its headquarters are at the main police station. The fingerprints look broad because they are what's called 'rolled off.' A detective has pressed the person's finger on an ink pad and then rolled it across a piece of paper. CFI uses nine points per hand when they identify on the basis of a print; it's supposed to be almost as precise as DNA. And a DNA profile is most likely what you have from the crime lab. Both items can be returned when a person, after imprisonment, for example, is deleted from the Criminal Registry, which is the National Police's central database, the database from which one gets criminal records. The KIF receipt is from Criminal Care in Freedom, a system of thirty-two very open prisons. Among the five closed state prisons, Horsens is the only one with high-security detention, if we don't count the rock-musician units. So what you're dealing with is a person who has served a long sentence, has spent the last part of that sentence in an open prison after good behavior, and subsequently, in accordance with police regulations, has gotten the fingerprint records back as proof that he or she is no longer listed in the Criminal Registry."

Kasper listened to the apartment. It had a new sound. Perhaps Sonja heard it too.

"It's the woman," she said. "You've discovered that she was in prison."

He did not say anything.

"It may have been for something relatively harmless," she said. "You and I, like most people, would be arrested if we laid all our cards on the table for the authorities."

She had always been able to comfort him, or anybody, even when they were very young. This time it didn't work.

"Is it glogg?" he asked.

"Sake."

"Take care," he said.

He hung up.

The taxi had dropped him off on Strand Road, and he had entered the trailer quietly. Stina was asleep; he sat in a chair listening to her sleep. Her body was completely relaxed; he wasn't able to hear her dreams.

He sat there perhaps a quarter of an hour. Then she sat up in bed. She woke up like a cat, one moment deep unconsciousness, the next total presence.

"There's something I want to tell you," he said. "And to ask you. It will take some time."

She reached for the telephone and reported that she wasn't coming to work. No clever excuse that could have made life easier for the person at the other end, just a laconic report, and then she hung up.

They drove south; at Bellevue he turned off the road and parked by the train station. Without saying a word they walked north, skirting Bakken amusement park, through Ulve Glen in Deer Park, across Eremitage Plain toward Hjorte Pool, past the castle. At the top of the hill they sat down on a bench.

Eremitage Plain didn't have Nature's usual dry tone, perhaps because of the trees, perhaps due to the Sound's shining surface; a quiet body of water is as hard as stone. The acoustics were like those in a concert hall, all the surfaces hard and reflecting.

Somewhere Martinus had said or written that Eremitage Plain was an earthly reflection of a spiritual fact in a better world. At this moment Kasper understood him; from the place where they now sat it was possible to live with the sound of the Charlottenlund and Hellerup suburbs as well as the central city behind them.

"When I was twelve I broke my back," he said. "I was part of a classic barrel act. You hop blindfolded with your legs tied together up a stack of three-foot barrels to a height of about twenty-six feet, receive applause, turn around, hop down again, and finish with forward somersaults and a twist. At a height of twenty feet I jumped incorrectly, grazed the barrel, hit the next one. The stack fell over and tumbled down on top of me. They were sixty-six-pound beer kegs from Carlsberg brewery. I broke my back and hip. At Rigshospital they said I would never walk again, and that I would have to be spoon-fed the rest of my life, and the rest of my life might be very short. They closed two doors before they said that, but I heard them anyway."

He heard her empathy.

"It wasn't so bad," he said. "It was like starting to fall—a weight was taken off me, the weight of being an ordinary twelve-year-old boy in the mid-seventies. An interlude had begun, and in that interlude I *heard* for the first time. I heard the hospital, the trip home, the car, the winter quarters, as I'd never heard before. It wasn't just the physical sounds; it was their context. Usually we never hear the world as it is. We hear an edited production. The sounds we like, we draw forward. The ringing in the ticket booth when they balance the cash. The fanfare that announces the little circus princess we're in love with. The bubbling sound of eight hundred people in a full tent. Whereas the sounds we don't like, we push away. The sound of leather reinforcements on deteriorated canvas. The sound of frightened horses. The sound of the toilets. Of the gusty wind in August that tells us summer is soon over. And the rest of the sounds are irrelevant—we tone them down—the traffic, the city, the mundane. That's how we listen. Because we've got things to do, because we're on our way somewhere, even a twelve-year-old boy. But suddenly I no longer had any projects; they were taken away from me. And for the first time I heard some of the world *alive*, unfiltered, unmuted."

He saw that Stina's eyes were gray now. But at other times they had been different. Turquoise, greenish. Sometimes flecked.

"When you really listen, all sounds begin to organize themselves into themes. They aren't haphazard. We don't live in chaos. Someone is trying to play something. Trying to create a piece of music. SheAlmighty. That's the name I gave to the composer. The one who creates the music. I lay in bed for three months; then they realized I was getting better and started to give me physical therapy. But I have only vague memories of the healing process. The joy was felt mostly by the others. What I was preoccupied with was the other thing. Being in my body and the world without muted sound—again and again, briefly, always briefly, always just for a moment. It sets an agenda. Even if you're only twelve years old, even if you don't have words for it, still you know that what will really matter for the rest of your life is to be able to really listen. To have a picture of the world that's true to nature. To hear it as it actually is. And with this longing comes the fear of not succeeding. That was twenty years ago. Half a lifetime is gone. And I haven't come much closer."

"So what keeps us from hearing?" she asked.

It took him a long time to reply. Only once before had he spoken about this to another person.

"In order to live in this world we need to keep an orchestra playing. Way in the foreground. It's a small dance orchestra. It always plays its own melody. It plays the golden oldie 'Kasper Krone.' Which has a series of refrains that are repeated over and over. Again and again it plays our bank account numbers, our childhood memories, our PIN numbers, the sound of our mother's and father's voices. The pale-green strophes we hope will be the future. The black noise we have good reason to suppose will be our actual reality. It plays continuously, like a heartbeat. But when the other sound begins to come through, you discover that you've been standing with your back to the true concert hall the whole time. We live in a sort of lobby. Where we can faintly hear the great orchestra. And that sound, just the embouchure to a sound from the real concert hall, makes the Mass in B-Minor disappear. Like a whisper in windy weather. It's a sound that sweeps away the din of war. It drowns the music of the spheres. It takes away all the sounds of reality. And at the same time as you vaguely hear the great orchestra, you vaguely sense the price of the ticket. When the door to the real concert hall begins to open you discover that perhaps you were mistaken. That Kasper Krone exists only because your ears continue to isolate the same little refrain from the collected mass of sound. That in order to preserve Kasper and Stina we've turned down the input from other channels to pianissimo. But that's about to change. And you can feel it. If you want to go inside, it will be the most expensive concert ticket anyone has ever bought. It will cost you the sound of your own self."

She stroked his arm. He had never been able to create a picture of her body in his mind. Sometimes she seemed as frail as a bird, sometimes as solid as a freestyle wrestler. But always when she touched him he could hear the earth, the earth and the sea.

"Where are we in all this?" she said. "You and I?"

"With you," he said, "the volume controls are lost. And I want to run away."

She was quiet. The woods were quiet. The wind had stopped blowing. The concept of an artistic pause is not unknown to SheAlmighty.

"I'm afraid too," she said. "Couldn't we run away together?"

He waited. She had her first chance to be candid; the possibility was there, and then it passed.

"To be twelve years old," he said, "or sixteen, or nineteen, and to have experienced that we live in an illusion, that in reality the world doesn't consist of material but of sound—that's not easy. Where do you go? In the mid-seventies. Having experienced something that no one else in the surrounding two thousand miles has heard. It makes you lonely. It creates a combination of loneliness and megalomania. You know you won't be understood. Not by your family. Not by your artist friends. Not by pastors. Not by physicians. Not by wise people. By no one. Nevertheless, you keep looking."

She had become absolutely quiet. Perhaps she sensed it was getting close. Her second chance came—he could hear it; she muffed that chance too. The moment was open, and then it closed again.

"Artists are believers," he said. "Deeply religious, like Gypsies and sailors. Perhaps because they live close to death. Perhaps because they travel light. Perhaps because they work with illusions. Each evening, while music plays, you unfold reality and exhibit it in the ring, and fold it up again, and carry it outside. When you've done this five thousand times, you begin to sense that the world around us is a mirage. That no matter how much one loves another person, a woman, a child, sooner or later that person must be carried out of the ring to rot away. And if one is completely honest, one realizes that all of us already stink a little. So one turns to some sort of God. In the heart of every artist is a longing, an empty space, something like SheAlmighty.

"And the Danish State Church didn't really help with that; the only ones who took religious experience seriously were the fundamentalists in the Indre Mission Church, and they didn't like the circus. So some artists developed their own religion, like my father; he's a believing atheist and proud of it. Others used one of two shops, the Catholic Church on Bred Street or the Eastern Orthodox Church. My mother took me along to the church on Nevsky Street. We spoke with a woman. The woman was wearing a habit. My mother told her that my father had left the circus and wanted her to leave too. What should she do? I wasn't more than eight years old—still I knew what the woman should have answered. She didn't do that. She spoke only one sentence: 'I like the circus very much myself.' We sat there perhaps ten more minutes, in complete silence. Then we left. When I was nineteen, and things weren't going well, I wrote to her."

He stopped speaking; the silence was Stina's final chance. In the fairy tales and in this so-called reality, there are always three chances. She missed this one as well.

He took out the folded letter and laid it on the bench.

"Her name was Mother Rabia," he said. "I did some investigating and found out that she was a deaconess and head of a convent. I wrote to her. In that letter I revealed for the first time to any human being what I've told you today. Will you read it out loud, please?"

She did not move. He stood up.

"I've forgotten my glasses," he said, "but I still remember it by heart. It begins like this: 'SheAlmighty has tuned each person in a musical key, and I—Kasper Krone, the clown—am in the difficult position of being able to hear that.' It's twelve years since I wrote that letter; I didn't save a copy. This morning I saw it again. In your apartment. I thought I'd find it. That's why I went there."

"She answered you," said Stina. "Mother Rabia answered you. Why didn't you respond to her answer?"

He had circled around her; now he stood next to her. His hands closed around her forearms.

"I'm the one who's asking the questions," he whispered. "How did you get that letter?"

"Will you please let go of me?"

Her voice was husky, amicable, pleading.

He put weight behind the pressure; she was forced to her knees.

"You'll find out," she said. "But not now."

"Now," he said.

"I've had some experiences in the past," she said. "With men and violence. Bad experiences. I get very frightened."

Her face had turned gray. Fatigued.

He squeezed harder. Something—he didn't know what—had seized and possessed him.

"Let's hear about the letter," he said.

He had underestimated her physical strength, now as in the past. From her kneeling position she kicked his shin with an outstretched instep. The blow was so hard that at first there was no pain, just paralysis. His legs buckled under him. As a child she had climbed trees and played with boys—he could hear that. She locked his wrists as he fell, so he couldn't cushion the fall. He hit the ground with his shoulder, like cyclists and artists, to protect his head. He heard his collarbone break with a sound like a dry branch cracking off an ash tree.

She was on her feet, but he threw himself forward from a prone position. He got hold of her ankle and pulled, then crawled after her until they lay beside each other.

"When you found me on the beach," he said. "That wasn't accidental. I'm part of something very big. You want something from me."

He took hold of her jaw. His fingers pressed the nerve centers behind the jaw muscles.

"My basic psychological problem," he said, "is that I can't trust women. Women always want something besides love. A man's body, maybe. His fame. His money."

She twisted her head free.

"I'm glad I don't have to hide it any longer now," she said. "That it's your body I want."

He shut her jaw again.

"There's something more than that," he said. "You've gone very far. Given a performance that's lasted three months now. Tell me what it's all about."

He squeezed.

"You've ruined everything," she said.

Then she head-butted him.

That was the one thing he hadn't expected. She hit perfectly. Not on the nose, which causes heavy bleeding. Not too high up, where the skull is thick. But right above the ridge of the nose.

He went out like a light. Only for a few minutes, but when he began to hear and see again, she was gone. There were people around him, but at a distance. Respectable citizens who were walking their dogs and staring at him. He could hear their thoughts. They thought: "There lies another addict who picked psilocybin mushrooms on fertile lawns and has drifted off to dreamland now."

He would need to adjust his self-image yet again. He had always imagined that in Deer Park he would ride in a carriage with a princess.


He had driven home with one arm. He had parked beside the trailer and sat in the car for a while. Nature had played the last part of *Die Kunst der Fuge*. And he had understood that he would never see her again.

**4**

He could remember the telephone number for Rigshospital. He wanted to say goodbye. He dialed the number. Maximillian answered the phone himself.

"It's me," said Kasper. "I'm calling from the airport."

"So we're both about to leave on a somewhat bigger trip," said Maximillian.

They were quiet for a while.

"Can you remember," said Kasper, "when we children were small. When we ate lunch after morning rehearsals. There were always children visiting, and the children didn't have to sit down for lunch; we ran back and forth from the table. Took bites. We didn't have to stop playing. And when we rehearsed, you never pressured us, neither you nor Mother. Never. I never said thank you for that."

He searched for a word, then it came to him. It was old-fashioned, outdated, but nevertheless exactly the right word.

"Respect," he said. "There was always a kind of respect. Even if you and Mother fought. Even when I was very little."

When Maximillian answered his voice was hoarse, like someone with a very bad sore throat.

"We did our best. And usually—usually it wasn't good enough. My fondest memories are of the nights. After we'd taken off our makeup. When we ate together. Outside the trailer. And your mother had baked bread. Can you remember that?"

"We burned our fingers on the crust."

"We were completely happy. Some of those nights."

They were quiet together, for the last time.

"When the plane takes off," said Maximillian, "what will you think about?"

"About you and Mother," said Kasper. "About Stina. About the little girl I tried to find. I didn't find her. And you?"

"About your mother. And you. And Vivian. And then I'll prepare myself, like in the horseback riders' gangway. Just before the curtain goes up, when you have your act ready. The tickets are sold. But still, you have no idea what will happen."

"Neither one of us will hang up first," said Kasper. "We'll hang up simultaneously. Timing, that always meant a lot to both you and me. I'll count to three. And we'll hang up."

He heard the door open behind him. They were coming to get him. Without turning around, he counted slowly and clearly to three. He and his father hung up at the same time.

Kassander entered the cell. Behind him stood two women. White and compassionate, like the figures of light Elisabeth Kübler-Ross writes about. But more attractive. More sexually defined than angels.

They leaned over him. Took the violin from him. Took his pulse. Pulled up his sleeve. Wrapped a blood-pressure cuff on his upper arm. He felt a cold stethoscope against his chest.

One of them was the African. Now wearing a white coat. With her hair in two hundred tiny braids. But it was still her. Her forehead was rounded like an orb. Above a beautiful mocha-colored continent.

"His heart is about to give out," she said. "He won't be flying today. We'll take him back with us. He needs immediate surgery."

Kasper put his hand on his heart. Now he could feel it too. The pain of being rejected by his beloved. Expatriated from his fatherland. Sorrow over the uncertain future. Over the beauty of the "Chaconne."

Kassander blocked their way.

"We have orders directly from the Ministry of Justice," he said.

The African drew herself erect. She was taller than the officer.

"His pulse is thirty-six. Irregular, extremely weak heartbeat. He's very close to throwing in the towel. Either you move, or we'll take you to court. Disciplinary action, dereliction of duty. You'll get at least six years. For gross negligence and manslaughter."

"I'll make a phone call," said Kassander.

There was not much left of his voice.

He made the call from a telephone at the back of the premises. Returned. He walked like a zombie. Laid a form on the counter.

"Twenty-four hours," he said. "He's booked on Iberia's morning flight at seven-twenty. He's a repatriation case. They're under the purview of the ministry."

The African signed. The women took hold of Kasper under his arms and lifted him up. He pulled them close, for reasons of health. And cautiously took the first tentative steps back toward freedom.

# Part
# Five

They had an ambulance waiting and helped him into it. A frosted glass divider separated them from the front seat; it was pushed to the side. The driver and the woman beside him were wearing white coats too.

The siren started, the ambulance drove across the area reserved for taxis, then across the parking lot, and made a U-turn. The driver's jacket had a high collar, but above it a dozen scars crawled up to the man's head like white flames; it was Franz Fieber.

A police car with flashing lights passed them going in the opposite direction. The women had drawn away from Kasper, and their solicitousness had disappeared. That was what one could expect. Somewhere Saint Gregory writes that one of the reasons many of the desert fathers became celibate was the discovery that when women had achieved what they wanted, their motherliness disappeared.

They passed Ørestaden. And turned right at the Transport Center exit. The siren got turned off. The ambulance drove across the grass, without slowing down, and came to a stop next to a large Audi ambulance behind a restaurant shut for the evening. The women lifted Kasper into the back of the new ambulance while Franz Fieber swung himself from one front seat to the other, like an ape, without using his crutches. The Audi accelerated and headed out onto the highway, out into the passing lane. The speedometer showed 110 miles an hour; Kasper could hear sirens both in front of them and behind them. Somewhere ahead and above them a helicopter approached.

"They're about to close off all of Amager Island," said Franz Fieber. "What does your fine hearing say?"

"Let us all pray," said Kasper. "For fog. And for an open lane crossing the Zealand Bridge."

The car turned off the highway. Into a wall of fog. The road disappeared. The approaching cars dwindled into twinkling yellow dots. The women stared at him.

"There are two possibilities," said Kasper. "Either I have a direct link to SheAlmighty. Or I heard the fog. And heard that there are no sirens in the direction of the bridge."

He felt his body collapse. Hands supported him as he slumped onto the stretcher. He tried to stay conscious by determining their route by the sound: the incoming planes on Runway 12, a shorter runway—for strong north or south winds—which gave the landings a particular sound and rhythm. The seagulls when the ambulance crossed the bridge. The social realism of outer Valby. Outer Frederiksberg's tone of a semipermanent home for the elderly. The special blend of bird sanctuary and traffic hell where the Farum highway cuts through Utterslev moor.

He was in and out of consciousness. They had gotten away and the traffic had thinned out when the ambulance turned onto a gravel road. Without slowing down, they passed a gate that he recognized; it was part of the fence around Rabia Institute. The Audi stopped, reality was tuned down, it faded, and was gone.

# 2

The world took shape again. He was being pushed on a gurney through the white corridors, past the icons, into an elevator. The African stood beside him holding bags of fluid in her hands; tubes connected to the bags went to his wrist. They had attached him to an IV. He could hear that the woman was afraid, but he wasn't able to hear why.

The door opened, they went down long corridors, up in an elevator, along yet another corridor, into an operating room. Now he could hear why she was afraid. She was afraid he was going to die.

There were six women around him. Every man's dream, but he could no longer feel his body. Everyone was wearing green surgical gowns; all of them, except the African, were wearing masks.

"We're going to give you a painkiller," she said.

"I'm an artist," he said. "I want to feel my nerves flutter."

His voice had no sound; they didn't hear him. He saw the needle glide into his wrist. The Blue Lady was within earshot. Now he could see her.

"I've come to get paid," he said.

His words made no sound, but she must have heard him anyway. She leaned forward to him and smiled.

"That will be a pleasure," she said.

He lost consciousness again, slowly, like a young girl strolling downtown.

He came back. Not completely into his body. But near his body. The African was speaking, but not to him.

"I'll check for internal bleeding," she said. "We've got both the bullet path and the blows."

He opened his eyes and watched her work. He would have liked to reassure her. To have said it doesn't really matter whether a person lives or dies.

"Percussing belly and lower abdomen," she said. "No tension. But pain. Low blood pressure and pulse. Hematocrit at stipulated blood percentage. Hemoglobin four to five. We'll do a transfusion."

He wanted to say something. "Absolutely not!" he wanted to say. "I agree with Rudolf Steiner. Blood is *eine sehr geistige Flüssigkeit*."

No sound came. They began the transfusion; he could hear the unfamiliar blood gurgle in his veins.

"One hundred milligrams Pethidine," said the African. "Ephedrine. I'm trying to keep him conscious, but no success."

She was talking to the Blue Lady.

"He's out," she said.

He laughed blithely. Within himself. He was about to be freed from the burdensome identification with his body. But hearing is eternal—that's what he was laughing about.

"A small-caliber bullet," said the African, "with low exit speed, fired at close range. A steel bullet, the kind police use to shoot through doors and cars. We'll take X-rays now, ankles, foot joints, skull, wrist. Overview of the abdomen. *Columna cervicalis*."

Someone placed a lead protection pad over his abdomen and thyroid. On the body that was no longer his.

He found himself in a place that seemed almost timeless. Bodies and physical forms were gone, and all that remained were sounds and the beginnings of sounds. Somewhere, in a distant province, part of him was undergoing surgery.

"Soapy water," said the African. "We'll sew intracutaneously, butterfly and histoacryl for the gashes. We've got the X-rays. The liver, spleen, and kidneys weren't hit. His pulse is still falling. Forceps. He's still bleeding. He has a Colles' fracture. I want a block analgesic in the axilla. Local anesthesia around the break."

They did something with his wrist. If he'd had better connection with his body he would have fainted from the pain.

"Plaster casts," said the African. "Splint for the arm. Circular for the ankle. We'll cut it up; the break is still swelling. His pulse is still falling. Do we have an EKG?"

He had once been a consultant, in the psychoacoustics section of the Sound Quality Research Unit at Ålborg University, on how to furnish an operating room; he had advised them to find a sound that combined the somewhat firm spatial tone of a convent with the intimacy of a living room. To give the sick person a sense of both home and religious authority. It was exactly the sound that surrounded him now.

The operating-room sounds got tuned down and sent to the edge of the picture. He fluttered in the wind. A warm, gentle wind. He was just a tonal structure, just an obedient bearer of consciousness. And of love. He heard the African speaking to the Blue Lady. They were far away, behind closed doors, so he wouldn't hear them. Like the time he broke his back. He laughed happily; he had a secret: His hearing had few or no physical limits.

"We're going to lose him," said the African. "The combined pressure on his system. The bullet wound. The violent beating. The broken bones. The skull fracture. The loss of blood. The psychological strain. There's nothing more we can do."

He half walked, half floated along a beach. He could hear a pulse, very strong and calm—perhaps it was SheAlmighty's pulse, perhaps his own. The doors into the large concert hall were about to open. He stood with the definitive ticket in his hand.

He discovered that the Blue Lady was walking beside him.

It was real. He wasn't hallucinating. Somewhere in the physical world she was speaking to Sister Gloria. But still, she was walking here beside him.

Her signal was far-reaching. And at the same time incredibly discreet. Both omnipresent and anonymous. He had never heard anything like it. It encompassed the beach, the sea, and himself. It encompassed the audible universe. With complete respect.

"I'm about to go away," he said. "Into the great freedom."

She nodded.

"Free of contracts," he said. "Free from needing to perform. Free of accountants. Of Customs and Tax authorities. Of having to think about money. Of having to take off makeup. Of going to the bathroom. Of having to shave. Free of attraction to, and troubles with, women. Of having to put on clothes. Pay bills. Free of sound pollution, of the world's noise. Free of music. Except perhaps Bach's—perhaps Bach lasts through death."

She listened. Only very rarely had anyone listened to him that way; it happened maybe once a year. And then it had always been a woman or a child. Those evenings he had performed far better than average.

"Still," he said, "something seems to be missing."

They were standing at the edge of the water. Far away, somewhere inland, he could see his body. Attached to machines which measured an electrical signal that was about to die out.

"Maybe it's KlaraMaria," she said.

"Maybe that's it."

He let his hearing expand into a sphere; he heard the quiet girl. The other child too. He couldn't determine where the sound came from—all the coordinates were dispersed. But he heard from their breathing that they were asleep. He could have stood there listening for a long time, perhaps forever. In his life there had been all too few opportunities to listen to sleeping children.

He heard that in a little while someone would awaken them and hustle them out. Somehow it wasn't in a little while; it was now. He didn't hear in temporal succession—he heard everything at the same time.

He understood what was missing. In order for his life to be complete, a finished performance, so he could leave the ring feeling he had fulfilled his contract. He needed to carry the children out into the night and into safety.

He decided to live.

He began to move back toward his body. The Blue Lady walked beside him.

He did not hear her smile. But he thought he heard a hint of satisfaction. As if this was what she had most deeply desired. That irritated him. It provoked an unwillingness to be manipulated by women. Unfortunately, a man who returns to his body also returns to the basic aspects of his own personality.

"It's a well-known fact," he said, "that someone who is approaching a spiritual breakthrough goes through periods of intense physical pain."

"It's a well-known fact," she said, "that angry cats get ruffled fur."

"I can't leave my fans," he said. "I managed to get one American talk show, for CBS, before being blacklisted. It had twenty million viewers. I can still hear them weeping. And longing for *da capo*. Moreover, isn't that what you said the saints did? They returned to give joy to the seekers?"

"They had something that would give the seekers joy. Do you?"

For a moment he was shaken. To speak that way. To a listening soul who has left his battered, dying body.

"For one thing," he said, "my modesty will give them joy."

That made her stop short. He felt a sense of satisfaction. If one can close the mouth—even if only momentarily—of enlightened Mother Superiors in their nonphysical manifestation, one cannot be completely dead.

# 3

He returned to a kingdom of pain.

It was everywhere. A numb, paralyzing pain in his stomach and lower abdomen. The dull surgical pain from his brain concussion, constant, throbbing. The hot torment from the swelling around his broken bones. His body's unfamiliarity with the new blood. The pain when the dentist put his loosened teeth back in place. An intensified pain when they began to fix his jaw.

He could remain conscious only for short periods. During these periods he prayed. He had no extra energy for words; he simply leaned in through the loving care around his body and out toward the great loving care beyond, out toward SheAlmighty.

Once in a while he opened his eyes. Sometimes he saw the African. Sometimes the Blue Lady. Then he went out again, toward the sea. But each time he came back.


Someone gave him something to drink; swallowing burned his throat. He saw the white corridors disappear. A door opened, a heavy sound-proof door with rubber flanges. They rolled him through it.

He could not turn his head. But he was lying in a hospital bed, and the African raised his upper body very slightly. He saw he was in a convent cell.

It was like coming home. Out in real life, people could set the table for up to twelve with blue fluted china. They had a large house, a chesterfield coat, two stereos, three televisions, eight hundred books they would never read again, forty-eight bottles of red wine saved for their sixty-fifth wedding anniversary. And so much junk stuffed away in the basement that they were desperately looking for a bigger house. Whereas every circus performer and ninety-nine out of a hundred artists wanted to avoid everything that could not be packed up and moved in an afternoon. The space around him was like that. His bed, a table, a washbasin, a door that opened to a small balcony facing the lake. That was all.

Except for the electronic devices. On the table was a monitor attached to electrodes on his chest. He could feel several electrodes fastened to his temples.

"KlaraMaria?" he said.

The African shook her head.

"How long have I been here?"

His voice was unrecognizable. She must have understood him anyway.

"Eight days."

"Bring me my clothes," he said. "I've got to get up and leave. I'm the only one who can find her."

"You just relax," she said. "Or we'll strap you down. You should be glad that you're even alive."

She put a clip on his finger; attached to the clip was a cord connected to yet another screen.

"A pulse oximeter," she said. "Measures oxygen saturation in the blood."

"A telephone?" he whispered.

She shook her head. More electrodes were placed on his chest.

"A scope," she said. "Monitors heart functions."

He felt his consciousness fading.

"Gandhi," he said, "continued to sleep beside naked women. After he made a vow of chastity. To test his sexual continence. Would you be interested?"


The African wrote numbers from the screens. There was another woman in the room. They spoke together. His body hurt all over. He heard his mother. Is there anything wrong with a healthy young man thinking about his mother? Even if he is forty-two. When he has been close to death.

He heard her very clearly. Now he saw her in his mind. He would not have been able to get up from the bed to go to the toilet. They had undoubtedly put a diaper on him. But his childhood memories were unharmed.

It was delightful. When you have reached the age of forty-two, you live an ever greater part of your life in memories.


It had been night, the performance over, Helene Krone still in tulle with a towel around her hips; he could hear the whisper of terry cloth. He had known that her shoulders must be naked. Most of the other women protected themselves from the sun; his mother inhaled the light. It was shortly after the accident and he was completely blind. He heard the sound of her silver jewelry. They told him it was a night with a moon. He knew that in the moonlight the silver against her brown skin would be white. No one had ever said so, but he knew she had gotten the jewelry from earlier lovers. That its constant, melodic tinkling was an ongoing challenge for Maximillian, a memento mori, as if there were a skull lying on the little table where she placed the soup.

She had baked food in a cast-iron pot that she set directly on the coals in the little Morsø wood-burning stove. It was the mid-seventies, and half of the circus grounds didn't have electricity for the trailers.

The air was fragrant with flowers. And around them were many herb pots; they filled most of the trailer when they were traveling. Helene Krone had loved flowers. Everywhere they performed for more than three days she had planted something or other, just to see the sprouts come up before they had to leave. Maximillian had known that his only chance to draw her away from the circus was to tempt her with a garden. He had tried, but did not succeed.

They carried Kasper outside. His mother gave him soup and bread. He was only able to use his right arm.

He was able to hear her movements; they were easy and natural. Even though it was night. Even though she had already had a sixteen-hour working day, including four hours of hard physical training. Even though anxiety about him sang in her constantly. Despite all that, she was natural. In the way wild animals share qualities with

Bach's music: a naturalness where one doesn't dream of changing a single note because it simply cannot be any other way. True freedom is freedom from having to choose, because everything is perfect just as it is.

Maximillian Krone leaned back and accepted the food without ever saying thank you. Appreciation was built into the situation.

Kasper could hear the intimacy between his parents, and also the passion, the caution. He would not have had a word for it. But he was able to sense that if you want to have the experience of a home that's meaningful and open and natural, like Bach's music and the big cats on the savannah, it costs something; it costs the risk entailed in living your life near two poles with highly different voltages.

Maximillian fell asleep. He collapsed with exhaustion. Helene Krone awakened him gently, very gently. Without fully waking up, he rose, staggered inside, and tumbled into bed.

Kasper listened to his mother as she cleared up. He could hear her weariness. But behind it there was a more powerful sound that he wasn't able to decode.

She picked him up, carried him inside, and put him to bed. He heard her lift the chimney glass and blow out the candle.

He wasn't able to sleep. He lay in the dark and thought about death. He was afraid to die.

So it had not been true, what he told Stina. That the sound of SheAlmighty had made him fearless. That had not been true. He had lain in the dark and been afraid.

Then he had heard a sound, right next to him. It was his mother.

She seated herself on the edge of the bed and he heard the soft rustle of her nightgown. He knew that if he had been able to see, it would have looked as if she were wearing moonlight.

Perhaps it hadn't been one particular night; he felt there must have been many. But nevertheless, behind them all somehow there had been just one long night.

She sat there a long time without saying anything, just holding his hand. Then she began to sing, very softly. She sang often, but she hadn't sung to him since he was a little boy.

When she began to sing, the sound behind her came again. It was huge, larger than any single person. And it was all-pervasive. He identified it now. It was the full volume of a mother's love for her child. And not just one mother. All mothers' love for all children.


Perhaps he had slept. And then awakened. Perhaps he was in the sickroom. Perhaps it was another night with Helene Krone.

She hadn't sung anymore. She had told him things.

About her childhood. About animals they had owned, and ones she had heard about.

"My mother, your grandmother," she said, "had an act as a white *clownesse* in Austria, before and during the war. There were dogs in the act. They had a terrier. She brought it along to Denmark. I remember one of her puppies. When that puppy and I ran through tall grass or grain, every fifteen feet or so it had to jump high into the air to see me."

As she talked, Kasper listened through her voice. He was able to hear the artists she talked about; he was able to determine their musical key. He discovered that in this universe every person's sound offers access to all other sounds.

He understood that those his mother talked about were dead. His grandmother was dead. The other people were dead, the dog was dead. Nevertheless, his mother's voice was a door into their sounds. He could hear that. But he did not understand it.

"There was a girl," said Helene Krone. "Karen. We were the same age."

Kasper listened in through the name. He sensed that his memory had taken him to this tonal location so he would remember this.

"She was the one who got me to switch from tightrope to slack line," said Helene Krone. "We had winter quarters by one of the lakes near Holte. Opposite the grounds was a marlstone quarry; a rope was stretched across it. She said she wanted to learn to walk across the rope. She got me to sail across the quarry in a floating wooden box. We couldn't swim. The grown-ups discovered what we'd done. They were frightened, and decided we should learn to swim. The closest swimming pool was by Fure Lake. We bicycled over there, just past Gammelgård and Skovbrynet. One day Karen said, 'You should meet the sisters.' They lived in a convent by one of the lakes. It was actually just a big house. They gave us tea and hard cookies. Which became soft when we dunked them in the tea. There was a woman. I remember her as being old; she must have been fifty. 'Is there anything you want to ask about?' she said.

"I trusted her. She smelled good. That was how I knew if I trusted grown-ups."

Helene Krone had laughed in the darkness, softly, so as not to awaken her husband. Then she continued speaking.

"'Yes,' I said. 'There's something I'd like to ask about. Sometimes I'm afraid the world is a dream.'

"'What do the grown-ups say?' the nun said. 'When you ask them about that?'

"She said 'the grown-ups,' not 'father and mother.' She understood how I looked at the world.

"'They say I can pinch my arm,' I told her. 'They say that if it hurts, then I know I'm awake.'

"The nun dunked a cookie in the tea. Slowly. Perhaps it was the first time I met a grown-up with absolutely no impatience. 'And what do you think about that?' she asked.

"I told her I wondered: What if the fact it hurts is something I'm dreaming too?

"I don't think she answered me. But when we were going to leave she walked with us out to our bicycles. They had real rubber tires, even if it was during the war. The circus had a stock of wheels on hand for the trick cyclists.

"The woman stroked my head. 'If this was a dream,' she said, 'would you want to wake up?'

"'Only if I was sure my mother and father would be there,' I said.

"She laughed quietly, in a friendly way. I didn't understand why she was laughing. 'You're welcome to come back again,' she said. 'Whenever you wish. You can come with Karen.'

"But I never went back. Until I took you with me to the church on Bred Street. To see her. The nun. Mother Rabia."

# 4

He woke up; someone was sitting on his bed. He thought at first it was his mother. But it was the African.

"How long have I been here?"

"Fourteen days. You've had a high fever. The bullet wound became infected. You've been given penicillin. The infection is improving."

He didn't ask about KlaraMaria. He could hear the tension in her system. Next to the bed was a folded wheelchair.

"A signal," he said. "A sound, once it's sent out, never stops. It goes out to the most distant parts of the universe. Perhaps it changes its form, from mechanical vibrations to heat waves to light, but the impulse continues. I can hear other people, certain other people, even when their bodies are somewhere else. It seems as though part of their sound is within the audible frequency field. Another part is ultrasound. Another is infrasound. And some of the sound is non-physical. I can hear KlaraMaria. She's under a lot of strain. She's at the limit of what her system can stand. Even hers."

"Nobody can hear so far away."

"Separation. She's afraid of separation. From all of you. From me. From something I can't identify. Maybe they want to take her away."

The African could not grow pale; her skin was too dark for that. But he could hear the life drain out of the surface of her skin.

"The police can do nothing more," he said. "You people can do nothing more. But I can do something. With your help. We'll need to take a little trip away from here."

"You're confined to bed."

"Help me get into the wheelchair. People have achieved great things from a wheelchair. Hawking, Ironside. Ireno Fuentes."

She was no longer there. Two other nuns had taken her place.

Far away he heard the sound of the great pulse. Perhaps it was his own. He sank toward it.



KlaraMaria was sitting with him. At first he thought she was real and he felt very happy. She must have escaped. Then he noticed that she was sitting on a church pew. And there was no pew in his sickroom; it must be a hallucination, a memory. But sometimes it is precisely the memories that keep us alive.

She sat with her profile toward him. As she had sat the third time he had seen her. The third, and next-to-last, time.



It had been two weeks after her second visit, after his first meeting with the Blue Lady. He had gone to Bred Street, to Nevsky Church. The church was locked; a plaque on the door said the building was open only two days a week for visitors to the church, the Russian library, and the bathhouse. He had gone there again the following day. At first he was the only visitor. A man with white hair and beard and a thick Russian accent had shown him around the church.

The acoustics had a softness that was very unusual for churches; he felt an urge to recommend it be included in Beranek's *Concert Halls and Opera Houses: Music, Acoustics, and Architecture*, which was—along with Eckehart—his favorite reading, a kind of acoustic pornography filled with profound sweetness. The old man who guided him exhibited a spirit of gentleness unusual for men. But also weariness.

On the way out, Kasper heard the silence.

"Who is in the building besides us?" he asked.

The man's face was expressionless. Kasper repeated the question.

"Nobody. Just a child."

Kasper walked back through the church. KlaraMaria was sitting far up near the altar. Her eyes were closed. He stood behind her for perhaps two minutes.

"Well, Cousin Gus," she said. "What are you staring at?"

———

They had walked back together to the old man. By the door Kasper pulled out a thousand-kroner bill, folded it slowly, and put it in the collection box.

"How is this place administered?" he asked. "Who is the highest religious authority?"

"The church is under the White Russian patriarchate."

Kasper waited. The man looked around. As if to make sure no one else was listening.

"Before the Revolution, the congregation belonged under the metropolitan of Moscow, the head of the Russian Orthodox Church. There's a controversy going on now."

Kasper heard the sorrow beneath the old man's weariness.

"And the other Danish congregations?"

"They've joined other synods."

"Won't they be expelled? Excommunicated?"

The man opened the door.

"The Eastern Orthodox Church doesn't excommunicate. It's decentralized. The patriarch in Constantinople is primus inter pares. But each congregation can, in principle, declare itself autonomous."

"And the Rabia Institute?"

The sorrow and fatigue turned into fear.

"They've chosen a woman as the metropolit. That means they have left the Church. A woman can't rise higher than deaconess. They're in conflict with the Holy Scriptures."

For a moment the three of them stood in the doorway. On the border between Bred Street, with its traffic, restaurants, auction houses, hotels, and glittering prostitution. And a church building that leaned back toward a two-thousand-year-old tradition and a Middle Ages reality that was on the verge of disappearing forever. Kasper found it hard to resist an impulse to pick up the old man and rock him in his arms.

"Thanks for the guided tour," he said.

He had parked on the top level of the parking garage on Dronningens Tvær Street. KlaraMaria walked close beside him. He had always been fascinated by the different ways people walked with someone else. The girl was self-contained as she walked and, at the same time, totally attentive to the rhythms of his system; it felt as if they were singing a silent duet.

In the parking garage they stood for a moment by the car. Beneath them they could see the Nevsky Church dome.

"Our friend," said Kasper. "Little Mother Maria. There must be hair on her chest. Under her push-up bra. She's a politician who has broken away from the party."

The girl looked up at him.

"Big Mother Maria," she said. "And she hasn't broken away. It's the others who haven't been able to follow along."

He heard himself blushing before he felt it. At first he didn't understand why. Then he realized that he had been reprimanded by a child.

They drove north along Strand Road, and didn't say a word until they reached their destination. Outside the grounds of Darf Blünow's Stables and Ateliers the girl spoke.

"I'd like to park the car."

He stopped, pushed the seat back; she sat on his lap. She could just see out the windshield.

She could not reach the pedals. But she had no problem with the gearshift. She must have driven before.

"I'm practicing," she said. "For when you give me a spaceship."

They stopped by the trailer. The car's motor was still running.

She leaned back against him, her head resting against his chest. A deep peace enveloped him, a feeling of both freedom and release, as in the last movement of the "Chaconne." The deep intimacy between them had no restrictions, no relation to physical reality. He thought perhaps it could sometimes feel like this to have a child.

"Will you go in the spaceship with me?" she asked.

He nodded. They let their imaginations play together; it was her delightful little joke. Right now he would have said yes to anything whatsoever.

She pulled back the steering wheel. Then he heard the silence.

It spread spherically around the girl, reached his body, enveloped it, reached the chassis of the car; the chassis faded to a pastel color. He gripped the steering wheel as if to avoid a collision. There was nothing to avoid; the phenomenon was gone, as if it had never existed. But for a moment, an infinitesimal moment, there had been no physical limits, only the silence. That, and the deep solidarity with the child in front of him.

"What was that?" he said.

She got out of the car. Her face was expressionless. He came after her, though his legs could barely support him. He had to speak. Isn't that what we should use words for first and foremost: to preserve reality, so we don't have to see what's hiding on the other side?

"Danish culture," he said, "is full of musical jewels about small boys who ride away on a horse with their mothers. But there aren't many about small girls. Who fly away with middle-aged men in a Lotus Elise."

"I'm hungry," she said.


He fried vegetables for her, cooked truffle rice, added a little cream and a curry blend of fennel and dried onion that thickened the sauce. He had learned to do this from Stina. Each time he prepared and consumed one of the dishes she had taught him he felt both joy and sorrow, as if he were taking part in some sort of erotic communion.

"I want to teach you a song," said the girl.

She began to sing. Her voice was a little hoarse, but she sang perfectly in tune. He stiffened. The song was "Bona Nox." He had taught that to Stina; she had loved it. It encompassed both Mozart's ancient refinement and his newborn innocence. And his love for Bach's fugues.

He joined in; they sang together. Tears came to his eyes, but he didn't understand why. He wept as he sang, his tears dripping into the curry sauce. He listened into the fact that every person will lose everyone else. In a little while the girl before him would be gone, and he could not bear it.

Someone touched him—it was the girl. She reached up and stroked his wet cheeks.

"Actually," she said, "there's really nothing to fear."

———

He had driven her home; it was May and the night sky was still light. They stood outside the fence around the Institute.

"Who taught you the song?" he asked.

Her face became expressionless. He heard the springtime around them. All his life he had loved the heavy, turgid sound of growth. But not now. Now it reminded him of separation.

"What's the opposite of never seeing someone again?" she said.

"Reunion."

She took his hand.

"For us," she said, "there's really no goodbye. Only reunion."

He had no idea what she meant. It was a solemn moment. He was aware of feeling anxious; when you're up high, you get smashed flat if you fall.

"You'll come back," she said. "Mother Maria says you will come. She says she has promised you something. She says you're going to get a carrot. Like a donkey, she says. In order to know what direction you should go."

He grew dizzy with anger.

The girl straddled the fence.

"I've got a carrot for you," she said. "Come back. And I'll tell you who taught me the song."

Then she was gone.

# 5

He was forced up toward consciousness; his hearing was being intimidated by one of the sounds he had gotten too old to tolerate: the outlandish cooling fan of a laptop computer.

The African was sitting in the room in front of the screen.

"Why the Eastern Orthodox Church?" he said. "Why not a little shamanism? Exorcism? Or Catholicism? If you need to have something."

"It was because of the joy," she said. "The Orthodox Church is the most cheerful. The emphasis isn't on the Savior's suffering. It's on the transfiguration. The resurrection. Sanctification in this life. I could tell that from the time I was a child. There were all sorts of congregations in Addis Ababa. The Coptic congregation was the happiest."

He heard a new aspect of her. An entrance to her rich spiritual depths. He would have loved the sound. If he had been feeling better. And if he hadn't needed to clear his mind of bitter jealousy while she was talking. Jealousy at the thought that women can find something approaching complete happiness without involving any man but the Savior. And perhaps not even Him.

"I found something Kain wrote," she said. "On the Web."

At first he didn't hear her. He had tuned into her sexuality. It had the energy of an Olatunji drum solo, of a gnu trampling through the rain forest. How had she survived the first thirty years of celibacy?

Then her words reached him.

She turned the computer toward him.

He was too old for the Internet. Not that he didn't love the sound, a limitless cacophony; it had the tone of the cheapest popular entertainment imaginable performed on a public toilet close to the beaten track. All the sounds in the world. Linked together on the lowest organizational level possible. The con man in each of us adores the Internet.

But to go from there to the point of abandoning natural dignity to acquaint oneself with how a computer works is still quite a leap.

Text sounded onto the screen. He tried to focus, without success. He had always read at a snail's pace. Not musical scores. He could take in six staffs from Beethoven's Concerto in D-Major right from the page. But books were different. Musical notes were the only written language with which he had made peace.

"Read it for me," he said. "Let it be my bedtime story."

She scanned the text. He could hear how she formed a quick overview. Pulled out key words.

"It's a fragment," she said. "The title and introduction are missing. Perhaps the intention was to delete the whole article, but that succeeded only partially. It's about warning procedures in Danish waters. A review of Lyngby Radio's NAVWARN; the Norwegian vessel traffic–management information system, NAVTEK; Shippos, the Danish Maritime Authority's ship-reporting system; and Denmark Radio's waterway information service and teletext. A description of changing transit routes through Danish waters. VTS, the Vessel Traffic Service; radar and reporting services in the Great Belt Strait and the Drogden Channel."

He could hear the ease with which she oriented herself in a foreign language.

"There's a description of the warnings that go through the Sea Sport Security Council in an emergency. Duties of the buoy service. Authority of naval officers, in particular the scope of their maritime policing powers. A review of assignments for the Coast Guard's MHV 951 cutters. The Danish Maritime Authority's responsibility for safe navigation during rerouting of all traffic from the Sound to the Great Belt. Procedures for transferring key personnel to the Naval Operations Command in Århus. Guidelines for maintaining traffic separation for vessels in the Great Belt. Assessment of the strait's capacity to handle a shutdown of the Sound. And so forth; it continues for fifteen more pages."

"What is it?" said Kasper.

"It's a memorandum," she said. "Written ten years ago. By Kain. For IMO, the International Maritime Organization. It's an analysis. Of the possible consequences of a natural catastrophe or terrorist act that would shut down the Sound."

He listened into her.

"It must be a secret document," he said. "You didn't find that on the Web."

She stood up.

"You got that from Moerk," he said. "He must have asked you to show it to me. Otherwise I wouldn't have seen it. Nobody ever tells me anything."

She remained standing in the doorway.

"He had good intuition," said Kasper. "Kain. If he was already on that trail ten years ago. Maybe he's clairvoyant. Maybe I'm the only one here who's shut up inside ordinary reality."

She was gone.

# 6

He felt sun on his skin, like a caress. He opened his eyes. They had rolled his bed out into the yard. He half lay, half sat, with his face toward the pond. The water was hidden by rhododendron bushes. His mother had loved that particular plant. Because of its hardiness and fertility. Other men brought their wives bouquets; Maximillian had come home with thirty-five cubic feet of *Azalea diabolica*. Contrary to nature, it had budded and bloomed in the middle of January.

Someone was sitting beside him. It was the Blue Lady.

"We're inspired by the convent gardens in Alexandria," she said. "The principle is—in translation from the Coptic—*hide and reveal*. One always senses the water, the source. But never sees it. It's a kind of spiritual striptease. It's meant to give the seeker a passionate longing for God."

"KlaraMaria?" he said.

Her sound grew dark, affecting everything around them; it was as if a cloud covered the sky.

"We had a telephone call. Heard her voice. And a man's voice. They say she's coming back soon."

"Do you have a tape recording? Can I listen to it?"

She did not reply.

"When I came here," he said, "while they were operating on me, I was very close to saying farewell. It seemed that you were with me. On the departure path. Going to a place *beyond*. Was that a fact?"

"Several of the Church's great female figures," she said, "have said that a sanctified person—that is to say, not insignificant agents like us, but people who have manifested the Divine—can act in three different forms, like three different aspects of the Savior. An acoustic form. A physical form. And as an aspect of love."

"I was raised outside the Church," he said. "Am neither baptized nor confirmed. I don't know how politely one usually speaks to an abbess. But if I could speak candidly, I'd say you're beating around the bush."

They listened to the splashing of the hidden water. He didn't know if he could trust her. Usually one can't trust people. Usually that doesn't matter. This time it was crucial.

"When I was a child," he said, "my mother once took me to the Nevsky Church on Bred Street. She had a conversation with a woman who must have been your predecessor. A woman she must have met here as a little girl."

"That would have been Mother Rabia."

"Many years later I wrote to her. I was sick as a child. For a while I was blind and partially paralyzed. During that time my hearing changed. I had nowhere to go with what I heard. So I wrote to her. Twelve years later I saw my letter again. In the apartment of a woman who left me."

"The letter must have been lying in an archive. She must have gotten it there. Is there anything wrong with that?"

He could not turn his head. But he could tell that she was looking at him.

"Was there violence involved?" she said.

"I was pushed to the breaking point."

"Women rarely like violence."

"Women want to use me. That's my experience. That was the fear it awakened. The fact that she had the letter. Women want something. My money. The fame. The high energy."

"Perhaps," she said, "they just want to be near your modesty."

He managed to turn his head toward her. In spite of the pain. In spite of the electrodes.

She was gone. On the chair where she had been sitting lay a cordless phone.


He got the telephone number for Rigshospital from Information. Maximillian answered the phone.

"Are you in Spain?"

The voice had no volume; there could not be much body left.

"I didn't leave. I'm in the hospital. On a false medical statement. Healthy as a sea eagle."

He could hear his father listening through the lie. He could hear his sorrow. Parents never stop worrying about their children.

"You're on the trail of something or other," said Maximillian. "In Copenhagen, the inner city is owned by pension funds, real estate companies, and private individuals. So far, the pension funds have taken things calmly. That is to say, the engineers' pension fund, the Danish supplementary pension fund, the physicians' pension fund, the lawyers' and managers' pension funds. All their investments are long term, and they've got huge amounts of capital. We're not interested in flagship real estate—for example, the headquarters of banks, insurance companies, and so forth. For the time being, they won't be for sale. The biggest real estate companies are Norden Corporation, Gutenberghus Properties, Jeudan, and Danbo. They and the pension funds have urged the government to help by purchasing some of the damaged property. As the government would do, for example, if dikes had burst and flooding had reduced the value of farmland. The state has gone in and bought an estimated five to ten percent of the inner city and Frederiksstad. The price hasn't been disclosed, but it has undoubtedly been at the officially appraised value. The National Bank has coughed up funds and the Ministry of Justice has made the purchase. That leaves the private individuals, the owners of condominiums and rental properties. I've asked around. People say there have been many sales, some panicky, which was to be expected. But nobody has sounded an alarm; no one has tracked the overall purchases. So I contacted the Copenhagen Building and Technology office to see if they had gathered data on inquiries. Before setting a price for a piece of property in the inner city, one would investigate existing development, the condition of the foundation, and possible pollution, even in a situation like we have now. The Building and Technology office has been terribly busy. It's had inquiries from all sides. So I kept probing. From my deathbed. All transactions are registered with the Municipal Records office. Of course, your old father has a direct connection to the land registry in the Municipal Records office on Hestemølle Street. It turns out that twenty-seven companies have systematically bought up property since September last year, three foreign and twenty-four Danish. In no instance was the price disclosed. But we're talking about billions of kroner. Perhaps fifty. Perhaps a hundred. The price was determined before the rent catastrophe. Around Strøget Street it was about two hundred seventy thousand per square foot. Now comes the interesting part. I forgot about the foreign companies for the moment. And telephoned the central business registry. In Denmark we don't register who owns companies. But there needs to be a managing director and a board. I wrote down those names. Along with the date the company was established. So listen to this. The twenty-four Danish companies were founded during the month of September last year. And all the board and managing director positions are held by the same twelve people."

Kasper's heart beat faster. The more rapid pulse sent a wave of pain through his head.

"Don't they have to pay tax on their profits?" he asked.

"They don't have to report any profits. Denmark has the right to tax income from real estate transactions. But not from the sale of companies. Our twenty-four companies bought the property for two billion, perhaps. But it's not the property that was sold. It's the companies. For sixty or a hundred billion. There's just one thing they need to avoid. Any evidence that there was a previous agreement about the deal before buying the companies."

Kasper tried to think.

"And that's not all," said Maximillian. "Though you'd hardly believe it, I still have some friends. One of them, a woman, is on the supervisory board at the Copenhagen Stock Exchange. I gave her the twelve names. Without saying where I got them. Asked her if she knew them, if she could think of anything that connected the twelve people."

Kasper knew what was coming. But no empathetic artist would take from a partner in the ring the joy of bursting the balloon.

"All twelve are—or have recently been—on Konon's payroll."

"Kain," said Kasper. "With his past experience in the navy and with the Navigation and Hydrography Administration. He'd know something about floods."

"And about how to operate in catastrophic situations."

"The dates," said Kasper. "What are the dates when the companies were established?"

He could hear the paper rustle.

"Between September second and September twenty-fourth."

There was a silence. In the silence Kasper heard his father's shock; it started at a single point, at an epicenter, as a tone of intellectual awareness and from there it expanded into a sphere.

"Good God," said Maximillian. "That means . . . that they knew the earthquakes would occur."

## 7

Kasper awoke to the song of the Sirens, the "Ride of the Valkyries," in a churchlike mode. He had no idea where he was, perhaps in hell. He stumbled into the darkness and fell against the night table. Reality returned and found him lying on the bare floor, tangled up in cords.

The singing was filtered through perhaps ten feet of masonry and must have come from more than two hundred feet away. It sounded like there were between twenty and thirty women, and their intonations would lead one to believe they were on their way to Brocken Mountain. His watch lay beside him. It was three o'clock in the morning.

He ripped off the electrodes. Held on to the bed. And managed to get to his feet. For the first time in more than two weeks, he stood up.

He made his way over to the washbasin. Turned on the light above it. His electric shaver lay on the shelf. Along with shaving cream and a razor. And the leather strop to hone the blade. All laid out with wisdom and care. If one's mother had done it, one would have been happy. But his mother had been dead for twenty-eight years; she hadn't lived long enough to see him shave.

He shaved himself slowly and thoroughly.

He faced himself in the mirror. Every man who shaves wishes a woman would watch and evaluate the result. In his case, it was eleven years since anyone had watched him shave. Stina had been the last one. Since then the only observers had been the dressers at the theater.

There was someone now.

It was the Blue Lady. She was leaning against the door. He hadn't heard her arrive. He looked down at her feet. They weren't animal pads. They were bare feet in sandals. With nail polish. Clear nail polish. A gloss. The singing grew more powerful.

"The canonical hours," she said. "The second matins. From three to four in the morning."

He rinsed off the last foam with cold water.

"Two things," he said. "Will you look and see if it's smooth enough to enter Paradise?"

Her hands were cool, with a fragrance of something that might have been sandalwood.

"It's fine. And the other thing?"

"Why are they here? The women. What does it give them? Being up at this ungodly hour of day. Greek mantras. Wool directly on your skin. Ugly pictures of pale young men on a cross. Total obedience. What does it give them?"

She walked in and closed the door behind her before she replied.

"Love," she said.


She pulled the wheelchair forward; he sat down in it. She seated herself across from him. They listened to the singing. No normal hearing would have been able to pick it up at this distance. But he knew that hers could.

"You'll come to understand," she said. "Why she disappeared, and also why she had the letter."

He didn't know how she could have known that. But he trusted her. Because of the tone of her voice. He could hear the expert knowledge. The world is filled with people who express themselves about things they don't understand. It was different with her. His trust felt like physical tension that pulled at his wounds.

"They were hard on you," she said. "Those last two days. Before we brought you here."

He could tell that a great performance was on its way. He had thirty years of experience in hearing beforehand that great performances were about to begin. But this one was without curtains. Without music. Without lights. Without an audience. Without blocking. Something came creeping up from the large orchestra pit. It was anxiety.

"They aged me," he said. "Those two days. They aged me fifteen years."

"On the other hand, they were certainly predictable, weren't they?"

He didn't believe his own ears.

"Wasn't it just a series of repetitions?" she said. "The same meeting. With the same two people?"

He listened into her system. There was nothing to hear. Body sounds, of course. But there was no sound of the mind. No whisper of thoughts. No aggression. No purpose. She was quiet, like complete absence.

But she was not absent. He met her glance. He tried to create a mental picture of her body. It was as solid as a cliff, as a block of bedrock. And at the same time, it was frail, like a flame that a draft can extinguish in an instant. His hair stood on end.

"In those two days," he said, "I met more people than I can remember. And I was in mortal danger. Everyone has been tracking me. Because I'm trying to save a child's life. And fulfill an agreement. It's been a series of nightmares. So what are we talking about?"

"Hasn't it just been a series of variations on a very simple theme?"

He stared at her.

"A man and a woman," she said. "To provide some variety for you, they are found in two versions. Those who help children. And those who harm children."

With great resistance, he listened to the two days in slow motion. He heard the meeting with Brodersen and the blond woman. Moerk and Asta Borello. Maximillian and Vivian the Terrible. Lona Bohrfeldt and the men around her. Kain and the woman in the sauna.

"In a few instances they may have been separated," she said. "So you met the man by himself, the woman by herself."

He heard Daffy. Franz Fieber. Stina. Sonja.

"But still, quite alike," she said. "With you, or against you. But otherwise quite alike."

"It wasn't only meetings," he said.

She nodded.

"There was escape. Into freedom. You're a refugee. And there was forced entry. Intrusion. You're a seeker. But always in the same tracks. How many essentially identical barriers have you gotten past in basically the same way?"

He heard the sound of Little Jack Horner at the tax office. The angel in the booth at the barricaded area. The Bad Mother at Lona Bohrfeldt's clinic. The entrance to Taarbæk Sanatorium. Women who guarded telephones. Who guarded the Map and Land Registry. He heard the officer behind the counter at Slotsholm Island. The man in the glass booth at Konon.

His anxiety became concrete, became fear. Panic-stricken fear, panic-stricken and deaf. Fear of being shut in.

"It was like that only for those two days," he said. "Otherwise my life has been as varied as a painter's palette."

He heard his voice from outside. It belonged to a person he didn't know.

"I've done five hundred performances," he said.

"But they were all quite similar, weren't they?"

He looked her in the face. He had never seen such a look. It was absolutely calm. And absolutely alert.

"That's all right," she said. "We all try to camouflage the monotony. But it takes a lot of energy. To insist on being special all the time. When we're so much like one another anyway. Our triumphs are the same. Our pain. Try for a moment to feel what relief there is in the ordinary."

He looked at her. She was transparent, like a watercolor. As if she were about to dissolve in sound, in tones not yet created.

He heard how few themes there were in his life. How few strings there had always been to play on. He let them go.

It was silent around him. Within him. More silent than it had ever been before.

The door began to open. The door to the great music. He knew she could hear it as well.

"That door too," she said, "even that will become monotonous in the long run."

He let go. He was behind the concert stage. In the wings with SheAlmighty. There was a hole. In the sound wall. Silence flowed through the hole. For the first time ever, his hearing had peace.


He did not know how long it had lasted; there was no extent to the moment. Extent in time requires that a metronome ticks, a pendulum swings. The moment had been silent.

"What did you do?" he said.

He couldn't make himself look straight at her.

"In a way, nothing," she said. "Played the silence game."

He looked at her after all. She smiled. Her smile sounded the way Ella Fitzgerald sang. The sound of a playful child, but also of timeless maturity. Was she an old woman or a very little girl?

"Mother Rabia," she said, "my predecessor and teacher, often said she experienced people as being trapped inside bubbles. One or two tiny little holes were pricked in the bubbles. And only through those holes could the bubbles connect to one another, only through them could people communicate and experience reality. Those holes ensure that we always experience the same few basic situations. Each of us carries around our own reality. But we have very little contact with other people's reality. Now what was the reason you never answered her letter?"

He did not say anything.

"The desire to be something special," she said, "is very strong. In all of us. It doesn't matter that life is painful. If only it's a special kind of pain. But when you meet someone who is wiser. Who listens more deeply. Then you risk having to put your specialness into perspective. Was that it?"

"That was part of it," he said. "But I was also afraid. That it would . . . weaken my hearing."

He could tell that she understood him.

It had gotten light outside, though he hadn't noticed the daylight come. He heard children's voices, children and young people. He got goose bumps.

"They aren't ordinary children," he said. "I've seen them stop time."

The voices came nearer; they were below the window. He recognized two of them, which couldn't be true. All the same, he put on his glasses and rolled the wheelchair over to the window. Beneath it were permanent tables and benches; the children were eating breakfast outdoors.

The closest child was the boy from Slotsholm Island. With water on his brain. One year older. But the same boy. In the child's shirt pocket Kasper saw the predecessor of his fountain pen.

His fear returned. He could feel sweat running from his armpits and down his sides. The other sound came from a group of children farther away. A big boy was serving them—hardly a boy, a young man.

His voice was husky, deep-throated like those of the boys in the St. Annæ choir. It was the boy from the Rungsted Hotel.

"I know two of them," he said.

"That must be a coincidence."

"I'm a card player. I know the odds of coincidence. This is outside those odds."

She sat where she had been sitting the whole time.

"Simon," she said. "He goes to the daycare center where you picked him up."

He shook his head to ward off her words.

"He was waiting for you," she said. "Not that moment. But sooner or later. All of us were waiting for you. Among the things I learned from Mother Rabia was that the tenacious people, those who lead, will come to us sooner or later. One can just wait for them."

"And the other youngster. The tall one. He served me at a hotel."

She shrugged her shoulders. Stood up.

He felt furious that she wanted to leave him. At this moment.

"We've just started," he said.

She shook her head.

"What we were looking at was a glimpse of the silence. Not a lexicon about the mysteries of life."

If he could have risen he would have grabbed her.

"You're a great egotist," she said. "In my opinion, that's positive. A great egotist is a great sinner. Great sinners have the opportunity for great remorse. Remorse is a springboard."

She drew down one shoulder of her smock. He stared at a piece of lacy black material, probably silk.

"I grew up accustomed to a degree of affluence," she said. "I could never live with wool next to my skin."

He managed to preserve his centeredness.

"And what about everyday life?" he said. "Two children have disappeared."

All humor drained from her face.

"That," she said, "is even worse than you imagine."


The African brought some soup and sat with him while he ate.

"Most things," he said, "are outside our control and in the hands of SheAlmighty. If a child disappears, or comes back again. Whether it lives or dies. Perhaps in the end we can do nothing either for or against it. But if we're going to be able to endure looking at our own powerlessness, there's one thing we must have done. We must have done our utmost."

He did not reach her; her mind was closed. She gathered up his dishes. In the doorway she paused.

"I'll get a car," she said. "Tonight."

"How about a bottle of Cognac? A couple of glasses. Some painkiller, a little morphine for when I have to perform?"

# Part
# Six

It was all over in three hours.

She arrived just after midnight, helped him into the wheelchair. The elevator took them down into a parking garage. He counted twelve parked vehicles: two four-wheel drives, the ambulance he had come in, another ambulance, a trailer truck, two pickups, a station wagon, three Volkswagen Polos, perhaps for the nuns' power shopping, and a delivery van.

Sister Gloria lowered the delivery van's lift, pushed him onto the platform, hoisted it, wheeled him into the van, and secured the wheelchair. Franz Fieber sat behind the steering wheel.

The garage door must have had a sensor or a remote control; it glided up by itself. Outside, the night was like a wall. The wrought-iron gate in the fence opened, the vehicle's headlights caught wisps of fog.

"We have three hours," said the African. "After that, somebody will begin to wonder about us."


"You said you had a driver," said Kasper, "who had a boat."

Franz Fieber wrote something on a small tablet under the icon, without taking his eyes off the road. He reached back and handed the piece of paper to Kasper.

Kasper tried to dial the number, but wasn't able to; his hands were shaking. He pointed to the number and the African dialed for him. He had to push the bandages aside to get the telephone to his ear. It took an eternity before the phone got answered. By a large person.

"This is Fieber's big brother," said Kasper. "Fieber says you have a boat you can have ready in fifteen minutes."

The man gurgled into the receiver.

"Get a doctor! It's the middle of the night!"

The motive for our actions doesn't lie ahead of us. It's something behind us that we're trying to escape. The voice on the telephone had memories of disappointment and abandonment. It had protected itself against those memories with material things. The words came from a fleshy body in a huge house.

"It pains me," said Kasper, "to think that you could have kept your job. And been ten thousand kroner richer."

They were driving along the Bispebuen highway. The telephone receiver was silent. Perhaps it was all just imagination. And the man was about to hang up.

"In cash?"

Kasper took the Institute money out of his bathrobe pocket and held the bills up in the light from the highway. He counted twenty bills. With a picture of Niels Bohr on them. The quantum mechanic had large bags under his eyes. It must have been hard on him. To live with a saint's heart and intelligence. And yet have lent a hand to the bomb.

"In slightly used five-hundred-kroner bills," he said.

He heard a lamp get turned on, the bed groaned, something heavy growled. His wife or the Rottweiler.

"The harbor is closed at night," said the man.

"Have they really managed to convince a true sailor that the Sound closes at sunset?"

They entered Åboulevard Avenue.

"The Kalvebod pier," said the voice. "Diagonally across from the sluiceway."


They drove past the central railway station and the main post office. Then turned south along the harbor and past the new fish market. When Kasper was a child there had been coal storehouses, houseboats, and manufacturing industries here; now there were shopping centers and nightclubs.

They passed the H. C. Ørsted power plant and Belvedere Wharf. He hadn't been here for ten years. When he was a child 250 cutters had been moored here, and there had been community gardens where people lived year-round. Now there were bowling alleys, mixed-use housing, and porn-film studios. A number of the small and medium-size circuses had stayed here; he remembered several winter seasons in South Harbor. At that time, the city had ended here, and southeast of the Zealand Bridge it was all tundra. Now there were golf courses, a soccer stadium, gas stations. Three houses he remembered from those days had been designated as historic landmarks and now stood inside a fence on the golf course grounds. What is one to think, that in half a generation we have gone from the jungle to the zoo?

"When I was a child," he said, "this area was the seedy side of the city. Now it's all respectable. I don't understand it."

It's always nice to have an audience. But he was speaking to himself. He had not expected an answer.

"The seedy side is intact," said the African. "As much as in those days. Or more. It has simply put on makeup."

He was seized by anger he did not understand.

"How," he said, "has an underage nun who grew up in the bush acquired such wisdom about the shadowy sides of life?"

She leaned over, kicked away Franz Fieber's leg, and jammed on the brake. Kasper was almost jolted out of the wheelchair and thrown through the front window. Franz Fieber was white as a ghost.

She pulled the medallion over her head, handed it to Kasper, and turned on the overhead light. Kasper saw a photograph of two children and a man on a green lawn. The children were arms and legs and wild, white smiles. The man had a gentle mouth and a look that salted the gentleness.

"I'm thirty-five," she said. "I have a husband and two children."

The silver medallion was warm against his hand. It had her fragrance. He knew that somewhere in the tropics there must be a plant that exuded precisely this aroma in the midday sun.

He turned over the flat piece of metal. On the reverse side were engraved two Zulu shields, two crossed Asagai fauna, and the words FIRST PAN-AFRICAN AIKIDO CHAMPIONSHIP.

"I'm becoming more and more attracted to the life of a nun," he said. "Can one aspire to that?"

They parked opposite two shallow basins between two piers; at the end of one pier they saw some movement; otherwise everything was quiet. Sister Gloria wheeled him onto the lift and set him down on the ground. She pushed him slowly, calmly, across the road, and toward the pier. There was no traffic. He loved the night. When he was a little boy his mother had read to him—not often, because there hadn't been time or extra energy, but sometimes. She had read *Palle Alone in the World*. He had heard the silence in the book. Behind the drawings, behind the words, behind the book's apparent loneliness, he had heard the refreshing silence in a city where everything is at rest.

He had the same feeling now: that the city around him was completely quiet. And that a capable female presence moved him forward.

On the farthest cement bollard sat a man wrapped in a horse blanket. Already halfway out the pier Kasper knew he had seen him before, seen him or heard him.

The Beet stood up, but his turquoise eyes gave no sign that he recognized the figure in the wheelchair. It would have been strange if he had; Kasper was bandaged like a mummy. The man was the person who had operated Stina's boat outside the National Bank an eternity of fourteen days ago.

"If we're going inside the barricaded area," he said, "it will be five thousand extra."

Bohr looked even more debilitated under the sodium lights. Stina had once told Kasper about Einstein's opposition to the quantum mechanic's theories of probability. Like all great poker players, Einstein had a sense of the limits of random chance. To meet the Beet here in South Harbor was outside those limits. Kasper shuddered a little. For a moment he had a sense that SheAlmighty was playing with a marked deck.

He opened the Cognac, the African handed him two eyecups; he managed to pour despite his trembling hands.

"Sister Gloria and I," he said, "live at the same convent. Monks and nuns are separated by a grill. For a whole year we've looked at each other through that grill. We can get out only for tonight, which is her eighteenth birthday. So we'd like to celebrate alone."

The man looked at the bandages. At the plaster cast. At the wheelchair.

"That's five thousand extra. As a deposit. I'll return it when you get back."

Kasper put on his glasses. Counted out half the amount. Not without difficulty.

"We'll leave the boat in there," he said. "Nyhavn Canal. No risk for you in that. And I'm sure you remember how it was to be eighteen and in love."

The man stared at Kasper. Kasper raised his glass for a toast.

"To the Savior," he said. "The first toast is always to the Savior."

Sister Gloria laid two aluminum planks from the pier to the gunwale, and wheeled Kasper onto the boat.

"It's a Yanmar," said the man. "How are you going to get it started?"

The nun opened the engine compartment, set the choke, opened the compression release, turned on the ignition; the engine started. She released the clutch, put it in gear, gave it gas, and the boat slowly glided past the man on the pier.

Kasper raised his glass.

"She took the boiler-attendant exam," he said. "Before she studied to be a doctor. But after she had recanted her eternal promises. And graduated to black belt."


The boat glided out of the sluiceway; the harbor channel widened.

"We trained back there," said Kasper, "when I was a child. The smaller circuses that couldn't afford real winter quarters, they camped here or in North Harbor. When spring came, at lunchtime we would go down and sit on the pier by the spice warehouses. I had a dream, a daydream, then and for many years afterward. An image that came by itself. I imagined I'd have children, I'd show them where I had lived and worked. It was always this harbor I saw in my mind. And one day I'd stand with them in the stern of a sailing ship gazing in toward South Harbor, and we'd be on our way to some distant place. And there would be a feeling of great freedom."

"Was there a woman too," asked the African, "in the dream?"

He thought about that.

"No," he said. "It was, in fact, just the children and me."

They passed Teglholmen and Tømmergraven appeared to port; they neared the barricaded area. A nylon net hanging from a cable attached to orange buoys had been stretched across the channel, interrupted only by a boom beside a platform with a small shack on it.

He recalled the other barriers he had encountered in his search for KlaraMaria. He thought about the Blue Lady. He knew he was seeing something projected from his own mind. The knowledge gave him a brief feeling of deep serenity.

He thought about the man whose boat he had now rented, another instance of something that was both a hindrance and a help on his way toward the quiet girl. He looked at the African opposite him, who was yet another manifestation of feminine nature. He could feel the repetitions; he was trapped in tonal repetition, a form of erasing the tape. But for the first time in his life, he knew it. Freedom would come through this knowledge; he could hear that.

"We'll be stopped," said the African.

He listened. There was no one in the shack.

"We're on a nonviolent mission for SheAlmighty," he said. "We have the cosmos with us."

She helped him out of the wheelchair and into the bottom of the boat; she lay down on a thwart. The boat glided under the boom. There was no one to be seen on the platform; they were in Gasværk Harbor.

"Why didn't you have any children?" she asked.

To his amazement he heard himself telling the truth. Or the tiny bit of the truth that can be expressed.

"Maybe I never believed I'd have enough stability to be able to offer to a child. I knew I could do something for children for half an hour or forty-five minutes. In the ring. Under the lights. But maybe I wasn't really suited to anything more than that."

"Was there ever a woman?"

"Only once that was serious. And that was very brief."

One must be careful about being honest. Suddenly he heard the loneliness close in around him. He felt her listening. He could tell that at this moment she heard and understood his system.

"Even with children one is often alone," she said. "Even in a family. Children change very quickly. There's no stability. One is constantly reminded that in a little while they will be gone. I've been away for a month this time. When I come home in three weeks, they will have changed; it will be as though I'm seeing them for the first time. As if they are strangers. In everyday life too. Perhaps it's true that love is eternal. But its appearance changes all the time."

Just ahead of the boat was a fog bank; they sailed into it.

Lange Bridge emerged from the fog. It was closed. But a car was parked by the HK building. When your driver's license has been revoked in two European countries you instinctively keep an eye out for the man with a camera. Kasper found him on the bridge, on the walkway next to the control tower. The African saw him too.

"They've seen us," she said. "We'll be picked up; the whole area is patrolled by the navy."

Kasper pointed; the boat turned into Christianshavn's canals. Most of the neighborhood had been evacuated, the office buildings were dark, the vacant apartments were dark, the streets were empty. The boat glided under the arch of the bridge below Torve Street. The arch concentrated all sound, since concave surfaces focus sound at a central point; bridge arches are acoustic crystal balls, condensing all the surrounding sounds. Kasper heard the echo from the empty apartments. He heard the sound of water being soaked up through the masonry. The sound of incipient collapse. And some distance away: an incomprehensible sound of the tropics.

On the top floor of the last house on Overgaden Neden Vandet Street, narrow strips of light sifted through the heavily curtained windows.

The rain-forest birds did not sing; they laughed, they screeched, they gurgled. Behind it all one could just make out the towering blue shadow of Kilimanjaro swimming in the mist. At the foot of the mountain, the succulent greenness of the Serengeti. In front of the savanna, the rain forest and the birds. In front of the rain forest, a woman sitting in an easy chair by a table with two bottles of liquor and one glass.

Perhaps she was 95, perhaps 295. At some point in prehistoric times she had merged with the chair; you could no longer tell where the person stopped and the massive piece of furniture began.

Kasper rolled his wheelchair over to the table. He still didn't dare to breathe. The smell was too strong, the smell of death and liquor.

The African remained standing by the door.

"It's mealworms," said the woman in the chair. "For the birds. They crawl under the carpet, where they lie and rot. There's nothing to do about it. Have a drink, dear friend. How did you find your way here? Who's the little black sweetie?"

The room could have been light, the air could have been fresh; there were six windows facing the canal. But they were covered with shades and curtains.

"I'm the son of Maximillian Krone."

"Can you prove that, dear friend?"

The skin on her face was as lifeless as that of a wax doll. One mottled gray eye stared blindly into the jungle; the other was black and intensely alive. It examined Kasper's passport.

The room was vast, but inaccessible. The jungle was contained in large ceramic pots placed on synthetic felt carpet before a photocopy of the African scene. In front of the plants were the table, the chair, and a stand for grow lights. Flitting around the plants were at least a hundred birds. The remaining two-thirds of the room was filled with a dense mass of paper and cardboard. Rows of books, photograph albums, bundles of letters, newspapers, postcards, file boxes, catalogs, oil paintings, and posters were stacked and stuffed from floor to ceiling.

"This is only one third," she said. "The rest is in the Royal Library's archives. Also films and videos. There are fifteen hundred hours of film."

"You knew my grandmother."

She held a bottle with both hands and pushed it toward Kasper; he shook his head. She poured some liquor into the glass. First from one bottle, then from another—green and yellow chartreuse. She mixed them in equal amounts.

The glass was narrow. But what it lacked in diameter, it made up for in height; it was as tall as a flower vase. Perhaps to shorten the long way from the table to her mouth. If it was to go down fast.

It was to go down fast. She drank like a dockworker, poured the liquid down without swallowing. Then she set down the glass and smacked her lips.

"One should be good to oneself. Especially when one is alone. Henry died ten years ago."

On the floor Kasper could see how good she was to herself. Two rows of bottles were carefully lined up, like props before a performance, twenty-odd bottles of each color. Her brain must be pickled in alcohol and sugar, like a green walnut. He would never be able to connect with her.

"Your grandmother was among the thousands of 'Vienna children.' They had a special passport around their necks. In Austria they would have died of hunger. She came to Denmark in March 1920. In the same shipment as Ilona Wieselmann. Who made her debut in *Cradle Song* at the Royal Theater when she was eighteen. One of Ernst Rolf's numerous female acquaintances. Married Aage Stentoft. Who wrote that song 'Your Heart Is in Danger, Andresen.'"

The birds had become quiet. A new sound began to fill the room. The sound of an extraordinary memory that had been activated.

"Your grandmother was taken into service. In an embroidery shop. In the town of Ærøskøbing on Ærø Island. That sure as hell didn't fit the young lady. It was undoubtedly some kind of forced labor. The first winter she walked across the ice to Svendborg on Funen Island. At that time the circus included a musical revue. Inside the tent. She traveled with one of the actors in the revue. There's a picture of her from those days. She's wearing a coat, half sheep's wool and half camel hair, ugly as an accident. The coat, that is."

A bird landed on her shoulder, an Amazon parakeet, a fifty-thousand-kroner bird, enameled blue, gold, and red. It cooed; she answered it with an identical sound from deep down in her throat. It laid its beak against her hand.

"I know what you're thinking, dear friend. You're thinking: 'Why doesn't she find herself a new friend. To go walking with in Deer Park?' I'm only a good eighty years old. But you say that because you're so green. You haven't experienced a great love. It can never be like with Henry. I can't even have his photograph up. The big one, from '52, taken by Peter Elfelt's studio. It seems to call to me. The psychologist said I should put it away."

"Was there anything to do with religion? Anything with the Orthodox Church?"

She dipped her finger into the glass and held it up to the parakeet. The bird licked off the liquor with a grainy tongue.

"The police asked me about that too. The answer is no."

She drained her glass.

"They didn't pay anything. The police. I have very large expenses. I'm collecting things for a museum. It's the world's largest collection. Normally I charge four thousand kroner. If it's something I can respond to here and now. If you also want to borrow a photograph, that's an extra two thousand. If a book comes out of it, I must be given credit."

He took out the envelope with the rest of the Institute's money.

"Was there anything to do with training children?"

"Nuns don't travel with the circus. Let's see the money."

He counted out the bills on the table.

"I didn't mention nuns," he said.

Her hands felt the bills. He recognized her tone, the tone of an artist. She was a sister. In spirit.

"Several of the children had gone to convent schools. During the winter. When the circus wasn't traveling around. No problems in the East. No enmity between the Church and the circus. The children stuck together when they came to Denmark. Kept contact with the

Russian Church. There was a woman who got them together as a group."

The black eye gave him a blinking look.

"There may be a picture," she said.

He put another bill on the table.

"Try the middle aisle."

He rolled his wheelchair into the mountain of papers. The middle aisle was an opening in the piles. Her voice followed him, penetrating as a bird's shriek.

"You are now by a signed portrait of my very, very close friend Charlie Rivel. The albums begin just to the right of him."

There were six shelves, continuing into a distant darkness. There must have been at least a hundred feet of shelving.

"One of the first albums is red with gold printing."

The volume was as heavy as an illustrated Bible; there were bird droppings on it. He laid it in front of her.

She could have found the picture immediately, but she did not do that. She paged through the album slowly. Through an endless series of carefully pasted black-and-white photographs signed with unreadable signatures. Men with their arms crossed and waxed mustaches. Women who could have gone into the ring against a sumo wrestler and one would not have bet even five øre on the wrestler.

"She got them together on Sunday. There was some sort of convent outside the city. In Bagsværd. Maybe it's still there. She ran into trouble. Had to give up. Sunday isn't a day off for artists. And what did she want with them? She ran into trouble with the foster parents."

Kasper's eyes scanned the photographs. He listened into them. Into her voice. He heard the passage of time. The history. It was a diminished tone. Most events leave only the faintest echo; the people in the pictures were dead, lived now only in the mental archive in front of him. And in a little while she would be gone too.

"Was there anything special about the children?"

Her tone shifted. The dust of time left it. He had tuned into something that wasn't the past. Something that was the present.

He placed another bill on top of the small pile. She licked her lips.

"I'm not so old. I was a little child. But there were rumors. Persistent rumors. People said some big tent owners paid some of the children. Just to be present. During the performances."

She pushed a bottle toward him.

"Would you be so gallant, dear friend? I have osteoarthritis."

He poured. She spoke to the African.

"You've found yourself a nice piece of meat, sweetie. Even if he's in a wheelchair."

She took a big drink.

"I've seen them all. From Erik Truxa and before. Illusionists from other countries too. It's all skilled craftsmanship. There's no magic. But still, some of the children were paid. People said that whenever the children were there, the circus tent was full. The tickets were sold out. No accidents in the ring. That's just superstition, of course. Artists are superstitious. Two of the girls died. One traffic accident. And one drowning. There were rumors. That they were murdered. Jealousy. On the part of other managers. There are always rumors. But still, as Henry always said to me: There are only two things that can make people commit murder—sex and money."

Her fingers stopped at a picture.

"There can be an atmosphere around a person. Like around me. The birds love me. And men. Men and birds. They've fought to come sit on my lap. Maybe it was an atmosphere. Around the children. I can remember some of them. From the late fifties."

Kasper drew the album over to look at it. The picture was taken in what might have been a community garden. Sunshine. Summer flowers. Twelve people around a table on a lawn. At the end of the table, a woman in a nun's habit. Tall as a giraffe. Mother Rabia. Beside her, a younger woman. The tone rang out from the photograph as if it were a DVD with a sound track. It was the Blue Lady. As a twenty-year-old. Already with a powerful tone. Like the young Bach. Still close to Buxtehude. But the great motets are waiting ahead.

Seated around the table were women and men in their forties. And a boy of about ten years old.

Kasper put his finger on the boy. He heard a refined sound. Like that of the young Beethoven.

"Boras's heir," said the woman. "Disappeared."

The boy's hands were lying on the table. Not the way children's hands usually lie. Alive. With awareness right out to the fingernails already. It was Daffy.

"What was the rumor?" he asked. "What was it about?"

She cleared her throat. He placed his last bill on the table. The atmosphere in the room was magical. True intimacy is always fleeting. He could hear that she had kept silent about this all her life. And he could hear her pain over that silence.

"It was said that one time the woman called together the foster parents. As well as the parents of some of the other children in the group. And she told them the children had a chance to do something. Sort of the way one can do something in the circus ring, she said. The circus ring is kind of a holy place. Where at times something divine happens. When the artists are trained. And brought together. And the lights go on and the music plays. And God's grace appears. In a similar way, the children could do something. Children and certain adults. If they were trained. And brought together. She didn't get through to them. Maybe they didn't believe her. And think of the times. The twenties and thirties. Poverty. The Danish mentality. Spiritualism. Exorcism. She had to let the children go. Which was a good thing. It was just entertainment."

Kasper gazed into the black eye in front of him. He recognized the woman. She was the Oracle of Delphi. She was one of the volvas. She was the witch from "The Tinder Box." The old Fury who struck Hakuin to the floor with a broom. The hetaera who knocked down Marpa.

He wanted to tell her about that. To tell Sister Gloria. But perhaps this wasn't the right time.

"Josef Kain?"

She shook her head. But her sound nodded.

"The woman said a person can become like God," she said. "And can meet God. Is that true?"

Today even oracles are searching for the ultimate answers. He pointed toward the jungle.

"Your little bird has gotten caught."

She turned like lightning. Now only the blind eye rested on Kasper. With a smooth unhurried movement he retrieved his money from the table. Divided the stack in two. Laid half in front of her.

"For your sake too," he said. "We need to find an amount that's acceptable to both your heart and mine."

The black eye grew evil.

"You're a damn fool," she said. "With bad taste. When I was a child, Negroes were something we exhibited in a circus. Behind bars."

Kasper did not see the African move. One moment she was standing by the door, the next she was leaning across the table. One hand held the Amazon parakeet, the other gripped the old woman's neck. The two women looked at each other.

"Will you accept an apology?" said the woman in the chair.

"What about Kain?" Kasper asked.

The black eye was afraid. Generally none of us reaches the point where we want to die; we all want to live, no matter what our age.

"There's a rumor," she said. "They say someone went in and tried to buy up several of the medium-size circuses. That name was mentioned."

Kasper took a final look at the picture. One of the men stared into the lens as if he were ready to give someone a beating. Kasper pointed to him.

"This is in black-and-white," he said. "But someone who knows men as you do, you would be able to remember if these eyes were blue."

"Turquoise," she said. "Like a lagoon in the Pacific."

"And you would be able to remember a little about the man."

"Gert. Suenson. Navy. I remember the first time I saw him. In Tivoli. He was passed out drunk on the bar at Wivex. In his white naval officer's uniform."

The African straightened up. Let the bird go.

"Was it true?"

The old woman had whispered. Kasper heard her longing. The longing that can be heard in all people. But in most people it's shoved into the background. With her, it suddenly filled everything.

"It would be quite different," she said. "To be about to die. If one knew there was love on the other side."

Kasper rolled his wheelchair backward.

"The hell with the psychologists," he said. "Put Henry's picture back on the table."

# 3

The African pressed the elevator button, but the panel did not light up; the electricity had gone out. She helped Kasper out of the wheelchair to start walking down the stairs.

He heard the outside door from Overgaden Neden Vandet Street open, and a moment later, the door to the stairway. The African put down the wheelchair and gave him a thoughtful look. They hadn't seen anyone coming here.

Kasper enjoyed the sound of movement up the stairs. Most people walk up stairs as if they want to be done with it. As if it's a kind of exercise one would prefer to do without. The man coming up toward them moved leisurely, pleasurably, resolutely, almost soundlessly.

He rounded the corner; it was Kain. He had climbed six flights of stairs, but his breathing showed no sign of it.

He stopped short when he saw them.

Kasper did not take his eyes off him. He listened to Sister Gloria. Her sound showed no recognition. She had never seen him before.

"Kain," said Kasper, "is a fellow member of the Naval Officers Club. While you hoist sail and ready my life jacket, he and I will exchange a few words."

The African looked from one man to the other. Kasper could hear the conversation between her mind and her instincts. They told her that something was wrong. Nevertheless, she obeyed.

The door at the bottom of the stairway closed behind her.

"The police said you had been sent to Spain," said Kain.

Kasper handed the folded wheelchair to Kain. Took hold of the railing. Gave the businessman his free arm. Kain took it. They began going down the stairs, slowly, very close to each other.

Kasper felt the other man's body tremble slightly; his own did as well. He sensed how dangerous Kain was. He knew that he was closer to death now than he had ever been in the ring.

"I can save you the trip upstairs," said Kasper. "You and I should be able to do business. I've talked with her. The bird lady. I got a little background information. What I know, I'll tell you. In return, you'll tell me a little about the children."

Kain's hair had been trimmed very short. To repair the crew cut on the back of his head. An attempt had been made to remove the henna, but it had not been completely successful.

Kasper increased his weight on the other man's arm imperceptibly.

"In the twenties the Russian Orthodox nuns in Denmark get an outstanding leader, Mother Rabia. She must have been what they call an extraordinary mind. She has an idea of training children. She starts among artists. Perhaps because many artist families go to the Orthodox Church. Which has a lay order. Perhaps because after World War One many Eastern European children who had attended convent schools came to Denmark."

"What did she want to train them to do?"

"She had the idea that, under certain circumstances, small groups of children and adults could raise global compassion. Send out a signal to the heart. Is that crazy?"

Kain did not reply. They stopped on a landing by a tall window. The pane was a glass mosaic, the windowsill just above knee height. Kasper knew he could toss the other man out through the window. And they were on the fifth floor. He could hear Kain's mind deliberating over the same thought.

There were two chairs on the landing. To allow residents of this home for the elderly to rest their degenerating legs if they walked up the stairs.

"In a little while," said Kasper, "you and I will complete the course of our lives. Perhaps in the same psychiatric nursing home. Sitting in a couple of chairs like these. There we'll meet all the flowers we've trampled. Also the crimes we've committed against children."

"They weren't kidnapped. The girl came to see me. She offered a deal. I was to find the other eleven children. And bring them here."

Kasper listened into the other man's system. Perhaps he was telling the truth.

"What did you get in return?" he asked.

Kain did not answer.

"Mother Rabia wasn't successful," said Kasper. "Someone started exploiting the children economically. For money, instead of for compassion."

"Does it have to be 'instead of'? Can't it be 'both . . . and'? I'm very fond of your recording of the solo partitas. For Bach it was 'both . . . and.'"

They descended another floor, in silence.

"Everything could end here," said Kasper. "End happily. You bring back the children. And the money."

Kain laughed quietly.

"It will end happily anyway."

"What did the children want?" Kasper asked.

"The world will discover that. In due time. It has to do with compassion too. It's very beautiful."

"KlaraMaria had been hit. When she came to see me."

Kain looked at his right hand. Kasper could hear that the man was shaken somehow.

"They're extraordinary children," he said. "And it follows that they're also extraordinarily apt to invite a smack in the eye."

Kasper listened into the resounding tone beside him. Kain was truly moved. In the coherent aspect of himself. The other aspect was pushed to the side for the moment.

"You and I," said Kain. "We could achieve something together. I've assembled a very special circle of people. Who are my contacts to the children. I have a huge business operation. We could earn money. And help the world go in the right direction. Come and join me."

The stairwell spiraled down before Kasper's eyes.

"Think about it," said Kain. "I'll give you my telephone number."

Kasper automatically held out the lottery ticket. The other man had a kind of magnetism; you couldn't resist him. The ticket was about to be filled up; like the major-minor tonality that could hardly last longer, the dance card was about to be oversubscribed. Kain wrote down his number and handed back the ticket.

He took out his handkerchief. Wiped his nose.

"I get emotional easily," he said.

"I can see that," said Kasper. "Do you cry all the way to the bank too?"

The other man's sound changed. They stood together at the brink and looked down into the abyss.

"I operate from a societal point of view. I'm the best thing that's happened to those children in a long time. What happened to the girl was an accident. It will never happen again. All of this is extremely demanding. It's a phenomenon unlike anything the world has ever seen. The children need to be helped. Helped and guided. And I can do that."

Kasper heard the hole in the other man's system begin to open. The healthy side of his personality got tuned down. And something else took over. He realized he was about to lose control himself.

"I've listened to many people," he said. "And right now I can hear that you'd be a real find for any madhouse."

They grabbed each other simultaneously. The door opened. The African stood in the doorway. Behind her stood the stocky man with the hearing aid. Ernst.

Kain let go of Kasper. Walked around the woman. Kasper shouted. Kain turned around.

"In two weeks," said Kasper, "I'll come to visit you in jail. And trim your hair."

**4**

Kasper unfolded his wheelchair. Sat down in it. The stocky man just stood there. His nose was bandaged. But with just a thin bandage. Fate must have brought him to the right plastic surgeon. Kasper rode over to him.

"You and I, Ernst," he said, "we're the strong silent type. Who use roundabout ways to manage things."

The man walked ahead of him. Out the front gate and down the sidewalk. Kasper wheeled himself alongside. Ernst looked at Kasper's stomach. At the spot where he had seen the bullet enter.

"I always have my illustrated Bible stuck in the front of my underwear," said Kasper. "It lessened the impact."

There was no echo in the other man's system. No sense of humor. That makes a clown's job harder. But not less important.

"There's a place, "said Kasper, "where the lungs end. And the kidneys and liver and spleen haven't yet begun. It went through there. Next time you should aim a little higher."

Ernst nodded.

"I'll remember that," he said. "I will definitely remember that."

A very small helicopter, like a large fish bowl, was waiting on the bridge at the end of St. Annæ Street. Kasper saw Kain open the window in front of the cockpit and get in. Aske Brodersen was in the pilot's seat.

The building behind Kasper and Ernst had been a café; the windows were broken, but there were still tables and chairs on the sidewalk. The man sat down on a chair.

"What did you cut them off with?" said Kasper. "The girl's fingers?"

That was to open the other man's system, and it succeeded. Kasper began to hear him; it was not a pretty sound.

There was no yielding; what Kasper heard was fearlessness.

There are two kinds of fearlessness. The first is the fearlessness of lovers, of mystics, the courage from *Die Kunst der Fuge*. The courage that comes from having opened up completely, totally given of yourself and not held back anything, and now the world streams into you and fills you, and you know that everything is safe and there will never be anything to lose.

The man's courage was something else. It was what comes from having found the life-giving source and shut it off once and for all, so it's worthless now. Therefore, even if life is at stake, one is calm, because there isn't really anything to lose.

Ernst looked at Kasper.

"You're not upset about it," he said. "I'll give you that."

"Why?" said Kasper. "Why kill her?"

One of the things that characterize those of us who love danger is our attraction to situations where we have left the farthest outposts of reason behind us and have entrusted our fate to what we call chance.

"I loved her," said Ernst. "So I had to do it."

The instant the words were spoken Kasper heard the love appear. Not worldly love, not the longing for sex or money—those longings are vague and weak compared to the feeling that resounded for a moment around the man beside him. It was a deep inner longing, a craving for the Divine, that he heard.

"She had it. And she wouldn't give it to me. What was I supposed to do?"

For a moment, a world stood open. A continent. In the middle of Overgaden Neden Vandet Street. Beside the abandoned canals and crumbling buildings. The mad world of those who have tasted a little of the great silence, and now cannot get the next drops. Kasper thought about the Savior. At around this time He had been busily preparing for His resurrection and return to earth. After the disciples had betrayed and deserted Him, after He had been tormented and crucified.

Kasper looked at Ernst. He knew he was listening into aspects of the special feeling a spiritually fulfilled person awakens in her admirers, even if that person is a child.

Then Kasper heard the other man's sorrow. It was far away, out near the borders of the Milky Way, twelve incarnations in the future. But it was immense; it could easily have enveloped Christianshavn and the whole surrounding area. It was the sorrow of one who has committed an offense against his deepest longing.

"Please wheel me over to the boat," Kasper said.

Ernst stood up, pushed Kasper over to the canal. The African was standing at the bulwark. She and the man watched each other intently, like a cobra and a mongoose. But Kasper could not determine for certain which was which.

Sister Gloria rolled Kasper onto the boat. She started the motor. Above them the man leaned forward. He cut the air with two fingers.

"With a wire cutter," he said.

# 5

The boat passed under the bridge that connected Christianshavn with Arsenal Island. The sea channel had disappeared in gray clouds.

The African helped Kasper onto the aft thwart and put the tiller in his good hand. She opened a stow space. Pulled out a rain poncho, a sou'wester, work gloves, wristlets, a flat liquid compass. She laid the compass on the thwart; the fog came and went.

He felt her calmness. He thought about Grock. About his Inez. Who had stayed by him her whole life. Backed him up. Loyal as a lapdog. Brutal as a bodyguard. Solicitous as a nurse.

Why had he never succeeded himself? In finding the right woman. Gentle. Patient. Loyal. Why were the women in his life Furies? Like his mother. Like Sonja. Like Stina. KlaraMaria. Like Sister Gloria. Women who were slack-line virtuosos. Mechanical experts. Hydrologists. Monster children. Martial-arts nuns with husbands and children.

A gust of wind opened a corridor in the fog. At the end of the corridor lay what must be Pylon 5. Three-stories of aluminum and wood, rectangular, built on a cement landing platform that had been part of Bornholmer Wharf before the earthquakes. The building was protected against new earthquakes with steel wires, like the guylines on a tent. A forest of antennae and two rotating radar sensors were visible on the roof. Tied up by the platform were two of the navy's low, dull black speedboats.

Kasper gave Sister Gloria the tiller. Put the wristlet on his healthy hand. Took his violin out of its case. They glided along the bridge piers under Christian the Fourth Bridge.

"Everything is guarded," she said. "We'll have to turn around."

He tuned the violin. He could suddenly hear what he had to offer women: his motivating force. No woman, of her own free will, steers into the Danish Frogman Corps arrayed only in her indomitable optimism and Partita in E-Major.

A searchlight went on.

"May I rest my cast arm against your shoulder?" he asked.

He closed his eyes and began to play, all the while speaking to calm her.

"The military loves music," he said. "Some sort of music is always played when people fight. But until now they've chosen the wrong pieces. They should have thought about Bach; they could have avoided bloodshed. Music like I'm playing now leads straight to a cease-fire. To legal mediation rather than lawsuits. We'll be inside shortly."

He leaned into the music. It opened the heart the way one opens a can of peeled tomatoes. His own heart, the guards' hearts, Stina's. He knew she had come out onto the platform.

The boat glided along the tires hung on the platform as bumpers. It was quiet all around them; the closeness of the fog and the music created some of the intimacy that can be lacking when one plays outdoors. It gave one the feeling that there was a concert hall extending around the Foreign Ministry, the bridge, the platform, and the National Bank.

Sister Gloria laid down the aluminum planks. At first there was no life on the platform, then two guards moved, like robots. Kasper was pulled up onto the cement.

Standing next to Stina was a young man in civilian clothes who had a sound like a brass orchestra. Kasper had heard that sound somewhere before. Stina's eyes were drugged with the music. They stared at him. At the wheelchair. The planks. The plaster cast. The Egyptian bandaging. At Sister Gloria.

"Five minutes," he whispered. "It's a matter of life and death."

Slowly, her soul worked its way up to the surface. Then she got her breath.

"Never!" she said.

He pulled out of his bandages the receipt for the registered letter that had contained KlaraMaria's drawing. Stina read it. Grabbed for it. It had disappeared.

He nodded toward Sister Gloria.

"She's from the Morality Squad," he said. "You can invite me inside. Or we can talk further at police headquarters."

# 6

The elevator was made of Plexiglas. The young man tried to squeeze himself in, but there was only room for four, and the wheelchair took up space for two. Kasper blocked him discreetly, the doors closed, and they sank into the depths. Because of the difference in pressure, all sounds are displaced when one moves downward. It was a normal situation in view of the fact that he was with Stina. With her it had never been very long before one was headed down below or up above the normal range of the register.

They passed a communications room, where people wearing headsets were sitting at digital switchboards. The elevator stopped. He let Stina go out first. As Sister Gloria wheeled him forward he stuffed two fingers of a work glove into the groove of the elevator door catch. It would block the electrical contact and delay the young man on the platform. It's good for young people to learn to postpone gratification.

They went through a small cafeteria; Kasper hastily took a dinner plate from a stack. You never know what you will have use for; haven't we all learned that from "Clumsy Hans"? Everything was quiet behind them, the elevator blocked.

They entered a beautiful room, large and rectangular like a gymnast's Reuther board, but packed like a spaceship. One wall was covered with flat screens showing ocean surfaces. Another with ten three-foot-square meteorological overview maps. Radar display consoles. Some thirty feet of granite slab holding perhaps fifty seismographs. A dozen barographs, the largest as big as the Danish Class Lottery's revolving drum. Three rows of computer tables. Sitting at the computers were young people with bodies for a tawdry music video and heads for a Ph.D. in Riemannian geometry. The remaining wall had a six-foot by twelve-foot aquarium window opening onto the harbor; the ocean floor was illuminated. In spite of the sludge, Kasper saw schools of fish.

The room had a dense sound, of ventilators, of megabytes, of swarms of numbers, of murmuring liquid-cooled processors. Kasper had a sudden feeling of joy. He stood in the twenty-first century's answer to the bridge of Captain Nemo's ship. He loved science. And it didn't matter that science did not love him. There can be great depths of love that are not reciprocated.

Stina looked at his bandages.

"I've been at a meeting," he said, "with a couple of individuals who have kidnapped KlaraMaria."

She braced herself against the granite slab.

"She's been gone for more than two weeks," he said. "The prognosis is poor for little girls who disappear for more than twenty-four hours. So I was wondering if you could help me."

Stina turned around mechanically and walked ahead of him along the row of monitors. She sat down. The African pushed Kasper's wheelchair to face her.

This was her workplace. There was a bottle of Italian mineral water. A hyacinth in a Pyrex distillation flask; if she had received it as a gift, he didn't want to know from whom. Three short carpenter pencils, sharpened with a knife. Next to them lay the knife that had sharpened them. A basket of braided birch bark for the shavings. A small jar of moisturizing cream.

It was a desk like all other desks. Ten square feet of laminated wood. Nonetheless, it had an atmosphere that made the visitor want to set up camp. It had her aroma; he breathed it in.

"We're part of a web," she said. "We have connections to the Seismic Station in Uppsala, to the Institute of Solid Earth Physics in Bergen. To all the NORSAR seismological observatories. The British Geological Survey in Edinburgh. European-Mediterranean Seismological Center stations in Nice and Madrid. We have a seismic station on the Vestvold embankment. Another in the lime mines in Mønsted. Directly beneath us we have a measuring well, twenty-three hundred feet deep, drilled and installed after the first tremors.

In it are seventeen hundred sensors. In the next room we have more equipment than San Francisco. RefTek recorders. Meissner seismographs. The army detonates eleven hundred pounds of dynamite for us each week, and the vibration is collected by eight hundred geophones. So we can measure the movement of pressure waves underground. We measure stress fields. Elastic pressure changes in the earth's strata. Local changes in magnetism. Groundwater changes and deformities in a square-yard net that stretches from Dragør to Farum. We have four biologists to observe changes in the behavior of small rodents in the woods around Copenhagen. Testing a Chinese theory—that animals react to earthquakes before they occur. We have a flying squad from GeoForschungsZentrum in Potsdam. I have a hundred assistant geophysicists, engineers, and technicians. They handle six million measurement results each day. Twice a week one of our geodesists with popular appeal appears on all the television channels and talks about the progress we've made toward understanding the situation. About the likelihood of new earthquakes. About the risk that large parts of Copenhagen and Zealand might need to be evacuated."

Someone must have removed the work glove. Kasper heard the elevator go up.

"We've put forward a series of possible explanations. Tomorrow evening I'm going on television to summarize them. This is what I'll say: Like Iceland, Denmark is headed southeast in a conditional geologic system. But we can go no farther; Africa is headed north and is pressing on Eurasia. The alpine collision zone is about to shift toward the north. This has created an explosion in the crystalline crust. About two miles beneath Copenhagen. The area where the explosion occurred is surrounded by a layer of heavy rock, similar to the Silkeborg anomaly. That prevented the pressure wave from spreading. Which is why the earthquake wasn't registered anywhere else. The only harm that occurred is the superficial collapse. We have reason to believe that there will be no further quakes. It's difficult to predict earthquakes. We have no guaranteed methods. We can't measure stress accumulations at great depths. We don't know what the earth's surface can withstand. Nevertheless, we're confident. We remain vigilant. But we see nothing to indicate that it should be necessary to evacuate. We don't think there will be further real earth-quakes. That's what I'll say tomorrow evening."

"That will be reassuring," he said.

She leaned toward him. Under different circumstances he would have enjoyed every inch. But not now.

"Yes," she said quietly. "And that's the intention. But there's just one thing wrong. And that is: It's a lie."

For a moment Kasper's peripheral hearing had failed; during his lack of attention, the young man from the platform had reached them.

"He is to be deported," the man said to Stina. "He was supposed to have been flown out of the country."

Kasper now recognized him; it was Moerk's page.

"Lieutenant Colonel Brejning," said Stina, "is responsible for our security."

The officer stepped in front of Kasper.

"There's a warrant out for his arrest," he said. "He's violent."

They did not look at Kasper. That was careless. You should not take your eyes off great clowns. He still had the dinner plate. From a tray under one of the whiteboards he took a wooden pointer, spun the plate in the air, caught it with a nail delay, centered it on the pointer, set the pointer on the desk, and moved the wheelchair for-ward. The young people and the African watched the whirling gyro-scope as if hypnotized.

He wheeled himself in front of Stina.

"We'll take him with us now," said the officer.

Behind Stina and the officer, the lively kitchen exploded; the plate wasn't earthenware—it was real porcelain and you could hear that the moment it broke into a cloud of ceramic splinters.

The instant the officer and Stina turned around, Kasper opened the top drawer of her desk. She had never locked anything, not then, and not now; she had a blind trust in the world. Unfortunately, such trust is not always well founded.

On top lay some kroner bills, under the bills a small pile of handkerchiefs that smelled like lavender. Under the lavender lay an old acquaintance. From a three-inch-square black-and-white photo-graph in a plastic pocket KlaraMaria stared up at him. He stuck it in-side his bandage and closed the drawer.

They turned around and looked at him. The young people looked at him. The African looked at him. Nobody thinks that a man in a wheelchair, wrapped up like a sausage, has any vigor. The situation dissociated into unreality. In this limbo the clown functions well.

"Could we be alone, please?" he said to Stina.

The officer shook his head.

"There are things," said Kasper, "a man can do for a woman only in private."

Behind Stina was something that looked like a sluice door. She pushed it up and stepped inside. The African lifted Kasper and the wheelchair over the doorsill; it was twelve inches high. She came in too. Closed the massive door as if it were cardboard.

"Brejning is from the Intelligence Service," said Stina.

"That's why I'm so nice to him," said Kasper. "We must try to help talented young people in the next generation have an easier time growing up and maturing than we did."

The space around them was like a huge broom closet with an industrial sink, water vacuums, shelves of cleaning materials, and narrow metal tables bolted along the wall. The walls were light-colored granite, as in a luxurious bathroom.

"This is the beginning of the basement," said Stina, "under the National Bank."

He took out the plastic pocket, removed the photograph, and laid it on a table.

"There was no earthquake," she said. "Not at any time."

Love has something to do with recognition. We can be fascinated by the unknown, we can be attracted by it, but love is something that grows, slowly, in an atmosphere of trust. From the first time he saw Stina, on the beach, he had heard it repeatedly, confidence and trust; it was there now too. But there was something else, now as then, which was strange, insurmountable, like an unexplored continent. It hadn't diminished with time.

"We felt the earthquake ourselves," he said. "At the restaurant."

"We felt a vibration in the earth's surface. Locally."

"But the big earthquakes. Eight on the Richter scale. I read about them in the newspaper."

"The Richter scale is a measurement of the combined energy discharge. The sum of a series of locally variable constants, plus the log-arithm multiplied by the oscillation amplitude measured on the seis-mogram divided by the number of oscillations. But there was no amplitude. No oscillation in the earth's crust. The two huge events were not earthquakes."

"Collapses, perhaps?"

"A collapse is uneven. It starts at one point and spreads exponen-tially. These were absolutely even movements."

She took hold of his lapels.

"The so-called fault zone. It's a rectangle. Five thousand feet by over two thousand feet, plus a depression through the whole Nyhavn area. Straight. Horizontal."

Her face was right in front of him. She had a tone he had never heard before. An amalgam of wonder and desperation.

"An earthquake is a sudden shift in the earth's crust, plus the consequences of the shift. Primary waves followed by ring-shaped secondary waves that cause the damage. In these instances, there was no explosive displacement. One moment everything is normal. The next, a seven-hundred-by-five-hundred-yard rectangle sinks ten feet. And is covered with water. And stands still."

"Holes in the lime?"

"Cave-ins are uneven. They don't go off according to a brick-layer's line. They don't end horizontally."

Someone pounded on the door. He laid the postal receipt in front of her on the table, on top of the photograph. Addressed to her. And signed with a ten-year-old girl's surprisingly steady hand. He wasn't sure she had seen it.

"Even so, we could perhaps explain ourselves out of it," she said. "That's how natural science works. We predict events backward. I'm sure we would have succeeded. If it hadn't been for the number of victims."

"No one was injured."

"True. No one was injured. What do you make of that?"

"It was a great blessing. One feels the hand of God."

She stopped short.

"That's new," she said. "In your vocabulary. About the hand of God."

"I'm growing. Developing rapidly."

He could hear the concentration in the next room. Someone was getting ready to do something vicious to the door. He thought about the Blue Lady. He could hear that one of his life's refrains was about to repeat itself: Just when one is establishing deep contact with feminine nature, the collective unconscious outside the door prepares itself with an angle grinder and a large diamond blade.

"Too great," she said. "The blessing, that is. Too fortunate. We asked the police, Civil Defense, and the Accident Investigation Board under the Council for Greater Traffic Security what the predicted consequences would be. We asked them to calculate the expected loss. Based on material from UCLA, which has experience with earthquakes in large cities. The estimate we got: at least ten thousand dead. Three times as many injured. Damage to the cable system, one billion kroner. To the sewer system, one billion. Ten billion in damage to buildings, primarily from fire and collapse. The first depression caused a ten-foot pressure wave. It cleared away sidewalks and streets along the canals. Dragged with it eight hundred fifty vehicles. More than a hundred fifty feet of roadway on Knippel Bridge. It glided along eight hundred buildings. With more than thirty thousand people in them. And nobody was hurt. Not a single baby drowned. Not one person had a car accident. Not even one old woman's corns got trampled."

The door began to vibrate. Powerful forces that wanted to prevent the prince from getting the princess had begun cutting.

Stina picked up the plastic pocket from the table; on the back of the photograph was a child's drawing.

"I got it two days before the first tremors. In a letter. Registered mail."

The drawing was colored very carefully. Kasper saw a castle. With three towers. Fish in the moat. Houses and cars. A baronial castle. A drawbridge.

"It's the new Foreign Ministry," Stina said.

He could see that. The steps. The bridge. It wasn't a bridge across a moat. It was Knippel Bridge. The castle wasn't a castle. It was the large white building on Amager Island that people called the Desert Fort. The city wasn't a city, it was part of a city; the area around Bremerholmen Harbor. She must have had a model, perhaps a map of Copenhagen. In the right-hand corner she had signed it *KlaraMaria. Ten years old.* And a date. *September 24.* That was unusual. He had seen thousands of children's drawings. Sometimes they had the year. But never the specific date.

The preciseness of the drawing was unusual too. There had been the same preciseness in the depiction of Lona Bohrfeldt's clinic.

"It's a map," said Stina. "It's exact. When you examine it closely. There's the National Bank. The Svitzer maritime services headquarters in Nyhavn. The Admiral Hotel. The rigging sheers. The dry docks.

She brought her face close to his.

"It's a map of the first depression," she said. "Exact, in every detail. And mailed forty-eight hours before the event occurred."

A new sound came through the door, the hiss of a compressed-gas cylinder. The angle grinder now had the company of a cutting torch.

"We're going to leave now," said the African.

She opened a door that led to a smaller room with yet another door, and opened that too; a stairway seemed to fall forward into bottomless darkness.

Kasper tried to pull himself together, to listen, but his hearing was out of order. He felt like a child, an infant in swaddling clothes. He chose a prayer to the Virgin Mary, leaned into the prayer, and left the practical things to Mother.

The African picked up a telephone on the table and called someone. Kasper heard Franz Fieber answer on the other end.

"And then pick us up on the surface," she said.

"The photograph," said Kasper. "In your drawer. We don't have a scientific explanation of that."

She had always hated to be asked for explanations. To be asked for appointments. She hated everything that seemed to threaten her freedom.

"She came to see me."

"Where?" he said. "I—your counterpart, your soul mate—haven't been able to find you. How would a ten-year-old girl be able to do it?"

The African hung up the telephone. Stina walked over to the door by the stairway.

"This leads down to the metro," she said. "Via a sewer system and the main cable conduit from Havne Street to Holmen."

They carried him down the stairs, pushed him along an underground canal, lowered him down a skid. He had put an arm around each woman, well aware that yet another existential monotony was about to set in. But an unbroken stream of healing vitality emanates from femininity. Precisely in his situation, during a period of convalescence, this healing quality was crucial. Bach would have done the same.

They came out into the metro tunnel. It was illuminated by emergency lights, the rails covered with water. Stina knelt in front of the wheelchair.

"This is the last time," she said, "that the two of us will see each other."

She ran her fingertips gently over his wounds and stitches. Over the swollen parts of his face. The touch was so careful that there was no pain. Already back then, before she disappeared, when she touched him he had felt that the greatest performances were not those on a podium or in the ring. The greatest performances were when fingertips took away a very thin veil between people and uncovered the universe in its entirety.

"It's usual," he whispered, "for severe illness and injury to precede a great breakthrough in love."

"It's usual," she whispered, "that a person who can't learn has to feel."

For most of us, our relationship to our beloved is expressed in a particular piece of music. Mahler used one of the adagios when he proposed to Alma; for Ekaterina Gordeeva and Sergei Grinkov it was the "Moonlight Sonata"; for Kasper it was the "Chaconne." He heard it now, in the water dripping from the walls, in the echo in the tunnel, in the African's breathing. She took his pulse without slowing down and without saying anything, but he could hear her concern. He drifted in and out of consciousness.

They went through an unlighted area, she pushed him up a skid, opened a door, and wheeled him out into the dawn. They were at Nørreport Station. There were people around them, a growing number. He had always avoided crowds of people; a crowd has too many sounds, which was one of the reasons he had stayed with the circus. Had stayed in the ring. Had stayed with music. A performer tries to synchronize everyone else's sound with his own system. When his performance as a silver clown won at the circus festival in Monte Carlo the first time, after the award ceremony he had walked slowly from the Grand Palais next to the big state casino down to the ocean. Nine out of ten people he passed had recognized him. He had wondered if this might be another way to solve the problem. If only you are famous enough, if only you are the king, if only your signal is strong enough, then you drown out all the others.

The next twenty years had pared down that position, especially the last five years. He had realized that in a large gathering neither the virtuoso nor the king is safe. It's only if you are anonymous. As he was now. Nobody looked at him, and if anyone did, it was to understand why a princess like the African had taken the stable boy out in a wheelchair.

Somebody whistled three notes, a pure, broken C-major chord; he was the one whistling. That's the drawback for those of us who are victims of our own charisma. He was wheeled forward onto a lift, hoisted up, rolled into place in the delivery van. Franz Fieber sat in the driver's seat.

"I, who am childless," said Kasper, "was about to develop a love for you that could be compared to what a father feels for a son. Until a little while ago, when I got some information that makes me think I've caught you in still another lie. The man whose gondola Sister Gloria and I borrowed, the man with turquoise eyes and a complexion like a tournedos, isn't one of your drivers. He's a naval officer. Who is connected to all this."

Franz Fieber hesitated. Kasper drew his wheelchair closer to the front seat. The young man edged away.

"Gert Suenson," said Fieber. "He's from the Navigation and Hydrography Administration. He's connected to the lay order. He's responsible for all the traffic in and out of the barricaded area. He has helped the police. In the hunt for Kain."

Kasper closed his eyes. It's terrible to be shut in, regardless of whether the cell is called a circus ring or the generally accepted version of reality.

"We haven't had breakfast," he said. "Is there any espresso left? And a drop of Armagnac?"

His consciousness phased out on its own; he tried to tune into the sound of his absence, and then he was gone.

# Part Seven

He woke up in the hospital bed in his cell. The Blue Lady was sitting on a chair by the head of the bed.

He had a headache that made the combined hangovers of his entire life mere hypochondria.

Something tugged at him from deep down; he was dragged beneath the border of alert consciousness. He could hear someone singing; it was Stina.

All the women in his life had sung: his mother, Stina, Klara-Maria, the nuns, Sonja, the Police Women's Chorus; there was no end to the delights. All he needed was the Blue Lady. To make the cast complete.

Stina laughed toward him. He realized it was a dream founded on actual events, and chose to remain in the dream; he was not yet in shape to confront reality.

She sang as she had sung back then, spontaneously, with no announcement. She had gently drawn him backward and laid his head in her lap. Then she had touched him. Had stroked his skin, and sung.

It had been the classics, pop singers like Kim Larsen and Shu-Bi-Dua, the great operas. Her voice was husky, lingering; he wished Rachmaninoff, and brain researchers Larsen and Bundesen, could have heard her. They would have felt completely understood. She glided over into the "Jewel Song" from Gounod's *Faust,* "Am I awake, or is my head whirling in a marvelous dream?" She hummed Rachmaninoff's "Vocalise." She sang like Renée Fleming. With only a semitone span. But just as effortlessly, she adapted the melody on the spot.

Her fingers against his skin had followed the music. He had begun to understand what the Savior meant by saying that God's kingdom is here and now; her touch and her voice created a Paradise on earth all around him.

He flowed into the feeling of being a child. He heard his own tonal space, it was 90 percent feminine; he felt like a woman, utterly receptive.

He heard the momentary relief of not having to be only a man. Not having to persevere. To keep things going.

He felt the love in her fingers. Right now, for a brief moment, he was accepted. For the sake of his honest face. For the sake of his clear blue eyes. For no reason at all. Just because he existed.

Perhaps love begins when it is all right, both for another person and for yourself, to be the way you are. Even if you are named Kasper. And have told women, including the one touching you right now, so many untrue stories that you no longer know where SheAlmighty's reality begins and your own fabrications end. And even if you have crossed so many boundaries that you no longer know if you can find the way home.

His legs had itched. To run away. From the unbearable knowledge that there was almost a 100 percent probability that a moment like this would never come again.

She modulated to "Bona Nox." Her voice was both affectionate and protective.

He felt the silence open. Like a great hand that was preparing to pick him up. He opened his eyes. The Blue Lady leaned over him. She wiped his forehead with a damp cloth.

"You've slept for twenty-four hours," she said. "You will survive. Again."


He expanded his sense perception. The surroundings were only faintly audible, almost gone. He knew that was due to the presence of the abbess. He had experienced the phenomenon a few times before, first with his mother, and several instances with Maximillian. With a few partners in the ring. Then with Stina. With KlaraMaria. He had turned forty before he dared to fully believe it. That hearing is collective. When the contact between two people intensifies, the outer world first grows fainter, and then begins to disappear altogether. Because for these two people at that moment, all that exists in the universe is the other person. This is what began to happen now.

A voice whispered; it was his voice.

"They've used her, perhaps also the boy, to predict the earthquakes; the children must have some sort of clairvoyance. They've bought up property in the inner city and they're going to sell it now, soon. They will keep the children alive at least until then. They need her—they need both of them. To make it seem credible that there won't be any more earthquakes. We have to get hold of the police."

"That won't be a problem," she said. "They can be here the moment we need them. You and Sister Gloria were seen."

The morning sun was very low, the color of white gold. The surface of the water was motionless, like tightly stretched tinfoil. The unmoving surface mirrored a second sun. The outskirts of the city were hidden by a narrow band of white mist. All outer sounds were drawn into the woman's listening.

They could have been in any mythological place in the world. She wanted to tell him something, without words, with her silence, but he did not understand.

"You have to eat," she said.


Sister Gloria brought him a tray, soup and bread. He said a short prayer, and then bit into the bread.

"It's good to say grace before you eat," he said. "The prayer allows you to go through a microscopic death and rebirth. You let yourself go into divine formlessness. And then you are re-created and resurrected as a newborn, with all your brain cells and all your taste buds and potency and hearing intact. Ideally, that is."

"Even if an archangel stood before you," said the African, "you wouldn't stop talking."

He took another bite of bread and thought about his mother. The bun was fresh from the oven; its crust was thin, smooth, and hard as glass. The crunch when his teeth bit into it told him that it was baked in a hot ceramic oven after having been brushed with a mixture of yogurt, oil, and sea salt. The smell was deep and complex, like a human body's.

"The first time I was here," he said, "a year ago, at night, you waited outside the Blue Lady's door. Why?"

"Mother Maria asked me to."

"When?"

"Earlier in the day."

It was beef soup; it tasted of eternal life and of the fact that all living beings consume one another.

"Earlier in the day she couldn't have known that I'd come."

"She knew it for years. We saw you on television. That was one of the first times I was in Denmark. Sometimes Mother Maria likes to look at television. Especially circus performances. We saw Cirque du Soleil. She asked who the clown was. One of the sisters said: 'He's Danish.' She said: 'He'll come to see us.' Just that. Nothing else. 'He'll come to see us here.'"

Kasper dipped his bread in the soup. Chewed mechanically.

"Mother Maria," said the African, "says some people think the great composers are saints who allowed themselves to be born among us. To help all of us. Then one can better understand. About Bach."

She was still dazed by the serenade. It was touching. On the other hand, it's important to help people get over their fascination.

"Also the great cooks," he said. "You must have one down in the kitchen. Now will you please leave Grandfather in peace? I need to digest my food."


The Blue Lady was in the room. He hadn't heard her come in.

"A person can't be in the circus for thirty-five years," he said, "without meeting killers. When I listened to the place within them from which the murder was committed, I never heard the killers themselves. I heard possession. By something else. The question of guilt is complicated. In an acoustical sense."

She did not say anything.

He felt his anger rise.

"I've identified him," he said. "The man who murdered the child. I wanted to be able to take him out of circulation. Once and for all."

"There's no doubt you're capable of that," she said.

His anger faded away. Leaving a feeling of sorrow. Of no escape.

"Kain," he said, "studied the consequences of a catastrophe outside Copenhagen. And now we have an earthquake."

"For those who pray," she said, "the number of remarkable coincidences increases."

It took him a long time to turn his head. When the feat was accomplished her chair was empty. She was gone. Had she even been there at all?

The African pushed him through the white corridors.

"I signed a contract with her," he said. "Agreed to risk my career. To try to stop those who were after KlaraMaria. To support all of you. If she knew I would come, why all the stipulations?"

They rode down on the elevator. She did not reply until they reached the bottom and were out.

"Mother Maria," she said, "has often said that it's not good for people to receive the mystery of religion too easily. They can't value it then. Especially bankers."

"Bankers?"

"When we saw you on television, we laughed a lot. Mother Maria too. Afterward she said: 'What we'll find out when the time comes is whether he is fundamentally a clown. Or a banker with special talents.'"

He prayed, "May SheAlmighty let me live long enough to make a voodoo doll and stick the Blue Lady full of pins." Then he realized what he was doing. He leaned into the pain of his anger; half of all anger is directed inward at oneself.

The movement had stopped; the wheelchair stood still.

A flat hand was placed against the back of his neck. Through the touch he felt the warmth, and was filled with gratitude. He could hear that this was the closest the African would ever come to apologizing. And it was almost enough.

They stopped in front of a door, it opened, and she pushed him out into the little park.

# 2

The Blue Lady was sitting on a stone bench, with his violin case under her arm. She stood up and took over the wheelchair. The African left, and the abbess began pushing him slowly along the path by the lake.

The spring light and sounds went into his blood like an unruly wine, like the first glass of a fully matured vintage Krug. The Creator Herself breathes life into great champagnes the moment they fill your mouth, and for years afterward this life returns to your memory, little by little, involuntarily and shockingly, like the aftereffects of a magnificent hallucinogen.

A mild wind rustled what would soon become birch leaves; it played *The Rite of Spring*, yet somewhere within creation's springtime music he heard winter. Somewhere in the champagne taste Angostura bitters lay waiting.

"Two men from the immigration police have come to get you," said the abbess.

She placed the violin case in his lap.

"In great spiritual traditions," she said, "the teacher cannot encourage the student to ask questions. Not even in pressured situations. Not even if one has reached the very last opportunity to ever ask."

Her voice was serious. But deep, deep inside he thought he caught a hint of teasing. He felt actual physical discomfort at this evidence of her lack of refinement.

"It's clear enough why," she said. "The teacher can't create openness in a student. No person can open another person. All we can do is wait. And then work with the openness when it occurs. Isn't that the clown's method as well?"

She stopped speaking. But he could still hear her compassion. It was far-reaching. It extended across Bagsværd and adjacent communities. It also included the teasing—he could suddenly hear that. And it included some rustic coarseness.

She spoke directly into his thoughts.

"Several of the world's religions have gone too far in trying to separate good and evil. Christianity as well. Not that we shouldn't make distinctions. But if the separation becomes too strong, it becomes inhuman. I always liked Leibniz a great deal. In the *Théodicée* he says that God is like a kitchen maid. When she has baked a loaf of bread, she has done her best. And that includes everything. The burned part of the crust too. Evil must also be from God somehow. Otherwise we couldn't be here. As human beings. With our failings. I've always felt that Leibniz was a great *staretz*. We just haven't canonized him yet. If he'd been available, he would have been a man for me."

Her words gave Kasper a jolt. He could have fallen out of his wheelchair. Impertinence is indispensable. But clowns have a patent on it. It doesn't belong within the Church. The Church should maintain the concert pitch. And then the rest of us can take care of the irregular intervals.

The wheelchair stopped by a bench and she seated herself.

"A disposable body," she said. "That's what Mother Rabia called our physical form. It's inseparable from sexuality. No person who still has a physical form is permanently asexual. I couldn't have gone without men. Still can't. And will never be able to."

She laughed happily, like a little girl. Kasper sensed champagne on his tongue. He heard a new sound. It was a deeper level of trust. The sound came from his own system.

"I have a question," he said.

He had opened the violin case and lifted out the instrument.

"It's about the 'Chaconne,'" he said.

He tuned the violin. Then he took a running start, and leaped. Into the music. Meanwhile he kept talking. Half spoke, half sang. Following the music. As if the words were a text to the chorales Bach had embedded in the musical sequence.

"The 'Chaconne' is divided into three sections," he said. "It's a

triptych, like an altar painting. I always knew this music offered a
door into heaven; it's an icon of sounds. That was clear to me from
the first time I heard it. I also always knew that it was about death.
From the first time I heard it, when I was fourteen, just after my
mother died."

The music demanded all his strength; there isn't a single measure in the "Chaconne" where the heading could not be "man or
woman struggles with a violin." Still, he felt the woman's concentration. It was wide-ranging. It drew in the lake and the woods and the
sky, and dissolved them in attentiveness. The surroundings faded
away; all that remained were him and her and the violin and Bach.

"She was the queen of the slack line," he said. "Slack line is the
most technically difficult discipline in the circus. It was the seventies, safety nets were not yet required, and once in a while she performed without them."

His fingers moved more quickly.

"D-minor," he said. "It's about death. Bach had lost Maria Barbara and two of his children. He loved them and her. The theme is a
death theme. Listen to the inevitability, the fixedness of fate; we will
all die. And try to hear how here in the first section he shifts the register, uses quadruple stopping to create the illusion of several violins
in dialogue with one another. They become the many voices that are
within each person, in all of us. Some of the voices will accept death,
others will not. And now begins the long, whirling arpeggio passage;
movement over three or more strings increases the sense of accumulating energy. Can you hear it? One would swear there were at least
three violins."

He saw only her eyes. Her tone had become colorless. Her compassion flowed around him on all sides; he was in an alembic, in a
concert space of complete understanding and acceptance.

"I saw her from the horseback riders' gangway. She performed
without a net maybe twice a year. My father hadn't seen any of those
performances. If she wanted the safety net removed, he left. But I
had always watched those performances. I had always understood
her. It's hard to explain in words. But on those evenings she had a
very special tone. It was completely calm. If you asked me why she
did it, I'd have to say she performed without a net for two reasons.

One was her love for the circus and for the spectators. The circus has always been close to death. There's very little deception in the circus. Very few pieces of scenery. No sloping boards to make the leaps artificially high. No stuntmen, no stand-ins. The circus is an extreme form of scenic honesty, and that honesty was crucial for her. In a way, the circus was an act of love for her."

The music's almost plaintive insistence intensified beneath his fingers.

"The other reason had to do with her deepest longing. She never talked about it. But I could hear it. Could hear the constant tone in her, the inner pedal tone, if you know what I mean. One can hear it in some of the great musicians. Some of the great comedians. Mountain climbers. I could hear it in Tati. In Messner. In your crazy driver. It's the longing for answers to the great questions. The longing for the Divine. Under the makeup. Under the totally artificial makeup. A genuine longing. And for those of us who feel it, it's the finest balance. Between heaven and earth. And that evening, when my mother was halfway between the masts, more than thirty feet aboveground, her sound shifted. And I heard something I hadn't heard before."

He neared the end of the first section, the number of simulated voices at a maximum; he had never fully understood how Bach did it—sometimes he thought perhaps there was not just one "Chaconne," perhaps there was a flowing tonal virtuality that kept multiplying and would never end. Perhaps people are like that—perhaps each of us is not just one person but an endless series of unique constellations in the present, or maybe that gets too complicated? That's the question great improvisers ask: Can we find our way back to the theme and the keynote?

"The longing for the Divine," he said, "for that which can never be completely contained in physical form, had gotten stronger in her. During the previous months. I could hear that. It was a small shift. But crucial. Normally I could always hear the part of her that continually listened for me. For my father. For the rehearsals and cleaning and shopping and food preparation and everyday reality. But at that moment, the volume for that part of her got turned down. And the volume was turned up on something else. I knew it before it happened. That she had forgotten everything else. And remembered only

God. I looked into her eyes. They were distant. But completely happy. And then she fell."

The theme returned, indicating the end of the first section; in the score there is no pause, but Kasper took a break.

"I went over to her. Everyone else was paralyzed; I was the only one who moved. I could hear her sound. Her body was dead. But her sound was alive. It wasn't unhappy. It was elated. This wasn't a mishap. Not from a higher point of view. From a higher point of view she had simply chosen a particular door. In a way, the best door to be found."

He met the Blue Lady's gaze. Her frequency was the same as his. He did not know what suffering life had brought her. But he felt that she knew his pain. And much more.

"It wasn't so easy for my father and me," he said.

The bow found the strings.

"The second section is in a major key. Compassionate. Deep sorrow. It was balm for my soul. Bach had suffered a loss, just like me; I could hear that. And he found a way through that loss. I played the piece again and again. Just listen: The consolation becomes almost triumphant. He makes the violin sound like trumpets. Here, beginning with measure one sixty-five, where he introduces a two-beat bar, he intensifies the fanfare effect by playing the D-string with the third finger while at the same time playing the open A-string. This reinforces the A-string overtones. Listen—it continues to measure one seventy-seven. Here the calm, deep joy begins. The rich use of musical suspension gives the feeling of great longing. He has made his peace with death. You'd think that would be enough. But it isn't enough. Something even greater is on the way. From measure two oh one the spaceship begins to lift off. The second section ends with arpeggio passages, as the first one did. And now listen to the beginning of the third section."

He played the broken chord.

"We're back in D-minor. The same chord that Brahms uses in the introductory theme of his first piano concerto. The 'Chaconne' radiates throughout all of classical music. We're approaching measure two twenty-nine, where it modulates into bariolage; Bach seesaws between the open A-string and changing notes on the D-string. The music mourns but, at the same time, is filled with vitality. Death from the first section reappears, but now in the light of the consolation and triumph and inner peace of the second section. This is music that surges through the ceiling. It's a way of living in which death is always present and yet there are great reserves of strength and energy and compassion. Just listen now, from measure two forty-one. The light of understanding shines through death itself. Bach doesn't only say that one can look at death with wide-open eyes. He does it himself; he does it in the music. What is the secret? That's my question."

"Forgiveness," she said. "The secret is forgiveness. Forgiveness isn't charged with emotion; it's a matter of sound common sense. It occurs when you realize that the other person could not have acted otherwise. And that you could not have acted differently either. Very few of us have a real choice in decisive situations. You've suffered a loss. For which you hold all women since then responsible. Including me."

She was silent. He would have liked to ask about more things. Where Maximillian was headed. Where his love for Stina originated. His love for KlaraMaria.

The questions had already been answered. He and the Blue Lady were standing inside the place where those answers were found. Or on the threshold. She had taken him there. He didn't know who was playing the music, but it was playing; someone or other was taking care of everything. He could see the woman in front of him, but she was quivering, as if she were part of the "Chaconne." He also heard KlaraMaria, Stina, Maximillian. And his mother. Because we are always entangled in a web of tones and feelings of the heart, and within that web it essentially makes no difference whether people are alive or dead.

He put the violin back in its case; someone or other put the violin back in its case.

He got out of the wheelchair, though he didn't understand how; it's true the Bible is full of stories of the deaf who hear and the lame who walk, but it's one thing to hear the stories and something else to experience it oneself.

He sat down astride her, the way a woman might straddle a man.

"Will you let me touch your breasts?" he said.

She opened her nun's smock. His hands glided over her skin. She was at least seventy. Her skin was like parchment and at the same time vibrating with life.

The firmness of the tissue under Kasper's hands reminded him that she had never nursed a child.

"What has it been like," he said, "to never have had children?"

"There was a time," she said, "I must have been around sixteen, when a situation arose between Mother Rabia and me; perhaps we could say it was somehow comparable to your misfortune. It was the sort of situation where afterward nothing is ever completely the same. At that time I got the feeling that all children were essentially mine. That it wouldn't be really meaningful to say that a few children were especially mine based on a frail biological connection. From then on I belonged—I believe—to all children."

Her usual sound and color were beginning to return. The surroundings came back. With them came the African.

She stood waiting politely some distance down the path. Beside her stood a couple of the children. Kasper recognized his partner from Christians Brygge Street, the boy with DAMP syndrome or water on the brain.

He moved back into the wheelchair and rolled himself forward. The African came up behind him.

"Deeply serious students," he said, "have always required particularly intense spiritual guidance."

The children looked at him thoughtfully.

"I think you should tell that to the immigration officers," said the African. "They've been waiting for an hour."

There were five people in the room, besides him and Sister Gloria. The Blue Lady, Moerk, the woman from Strand Road who later had bandaged him at police headquarters, the Beet, with his turquoise eyes. And the well-dressed old man from the Church Ministry, Weidebühl. They sat around the rectangular table at which Kasper had met Mother Maria for the first time. A digital recorder had been placed on the table.

"We've spoken with KlaraMaria," said the older man, "by telephone, several times, and we feel reassured. We believe we can have her back at any moment. We know about the agreement you made with the Institute. You've fulfilled your part of it. A patrol car is waiting outside. They will drive you to the main convent in Audebo, where they're preparing a bed for you. You'll stay there until the two children are returned, and while your case is pending."

"Wiedebühl," said the Blue Lady, "is a lawyer, a consultant for the Church Ministry, and on the boards of both the Institute and its philanthropic foundation."

It is hard for men to dress up their appearance. And it becomes no easier with age. The lawyer must have been in his eighties, and time had removed his body structure. But his tailor had accomplished a Christian miracle. The light-blue suit had achieved resurrection of the flesh as far as his torso was concerned. However, tailors can't do anything above the collar. The man looked like a turtle. But one should not underestimate turtles. In the sixties, when entertainers still performed at fairs with trained reptiles, Kasper had seen hundred-year-old Russian turtles mating. They had bellowed like people.

"The Interior Ministry has promised to extend your residence permit," said the lawyer. "And to speak with the tax authorities. The Ministry of Immigration and Integration will get you included in the next draft of naturalization legislation. Parliament confers citizenship twice a year, in June and October. We can have a Danish passport for you on July first. An out-of-court settlement with the tax authorities before September first. Negotiations with the Spanish authorities during the fall. Before the end of this year you'll be back on the major stages."

The atmosphere in the room was pastoral, pale green, in F-major, like Beethoven's Symphony No. 6. Like when the whole family is gathered to tell Great-grandfather he is going to a home for the elderly and he has taken it nicely.

Kasper looked over at the Blue Lady. Her face was expressionless.

"Would we," he said, "by any chance have the conversations with KlaraMaria on tape?"

The woman from the police department leaned forward and started the digital recorder.

There was no buzzing on the tape. No sound of the telephone ringing. Just a slight scratching when the receiver was picked up. A woman answered; it was the Blue Lady. A man's voice spoke.

"KlaraMaria is visiting us. She's fine. She wants to talk with you. She'll be here for a week. Then she'll come back."

It was Kain's voice.

To those with ordinary hearing, the telephone line was quiet. To Kasper—or his fantasy—it sounded like someone moved across a carpet in a large room. The telephone changed hands.

"Maria. It's me."

She didn't say "Mother Maria." Just "Maria."

"I'm fine. I'm coming back in a week. You mustn't worry."

The abbess said something that Kasper could not hear. Her voice was flat. The man's voice returned.

"You'll get a telephone call every third day."

The connection was broken.

Everyone looked at Kasper.

"Let's hear the next call," he said.

"They telephoned again," said the lawyer. "As they had promised."

The woman changed the tape and wound it. This time you could hear the call made. That meant the first recording was from the Institute's answering machine. After that they had installed the recorder. And waited for the next telephone call.

The ring tone was slightly fainter and slower. The call was made from a mobile phone. The Blue Lady answered. There was a very brief pause. Then KlaraMaria's voice was heard.

"I'm fine. You mustn't worry. I'm coming back soon. In a couple of days. Bastian too."

The connection was broken.

Everyone looked at Kasper.

"The second call is a fake," he said. "They're playing a good digital recording, certainly a DAT, into a mobile phone in a car that's driving on a highway. To avoid being traced. It guarantees nothing. Not even that she's alive."

The pale-green sound in the room was gone.

"The children possess some sort of clairvoyance; KlaraMaria predicted the first earthquakes. She drew a map showing the extent of the quakes and sent it to a geodesist. People with a connection to Konon have bought up property in the inner city. There's going to be some sort of auction of the properties."

"You're from the circus," said the lawyer. "You've known busloads of fortune-tellers and astrologists. That's just hot air. Nobody can see into the future."

"These aren't ordinary children," said Kasper. "I've met them. They've had special training."

He looked at the Blue Lady. She did not move.

"You want something from me," said Kasper. "You haven't assembled in such numbers just to be here. Although that's part of the reason, of course. You wanted to hear what I thought of the tapes. And then there's one more little thing."

The lawyer nodded.

"We want to ask you to keep quiet. And *ask* isn't the right word. We want to make you aware that you don't have any choice. You're going to be taken away now. This case is coming to an end. Tomorrow we'll have the proper attorney for you. In fourteen days we will have you freed, with an apology from the police. And during those fourteen days you will refuse to say anything. The accused has that right. And you will make use of it. You will remain as silent and closed as an oyster. Because if you don't, you will have lost everything. You will not see this place again, you will not see the children again, and you will have forfeited all legal and diplomatic help."

He looked at Kasper and nodded. The gesture had finality.

"We thank you for your help," he said. "On behalf of the Institute and the police. And we wish you a speedy recovery."

"I've met those people," said Kasper. "The children won't be returned."

"Thank you for coming," said the lawyer.

The wheelchair delayed Kasper just a little. But not enough for anyone to react before he had leaned over the table and pulled the old man out of his chair.

"They'll disappear," he whispered. "They'll be taken out of the country. They're a limitless gold mine. And when they're gone, I'm going to come after you."

Two pipe wrenches mounted on a jack locked around Kasper's wrists from behind. The African sat him back in the wheelchair.

"You need me," he said. "I can hear her. I can hear both of them. Give me twelve officers. Twenty-four hours."

Everyone stood up.

"You're over forty years old," said the lawyer. "One's hearing decreases exponentially after birth."

"That's right," said Kasper. "I can no longer positively determine whether it's a Grande Complication. Or a thoroughbred from Schaffhausen. Your watch, that is."

Everyone in the room looked at the lawyer. His thin wrists emerged nakedly from his sleeves past the chalk-white cuffs. There was no watch.

"In your vest pocket," said Kasper.

Once again he rose out of the wheelchair before Sister Gloria reached him. In one flowing movement he took the watch out of the man's pocket and laid it on the table.

The watch case was gold. But the timepiece was otherwise unremarkable at first glance. It had a brown leather band.

Kasper turned the watch over. The unremarkable disappeared. Its back was sapphire crystal. Through the crystal one saw the minute diversity in a mechanism of pure gold. With fifteen hundred parts.

"Il Destriero Scafusia," he said. "From the International Watch Company in Schaffhausen, Switzerland. The sound is a little denser than the company's Grande Complication. Because of the gold. It's the most expensive watch in the world. How does that fit with Christian humility?"

The turtle started to blush.

"Let's get him out of here," he said.

The Blue Lady raised a hand. That stopped everyone in the room.

"He needs a blessing," she said. "That's the final part of the contract. I'll show him the church. It will take less than ten minutes."

# 4

She closed the gate behind him; they were alone in the yard. Even in this sheltered area he could tell the wind had risen. She helped him out of the wheelchair. Gave him his crutches. From a physical standpoint, he was improving.

"They know everything that's relevant," she said, "about the children. But they can't make it public. They don't expect the children to be returned. They're planning some action."

"They need me," he said. "I was the one who tracked down Kain. I know something they don't know. I have to be there."

They were standing in front of the church. It was diminutive. Like a large community-garden house.

"It's one of the world's smallest cruciform-dome churches," she said. "And one of the most beautiful. Built in 1865, the same time as the Russian church on Bred Street. When the Orthodox Church came to Denmark."

"Let me out of here," he said. "There must be a door in the fence."

"You can't walk without crutches. And even with crutches, you can't walk far."

That was correct. She opened the church door. They went inside.

"The narthex. Those who aren't baptized can't go any farther."

It was cool and quiet.

The church faced south. He considered whether he could break one of the colored-glass mosaics. Reach the edge of the lake. Find a boat. He knew it was hopeless.

She pushed open another door; he drew back a step.

At first it looked as though they were facing a wall of fire. Then he saw that it was icons. A wall of icons. Lit from above by sunlight flooding down from what must be openings in the dome. The light dissolved the pictures into flames of different colors. Flames of gold. Blazing silver. Crimson, a blue glow, green flames, like burning water. And within the fire, the intense motionless figures. The Savior, the child, the women. The holy men. More women, more children. More Saviors.

"We perform here," she said. "Every day. We warm the wine to eighty degrees. Pierce the bread with a spear. Sing. Dance. The cosmic circus. You would love it."

He edged away from her.

"Spanish criminal law specifies the chances of a pardon," she said. "If the accused enters a monastery for life, the chances increase significantly."

She blocked his way. Something forced him over the threshold, toward the wall of icons. Perhaps it was her tone.

"I'm not baptized," he said.

"In special circumstances," she said, "we have to be unconventional."

"I've always tried to avoid offending people," he said. "It's not good for ticket sales."

"You have five minutes," she said. "Perhaps you should forget ticket sales. And concentrate on essential things."

He walked in under the dome. Stood before the wall of light.

"We have two words for confession," she said. "*Penthos*, to regret. And *metanoia*, to change one's mind."

He followed her glance. In the diminutive aisle was a tiny Brazilian rosewood hut on wheels.

"We," she said, "and a few other Orthodox congregations, have kept the confessional. Is there any better place for you to spend the last five minutes?"

He walked over and opened the door of the hut. The floor was no more than ten square feet, like a standard lavatory in a trailer. There was a folding chair with plush upholstery; he sat down. Straight ahead of him was a tinted glass window with small perforations at the bottom. He closed the door. A faint light came on, like the safelight in a darkroom. Through wood and glass he heard the woman take her place on the other side. The situation was symbolic of the relationship between the masculine and the feminine. And between God and human beings. Totally ready to make contact, but always separated by a very thin membrane.

"I want to confess," he said.

"You are welcome."

It was not the abbess's voice. He gave up the attempt to identify it. He had not come to make classifications; he had come to give himself unconditionally.

"I have a very deep sorrow," he said.

"Have you tried to pray?"

"As much as possible. But it's not enough. A woman abandoned me."

"What was your part in that?"

The question bewildered him. He tried to collect his thoughts.

"I opened my heart too much," he said.

"What do you want us to do? Canonize you?"

At first he did not believe his ears. Then he opened the door and rose from the chair. Ignoring his crutches, he rounded the hut on all fours and threw open the other door, all in one quick movement.

She was wearing a blue-gray nun's smock, and at first he saw only that. Then she took off her headdress, and he saw her hair and her face. He had known it would be Stina. And yet had not known.

"You're abusing a believer's faith in God," he said.

"You're inside the convent enclosure. That's blasphemy."

He closed his fingers to slap her, but she leaped out of the chair like a cat, without tensing in advance. He hesitated, and then it was too late; violence must be fresh and spontaneous. Premeditated violence is inhuman.

The Blue Lady stood behind him.

"You have four more minutes," she said. "After that they'll drive you to Audebo. And Stina to work."

Then she was gone.

# 5

"You're part of it," he said, "part of this con trick. Back then too. You were a carnival nun."

Stina did not say anything.

He would have liked to sit down, but there was nothing to sit on. His body felt paralyzed. An old paralysis. That comes from being manipulated by women. Not only in this life. But in many lives before this one.

"You owe me a fantastic explanation," he said. "And you'll give it to me. But not now."

She did not say anything.

"They still haven't found the children. They want to keep me out of it. They're going to take me away now. There's a patrol car waiting outside."

He looked away. To avoid seeing her face.

"We will all eventually let down a child," he said. "One can't avoid that. That's why I didn't want to have children. That was the real reason. But now I've promised a child something anyway. KlaraMaria. I promised to come back for her. I've got to keep that promise."

"Why? You're almost a stranger."

He tried to find words for it; he looked at the bread on the altar.

"When I was a child her age and we were given bread right out of the oven, or something like that, we shared it with the others. There was always a flock of artists' children, and we were always hungry. Everyone shared. We knew something without it being put into words: We knew that bread tasted better when it was shared. We didn't try to explain it. But it was a very physical sensation. The taste was better. Later one forgets that; I'd forgotten it. But in the last few days I've thought about it. What we knew back then was that you can't keep the important things for yourself. If one person is hungry, everyone feels the hunger. The same with happiness. There's no private happiness. And freedom. If she isn't free, then I'm not free either. She could just as well be me. Maybe that's love."

He had reached her. He could hear that. The dome above them focused their sounds, as in a circus ring. It was a sonorous moment.

"What do you want me to do?" she said.

"I want you to take off your clothes."

Her sound turned off, as if she had been hit on the head with a crowbar.

He stripped off his jacket. Began to unbutton his trousers. He could use only his right hand. The woman before him had the look of someone hallucinating.

"We'll exchange clothes," he said. "That's the only chance. Two police cars are waiting outside. We'll each get into the wrong car. They'll drive you to house arrest in Audebo. When you get there, you'll tell them who you are. As for me, I'll be driven in toward the city. I'll find some way to get away from them."

She did not move. He stood there in just his boxer shorts. A sense of sacrilege began to sneak up on him.

"You must be absolutely crazy," she said.

He relaxed completely, as before a high-stakes bluff in poker. He adjusted to a feminine perspective. Prepared to lose everything if necessary.

"The folks in there," he said, "the police, they haven't met the people who took KlaraMaria. I have. This isn't Mr. and Mrs. Solid Citizen. This is the wicked king and the wicked queen. The children aren't on their way back. They're on their way to disappearing."

She stared at him. Then she lifted her hands and unbuttoned the first button.

"Turn around," she said. "And close your eyes."

He turned around and leaned his forehead against the fragrant wood of the confessional.

He focused his hearing on her nakedness, on her skin. He didn't have to see it to drown himself in it. That was one of the redeeming aspects of hearing like his. You could stand in front of the women's locker room at an indoor swimming pool and feel as if you were with the women inside.

"Put your hands on your ears," she said. "Otherwise this whole thing is called off."

He put his hands on his ears.

She touched his shoulder; he turned around. She was wearing his clothes. But she looked like herself more than ever. The jacket, shirt, and trousers emphasized her femininity. There are people whose being shines through every disguise.

He put on her blouse, then the blue smock, and tucked his hair under the nun's headdress. He caught a reflection of himself in the window facing the yard.

"Sunglasses?" he said.

She took a pair of sunglasses and a small mirror from a handbag on the floor.

If he'd had twenty minutes and a makeup kit he could have done something with his face. Now there was nothing to do but hide it. He found a handkerchief in her bag, put on the sunglasses, then unfolded the handkerchief and held it up to his face as if he wanted to hide that he was crying.

He put on her sandals; she wore the same size as he. He had always been fascinated by her feet: large, strong, flat, the toes spread out like a fan; he could hear how much she had run around barefoot as a child, around Skagen on herringbone parquet floors, on rolling lawns and private beaches. He cast a sidelong look at the crutches. Then they started walking.

In spite of the pain, he delved deep into his femininity. Felt the ovaries. Settled into the heaviness of a female gait, the elasticity of the stride, the slight roll of the hips. Stina opened the door. They were out in the courtyard. The wind hit them.

"This is grotesque," she said.

"You're very convincing," he said. "Totally mannish. My suitcase is inside the door. Carry it in both your arms. Walk as if it's heavy. Men and women walk the same way when they carry something heavy. Lift the suitcase so it partially hides your face. Get into the backseat without speaking to them."

"It won't work."

"It's doomed to succeed. This is an archetype with good fortune. As in *Fidelio*. She searches for her lover in the Underworld. Disguised as a man. When the lovers get close to each other in earnest, they're forced to explore the other sex in themselves. At the end of that journey they find a great love."

"At the end of this journey you'll find I never see you again."

"Get away from them somehow. Convince the African and Franz Fieber. They're my loyal supporters. Take a vehicle, the three of you. And pick me up at Rigshospital. In an hour."

The Blue Lady must have waited for them. By the pond. Behind the bushes. Listening to the water. Now they faced her.

She looked at them. For the first time he heard her lose her equilibrium and experience a real shock. But the silence returned almost immediately.

She did not want to shout. She wanted to turn around, cross the courtyard, and call for Moerk without losing her composure. The moment she turned around Kasper would have had the handkerchief around the lower part of her face. It would have been yet another step toward a breakdown in ethics: violence against an older woman and the head of a convent. But it would have been necessary.

She looked past Kasper and directly at Stina. At her men's clothing and pageboy hairdo.

"Kasper Krone," she said to Stina. "There are two officers waiting for you in the hall. Stina, just go out to the gate. A government car is parked there, and they've promised to drive you into Copenhagen. May God go with you both."

# 6

Two cars were parked outside the entrance, a police car and a Renault. There were two officers waiting by the patrol car. He walked toward the Renault. Hunched over against the wind. Out stepped the two monks.

He heard a twofold reaction when they saw him. An amalgam of surprise and sympathy because of the handkerchief and the weeping. And the quivering of awakened instincts that a woman like him would arouse in two men if they weren't castratos or angels.

They held the door for him, and he got into the backseat.

Stina came out of the building; she had pulled the jacket over her head. Moerk was right behind her, the Blue Lady beside her. The abbess spoke to the officers.

"I asked him to cover his head," she said. "He must be protected in case the press turns up. We don't want to risk having anyone recognize him."

The Renault, with Kasper inside, started up and drove out of the driveway.

He sank down into the seat, down into exhaustion. Exhaustion often waits for us in an automobile. He remembered the sweetness of falling asleep in the Vanguard as a child, the feeling of Helene Krone's bare arm against his cheek. He wished she could have been here beside him now. Is it shameful to miss your mother when you're forty-two and walking a tightrope stretched across a nervous breakdown? He had sand in his joints. His body had used coffee, had used Armagnac, had used a little organic chemistry to stay awake.

He had none of these things now. A prayer began instead. Prayer is a paper ship of wakefulness on the stream of worldly weariness.

He could give up. He could reveal his identity. Be driven to Au-debo. Give in to sleep. Wait for them to take care of his case. They would do what they had promised. He could be back in the Circus Building by November. With Benneweis at the Circus Arena in Bel-lahøj by the beginning of April.

He heard Maximillian's voice. It came to him across thirty years. As fresh as if time were simply an acoustic filter we put up to avoid facing the fact that all sounds are always present everywhere. It was tinged with an accent from having grown up in Tønder.

"I promised that if I had a child who fell asleep in the carriage, I would always carry the child inside."

Lyngby Road ended; they crossed Vibenshus Circle.

He addressed the two backs in front of him, speaking into the handkerchief in a voice choked with tears.

"We make eternal vows," he said. "When we become nuns. Total obedience. No possessions. No sexuality. The latter is the worst. That's why I'm crying. Just imagine being in my situation. A woman in her early thirties. Filled with an appetite for life."

The two backs stiffened, as if the spinal fluid had begun to coag-ulate.

"People outside don't understand us. You know the vulgar stories about nuns and sailors. They aren't true. What a nun actually dreams about when she's lying with her head on a bed of nails and her hands on top of the quilt is two handsome policemen."

Their sound was fading, as with people who are about to faint. For a moment their connection to normal reality was impaired.

"Take a left here," said Kasper.

They made a left turn, down Blegdam Road.

"In here," he said.

The car turned in toward the main entrance at Rigshospital.

"Stop here."

They stopped.

"I'll run into the shop in the lobby," he said, "and get two bottles of Bacardi. And a package of condoms."

He got out of the car. Hunched his body against the strong wind. Heard the Renault pull away from the curb behind him. Heard it sneak away. The driving was jerky and uneven.

# 7

The heavy drapes were closed, the shades down; the only light in the room came from the flat screen of a computer and from a night lamp beside the bed. Maximillian Krone's face looked like a leather mask; it looked like the Grauballe man preserved over the centuries. His eyes were closed. Behind the irregular breathing Kasper heard the weary heart. One foot stuck out from the quilt; the ankle was covered with stasis eczema.

The sick man opened his eyes.

"The transactions were recorded on Hestemølle Street ten minutes ago. That means they're officially registered. The auction has taken place."

Maximillian fumbled for the gold eyeglasses on the bedside table. His arm and hand were thin and wrinkled, like a bird claw.

He put on his glasses and looked at Kasper. Looked at the nun's habit.

"I'm glad," he said, "that here at my deathbed you're showing your best side."

"I just escaped from the police."

"That's what I mean by your best side."

Kasper could barely understand the words; the voice was a mere fragment.

"I have friends with offices that face the harbor," whispered Maximillian. "I telephoned them. They can hear I'm speaking from the grave. And they almost shit their pants. 'I'm calling to wish you Merry Christmas,' I say. 'Because I'll no longer be on the premises to do it then. And I'm also calling because you must cancel your board meetings and stand at the window with a pair of binoculars and look over at Tippen. At Konon. They say something is happening on the roof.'"

The door opened. Stina entered, still wearing men's clothing. Behind her were the African and Franz Fieber. The sick man hadn't heard them arrive.

Kasper took out the taxi voucher. He dialed Moerk's number. "Yes?"

"Something is happening on the roof," said Kasper. "At Konon."

"How would you know that? In Audebo, with no contact to the outside world."

"I've sprung a Houdini. I'm in Copenhagen. Close to everything."

Kasper heard the other man's breathing, stressful E-minor, wracked with sorrow and anxiety.

"I've been taken off the case," said Moerk. "The minister himself has taken charge. One more false step and I'll be forcefully retired. I wouldn't do so much as admit that I've taken this call."

"A police helicopter. Just twelve officers. It's the lives of two children."

"Go to Audebo. Enjoy the tranquillity. Plan the next escapade. Listen to Prokofiev's *Peter and the Wolf*. Or go to hell."

The line went dead. Stina crossed the room.

She embraced the sick man. Ran her fingers gently over the leathery skin. Maximillian's face began to glow faintly, unnaturally. As if a corpse were being awakened from the dead. Kasper had heard of it before. How sometimes daughters-in-law can build bridges over the Philippine Trench between fathers and sons.

"I always felt there was mutual understanding between us," whispered Maximillian. "In the pain. Of being fatefully connected with that borderline transvestite over there. But when I see you now in his recycled clothing, then I start to wonder, by God."

Kasper opened the brocade drapes. Rolled up the shades. At first the light was blinding. He looked out across North Harbor. Tippen was hidden behind the container port and the office buildings.

"I'll get a weapon," he said. "I'll force my way in. From the street. In some new way. There's never been a barrier I couldn't break through. I promised her."

He heard the compassion of the others. His father. Stina. The Blue Lady. He looked around. The abbess was not in the room. She must be somewhere inside him. Perhaps in his heart. It wasn't her voice he heard, but her opinion. That he had exhausted his energy. He would not survive the attempt.

Maximillian picked up a cell phone. His voice was too weak for them to hear what he was saying. They went closer.

"They telephoned," said Maximillian. "My lodge brothers from Holmen, that is. The Konon people are trying to land a helicopter on the roof. Even though the wind speed is forty-five miles per hour."

"How much time do we have?"

It was Stina who asked. He didn't understand why.

"One hour."

It was Franz Fieber who spoke.

"They can't land in this weather. But the wind is about to decrease. In an hour it will be okay."

"We can be inside in an hour," said Stina.

Kasper stared at her. Shook his head.

"You trusted me once," she said. "You can do it again."

Something in him gave up. Or leaped. Like a spring in a mechanical toy. Within him, a prayer began. To the feminine spirit. The Virgin Mary. Mary Magdalene.

"All right," he said.

She turned on her heel.

In front of Kasper, Maximillian was getting out of bed.

It was like looking straight into the grave. He was as skinny as a survivor of Auschwitz. Probably even less than a hundred pounds. Biological processes no longer drove him. It was his will, and a nonphysical enthusiasm.

"I'm going along," he said.

Kasper raised an arm to stop his father. Sister Gloria walked over to the sick man. Took his arm.

"Among my people," she said, "the Luo, we take at least one representative of wise old age when going to war."

"But do you choose someone with advanced Alzheimer's?" said Kasper.

They walked past him. Kasper shuffled after them. He took the hospital robe from the chair. Wrapped it around his father.

# 8

The convent's ambulance stood in the parking lot facing Fælled Park, next to the Patient Hotel. Now, for the first time, Kasper saw that it was identical to the Rigshospital ambulances, except for the Dagmar Crosses on the sides. Franz Fieber sat at the wheel.

Kasper's suitcase lay on the stretcher. Stina opened it. Kasper's things were no longer inside; there were several sets of thin blue coveralls, folded. Long thin gloves, folded.

Stina distributed the clothing. They put on the coveralls without asking any questions. Kasper too. Maximillian needed to take off his robe to get into his; he stood there for a moment in his underpants. Kasper had to look away.

Stina distributed headlamps, little plastic LED capsules that fastened around the head with an elastic band. Stina lighted hers. Even in daylight it filled the ambulance with a sharp blue glow.

She moved aside. The African took hold of a ring in the floor and pulled. A five-foot-square hatch swung open. Kasper looked down onto a shape he recognized, a meander pattern. The ambulance had stopped directly above a manhole cover.

Stina handed the African a long steel hook. She held a matching tool herself. The hooks fit into two holes on the massive iron plate. The women hoisted the cover into the vehicle and tossed it aside as if it were a piece of Tupperware.

Cold air from below filled the ambulance. Beneath the manhole cover a shaft descended into the darkness. A ladder was welded firmly to one side of the shaft.

Stina lowered herself into the hole and disappeared, as if by magic. Kasper looked down. She had grabbed the rungs of the ladder and was already ten feet below.

"Kasper is next," she said.

He could hear his confidence in her. It had never really been in question. Actually, he had always known that she was precisely the one whom he would dare to follow straight into the Underworld. The problem had been to get permission.

Nevertheless, he made the sign of the cross on his chest. Just a small one. Nothing extraordinary. He fine-tuned his prayer. Then he climbed down after her. It was colder than he had expected.

The African came next. She carried Maximillian in her left arm, effortlessly, like a rag doll. The two fluid bags attached to him with tubes and needles were firmly clasped under her arm.

The ladder ended on a narrow landing. Franz Fieber was the last one down. When they were all gathered, Stina turned around. The light from their headlamps revealed the surroundings.

The first thing Kasper noticed was the stench. It surpassed anything he had experienced aboveground, even in the circus. The next thing he saw was the beauty of the scene. It canceled out the stench in a way.

They were standing in a gigantic tunnel, the cross section of an oval. Along the bottom flowed a black, clayish river.

Stina sensed their silent prayers.

"It's a sewer line," she said. "Dug out by hand. At the end of the eighteen hundreds. Thirteen feet high, twenty feet wide. Concrete bottom. Brick sides. The tubes are small PVC sewer pipes."

Kasper saw them now, bundles of plastic tubes hung along the walls.

"A spillway structure," said Stina. "For the one time every ten years that the system backs up and the sewer overflows. The surplus runs directly into the Sound. The other main conduit goes from Nørrebro under Frederiksberg and the railroad yard, and flows into the old Teglværk clay pit."

She started walking, and they followed her slowly. In the darkness outside the beam of his headlamp Kasper saw small pearl-shaped lights, like a multitude of stars just above the surface of the water. He directed his lamp toward the galaxy, and saw the rats. There weren't hundreds of them, but thousands of them. On the cables, on the narrow path on the other side of the river, at the edge of the water. For the first time in his life he was aware of the creatures' elegance; he heard it, heard their agility, their broad intelligence, their ability to adapt. He recalled an experiment when he was a consultant for the Acoustics Institute at Danish Technical University; it had been carried out at the agricultural college's experimental station in Tåstrup. They had tested the effect of music on domestic animals. He suggested Handel for the cows. Large square barns of music. Saint-Saëns for the pigs. Somebody included rats in the experiment. The rats had loved Bach—Kasper could tell that. He heard it in their happiness. Bach's piano concertos had doubled the rats' fertility.

"I've always liked them."

Stina stood behind him.

"When I became chief engineer in my department, they put on a party. I was so young. And the first woman to hold that position. That morning I'd found two baby rats that had drowned in one of the system's depth pumps. I wore them for the party. As earrings. They hung by their tails. Swinging around my neck."

She wasn't joking.

"Why?"

She tried to find an answer within herself.

"Maybe," she said, "I've always wanted to show people what lay behind. What lay underneath. What the costs were."

"Could they take it?"

"Nobody could eat a bite. I had to take them off. Flush them down the toilet."


They had been walking for perhaps ten minutes. The gentle flow of the water indicated that the tunnel must slope down slightly. He heard the walls open outward. The sound expanded; they must have reached some sort of huge hollow.

A faint light shone from overhead. As if from a skylight in a church dome. The roof opened into a shaft.

"A ventilation canal and escape route," Stina said. "There are four hundred in this conduit alone."

The light from her headlamp pointed out pipe openings on different levels.

"Electricity, telephone, and broadband are closest to the surface; they don't require frost protection."

The light shifted down about three feet to a deeper conduit.

"Military cables. That one there is NATO's main cable for non-digital information. It goes along Roskilde Road to their administration building in Koldsås."

The light moved downward.

"Gas, water. District heating. And then the sewer system. Copenhagen's underground isn't solid. It's as porous as a beehive."

The beam of light became horizontal. It rested on a metal door with a high-voltage warning.

The African walked over to the door with a small crowbar. She pulled it open the way one opens a can of beer.

The door was just decoration. Behind it was the real protection: forty square feet of stainless-steel armor plate that could have withstood a rocket attack.

Franz Fieber gave a low whistle.

"Everything is controlled from here," said Stina. "We need to get in."

Franz Fieber opened his attaché case; lying on black velvet were shiny instruments, as if for jaw surgery. He pointed to a metal box the size and shape of a hair dryer located about three feet to the right of the door.

"The siren and the alarm," he said. "If we cut it, a telephone will ring to alert the police and Falck security services. We have to disable the phone line."

His fingers glided over a push-button panel to the left of the door.

"An electric one-channel lock. Which means that the pick gun won't work. And that the alarm covers the entire door."

He handed Kasper a black rubber hammer, the kind doctors use to test reflexes in cases of delirium tremens.

"Let's test your hearing."

He pointed to the wall; Kasper knocked on it carefully.

"We're looking for a contact unit for the panel. It connects the alarm to the station's network. And to a battery, in case of a power outage. If you can find that, I can go in through the wall."

Kasper pounded carefully.

"Can there be something in it that jingles?" he asked.

Franz Fieber shook his head.

"You must have found the key closet."

Kasper continued on the other side of the door. All eyes were on him.

He heard something.

"Electronics?" he asked.

"A circuit board."

"What else?"

"A battery. A loudspeaker for the alarm."

"Small springs?"

"Makes sense. The door must be spring-loaded. If it's opened, the sabotage alarm goes off."

Franz Fieber attached a long masonry bit to a drill. Bored a hole. Guided a dentist's mirror and two small forceps attached to a rod through the hole. He snipped. Attached a diamond blade to a small battery-driven angle grinder. Placed it against the door hinges. The disc went through the tough steel as if it were butter. The African caught the heavy door as it slid out of the rabbet.

The space behind the door was quite small. Kasper heard the dangerous hum of high-voltage electricity. Stina and Franz Fieber got to work with the circuit-breaker control panels.

"The train needs to keep running," she said. "And the pump station. And the elevator up to the surface. We'll shut down everything else."

She held a wire cutter; its insulation was as thick as a pair of heavy mittens. As she cut, a cascade of sparks poured over them.

"The rest are on the circuit breakers," said Franz Fieber. "A higher-level four-hundred-kilovolt cable supplies Copenhagen. Under that lies a one-hundred-twenty-kilovolt system. Under that, thirty and ten kilovolts. The surveillance equipment draws directly from the one-hundred-twenty system, to reduce the chance of it shutting down."

He turned off one circuit breaker after another as he spoke.

"We will now say goodbye to the Copenhagen environmental protection agency."

He switched off a circuit breaker.

"To National Telecom's cable monitoring office."

He turned off another.

"To the maintenance department at E2 Energy."

He turned off another.

"To NATO's head office. With overall digital surveillance of Copenhagen's underground."

Franz Fieber put two bypass wires across the circuit breaker. The tunnel became illuminated.

What surrounded them was not a hollow. It was a large space. More than 500 by 150 feet. The sewer line went through it about six feet above the floor. Above them was a vaulted brick ceiling. Below them, remnants of masonry, as if from small cubicles.

Stina followed his gaze.

"Graves," she said. "More than five thousand. This was a cavern under one of the earliest Catholic convents."

Close to their feet they saw two narrow tracks. And just ahead of them, a vehicle that looked like the roller coasters in Tivoli.

"Tipper trolley tracks," said Stina. "They laid them when they dug out for the freight railway. They dug through the old garbage dumps. They had to get rid of twelve million metric tons of contaminated Class Three soil. So they laid the trolley tracks. And transported the soil out to North Harbor. Built the Lynetten sewage treatment plant on it. Filled out beyond Tippen."

The tracks emerged from a black tunnel to their left.

"They go out to the Tingbjerg neighborhood," she said. "To the Copenhagen water-supply headquarters. They service both the water mains and the sewage system. Copenhagen's sewers are almost worn out. So the maintenance crews are kept very busy. Trying to postpone the system's collapse."

She opened the trolley doors. They all got in. Franz Fieber took the driver's seat. Somewhere a large electric motor came to life. The trolley began to move.

It accelerated powerfully, like a jet airplane. Ahead of them the emergency lighting was out. The trolley shot into the dark. The tunnel curved and twisted.

They were in total darkness, aside from a faint reflection from the instrument panel on Franz Fieber's face. Kasper's hearing registered an expansion of the tunnel, then a contraction. Registered that the material on the walls of the tunnel changed from brick to cement. Or else it was just the material inside his own nervous system that he heard.

He leaned toward Stina.

"You knew about me in advance. Before that time on the beach. You hadn't gotten separated from the boat. I was a pawn."

They came to a lighted section; he could see her face.

"Do they use drugs in the circus?" she said.

He had no idea where she was going with that question.

"Only in strength disciplines. Anabolic steroids. They're used in all international strength performances these days."

"Sister Gloria showed us a list. From *Physicians Weekly*. About the most habit-forming drugs in the world. They're created in laboratories. The few people who have taken them—the discoverer and a couple of laboratory technicians—spend the rest of their lives trying to get money. A fix costs a hundred thousand kroner and up. The effect lasts from one to ten minutes. It's described as an extremely heightened feeling of clarity and love."

The tunnel opened around them. Here the ceiling was arched like an airplane hangar. In the faint light he saw a vestige of something that looked like an altar.

"The remnants," said Stina, "of foundations under the first Jewish synagogues. Built on top of a heathen sacrificial altar."

She pointed to what looked like fallen timber.

"Old water pipes. Made from hollowed-out trees."

Kasper felt his impression of the city changing. He had thought it rested on lime and clay. It didn't. It rested on garbage and crumbling pieces of its religious past.

He fine-tuned his prayer. The only thing you could depend on. Besides love. And even that wasn't certain.

"Five thousand people."

Stina whispered the words in his ear. He had always loved her breath; it changed according to her moods, or was it his moods? Right now it had a hint of petroleum.

"That was Mother Maria's rough estimate. When Gloria told us about the drugs. There are five thousand people in the world who have taken them. Not the chemical drugs. But people who have experienced something similar. Who have discovered that reality is a birdcage. And who are looking for the gate that leads out of the cage."

He turned and looked straight at her. She and the Blue Lady and KlaraMaria could have founded a company. And leased their forthright gaze to a demolition firm.

"We saw you on television," she said. "The sisters and I. That's twelve years ago. During an intermission. When it was quiet. Mother Maria says: 'He's one who has tried those drugs. He's a seeker.' And then she looks at me. And says: 'You could meet him.' And I say: 'Why should I?' And she says: 'To help him by being a guide. And because he has a way with children.' That's why I came. In my own way."

"Why the unfriendliness, then? Why did you run away on Strand Road? To begin with?"

She hesitated.

"When I faced you, I could sense all the things you weren't able to control. Your inner chaos. And also something else. So it suddenly felt unpredictable. Overwhelming."

During the last few minutes he had heard some noise ahead. Like huge turbines. Now the sound got louder, became more powerful, like a waterfall. The trolley stopped. The tunnel ended in a cement wall. Below them the dark water was sucked through a grate.

"Lunch break," said Stina. "For three minutes."

Sister Gloria opened a backpack. Distributed bread and cheese. Kasper shifted the food from one hand to another. The sewer smell hadn't disappeared; one didn't get used to it as one could have hoped. In fact, it had gotten worse. And now it was mixed with the odor of rotting fatty substances, like the cesspool from a kitchen sink raised to brutal potency.

On the wall of the tunnel was a metal cover; Stina knocked it off with the red crowbar. Behind the cover was a lighting control console unlike any Kasper had ever seen before. Franz Fieber plugged a laptop into the console. He and Stina bent over the computer screen.

As she worked, Stina ate. Calmly. He remembered the first time she had come in while he was sitting on the toilet. He was having his morning bowel movement, his ritual time on the seat. From the little CD player on a shelf in the toilet Hans Fagius was playing BWV 565 on the restored baroque organ in St. Kristina's Church in Falun. Stina opened the door, walked in, and turned down the music. In one hand she was holding a sandwich, a little like now. Avocado and Camembert *lait cru*.

"I've got something important to tell you," she said.

He felt his abdomen contract. All living beings want to crap in peace. You can't expel from your body at the same time as you relax the bottom part of it. You can't do a head butt. Can't correspond with the tax authorities.

She took a bite of her sandwich. Completely unaffected by the situation. He suddenly understood that even deep inhibitions were culturally determined. And that somehow or other she was free of them.

"I discovered something this morning," she said. "Just as you opened your eyes. And the day was beginning. It seemed as if I were sitting at your deathbed."

He couldn't say anything. He was on the toilet. And she spoke as if she were in some Shakespeare play. He had no familiar reference point from which to respond.

"At that moment," she said, "I realized that I love you."

What should he say to that? In such a situation?

"Would you please leave," he said. "I need to wipe myself."


She turned her head away from the computer screen.

"We're at the main pump station, before the pipes go down under the ocean. On the other side there should be a new conduit they haven't put into use yet. But we're going farther than the pump station."

She turned back to the screen. Kasper heard his father beside him. Maximillian was leaning on a crutch, one of Franz Fieber's. The African had stuck the fluid bags into the breast pockets of his coveralls. Together the father and son watched the two women and the young man who were bent over the console and computer.

"They're like soldiers," said Maximillian. "Elite soldiers. But they have no anger. What drives them?"

Kasper heard his system synchronize with his father's. It happens in all families. Between all people who care about each other deeply. But it happens rarely. And usually no one discovers it. Discovers that for a brief moment the mask is gone. The neuroses. The inborn psychological traumas. For a brief time all the previous mistakes, which we carefully preserve in our memory for possible use against each other, are gone. They're gone for a moment, and one hears entirely ordinary humanity. Frail, but insistent. Among rats and pump stations and foul rivers of sludge.

"They're filled with something," said the sick man. "Something so powerful they're willing to die for it. I can tell that. What is it?"

Kasper heard the longing in his father's voice.

"Your mother and Vivian," Maximillian continued. "Those two women. That's the closest I've come to letting go. But still. When it comes right down to it, I didn't dare. The same with my love for the circus. I didn't dare. And my love for you."

They looked straight at each other. With no reservations.

"Having you," said Maximillian. "That was the finest thing Helene and I did. Many other things were good. But you were the best."

Kasper reached out his hand and laid it against the sick man's temple. Maximillian bore the intensity for a few moments, then turned away. But it was still the longest contact Kasper ever remembered having had with his father.

"It will empty in one hundred eighty seconds," said the African. "After that, we'll go through."

Kasper heard a change in the sound of the colossal pump. He turned toward the shiny cylinder; it was as big as a fermentation vat in a brewery. Its walls were gleaming with condensation. Where the water dripped onto the tunnel's cement, a plant with glossy dark-green leaves was growing, completely contrary to nature. Stina leaned over and picked a leaf. She held it up to his face. On the shiny surface lay a drop of water.

"It's a type of hazelwort. It can survive with just the emergency lighting."

She stood very close to him.

"I had a good childhood," she said. "Not one day in a wheelchair. Nothing more serious than two stitches and a little chlorhexidine in the emergency room. I had a game I played."

The drop of water began to wander along the edge of the leaf.

"I tried to understand a drop of water. Tried to understand what held it together. What kept it from separating into smaller parts."

The movement must have come from her hands. But they were motionless. Larger than his. Veined. Cool at first. But when she had touched him, stroked his skin for just a minute, they became very warm. But always calm. As they were now. But under the calmness he heard trembling, like the underlying tone of a Hindu raga. It took him a moment to identify what it was. Then he heard; it was anxiety for the children. But she still kept a firm grip on reality.

"What holds it together?" she said.

He had loved her curiosity. It was a hunger that was insatiable. It was like the curiosity of a clown. And of children. An openness, an appetite for the world, where nothing is taken for granted.

"I still play that game," she whispered. "Just a little differently. A little more concentration. A little broader scope. That's the only difference. Between the girl and the woman. Between the child and the adult. I collect in my mind everything we know about the bonding force in fluids as compared to air. The elasticity of the drop. Its attempt to find the least possible potential energy. Dirichlet's theorem. Normally we can hold only a couple of theorems at a time. I try to hold them all. As a form of professional intuition. And when I'm on the verge of understanding, am very, very close to it, and at the same time realize we'll never get there completely, and my mind is about to explode, I let go of all my understanding and go back to the drop."

The leaf was quiet. The drop existed. Nothing moved. He heard the last of the water being pumped out.

"And then, in brief, there seems to be no difference between the drop and me."

Carefully, very carefully, she laid the leaf down on the gray concrete.

"When that happens, on the rare occasions it happens, one has an inkling of what it will cost. To actually get there. It's a price no researcher can pay. And continue to be a researcher. Because it will cost understanding itself. You can't be right up next to something, and at the same time want to understand it. Do you know what I mean?"


There were steps on the outside of the cylinder. They went up about ten feet. Three conduits led from the pump station exit. The smallest had a diameter of about two and a half feet.

The cylinder's cover had an electric lock; it had sprung open. Stina must have opened it from the light console.

"Now they know in the surveillance center that something is wrong," she said. "In five minutes the city authorities will be here. Plus TDC telecommunications and the military. Falling all over each other. With dogs and firemen with their breathing apparatus. But by that time we'll be gone."

She hoisted herself over the edge of the pump case. Kasper tried to follow her. His body would not move. She pulled him up after her. Two of the conduits were closed by electric valves. The third was open. Stina turned on her headlamp.

They looked into a flawless deep-green world. The conduit was completely round, the inside lined with green material that gave off a muted reflected light, like soft-tone recessed lighting.

"Polyvinyl chloride," she said. "From Aarsleff pipe technologies. They've given the sewage system a life-extension treatment so it will last a little longer. They've pulled a PVC stocking inside the pipes."

It felt as if you could see infinitely far in and down.

"It's like looking into your own birth canal," he said. "It's very beautiful. Are the surveillance cameras turned off?"

She nodded.

"How about," he said, "using this unseen moment for a little kiss?"

She tried to get away from him. But she was standing on a narrow step.

"I know," he said, "that maybe you would say God sees us. But God is on our side. And Kierkegaard. Don't you remember what he says in *Works of Love*? Every love relationship is a shameless triangle. You, me, and Our Lord."

She twisted her head away.

"Goethe," he said. "And Jung. And Grof. And Bach. They're all in complete agreement. Before the great breakthrough, one stands mouth to mouth with the beloved facing one's own birth."

She freed herself from his hypnotic effect.

"Pure pop," she said. "You were never anything but pop culture!"

The sound of her anger was condensed, like acid, perhaps due to the alembic of the pump case around them. It functioned like an acoustic concave mirror, increased and concentrated the tone. She had a melodious voice. Enhanced in the Zahle School girls' chorus.

Conducted by Hess-Theissen. But at the same time it could be a whiplash. He had seen her quick-freeze an entire super-elliptical conference table of chief engineers.

"I'm thirsting for you," he said.

"Your source, please," she said. "That's borrowed. Stolen. Patchwork!"

She gripped the arm of his coveralls.

"Your feelings have no depth. You run, Kasper. You run away. One day it will catch up with you. The depth, I mean. Those declarations of love. You live and talk as if you're performing in the ring all the time."

He began to hum. The acoustics in the steel conduit were fantastic. The sound crept around along the wall and came back, as in a whispering gallery. He hummed eight bars, charmingly, irresistibly, fantastically.

"*Paris Symphony*," he said. "The development of the first movement. Where the main theme modulates into a crescendo. And in the final movement. At the end of the exposition. He simulates a fugue. Without developing it. That's pop music. He knows it himself. Writes from Paris to his father: I want you to know, Father, that I'm doing thus and so, in this and that measure; the audience will weep snot—they will love it. Pop music. But it works. It goes right to the heart. Technically it isn't anything special. No professional depth. But it's charming. It works. It works absolutely perfectly."

He leaned toward her.

"The heart. And the intensity. Those two things are why I went into the ring."

Their faces were right next to each other. He did not move an inch.

She climbed into the pipe's opening.

"Two people at a time," she said to those behind her. "This is the roller-coaster ride of your life. It goes down to almost two hundred feet below sea level. You brake by pressing your feet and elbows against the sides."

He got up beside her. They let go.

## 9

At first it was like free fall. There was almost no friction in the PVC; it was like riding on a pillow of air. He gave up tensing against it, leaned back, felt her body pressed against his. The only sound was a very faint echo of the fabric rubbing against the plastic pipe. And a distant, just barely audible sense of something waiting ahead.

The curve straightened out.

"A few more minutes," she said. "It's Northern Europe's longest roller coaster. Aarsleff invited the section leaders to try it when it was completed. They had us slide down holding a glass of champagne. It's a high-pressure pipe. No valves. No joints."

The air around them got colder.

"You visited my mother and father at home," she said.

It was when she had been gone for three weeks. He thought he was going crazy. He had circled around the address he had taken from her apartment, like a sick animal. Then he had driven out there.

The house lay on the outskirts of Holte, close to the lake, at the edge of fields and forest, far back in a yard filled with old fruit trees. Her mother invited him in and made tea. She resembled Stina somehow, which nearly knocked him off his feet. Her father remained standing throughout the visit, leaning against the bookshelves, as if to prop himself up. He did not say anything.

Kasper did not say anything either. It was the atmosphere in the room that spoke.

The house was unassuming in a way. Both the man and the woman had an unpretentious tone.

But it was the particular kind of unpretentiousness that comes when your family has surfed on a wave of bourgeois culture and financial capital for 250 years. Kasper had encountered the sound before, but not so close at hand. There was something limitless about it; the two older people before him were completely open—they had nothing to prove. For eight generations their background had variously been stockbrokers and pianists and Skagen painters and doctors of philosophy, and it was only about 125 years since Hans Christian Andersen had risen from the family's dinner table, and what shall we do with the Golden Age paintings with greetings on the back from the artists to Great-great-great-grandmother, because we have so many there is no room for them on the walls?

Kasper had listened for the costs. What was the price for refinement, for the height of the ceiling? The last time Charlie Rivel performed in Copenhagen, Kasper had shared the dressing room with him in the Circus Building, the green dressing room. Rivel had stayed in the ring too long; Kasper could hear it, Rivel could hear it himself. The old clown had tears in his eyes when he came out.

He had looked at Kasper.

"I've lost my timing," he said. "Twenty years ago they wouldn't let me leave. Now they humiliate me. With their boredom. Everything has a cost."


A girl had come into the room. Younger than Stina. Like a small fairy. With a wide mouth and a thin face. With some of Stina's sound. And beauty.

He pulled himself together after the shock. Tuned in. The connection between the intellectual and imaginative aspects of the girl's mind was disrupted. Her tonal unity was amorphous. But she had an open spirit, directed outward without reservation. He had heard it before, at charity performances. This must be Williams syndrome. A chromosomal defect.

"I'm a friend of Stina's," he said.

"You're her lover," said the mother.

"She's left me," he said. "I don't know where she is."

The woman poured the tea.

"When Stina was a child," she said, "she refused to be fed. Under any circumstances whatsoever. I ended up putting her on the floor with her plate. She wouldn't hold my hand either. When we went shopping. I had no idea what to do."

She reached out and touched her husband. Kasper heard the sexual vitality between them. Alive and healthy. After so many years.

"She's gone away," said the mother. "We don't know where. We get letters. But there's no return address."

"Could I see an envelope?" said Kasper. "I could track her down. I have limitless resources."

They looked at him. He knew they understood his desperation. He felt their sympathy.

"She would need to give her permission for that," said the father. "And we can't ask her."

Kasper could have committed murder. Choked them. Burned the house down on top of them. He just stood there.

The mother accompanied him to the door. Her resemblance to Stina was overwhelming. The words that were spoken came from Kasper's mouth. But he didn't know who articulated them.

"When you touch people. Do your hands get very warm?"

She looked at him in surprise.

"Yes," she said. "That's what people say. After about a minute my hands get very warm."


He had wandered the streets blindly, not knowing where he was going. When finally he could see clearly, he had lost his bearings, somewhere in the Vaserne bird sanctuary. By the time he found his way back to his car, night had come.


Behind them in the tube he heard the muted swish of the three others. And a sporadic thud when a crutch hit the wall.

"You missed me," she said.

She said it with amazement, candidly, as if it was only now that she really understood it.

The descent became steeper.

"We're almost at the end," she said.

The slope of the pipe flattened out and they came to a standstill. They lit their headlamps; the tube ended at their feet.

They came out into a square space, about sixteen by sixteen feet. It was crisscrossed by cement and plastic pipes; Stina placed her hand on the largest one.

"The central cable line. From Copenhagen to Amager."

There was a steel panel on the wall. She touched the panel with her fingertips. It slid to the side.

"Escape routes are mandated by law," she said. "I was involved when the Building and Technology office in Copenhagen granted permission to create the landfill beyond Tippen. We mandated this emergency exit elevator. We'll come up directly under Konon."

Franz Fieber emerged from the pipe. After him, the African. She had strapped Maximillian to her with a harness. His father held a telephone in his hand.

"They've landed the helicopter," he said. "Despite the gale."

A distant whistling came from the tube they had just left. Stina's face went blank.

"Water," she said. "They've connected us to the main line from Tingbjerg. They want to drown us."

She shook her head.

"Who?" she said.

Maximillian laughed quietly.

"No matter who pushes the button," he said, "there's a system behind them that maintains reality."

They all crowded into the small elevator. An inner door with glass windows glided open. The outer door began to close. A stream of water shot out of the vinyl tube. It became a huge torrent; the water hit the wall overhead with a sound like thunder. The elevator was lifted upward.

"Let us all pray," said Kasper, "just for a moment."

They stared at him.

"Prayer," he said, "is the real Jacob's ladder where God's angels ascend and descend—it's the really big elevator. Besides, we need it."

They all closed their eyes for a moment.

It was a high-speed elevator. They felt pressure in their knees and after thirty seconds experienced a moment of actual weightlessness.

They came out into a room of polished granite. Kasper recognized the structure of the stone surfaces. They must be in Konon's basement. Opposite them, double doors to the building's elevator opened. They entered it. The elevator car was big enough to hold a party in.

Stina hesitated. With her finger on the button.

Kasper heard her relinquish her authority. They were nearing other people now. The clown's bailiwick.

"Let's take off the coveralls," he said. "They look like uniforms."


He counted twenty floors, plus a few unnumbered ones; finally, the elevator stopped.

The door opened to one of the most tasteful rooms he had ever seen. In front of him was an oval wall decorated with pieces of driftwood. Seawater had smoothed their shapes on the beach and given the wood a silver-gray patina; the impression created was both rough and incredibly refined. The floor was marble. Under other circumstances he would have just stood there quietly. To enjoy the scene. And the very unusual sound of the room.

But not now. Outside the elevator stood a man in a green uniform. Holding a machine gun. It was Aske Brodersen.

Kasper had never cared for weapons. He refused to have so much as a prop pistol in his performances. Not even the kind where a flag pops out of the barrel with the word BANG!

He recognized the weapon in front of him as an automatic Bushmaster only because he had seen them in marketplaces when he toured the eastern-frontier provinces with the Russian state circus. Piles of machine guns and piles of opium had lain side by side in the markets; he would never forget the aroma of fresh curry leaves and raw opium and acid-free gun oil.

He let the blue nun's smock swing around his hips. Adjusted his voice to a high pitch.

"Where's the ladies' room?" he said.

The man in front of him stopped short. Courtesy is deeply rooted in Danes; it's karmic, and goes back to the feudal structures of an absolute monarchy. Kasper glided across the floor.

"Follow me," he whispered.

Then he gave the man a head butt.

Aske Brodersen sank to his knees, as if to pray. The African took the weapon out of his hands. She held the barrel with the stock down.

In the wall ahead of them was a door made out of monkey-puzzle wood. Curved like the wall. Six feet wide. It was fitted with a pneumatic hinge and opened without sound or resistance. They walked into a room flooded with light.

The walls were glass. The roof was glass. The floor was glass. Supported by narrow, chrome-plated steel beams. The space was shaped like a flying saucer. Beneath them was a drop of perhaps 250 feet down to the sea. Beyond the curved windows lay Copenhagen. The room was so high up you could see the city's weather laid out before you. They were above the clouds that covered Frederiksberg. Above something that could be thunder toward the south. And the inner city glowing in the setting sun.

The silhouette of a gigantic wheel floated through the room. It was the shadow of the helicopter's propeller. The chopper was directly above them; the landing pad was on the glass roof.

Beside a grand piano stood Josef Kain.

Every clown has broad experience with expressions of surprise. Kain's was something quite special. Kasper had seen the look a few times before. On some of the truly great figures in show business. Once you accept the premise that only the Lord Himself can take you unaware, you have somehow made yourself vulnerable.

KlaraMaria sat on a sofa; beside her was a dark-haired boy.

She got up and ran over to Stina. Hugged her tightly around the waist.

"Mother!" she said.

She pressed her head against Stina's stomach. And repeated the word. The scene was beautiful. But bordered on sentimentality, perhaps. The girl's face turned toward Kasper. It was angelic, until it broke into a wide grin. The cosmos doesn't suffer sentimentality for very long.

"Father!" she said.

Kasper looked around. To see whom she was speaking to behind him. There was nobody.

"I was pregnant," said Stina. "When I left. She's your daughter."

There must have been an entry in the ceiling that Kasper had overlooked. And for a moment, his hearing had failed him. The man who landed on the floor must have jumped from a height of about twelve feet. Nevertheless, he landed like a cat. It was Ernst. His bandages were gone. The bruises appeared to have healed very nicely. With just a little powder he could have posed for a health club ad. His tone was soft and alert. His lips moved as if he were talking to himself. Kasper suddenly understood that what looked like a hearing aid was a headset. The man held a weapon in his hand. The instant he touched the floor he shot the African.

A series of shots rang out, so close together they sounded like a cough. The force of the bullets lifted the woman and threw her against the wall. For an instant it seemed her body would hang there; then she fell to the floor facedown.

The man turned the weapon toward Kasper. For a moment the woman's clothing confused him. Kasper tensed against the impact. He felt a particular sweetness at the realization that his prayer had never stopped. He would die in a petition to the great spirit of love. Following the best examples. Jesus. Gandhi. Princess Pemasal.

Maximillian threw down his crutches and stepped in front of Kasper. The bullets came in an upward curve, striking him in the hip and across his chest; he seemed to float backward. The exit path of the bullets opened his back like a zipper, blood and tissue bursting out over Kasper. Then his father fell against him, and they both toppled to the floor.

The stocky man looked around the room. To be sure everything was calm before he finished his project. Kasper felt a wave of admiration. Every great improviser can recognize another. By the ability to remember the whole picture in the midst of a fortunate flow of actions.

The machine gun was aimed at Kasper.

At that moment he realized the African was alive.

When he saw her get hit and fall he had been sure she must be dead, so his hearing had shut her out of the sound picture. It's this kind of matter-of-factness that limits us human beings and restricts our receptivity to the truly miraculous.

In Morocco, with the Cirque du Maroc, at the edge of the Sahara, he had seen two circus lions mate. It happened on the way from the gangway into the cage. Everyone had scrambled out of the way, including the animal trainer; all the doors were closed and locked. Kasper got into a circus Land Rover with a technician. In the rush the technician dropped his cap; he opened the car door and leaned out to pick it up. The vehicle was 250 feet from the lions. In the time it took him to lean over two and a half feet, the male lion reached the Land Rover. As Kasper pulled the man back into the vehicle and slammed the door, the lion's claws hit the water can above the running board.

The sound Kasper had heard from the lion was one he never wanted to experience again.

But he did now. And from a woman.

The African sprang directly from a prone position. And she reached Ernst in one movement.

She hit him in the head with an outstretched arm, as if with a connecting rod. Then she grabbed him around the neck and slammed his head into the grand piano. It made a sound like a Chinese temple gong. The man's body grew slack; he sank down in a cross-legged position.

The African's smock seemed to divide into two pieces, sliding down on each side of her. It was her carrying harness, slashed as if with plate shears. The leather-and-steel insert must have functioned like a bulletproof vest.

Her hands clenched.

"Thou shalt not kill," said Kasper. "We must try to hold evil in check. It will haunt you the rest of your life. Eckehart says somewhere . . ."

The African looked at him. He had reached her. Perhaps not with his wisdom. But perhaps with the surprise effect. Her jaw began to drop.

The man at her feet got to his knees and struck her with the slim barrel of the weapon. Kasper heard her thigh bone break.

Her eyes grew reddish. As if blood were flowing to the white membrane around the iris. She leaned over. Put her arms around the man beneath her. Lifted him up.

She began to squeeze him. She held a man of two hundred pounds plus her own weight upright. With a broken thigh bone. Kasper realized that he was listening into the future. That he heard a foretaste of what can happen when Africa soon loses patience and rises up.

The man's eyes began to bulge out of their sockets. Kasper heard a wrist break. Ernst's fingers were pressed hard on the trigger guard.

The machine gun went off. The swarm of bullets drew half a heart on the plate-glass window. The window cracked and blew in.

It splintered into pieces of glass the size of dinner plates. Just then Kasper heard the wind.

It had gotten stronger. He had let himself be fooled by the sunshine. By his unfamiliarity with being up so high. It was no ordinary wind. It was a jet stream, an April storm.

The shattered glass wall swept through the room and pulverized behind Kasper. After the glass, the wind grabbed the furniture, the children, Kain, the African, and threw them against the wall.

Kasper saw the grand piano rear up as if it wanted to stand on two legs. Then it was tossed across the room and splintered against the wall.

For a brief time, things were in limbo. During which, Kasper grabbed the two children. He laid them on top of Maximillian and fastened their feet to a pillar.

Then came the suction; the wind withdrew like a tidal wave after it has struck the coast.

It created an outward pull, as if an exit door had fallen off a jet plane. Kasper looked for Stina. She was sitting down holding on to a pillar. He saw Kain working his way toward the door.

The African let go of Ernst. Kasper saw him struggle to get the weapon into position. Saw him realize that his hands no longer obeyed. Then the undertow pulled him backward, slowly at first. He got down on his knees to try to escape the powerful current, without success. He grabbed for a pillar, but his hands weren't strong enough. Then he was sucked out over the sea.

Above them Kasper heard the helicopter propeller accelerate. He heard the mooring line's snap-lock pop open. Then the wind tore the machine away from the building.

He did not look up. He looked into his father's face. They were lying next to each other. Maximillian smiled.

He managed to lift one hand. He stroked Kasper's cheek.

"I know what you want to say. That it was beautiful. Touching. That I sacrificed myself for you. To atone for some of the mess your mother and I got you into. And you're right. You're damn right."

He tried to draw a breath. Kasper saw two shades of blood in his father's mouth. The dark-red blood oozing from the vein injuries. And the bright-red blood from his arteries. The latter made a sound like microscopic oxygen bubbles quietly boiling on the fluid's surface.

"I'm a man with great reserves," whispered Maximillian. "I can afford to agree with you. Just once. Here at the very end."

Even if his voice was now only the faintest whisper, it was full of life. The way Kasper remembered it from when his father was about forty. Maximillian's body was a silk thread in the universe. But his mind was undiminished.

"Don't talk. One of the things I liked best was death scenes. Do you remember Basotto? That clown kept coming in and dying over and over again. We almost peed in our pants with laughter. But this now. This will be the last time."

"Are you really sure about that, Grandpa?"

It was the little girl who spoke. The dying man focused on her.

"Isn't it a little late," he whispered, "to introduce me to my grandchild?"

"It couldn't be done earlier, unfortunately," said Kasper.

"You shouldn't be talking," said the girl. "You should think about the fact that you're going to die."

"What the hell?" said Maximillian.

She leaned over him. Placed a hand on his chest. And a hand on the top of his head.

"Bastian," she said.

The dark-haired boy knelt by Maximillian's head. The two youngsters focused their attention with an intensity that Kasper had never heard in children. Hardly even in adults.

Kasper gently held his father's body close. He felt something move against his hand, like a small animal. He realized it was his father's heart. The bullets had opened the back of the chest cavity and exposed the pulsating muscle.

"Really," said the girl, "there's nothing to fear."

Kasper heard the silence. Beginning from a center between the two children, it spread into a sphere and dissolved all sounds. The storm disappeared. The glass room. The bodies. The present. Denmark. The last thing Kasper saw was his father's face. When consciousness left his eyes and was drawn back into a tunnel. Then everything was gone.

# Part
# Eight

# 1

They drove him to Værløse airfield, the part the air force had kept. To a complex of small barracks half buried in the ground beside a barricaded area riddled with drainage holes and surrounded by signs saying POLLUTED.

It started to rain as they drove through the town of Jonstrup. The rain continued steadily through the three days they questioned him.

They let him sleep about three hours a day; the time of day was something he guessed at—there was no clock. They gave him nothing to eat, but offered him coffee and juice; he drank only water, just in case they might have put something in the juice and coffee.

He heard the rain on the roof start to play—Bach's cantatas, perhaps. After two days and nights he could hear very clearly the six string quartets that Haydn had written after a ten-year pause. And later, Mozart's six quartets that were a response to Haydn's. By that time Kasper had begun to see his sleeping dreams with open eyes, and he realized that his thoughts about music and the rain were in order to survive. In order to create some coherence in a reality that was falling apart.

There were three sets of two-person teams, one man and one woman on each team. They must have understood how he related to women; the women were warm and motherly. Every interrogation team uses the contrast between the good and the bad parent; he felt like weeping at the women's breasts, and did twice, while the questioning continued.

"Why were the children kidnapped?"

"I don't know," he said. "Could it have had something to do with a ransom, something to do with sex?"

"You've mentioned clairvoyance."

"That must be a misunderstanding," he said. "Clairvoyance is superstition, and I'm not superstitious. Do you have that in writing or on tape?"

"Why did you come back to Denmark?"

"I'm forty-two years old. I've come home to die in my own nest. Like the elephants, you know. For me, Denmark is an elephant cemetery."

"Why did you cancel your contracts?"

"I don't have the energy I once had."

"Where had you met the children before?"

"I never set eyes on them before."

"The girl says she had met you before."

"She remembers incorrectly. That's how it is to be loved and idolized and in the newspaper. Children and adults think they know you. I've suspected you too. Of just wanting to be in the proximity of fame."

"You were at the convent for the first time in May of last year."

"I was there for the first time two weeks ago. I went directly from the airport."

"Why did they come to get you?"

"Ask them. They're compassionate sisters. Isn't it their job to nurse lost souls?"


After two days and nights the threats began.

"The woman," they said. "And the child. We can hold them for an unlimited time. The national state of emergency suspends the law."

"What does that have to do with me?"

"You will be sent to Spain tomorrow."

He laughed within himself. Quietly, a private laughter. He no longer felt any anxiety. There is only so much you can take away from a person. After that, the person is free.

"Kain," said the woman across from him. "What does that name mean to you?"

"Isn't that something from the Bible?"

"When did you first meet him?"

"Could I sit on your lap for a little while?" said Kasper. "To collect my thoughts. Maybe something would come to me."

They had given him a chair with a slanting seat. He kept sliding down. He had heard about that kind of chair—some of the Moroccan performers had been interrogated by the Foreign Legion in Ajaccio, on the island of Corsica. They said that the slanting chair was worse than the beatings. Kasper held out for some hours. Until the middle of Mozart's *Dissonance* quartet.

"I need a different chair," he said. "It doesn't have to be an Eames. But it has to be better than this one. Otherwise, I'm going to cause an accident for you."

They did not react. They didn't believe he had any juice in his batteries. He stood up and tossed the chair with his foot; it hit the man across from him in the head.

The next instant the room was full of people and he was handcuffed with black plastic clamps. But they gave him a better chair.

"Can the children do anything special?" they had asked.

"They seemed like talented children," he said. "I'm sure they can shit and beat drums. How about asking them yourself?"

There was an oblong mirror in the room, shimmering, as if coated with oil: a one-way window for identification of suspects. In his case, the money was wasted; he could hear every movement behind the glass. His only complaint was that the glass cut off some of the high frequencies, as damp air does.

Most of the time he heard Moerk. Sometimes the baroness from Strand Road. Men and women with a tone of authority. Twice he heard someone who was perhaps the foreign minister; he remembered the sound pattern from one of the loges at a gala performance. Or else it was all his imagination. The only thing he was certain about was the rain.

After two days and nights he realized that what they were looking for was not the truth. What they were looking for was a fabrication. Which they and the public would be able to live with.

"Were the children abused? Was that the reason?"

He raised his head and looked straight at them.

"That was the motive," he said. "But they didn't succeed. That, and the money, perhaps. The convent's philanthropic foundation is very well off. Since the beginning of the last century. Donations from upper-class Russian immigrants who came to Denmark fleeing the Revolution."

He could tell that he had reached them. From then on, he controlled them.

"What was the woman, the engineer, doing in the tower?"

"A former friend. I had to use what help I could get."

"And you yourself?"

He settled himself on a razor's edge. It was a matter of ensuring Moerk's help. And reassuring the man and woman across from him.

"The Foreign Ministry's police department contacted me. Because the girl had been my student. A routine questioning. I offered to help them. I hoped it could benefit my court case."

Their faces were expressionless. But their relief came through clearly.

At some point he must have fainted after all. He had been unaware of the transfer, but he noticed that the room was different; the walls were now yellow, like plasma.

He lay on a thin mattress. He could hear those who were questioning him, he could understand the questions, but he could not see who was asking them.

He knew he was experiencing some sort of psychosis. Between the undulating walls human bodies developed animal heads; he realized immediately that people who were thrown in here unexpectedly would lose their minds.

He sensed that his praying ensured a kind of equanimity. It went on steadily like a deep, musical, automatic acceptance of the lack of structure around him. Prayer is a raft that ferries us safely through divorces, through drunken sprees, psychedelic mushroom trips, grade-three interrogations, and even through death, they say.

Prayer and love. He thought about Stina.


She had been gone for several years. He had tried everything: threats and pressure on the Geodesic Institute, Interpol's missing-persons department, private detectives, lawyers with international contacts. He had put ads in the personals columns of Europe's biggest newspapers. All to no avail.

One afternoon he had driven out again to Holte, to her parents' home. It was winter; her father was out in the garden cutting fruit trees with a grafting knife. Kasper stood for a while watching the man work. Absorbing his sound. Some of it reminded him of Stina.

"One shouldn't be too sentimental about love," said Kasper. "Most of what people call love, also here in Holte, could just as well be with someone else. Love is a very practical arrangement, as I can hear, and that's fine in its way. But the better that people fit together, and the greater the risks one is willing to take, the fewer options there are. I can't explain it, but it's the same with my profession; I couldn't have been anything very different—there are few or no alternatives. That's how it was with Stina and me. It's like a performance that got interrupted while it was still at the beginning, and twenty-four thousand tickets have been sold in advance, and I have a responsibility to the spectators. The spectators are all those parts of me, and of her, that want to have each other; it's not just the inner prince and princess, but also the inner cripples, the dwarfs, the naughty inner children. They sit waiting because they know it has been decided that this performance should be completed. It was commissioned higher up. I feel that somewhere outside the usual pettiness a contract has been written, and it needs to be fulfilled."

The man looked up. He had tears in his eyes.

"There's nothing I can do," he said.

Kasper had then driven out to see his own father. Maximillian had moved back to the large house in Skodsborg. One should be careful about moving back to places where one has suffered great losses; the house was filled with echoes of Helene Krone.

They sat in a living room that faced the water; around them were all the right pieces of furniture, the right pictures, the right view. Unfortunately, material things are not enough; something needs to breathe life into them, someone needs to blow into the instrument.

"You've always kept many things secret," said Kasper. "I applaud that wholeheartedly. I have a closed side too; but there's something about Stina—I could always hear that. You know something or other. And you must tell me now."

Maximillian looked around without finding what he was looking for, a way out. That's one of the disadvantages when you set yourself up expensively but simply; the surroundings no longer offer pretexts and hiding places.

"The police have a central database, and I looked her up. She spent two years in the women's prison in Horsens. For manslaughter. I couldn't get the details."


He accompanied Kasper to the door.

"My problem," said Kasper, "is that even if she had killed and devoured a whole family, I'd still love her."

Maximillian opened the door.

"I would too," he said.

Father and son looked out over the snow-covered lawns. Their sounds were related. Very often a particular aspect of loneliness is transmitted from one generation to the next.

"Nevertheless, we have to live," said Kasper. "I'm about to set my mind to meeting a woman who is more a nurse type. It would be fine if she was a member of the Ethical Council. And did volunteer work in a church congregation."

"When you find her," said Maximillian, "if she has a mother or older sister, will you give your father a call?"


The baroness from Strand Road brought him out of the psychosis. Back to a reality that was not much better than where he came from. She took his pulse. Lifted his eyelids and shone a light into his eyes.

All the same, it reassured him, in a sense. It was obviously important to them to keep him alive.

At one point, near the end—although at the time he didn't know that—they left the room. Vivian the Terrible came in. At first he couldn't see her; his sight was poor and his memory too. But he recognized her A-flat major. The depth of the musical key. Its compassion. He remembered how Mozart had often composed for the theater. How he had tuned into the singers. And then written in their specific musical key. For this woman he would have written an aria about a broken heart. In A-flat major.

He did not understand how she had gained admittance. But if there was anyone who could do that, it was she.

He knew that he couldn't ask about anything. They were being monitored, as if for a studio recording. He did it anyway.

"The children and Stina?"

"They are safe."

She tried to maintain her mask. But he could dimly see his mirror image in her eyes. He must look like a ghost.

"Kain and the woman?"

"Disappeared."

She had a portable radio with her, which she placed on the table and turned on. Tom Waits sang "Cold Water" from *Mule Variations*, deep loneliness and deep compassion and deep spiritual longing that hasn't found its way home and probably never will in this life, at 140 decibels in a bunker from World War II. The sound would paralyze all their small condenser microphones.

She leaned down to him.

"I've seen the state medical examiner's certificate. Cause of death: heart attack. Shall I get it revised?"

He shook his head.

"What will the official story be?" she asked.

"A compromise. Children kidnapped. A combination of sexual and economic motives. The kidnappers did not succeed."

"Reality is created by compromises," she said. "That's what human beings can tolerate. Many of my patients prefer to die with the television turned on. Your father and I. We were beyond that. We were headed into unknown territory."

———

She was gone. The interrogation team was back. They asked something, he answered; he understood neither their questions nor his answers. Moerk entered the room. With a small knife in his hand. He cut the handcuffs; Kasper gratefully rubbed his swollen hands.

"Kain and the woman?" he asked. "They got away. Was that part of the deal?"

Moerk shook his head. Kasper could hear he was telling the truth.

"The Avedøre embankment is closed. They've started pumping out the water. The inner city will be reopened in seven months. In eighteen months Copenhagen will look like itself again. Scarred. But otherwise as if nothing had happened."

"The desert fathers," said Kasper. "And Hegel. And Karl Marx. And the authors of the Old Testament. They discovered that if a person or a city was warned. By the Divine Being. And did not listen. Then history repeated itself. First as warnings. And later as catastrophes."

Beneath the other man's fatigue Kasper heard the anger. But the point is to make people wake up. And it's quite all right that sometimes it's hate that awakens first.

"I was never interested in religions," said the official. "And I'm especially not interested in Karl Marx and the desert fathers."

"It's never too late to become wiser," said Kasper. "Not even at the point where you are. Three-fourths in the grave."

Moerk drew back. Without training in the ring, without five thousand nights with two thousand people who don't give up at the doors, it's hard to have the last word with a clown.

The door slammed. Kasper put his head on the table and fell asleep.

# 2

He awoke to daylight coming through the bars at the windows and managed to get to his feet. From his second-floor room he looked out toward Fælled Park and the outdoor swimming pool. He was in Section A of Rigshospital, a locked ward.

He was wearing hospital underwear. A T-shirt and pajama bottoms. On the table lay the lottery ticket, his fountain pen, and four kroner, seventy-five øre, in change. They had taken away his shoes.

He lay down, absolutely still. Tried to connect with his nervous system.

From the loudspeakers at the outdoor café in the park he heard a saxophonist tackle the hopeless task of repaying some of our communal debt to Coltrane.

On the radio of a parked car Chet Baker was singing in a recording from the days when he still had his Dean Martin looks, with teeth in his mouth and hair on his head. It was swing music, the likes of which, Kasper imagined, could otherwise only be heard from the heavenly hosts as they circled around God's throne.

From the paddleboat lake came the sounds of children's voices and laughter; they merged into snatches of *Brandenburg Concerto Number 2*. Bach's music could swing too.

He listened out through the wall. To the sound of two men who had not yet had deeper contact with the feminine spirit; it was the two monks.

The door opened. The Blue Lady walked into the room, followed by the monks. She held her arms out to the side; they frisked her and left the room, shutting the door behind them.

He sat down on the bed, and she pulled a chair over next to him.

For a while they sat there like that. The silence thickened around them.

"The children are safe," she said. "Stina is safe. They were questioned, which was no fun, but now that's over. Now they have peace and quiet."

He nodded.

"Benneweis Circus has announced its fall program; you're on it—posters are already printed. It appears that you've had a self-appointed impresario, a woman; she said on television that she's gotten a binding commitment from the Interior Ministry that your Danish citizenship will be restored. I've spoken with the patriarchate of Paris, and they have approached the Spanish king regarding the question of a pardon. We'll see how that goes."

The woman rose.

"I want to get out of here," said Kasper. "I want to see Stina and KlaraMaria."

"They want to put you through the extensive psychiatric examination ordered by the court. The Intelligence Service isn't finished with you either. Nor is Department H. They say it will take three months. You'll be out in August."

He clutched her nun's habit. She gently removed his hands.

"The time comes," she said, "when feelings between the student and the teacher have reached a depth that indicates there will be help and contact whenever needed. But we always have to be careful not to let it slip into mollycoddling."

Anger rose in him like a jack-in-the-box.

"Surely you can give me more than that?" he said. "Look at my situation. I need information. I need comforting and blessing."

"I can give you a bus card."

"They've taken my shoes," he said. "That's more effective than chains and handcuffs. Without shoes I won't get any farther than Nørre Boulevard."

"Before I came in here," she said, "I went to the restroom. In the hall just outside here. The ladies' room. In there, I somehow forgot the shoes I was wearing when I arrived. By divine coincidence, they were jogging shoes. Much too big for me. Size ten. They felt like clown shoes. Fortunately, I had these in my pocket."

She stretched out her foot. She was wearing a pair of white gymnast shoes.

She stood up.

"I'm not the one who told you that Stina and KlaraMaria are at the Institute. But only for twenty-four more hours at the most."

She was gone.


He opened the door.

"I need to use the toilet," he said.

The monks walked on either side of him, holding him under the arms.

"Would one of you please go in with me?" he said. "The past few days have been hard on my nerves; I don't like to have to sit and take a crap all by myself."

They edged away from him a little, which was what he had counted on. When he went into the restroom they remained outside the outer door.

He knew the restrooms. He had been on the locked ward several times during the good years, with students who had borderline diagnoses and schizophrenics who had scored 1.0 on the Thought Disorder Index. In those days he had gone along with everything if the parents had money. And sometimes also, already then, out of compassion. It was nice to think that this compassion came back to him now like a gentle karmic wind.

Both Francis of Assisi and Ramana Maharshi had said that, for the enlightened person, the world is a madhouse, while locked wards can seem refreshingly normal. Both men had called themselves "God's clown."

He went into the women's restroom. The shoes were behind the toilet bowl. They were his shoes. She must have found them in his suitcase.

They had a celestial tone. He reached inside them and felt the kroner bills. There were five thousand kroner, in five-hundred-kroner bills. Bohr looked healthier than before.

The mirrors above the sink were plates of polished stainless steel. One of Kasper's students from those earlier days had escaped from a restroom, through the ceiling; she was never found. What clients can manage must also be possible for the therapist. He climbed onto the water tank and then up onto the hand dryer. The panels in the ceiling were rock-wool slabs; many psychiatric disturbances cause increased sensitivity to sound. Like his own now, for example. He pushed up a panel and pulled himself into a ventilation duct.

He crawled out of the duct and found himself in front of an empty office facing Henrik Harpestreng Road. He jumped from a window onto the green lawn by the hospital laundry, reached through an open window, and fished out a pair of blue work pants from a pile of uniforms.

Spurred by a happy impulse, he went back to the main entrance.

He gave Lona Bohrfeldt's name at the reception desk, was told a floor, a section, and a room number, and took the elevator up.

The room was on a surgical ward and had several beds in it. In the bed by the window lay a man with a bandaged head, but the sound and general atmosphere around him were full of vitality. Above the bandages his black hair bristled like a clothes brush.

Lona Bohrfeldt sat on a chair beside the bed. She was in the last trimester of pregnancy, where both body and sound seem ready to burst.

"I came on duty now," said Kasper, "here at my second job as the medical director, in order to check up on your health. May I?"

He put his ear to the woman's abdomen; a spasm went through the man in the bed.

"Everything sounds stable," said Kasper. "He's had some shocks, that little fellow. But he's recovering. Children can stand an incredible amount. He'll be a fully developed troublemaker. How are things going with the gums?"

"He still needs to be careful about speaking," said the woman.

"Enjoy it," said Kasper. "As long as it lasts. We all talk too much."

"What about the children?"

"They're back. With their parents."

Tears came to her eyes.

"Kain has disappeared," he said. "Do you have any idea where I could find him? Just to have a polite exchange of opinions about what's happened."

She shook her head.

"The only thing he kept saying," she said, "was that there had to be a sauna nearby."

Kasper moved toward the door.

"We want to thank you," she said.

"Remember Beethoven," said Kasper. "When the audience blubbered too much, he said: 'The artist doesn't want tears. He wants applause.'"

"We want to invite you to the christening."

The patients in the other beds were following the exchange.

"A person like me," said Kasper, "must usually protect his private life from his overwhelming popularity. But in this case, I could make an exception. So I'll come. Like the fairy godmother. And as a baby gift I'll bring the little juvenile delinquent the best hearing. And the best manners."

"In return," said Lona Bohrfeldt, with a glance at his work pants and T-shirt, "perhaps we could help you with some nicer clothes."


He walked down Blegdam Road; when he heard the sirens he ducked into Fælled Park. He found the place within himself where the prayer went like this: "May SheAlmighty's will be done, even if it means I get nabbed. But I still pray to have just one hour."

A woman ran past him. She was wearing sharkskin and running shoes. It was the head of Department H, Asta Borello.

"I got out of the locked ward," he said.

Without losing speed, she turned her head. Saw the hospital T-shirt.

He couldn't have kept pace with her very long, but that wasn't necessary either, thank God; she slowed down and began to walk. Staring straight ahead. He empathized with her; he knew the feeling. Of hoping you are standing before a fata morgana. And at the same time knowing that, alas, that's not the case.

"I'd like you to know that I don't hold a grudge," he said.

She wanted to start running, but her legs refused to obey.

"I'll not only pay my taxes gladly," he said. "I'll pay them with quivering delight. But I'd like to help you go further. In your personal development. That's the danger, with the Customs and Tax authorities, and with excessive physical training. The danger of losing your natural, flowing, feminine spontaneity. Think about it."

He had to move on. He set out at a trot. By the rose garden, near the Østerbro post office, he turned and waved. She didn't return his greeting. But even at that distance he could hear that the meeting had made a lasting impression.


He waited in the bushes opposite the steps up to the post office. It didn't take even five minutes before a car stopped; a man got out to mail a letter, leaving the key in the ignition and the motor running.

Kasper got into the driver's seat. On the seat beside him lay a suit jacket in a carrying bag and an active cell phone. How lucky can one be? "For he that has, to him shall be given" (Mark 4:25). He locked the door and rolled the window down slightly.

The man was the blond Prince Valiant, Professor Frank.

Kasper listened into the situation. Into its divine improbability. He knew—knew, but without understanding—that he was on the threshold of the place where his life's storyboard had been mapped out.

"I'm an ethical person," he said through the crack in the window. "A devout believer. But I need a car. And I don't think it's a coincidence that it will be your car. I think you and I are getting a glimpse of compensatory karma in action. A kind of fateful payback. But still, I want you to know that you can pick up your car tomorrow. On the tent grounds at Bellahøj. The keys will be above the visor."

Then he stepped on the gas.


He drove across Langelinje Bridge and parked near the tollbooth. His good judgment told him that he ought to be weighed down under great unsolved existential questions: Where is the woman? Where is the child? What will the revenge be? However, good judgment is but one of the many voices in the internal boys' choir. Instead he heard the springtime. He heard the life around him. Even the people busy scraping together money on a walk along the beach, with no other perspective than being able to have an overweight retirement and leave a respectable amount of small change to the children—for whom a large inheritance is downright harmful, even when it sounds wonderful. And it wasn't only the people. Kasper also heard the migration of birds toward Falsterbro, as spring worked its way toward Sweden.

He dialed the number Kain had written on the lottery ticket. "Yes?"

A person must be careful when answering the telephone—someday it could be one of the great clowns calling. Kain should have let it ring; as soon as he took the call he was located. Kasper listened for a moment. Then he broke the connection.

He drove back past the English Church. On its grounds the Russian czar had once planned to construct a large Russian Orthodox Church; perhaps with a little more tailwind, Hesychasm could have been more successful with the Danish public.

Kasper parked on the square by Marmor Church. Put on the suit jacket. He bought a pack of playing cards at the kiosk on Dronningens Tvær Street. Outside Nevsky Church he stood for a moment enjoying Bronikov's portrait of Alexander Nevsky, then he took a deep breath, said a prayer, and listened to the Church. To its discipline. Its compassion. Its stubbornness. Its deep understanding of how experiences of the Divine require training. It was like the circus. To Kasper, Luther's idea that everything is preordained had always seemed completely contrary to everyone's daily experience. Shortly before Groucho Marx died, a journalist asked him to sum up existence. The great comedian had stripped the irony off his face like a latex mask; so close to the grave there was no time for anything less than the truth. "Most of us," he said, "must try to compensate for our low intelligence with hard work. It's all a matter of training."

Kasper pressed the doorbell; the deacon opened it.

"I need a bath," said Kasper.


They walked through the small assembly hall. The deacon opened a door and handed Kasper a large, coarse-woven towel; steam poured out toward them, as thick as smoke.

It was a Russian bathhouse. Kasper walked along a narrow tiled corridor; he counted five open doors leading to small rooms, each with its sunken bathtub. In several of the tubs men lay floating, weightless, breathing softly, like baby walruses. The corridor opened into a communal room with a small circular pool; six men sat on a ledge in the hot water, three of them with long beards.

Kasper took off his clothes and laid them on a chair. Then he walked through a glass door into the steam bath.

The walls of the room were painted with purification motifs from the New Testament: Jesus' baptism, Jesus washing the disciples' feet, Mary Magdalene washing Jesus' feet. The woman was portrayed with her face turned away, so she wouldn't see the nakedness in the bathhouse.

Along the far end of the room were three levels of marble ledges; Kain sat on the bottom ledge. Kasper pulled a chair in front of the other man and sat down.

Kain must have been sitting there for a while; his face was red and moist, the veins on the surface of his skin pulsating.

"It was you who telephoned," he said. "How did you find me?"

Kasper pointed to the surroundings. They heard the quiet hiss of the steam from vents under the marble ledge. The water murmuring in the pipes. From somewhere far off, music could be heard.

"Tchaikovsky's liturgy and vesper service," said Kasper. "I couldn't hear either the themes or the words. But the modal character came through. And the overtones from the bells. They must have bells. I haven't heard them ring. But they swing in rhythm when there's singing."

He opened the pack of cards, cut the deck, and shuffled.

"There are six bells," said Kain. "Constructed as a carillon. The last bell ringer who had mastered the technique died in '62. The Church and its mysteries are in danger of dying out. I'm going to be its salvation."

Kasper dealt the cards.

"How," he said, "did a wealthy man of honor like you, who owns spas and sanatoriums, develop an interest in a little Russian bathhouse with an adjoining chapel on Bred Street?"

"Mother Maria told me about it. It's a meeting place for the religious patriarchs. The priests from St. Ansgar Church come here. The Catholic bishop. The chief rabbi. The royal confessionarius. Mother

Maria says when the day comes that they also invite her and the imams, a new perspective will open for religious life in Denmark."

"And how do you know Mother Maria?"

"KlaraMaria introduced us."

Kasper felt a sudden, inexplicable, and irrational stab of jealousy. Men do not want to share women's attention with other men; it makes no difference whether the women are over seventy or under twelve—we want them entirely for ourselves.

"Pick up your cards," said Kasper. "We're playing Hold'em, two cards in your hand, five on the table, three rounds."

Kain picked up his cards.

"What are we playing for?" he asked.

"For your life," said Kasper.

Kain looked at him. Kasper heard again the physical threat of the other man.

"The stakes are parts of the truth," said Kasper. "Candor. I'll begin: Can you hear the sounds around us? The reflection from the marble walls? Slightly softer than granite. But still hard. Yet toned down by the steam. It creates intimacy. In the midst of the hardness. Can you hear that?"

The steam closed in around them, the walls of the room beginning to disappear.

"You and I," said Kasper, "are sitting within this intimacy. There's a special, almost jovial tone when men are naked together. You're free of your wing collar and bow tie and puttees. Free of your public image; clothing is a mask. You're a little bit closer to yourself. With distant happy memories of playing naked on the beach. With lively acoustic souvenirs from the soccer club's locker room. Can you hear it? Do you follow me? I'm reminded of Eckehart: 'Whom did God make love with in order to give birth to so many sounds?' And amid this tonal Eden is the sound of you. Your greed. Your manipulations and criminal offenses. Enough to merit lifetime imprisonment. And behind everything: maltreatment and murder of a child. Your bid. Your blind is the truth about the child. What have I heard wrong?"

"About the child," said Kain. "That was Ernst. Things got out of control. He's paid for it."

Kaspar dealt three cards face-up on the table: the queen of hearts, king of diamonds, and ace of spades.

"You're responsible," said Kasper.

"I've repented. Mother Maria says no sin is so great that it can't be repented."

"What about justice?" said Kasper.

"You're as furious as a one-man army. What about this bid?"

The fan of cards swam before Kasper's eyes.

"And what's made you gentle as a lamb?" he said.

"Meeting the little girl. And Mother Maria. I'm going to sell everything. I'm going to put it all at the Institute's disposal. I've repented. Am sorry for everything. I'm waiting for your bid."

"Help me with the chronology," said Kasper. "In August of last year all twelve children are gathered in Copenhagen. They contact you. You suggest something. Was it that they should cause the earthquakes? Could they make them happen? Can they manipulate the physical world? Or can they only predict what it will do?"

He cast aside the top card and turned the next; it was the two of diamonds.

Kain shrugged his shoulders.

"I work with options. For me there's almost no difference. Between making things happen and knowing they will happen. They said the earthquakes would occur."

"So you come up with the scheme of buying worthless property. And creating among potential buyers the idea—the true or false idea—that the earthquakes and the cave-ins are over. For that, you need to use the children. What they get in return is that you'll bring them here—is that correct?"

Kain nodded.

"But there must be more," said Kasper.

"I'll help to manage the publicity. And the media. When the children go public with all this."

Kasper shook his head slowly.

"They want to force the world to do something or other. By threatening that they can cause natural disasters. That's vandalism. That's child terrorism. That's criminal children. Is this true? Can they do that?"

Kain shrugged his shoulders.

"And you planned to cooperate in this?" said Kasper.

"I've been converted. I've seen the light."

"Where did the children live while they were here?"

"At the Institute. That was simple. I got an associate to apply to the Institute."

"The blonde," said Kasper. "Irene Papas?"

Kain nodded.

"The Institute organized transportation. But we picked them up outside the country. In some cases, the parents wouldn't let them go. That's why the reports. Unfortunately, I gave Ernst one of the tasks."

"Why didn't Mother Maria see through you?"

Kain cast aside another card and turned the final one over. It was the ten of spades.

"Saint Symeon the New Theologian," he said, "writes that it's important not to attribute omniscience to a spiritual teacher. Even the greatest ones are human beings."

Kasper found it painful to breathe. Perhaps it was the steam, perhaps it was the bitterness of no longer having a monopoly on citing the Church fathers.

"So you simulated a kidnapping," he said. "Why only two of the children?"

"That's all we needed. To convince the buyers."

"KlaraMaria sent a postcard to a hydrologist. A woman from the lay order. The card showed a picture of Copenhagen Harbor after the earthquake. Why was it sent?"

Kain's tone changed. An interplay of tics and tension suddenly came and went across his face.

"Those children, they're monsters. Kidnapping them is a punishment in itself. There's no need for legal prosecution. They wanted to prove that they knew about the earthquakes in advance. But they hadn't informed me."

"But my mistakes," said Kain, "are a fantastic starting point for a process of spiritual growth. I want to make a really significant difference. For the women and the children."

"First," said Kasper, "you're going to spend some time in jail. Showdown."

He laid the jack and seven of clubs on the table. Kain stared at the straight. He put his cards on the table. The king of hearts and the five of hearts.

"There's not much pigment in the red color," said Kasper. "A little lighter, a little faster than the black. On the other hand, the face cards are a little heavier. I could hear your cards."

Kain leaned toward him.

"I have a network like an American president. I'm resurrecting the Church. I support the Institute. I'm a tremendous ally."

"I'm the one who rescued the children," said Kasper.

"I have fantastic spiritual potential," said Kain. "Mother Maria has let me understand that. I've just had to take a roundabout path. Many of the great ones had to do that. Milarepa. The tax collector in the Bible. The rich man Jesus met. Paul. But now I genuflect. I make amends. I'm going to go forward like a galloping horse."

"You're going to go to Horsens state prison. I'm the nuns' star."

"I've found the way to humility," said Kain. "Deep humility. I give everything to the Church. To the Institute. I kneel before my neighbor."

"My humility is global," said Kasper. "I've sacrificed a global career. I wash everyone's feet. I even wash yours."

Kasper struggled to get off the chair and down on his knees. But he was weak, and Kain was headed in the same direction. It was a competition in humility. But the steam blinded them. On their knees in front of each other their heads banged together, inadvertently, but with damaging force nonetheless.

The difficulty for us beginners is that our good intentions have a hard time tolerating situations that are a little more stressful. When it comes right down to it, compassion often proves to be just a thin layer of gold leaf over a somewhat coarser metal. Kain put his hands around Kasper's neck. But Kasper just sat there. When a passionate poker player has settled himself somewhere, it takes a great deal to remove him.

He felt his eyesight and his hearing begin to fail. Kain slowly pressed him back toward the marble slab and the jets from which scalding-hot steam was hissing.

Kasper was aware of the prayer; it turned to Dismas, the good thief on the cross next to the Savior. Dismas is the patron saint of gamblers and all who serve long prison sentences.

Then he head-butted the man above him.

That threw Kain backward, his body sliding across the thin layer of water on the floor and crashing into the wall. His forehead was wounded, his face covered with blood.

The glass door opened. In the doorway stood the deacon.

"The bathhouse is sacrosanct," he said, "like the church."

He stepped aside; Kasper got to his feet, slowly, unsteadily, then lifted Kain and half dragged, half carried him past the deacon.

The deacon pointed. Kasper placed Kain under a shower and stood under another himself. The deacon turned on a faucet.

The showerheads were not just large, they were as big as mill wheels. And the water that gushed out of them was not only cold, it was meltwater from the Caucasus.

"Cold ablutions," said the old man thoughtfully, "have always been among the deepest spiritual techniques."

Kasper felt millions of capillaries contract. But the magnanimity of his heart swelled.

"Jealousy increases in proportion to one's closeness to great spiritual leaders," he said to Kain. "At the end, when one is within touching distance, it approaches insanity. I beg your forgiveness."

Kain's gaze was still blurred. Kasper took one of the large towels from a radiator and went toward the businessman.

"Come," he said, "and let Kasper dry your back."

Kain drew back.

"After that," said Kasper, "I'll rub you with moisturizing lotion. And massage your feet."

Kain grabbed a towel from a chair. The bearded men by the pool watched them silently.

Kain tottered backward. Without taking his eyes off Kasper, he wrapped the towel around himself. He staggered through the corridor. Kasper followed close after him.

"The head butt," shouted Kasper, "that I gave you just now. I take it back. I kiss your forehead. I weep over having lost control once again."

Kain managed to open the door to the street. He stumbled down the steps and onto the sidewalk.

Passersby stopped. At the bottom of the stairs was a woman. For a fantastic moment Kasper thought it was Asta Borello. That would have been monumental synchronicity.

Then he saw it was a stranger. And in a way that was a relief. When the cosmos dishes out artificial coincidences it's nice not to have an overdose.

Kain hurried past the woman and began to run along Bred Street. Kasper waved to the spectators. Bowing deeply, he glided backward toward the dressing rooms.


He walked down the corridor and put on his clothes; on the way out he stood for a moment opposite one of the small rooms. The man in the bathtub was hidden behind a newspaper. Kasper went into the room.

"Pardon me for disturbing you," he said, "but I'm following the sound. I'm driven by a desire to listen one last time to Il Destriero Scafusia from Schaffhausen. And to get a glance at your newspaper."

The man lowered the newspaper; it was Weidebühl. Both men looked at the teak chair beside the bathtub; on top of the carefully folded clothing lay the watch.

The lawyer handed over the newspaper. Kasper turned to the numbers from the last Class Lottery drawing on the back page. He took out his lottery ticket and ran his fingers down the numbers in the paper; he found a number that matched his own. His ticket had won. He stood there quietly, for a minute, perhaps.

"My lottery ticket has won," he said. "Six million kroner; it's a one-eighth ticket, which means I've won seven hundred fifty thousand. And I must confess that for a brief moment, a few seconds ago, I wasn't filled with gratitude toward the Divine, but with bitterness, because I hadn't gone back to my favorite bailiff, Asta, on Kampmann Street and borrowed a thousand to buy a whole ticket. Do you know what I mean?"

The lawyer shook his head.

"Greed," said Kasper, "is one of the trickiest obstacles to spiritual progress. But thank God, the next second I felt the prayer within my heart begin, and it's continuing now. I'm praying to Saint Cecilia; I wonder if you know her—she's the patron saint of music."

Kasper heard a movement behind him; the deacon stood in the hallway.

"I apologize for that incident earlier," said Kasper, "but how you can open the door to a fierce baboon like Kain is beyond my understanding."

"If a place or an atmosphere is, in the truest sense, divine," said the deacon, "then it can't be closed to anyone."

The three men looked at one another. Kasper felt he had been mistaken about the Orthodox Church. Perhaps in the end it would encompass and survive the modern world after all.

"Is that also true of our friend," he said, "Mother Maria, the metropolit of Bagsværd?"

The deacon took some time before replying.

"We're going to be working on that," he said.

Kasper folded the ticket.

"There are some numbers on this piece of paper," he said. "Telephone numbers and others. Also a winning lottery number. I have no use for any of them. Where I'm going."

He stuck the ticket into the breast pocket of the deacon's robe.

"A symbolic contribution," he said. "To the work of Christianity in integrating the more difficult women."


The deacon accompanied him to the door.

"What about a small word of thanks?" said Kasper. "It is, after all, close to a million kroner."

"Saint Pachomius," said the old man, "around the year 307, had a vision from God in which he received some of the monastic rules we still follow. In the vision it was also said that if anyone gives alms to the brothers and sisters, it is the giver who should say thank you."

Kasper and the deacon looked at each other. Then Kasper bowed.

"Thank you," he said. "To you. To the Orthodox Church. And to the Danish Class Lottery."

# 3

He parked on Nybro Road. Like the last time. But this time he went out to the edge of the lake, where the buildings ended.

He had to walk very slowly. He must have lost over thirty pounds. There was no fat left, not even on his rear end. He had blood effusions just from having sat on the chair while they interrogated him.

He found a spot opposite the little domed church where the view to the convent was blocked by a tree, and managed somehow to struggle over the fence. But afterward he had to lie on the grass for maybe ten minutes before he could continue.

He entered the main building by a side door. The corridors were deserted. Far away he heard a mass. They were singing something by Bach, one of the Easter cantatas, something with "Rejoice, ye hearts."

Behind the music he heard what he was looking for.

He took the elevator to the guest wing. They were staying in the cell that had been his. When he was still a nun.

He knocked, and walked in. Stina and KlaraMaria were sitting on the bed drinking tea. Between them lay a mountain of dolls. He sat down on a chair, the one the Blue Lady had used.

The tone around them was larger than the room; it was arched, like a cathedral. He had heard before that the variation of wave amplitude between parents and children could take that form when there was love between them. And when both the woman and the child resembled something from Greek mythology.

He didn't belong in the sound picture. He had no place there. He wasn't qualified. He would never be allowed in. It was too late.

"It's good you came," said the girl. "You're going to read me bedtime stories. And play music afterward. Both the violin and the piano. Something by that man Bach. Every night."

She edged closer.

"I'm going to sit on your lap. And you're going to hold me. Every night. I'm very affectionate."

She began to hum. "Bona Nox."

He started to sweat under his arms.

"It will take a long time," she said. "A long, long time. Until you've paid me back. For not being there when I was little."

She hit the dolls.

"Two hundred Bratz. They promised me five hundred. They promised!"

She stood up.

"I'm going outside to play."

She paused in front of him. Gently ran her fingertips along his jaw. Like a grown woman.

"She's mine," she said. "My mother. Just mine."

He nodded.

"I don't think you should say anything to her," she said, "that you wouldn't want me to hear."

He nodded again. The force of the girl's personality was unwavering. Like Karajan's. Nobody had been able to contradict Karajan. Not Richter. Not even Ingmar Bergman.

Then she was gone.


He waited until Stina's individual tone was established. It too was a space. But its form was slightly different from what she had with the child. He had heard that space from the beginning. On the beach. He had wanted to enter it. *Wanted* wasn't the right word. He had been drawn into it. And afterward had never found the way out. Never wanted to find the way out.

It was an open space. No furniture to bump into. No traps. No cautiousness. But still. There had been a place he was always forbidden to enter. But now he no longer had anything to lose.

"You were in Horsens prison for two years," he said. "Before I met you. For manslaughter."

He had sat across from all sorts of delinquents. The circus is like that. A world that includes many things. Murder had a particular sound. A sound of something ultimate. It was present in the room now. That's the remarkable thing about words. The mere sound of them activates part of the reality they name.

"It was a lover," she said. "He raped me. It happened when he came after me the second time."

He listened into her system.

"In that case," he said, "rape is a path I will never take."

She got up, went over, and stood behind him.

"I'm glad to hear that," she said. "Damned glad."

Her hand stroked the back of his neck. His relays switched off. His brain switched off. His synapses stopped firing. He was available gratis, waiting to be claimed. He had no defenses against her. Outside, he heard children's laughter.

"How long are they here?" he asked. "The children."

"They're flying home tomorrow. All except KlaraMaria."

"And the idea of their having predicted the earthquake?"

"I had to figure out something. To explain to you the contact between her and me."

Deep, deep within him a warning signal went off. But it was too far away. He felt the warmth of her palms. Almost like live coals. His hearing closed down.

**4**

He woke up and knew that the woman and the child had left him.

It had been a deep sleep. One haunted with apparitions, like an opium dream. His body ached, his eyelids sticky with the poppy glue of sleep. His hearing scanned the building; they were gone. He staggered into the hallway and opened the cell door. They hadn't slept in the bed. The dolls were gone. Their clothes were gone.

He splashed cold water on his face. The face in the mirror no longer attracted readers of women's magazines. It called for plastic surgery. At the Rigshospital hospice.

He could hear one of the matins. From the church. Filtered through the masonry. Sixty women in ecstasy. While he could barely stand upright.

When he was a child and all tent owners had been men and all mothers had been women, he had wished the world could be ruled by a feminine principle. Now, when that was starting to happen, he had begun to have doubts.

He stumbled through the white corridors. Feeling as if he were crawling on all fours. Outside the attic room he stopped and listened.

The African was speaking.

"There's a box," she said. "With three hundred dolls in it. From Fætter BR toy store. It can't have been lost. You must have it somewhere."

For mystics and clowns, every unexpected situation sparkles in the sunshine. Like a visual and auditory jewel. He opened the door.

She was sitting at the Blue Lady's desk. Her leg was in a cast. The stitches on her face shone pink in the darkness of her skin. They were healing.

He could hear that it was at least twenty-four hours since she had gotten any sleep. And that she could handle that.

"Where are they?" he asked.

He could hear dust and resin in his voice.

"They'll write to you. Within a month."

From anyone but her he would have forced a confession. But it wasn't the right time for self-mutilation.

The prayer began. He was aware of his breathing. His system prepared for the final entrée. Her eyes were on him. He knew that if he made even one false move she would take him off the stage.

He placed the car keys in front of her.

"I had to steal a car to get out here yesterday. It's parked by the Nybrogård psychiatric residence. A royal-blue BMW. I'm afraid all of you will get the blame when it's found. I'm still free strictly on the basis of your medical statement. The car needs to be delivered to the tent grounds at Bellahøj. Do you think we could get one of the little novices to run over there with it?"

She gave him a searching look. He let his tone and attention shift to her feet. That was how he had devastated Europe's poker halls. Not by going straight to the heart. Not by dissembling. Instead, he had let his attention go down to people's feet.

She rose.

"You'll get to see them again," she said. "Stina and KlaraMaria. It may be as long as a year. Things take whatever time they take. But you will see them."

"I'm not worried," he said.

She walked with one crutch. Weightless. For a moment he just sat there enjoying the scene. Bach would have done the same. Even if he had been in the midst of the final movement of *Die Kunst der Fuge*.

He turned toward the telephone. He listened to the prayer. Now for the last time he had to get past a female guardian of a threshold. For the last time surmount a barrier by means of a swindle. For the last time operate very deceitfully. He felt that it wasn't for his sake alone. That something greater was active in and through him. Was it SheAlmighty? We can hope so. But can we ever be completely sure?

---

He telephoned Fætter BR, the company's main store on Roskilde Road. A young woman answered the phone. He had not prepared anything; he acted according to the openness of the voice. People under thirty haven't yet stopped believing that something wonderful can suddenly happen.

"This is the Lord Chamberlain's office," he said. "We'd like to have five hundred Bratz dolls delivered. With cars and clothes and all the accessories. Packed in a large cardboard container. Can you do that within an hour? It's a gift for a diplomat. Have it delivered to the prime minister's official residence, between Bagsværd and Lyngby Lake. There's a separate delivery entrance at the back."

"That would be two containers," she said. "On one pallet. With a transport company. All our own trucks are busy now. And we don't have the dolls in the warehouse; the men will need a little time to collect them from the stores."

"That's all right," said Kasper. "We'll arm ourselves with royal patience."

"Where should I send the bill?"

Kasper's mind was in his feet. The prayer continued.

"Send it to Amalienborg Palace. The zip code isn't necessary. And we usually get a twenty percent discount."

He waited for the truck at the edge of the lake. It was springtime. Summer was on the way.

The vehicle arrived after an hour. It was as large as a moving van. And the driver had a sound Kasper recognized. From the distant past. He identified the face. It belonged to one of the young knifers who had helped him get into Konon. Beside him sat the dark-haired fourteen-year-old boy.

Kasper heard their tone expand in shock. But their faces revealed nothing.

He borrowed a hobby knife from them. Slit open a container. He dumped dolls and packing materials into the vehicle. Until the box was half empty. Then he took the knife and cut three holes in the cardboard.

"I'm going to climb inside," he said. "Then I want you to close the top. And tape me in."

He took two tire irons from the floor of the truck. As Augustine, and Ramana Maharshi after him, said: "We will be guided. Still, it can't hurt to take precautions."

"This is a fairy tale," said the younger boy. "I know the story. From school. A Danish fairy tale. Afterward we'll throw you in the river."

"Never-ever-no you won't, by God."

He gave them directions to the convent.

"There's an African woman in the office. She has eyes as big as one of the beasts from the Koran. But don't let that scare you. Tell her you have a delivery of dolls. Sent several days ago. But delayed. And ask where it should be delivered. She'll give you an address. You'll drive there. You'll put me on a dolly. And take me all the way inside."

Kasper crawled into the container. The boys did not move.

"You've gotten thinner," said the younger one. "Since we last saw you. That's not so strange. With the life you lead."

Kasper arranged a place to lie down. In the packing materials.

"But your finances must still be good," said the boy.

Kasper emptied his pockets. He found the last five thousand kroner. Handed them over.

"You're a desperate man," said the boy. "We could try to pressure you more. We need a little something for the tire irons too."

Kasper turned his pockets inside out; they were empty.

"A fountain pen, maybe?"

He handed the boys his fountain pen. They closed the top of the container and taped it up.

"We'll bring you all the way to the person who's supposed to get this box," said the youngest voice. "Even if the Devil is guarding the place. I swear it on the Koran. And I've always kept my part of a deal."

**5**

He felt the container being loaded onto a dolly. He heard the boys' labored breathing up an ascent. He heard traffic on main streets. The echo from open spaces in parks and market squares. The wind rustling in banana trees. They were by the Botanical Gardens. Next door to the Geological Museum. Going up to the Copenhagen Observatory.

They must have brought along skids; they got the dolly past a doorstep and into an elevator. He no longer remembered how many elevators there had been in the past months. Infinitely many. This, he somehow knew, would be the last.

He was rolled down a corridor and through a door; he heard the space around the container become dome-shaped, or else it was he himself. The box was loaded off the dolly. The boys' steps moved away, and everything was quiet around him.

Not the usual silence. But the silence that SheAlmighty must have been working with when she opened Her mouth and said: "Let there be light."

He summoned the last of his strength, pressed against the cover, and burst it open.

The room was shaped like a dome. It was the observatory itself. The ceiling was a perfect hemisphere, made of double-curvature copper plate. A gigantic telescope of polished brass and bronze next to the wall was mounted on a track that made a complete circle around the room. Josef Kain stood leaning against the ocular.

Beneath the center of the dome, in a circle around Kasper's box, sat the twelve children, Stina, and the Blue Lady. Andrea Fink. Daffy. The Beet. They sat cross-legged. Like simpletons in group therapy. Like Hindu nuns performing a *puja*.

One can't spend thirty-five years in show business without having had the opportunity to enjoy seeing naked women pop out of layer cakes on various tasteful occasions. But Kasper had never had a chance to really listen in to the situation from the women's perspective. He did now.

He felt deep contentment. For a moment the faces around him were blank with amazement. For a moment the silence retreated from the overwhelming women and the fantastic children. And the room resounded with defenseless astonishment. The word *thunderstruck* would have been appropriate. Even for the Blue Lady.

At that moment Kasper realized, and each person under the observatory dome realized, how even in the most sacred gatherings SheAlmighty holds back the clown until the last moment, as a trump card up her sleeve.

Then the silence was regenerated.

The Blue Lady stood up and went over to get a chair; the children made room in the circle. She placed the chair in it.

"Kasper Krone," she said. "*Avanti*. We're very happy to see you."

The suitcases were lined up along the walls with the tags of eleven different airlines already attached. He was witness to a farewell.

"The children were never kidnapped," he said. "They went along voluntarily. There was a skirmish. But no coercion. They made a deal with Kain. What was it?"

*Shame* was not a word he would have connected with the children in front of him. But the feeling was present now. Dissonant in a magnificent way. Like the beginning of the last movement of Beethoven's Ninth. The children, each and every one, resembled ten-to-fourteen-year-old sex offenders who have been caught in the act and now, like all the rest of us, must try to understand how to go on living and preserve one's dignity and belief in free will after discovering that we exist like beach fleas on a whale of submerged powers we can't control.

"They wanted to get together," said the Blue Lady. "Here in Copenhagen. They wanted to see one another again. It's very complicated, and expensive. To bring twelve children here. We do it once a year. With great difficulty. They got Kain to do it."

Kasper looked at the man by the telescope.

"You," he said. "You wouldn't even help a ninety-year-old across a highway without having investigated her credit worthiness. What did you get in return?"

He felt the woman weighing her words.

"He thought the children could achieve something. In the physical world. That the mind—if it can reach the point where reality is not yet created—can influence the physical environment. That was naïve, of course."

"Of course," said Kasper.

Concealment colors the edges of a situation like funereal borders of polluted sound. The room trembled with what was not said. Kasper knew that SheAlmighty would appoint somebody to liberate the moment. He hoped it would not be him.

It was the quiet girl.

KlaraMaria stood up.

"Josef," she said. "Mother Maria. Daffy. Andrea. Suenson. I want to talk with you outside. Alone. For a minute."

The words were spoken with profound seriousness. With great, innocent solemnity. In certain instances a child's insistence is so powerful that everyone has to comply: the little boy in "The Emperor's New Clothes," young Jesus in the temple. The Blue Lady stood up. Kain followed her. Daffy. Andrea Fink. The naval officer.

They should have stayed seated. From the moment they stood up, they had no chance.

The girl held the door for them. They walked out. Then she closed it from the inside. And locked it.

The door looked like it dated from the time the observatory was built. Solid oak. Heavy as a church door.

The girl turned toward the children and Kasper. Then she smiled.

It was a smile that made Kasper want to crawl back into the cardboard box. But it was too late. That's why you have to think carefully before beginning the journey out of your personality in earnest. Often there's really no easy way back.

"I don't know what you think about war," she said.

Kasper did not say anything.

"We thought that if we showed the world something, something really unbelievable, then maybe we could get the world to understand. Get grown-ups to understand. And to stop waging war."

Kasper's mouth was dry. But his eyes were moist.

"That's a very nice thought," he said. "What did you want to show the world?"

"We thought if it was something really big," she said. "That the whole world would hear about it. Something in a city. Where nobody got hurt. But where people would realize how much it could cost if we didn't stop. That's the only thing people are really afraid of. Losing money. Then maybe we could get through to them."

"And at the same time score five hundred Bratz dolls," said Kasper.

She smiled. It was not a daughter's smile to her father.

"The one thing doesn't rule out the other," she said.

Kasper nodded. His neck was stiff. As if he were rapidly developing meningitis.

"Bach would have said the same thing," he said.

She came close to him.

"You and I," she said. "We're going to have fun together."

He moved away from her. Her tone grew deadly serious.

"We thought that if it was important enough, there was nothing one couldn't do."

"Your father has always operated according to the same principle," he said. "If one is just able to reach their hearts."

She joined the circle.

"Did you children make the ground cave in?" he asked. "Can the mind change physical reality?"

Perhaps she didn't hear him. Perhaps she lowered the volume on his channel. His anger took his breath away.

"You remember that I want to be a pilot," she said.

She looked straight at Kasper.

"There's a prestart checklist," she said. "Before turning on the engines. Altimeters. Electrical system. Fuel system. Navigation. Route report. Radio frequency. I've read about it. In real books. Will you help me become a pilot when I grow up?"

He did not move.

"Let's start the engines," she said.

The expression on the twelve children's faces was completely open. Very alert. Relaxed, as in sleep. But with eyes wide open.

"Did you children cause it?" said Kasper. "Did you make the ground sink?"

She looked at Kasper.

"Maybe it just happened," she said. "By accident. And we just sort of felt it in advance. What do you think?"

He felt the density of the room increase. His hair stood on end. As if he were in an electrostatic generator.

"Some of it was in English," she said. "Cabin ready. Doors released."

She looked around at the children. One after another they nodded. Kasper wanted to run away. But he knew it was too late. His brain had lost control of his body.

"Ready for push-back," said the girl. "Copenhagen Observatory with Kasper Krone and Stina and their daughter and friends cleared for push-back."

She raised her thumbs.

For a moment the building shook. Not tremendously, but very noticeably. Or else it was his own shaking.

Then the room turned into light. Or his eyesight failed.

He felt the observatory rise and break through the sound barrier. He looked into the girl's eyes. They were utterly calm.

Perhaps they rose vertically. He looked out through what were perhaps the building's walls of light, perhaps a hallucination, perhaps a new form of visual perception. He thought he saw Copenhagen drop out of sight below them, as if the city were sinking into an abyss. But can we ever know for sure?

He felt bile pressing up from his stomach. He thought he had reconciled himself to death. Now, when it was right before him, in the figure of a child, he realized that wasn't so. When it came right down to it, he didn't want to die.

"Take us back," he said. "Put us down."

His voice was as furry as a pipe cleaner.

The girl smiled again. She had lost a front tooth. Or it had been knocked out. It was a toothless grin. Like those of great witches.

"Is it possible to convince you," she said, "to make another attempt? With Mother?"

His face was a mask of perspiration. Gleaming perspiration.

"This is blackmail," he said. "Spiritual blackmail."

"That's the best kind," she said.

He made a resigned gesture with his hands.

"Okay," he said.

"Swear. By SheAlmighty."

"That's blasphemy. That's taking God's name in vain."

"Can you afford to be hard to persuade?"

He raised his hand to swear.

At that moment the door was kicked in.

It was Kain.

Kasper was filled with a kind of respect for the man. Granted, the door was not what it had been a minute ago; it was shimmering like a watercolor painting, vibrantly luminous. But it was still made of oak.

The Blue Lady stood in the doorway. Most of her had been transformed into rainbow light. But not all of her. And what was left was anger.

It was a fantastic fury. Kasper realized immediately that he should appreciate the sound. That he would not have a chance to hear it very often.

"KlaraMaria," she said. "Shut that down!"

Kasper had never heard such a tone before. The voice was as authoritative as a true prediction of Judgment Day. It didn't ask for anything. It simply established a new reality.

There was no landing. One moment the shining alembic seemed to be floating thirteen hundred feet above the city, outside time and space, illuminated, transparent, in absolute silence. The next moment reality was reestablished. Everything was just as before. Nothing had happened. And nothing was any longer the same as before.

While it happened, Kasper's head had been empty. Now his psychological nature hit him like a tidal wave that had been restrained. And his first thought was: If only one could be the children's impresario!

Isn't that what we all strive for? That our children will be able to support us, so we can sit with our feet up, let our evening cocktail and joint pleasantly blend, knowing that we've employed people to pay the best possible interest on our savings?

Then the prayer broke though. He realized that if you are driving 250 miles an hour with SheAlmighty and you grab hold of roadside trees to pick fruit, there's a considerable likelihood that your arm will be torn off.

He met the Blue Lady's gaze. Her sound intensified. It was like gazing down into water that's tinkling with jewels.

"This," she said, "we will keep to ourselves. For a while yet."

Kain stood next to her. She put her arm around his waist.

Kasper was even more shocked than before. He let himself be drawn back into the prayer. There is nothing the Divine cannot endure.

"If Christianity is to survive," she said, "a decisive change must take place."

She could have had anyone. She could have had one of the fourteen-year-old boys. Under slightly different circumstances she could perhaps have had him, Kasper Krone.

"Why him?" said Kasper. "Why choose a crippled devil?"

Josef Kain drew himself erect.

"I'm going through an intense process of repentance," he said. "I want to be cleansed. Become a new person. I've spoken to Maria about making a general confession."

"That will take a couple of years," said Kasper. "Talking nonstop twenty-four hours a day."

Kain doubled over, ready to pounce. Kasper waved the tire irons. Gently, invitingly, like Chinese fans.

Somebody touched him; it was Stina. He landed in his own body.

She stood behind him. As when he used to remove his makeup. In a past that no longer existed. That could never come again. And that he did not desire. But that nevertheless would look good in the scrapbook.

"When it came right down to it," he said, "I never believed any woman could love me."

Her hands grew warm, almost burning, against his skin.

"I understand completely," she said. "I really wouldn't have thought so either. But against all odds and the laws of nature there's possibly one who does anyway."

He closed his eyes.

The moment had something of the ending of BWV 565 about it, Toccata and Fugue in D-Minor, great fateful pillars of music that stand there briefly before the curtain goes up again.

Yet it leaned slightly toward the romantic. And Kasper knew that the cosmos is not especially romantic. Romance is an extreme position, and all extremes get evened out.

He felt something against his body. It was the child. The quiet girl pressed herself between Stina and him. She smiled at him. A wolf smile.

He bared his fangs and smiled back. He listened into the future. He could hear it only piecemeal, divided up bit by bit.

What he could hear certainly sounded lovely. Certainly like a great gala performance. And certainly very, very difficult.